Look Now

STEPHANIE ROGERS

ISBN: 9798370735042

This book is primarily a work of fiction. Other names, characters, organisations, places and events are the product of the author's imagination or are used fictitiously. Any resemblance to actual persons, living or dead, events or locales is entirely coincidental.

Cover images used under licence from iStock

ALSO BY

Look Closer: The Webcam Watcher Book 1.
Look Again: The Webcam Watcher book 2

The Dark Place

1

Sarah

'ARE YOU REALLY SURE you don't mind us going out?' I asked Mum, swaying slightly as I entered the living room. I stopped abruptly, and Leanne bumped into me from behind.

Mum smirked as she picked up the remote and muted the TV. 'Looks like you two have already started on the booze. And of course I don't mind. How many times do I have to tell you?'

Lulu jumped off the sofa and danced around our feet, excited barks escaping her. She picked up her ball and dropped it at my feet. As I bent to throw it, I had to grab the table to stop myself overbalancing. The two large gin and tonics I'd slugged back had gone straight to my head, and Leanne, the lightweight, was no better. I took a step forward and bumped into the sofa, making Zac, who'd nodded off in Mum's arms, jump awake.

Mum slung him over her shoulder and patted his bottom until he twisted his head to one side and dropped off again. She grinned. 'Hmm, this ghost walk you're going on? Are you sure you two won't be the scariest things on it?'

'Very funny! Will you be alright on your own?'

She tutted loudly and rolled her eyes. 'I think I'll manage. Your dad will be back soon, anyway.'

I hadn't noticed he'd gone. 'Where is he?'

'He's just nipped out to get us some wine. 'We're watching that new drama on telly later.. She dropped a kiss on Zac's head. 'When this one is in bed.'

'I don't think we'll be out that long. The ghost walk is only an hour, then we'll be back after a bite to eat,' I said.

'Where does this walk thingy start from, again?' Lee asked, her fingers fumbling with the zipper of her coat.

'Outside The Jacobean pub,' I said. 'It's just a few minutes' walk.' A loud hiccup erupted from me.

Mum tutted. 'It's like you two are back at school, stealing nips of my vodka and then acting all innocent.'

'We never did that. I don't know what you mean,' I said, winking at her.

'Just go and enjoy yourselves. This little man will be in bed soon, anyway,' Mum said.

I opened my mouth to speak, but she cut me off. 'Yes, I know the baby milk is in the fridge.'

'How did you know I was going to say that?'

Mum just looked at me.

Leanne successfully zipped her coat up, picked up her bag, and slipped it over her shoulder, where it promptly fell straight back off.

'Do you know what?' she slurred. 'I'm just going to put my purse and my phone in my pocket and not bother with the bag.'

Zac let out a loud wail in his sleep and suddenly, I didn't want to leave him. What sort of mother got tipsy and swanned off out, leaving her baby with her mum, who wasn't in the best of health herself? But Mum glared at me as I took a step towards them.

'Don't you dare, Sarah!' she said, patting the sofa cushion beside her. Lulu was on it after a flying leap, spilling Mum's tea in the process. She pushed her arm forward, and I pretended not to notice the drips falling onto my new carpet. 'I'll clean it up. Now go, or you'll be late. What time does it start, again?'

The clock on the wall read seven twenty-five. She knew damn well it was due to start in five minutes.

'Okay, we're going,' I muttered, pulling my coat on and winding my woolly scarf around my neck. I threw my bag diagonally across my body, and we left, Leanne breathing down my neck as we rushed through the cafe and out of the main door.

We linked arms as we made our way down Lendal, towards Stonegate. With the Christmas period long gone, York was quiet, the Christmas shoppers now replaced with tourists and drinkers. Our boots clicked on the pavement as we hurried to the pub where the ghost walk was due to start.

Now free and looking forward to an evening out with my best friend, I swallowed down a bubble of laughter that arose in my throat. Outside a pub halfway down, a small crowd had gathered.

'That'll be them,' I said, pointing. 'Now, act sober and look interested. We don't want to get chucked out, do we?'

Leanne sniggered. 'Do you think they get many pissed patrons on the ghost walk?'

'I don't know. If we don't speak and just nod, no one will know, will they?'

She barked out a loud laugh, and a man walking by us turned his head.

'Sssh,' I said, the urge to laugh now becoming so strong I couldn't help giggling again.

We drew nearer to the group, and it was then I spotted her. She must be the guide taking us on the walk. She was dressed in what appeared to be black leather, or pleather maybe, with a corset top and long skirt. I think they called it Steampunk. A long, dark-red coat the colour of claret swept the floor. It was open at the front, revealing a giant, crepey chest that threatened to spill out of the corset. She was leaning heavily on a red-tipped cane, and I wondered how old she was under her thick make-up. A black, wide-brimmed hat with feathers all around the crown topped off her look.

'Oh my God!' Leanne muttered next to me.

A snort escaped me, and I quickly turned it into a cough. Mrs Steampunk saw us, and her smile widened even more. 'Are you for the tour?' she asked, blinking. She wasn't half bad at the old cat-flick, I thought, noticing the winged liner tapering from the corners of her eyes. Much better at it than me.

'Yes,' I said, pulling a ticket out of my pocket and waving it in the air. I made a concerted effort to not sway as I stood in front of a shop window that contained rows of handbags. Lee caught my eye, and I looked away quickly, fixing instead on the others in the group. There were twelve of us altogether; not bad for a damp March night.

'Right, I think that's everyone who booked,' Steampunk said, consulting a piece of paper. 'We'll be off, then. It takes about an hour, a bit longer on a better night. But we'll have fun, anyway. Is everyone ready?'

A few people chorused 'Yes', and she set off at a much faster pace than I was expecting, holding her cane aloft and shouting 'This way' in a booming, theatrical voice.

'I'm never going to keep this pace up in these boots,' I said to Leanne, who was hanging onto my arm as if for dear life.

'Me neither,' she panted.

Steampunk had now disappeared around a corner and was striding towards the Minster, her heeled boots echoing loudly on the pavement.

'Are we going to the pub after this?' asked Leanne.

I turned to her. 'Are you turning into an alkie or something?'

'No, course not. But it's been ages since we had a girls' night out.'

'Alright. You've twisted my arm. I haven't been out in ages, since I went with Claire to have a curry before Christmas.'

'Perils of being a mum, I suppose,' Lee said.

She was right. But I actually preferred being in with my little family: Zac, and my mum and dad, who kept saying they were going to look for somewhere of their own, and I kept begging them not to. I loved having them around. The thought of it being just Zac and me in the flat scared me, for some reason. But, deep down, I knew it wasn't practical for us all to live together in the long term. There were only two bedrooms, and Zac would soon need the one my parents were sleeping in. It wasn't ideal having him in with me, even though he slept through most nights. If I met some bloke one day, he wouldn't want to share our bedroom with a kid, would—

I bumped into a man in front of me and was jerked back to the present. The group had stopped in front of a small church not far from the Minster, and the guide looked like she was winding up to go on stage or something. She was strutting up and down, seemingly soaking in the attention of the group. I noticed some of the male members were quite taken with her cleavage as it weaved from side to side. On closer inspection, she looked younger than I first thought.

She was talking about Guy Fawkes being born in York.

Lee's head snapped round. 'I didn't know Guy Fawkes was from here, did you?'

I shook my head and shrugged. 'No. Unless she means a different one.'

Leanne scoffed. 'Yeah, that'll be it. There's probably loads of them!'

Steampunk smiled indulgently at us, and I realised she'd stopped talking.

'Sorry,' I said.

'Thank you. As I was saying…' she carried on. To be honest, what she was saying was interesting, but I just couldn't stop my mind from wandering off. I glanced up and down the dark streets. A man hurried by with a small dog and nodded at Steampunk, who nodded back but didn't miss a beat. He must live around here, then. Probably sees her every night.

'S'cuse me,' Lee said, putting her hand up.

Steampunk didn't look too impressed with being interrupted. Well, you know what these thespian-types are like, hogging the limelight.

'Yes?' she asked, somewhat snappily. Lee wouldn't like that.

'Where did you get your dress from? It's very nice.'

I rolled my eyes. Trust Lee to be thinking about clothes. She'd probably been eying the woman's costume up since we got here, wondering if she should run up something similar to sell in the vintage clothes shop she worked in back in London.

'It's specially made,' Steampunk said, softening a bit at the compliment. 'Now, follow me to a very special place for the next part of the tour.'

And she was off again, her hips sashaying as she strode away from the Minster and down a tiny alley I'd never even noticed before.

'How old do you reckon she is?' I whispered to Lee.

'Fifty-ish, do you think?'

'Dunno. Maybe, yeah. She's certainly keeping the blokes' attention, isn't she?'

Lee sighed and looked down at her chest. Even in the padded anorak, there wasn't much there. 'I'd love boobs like that,' she said.

'Don't be daft. I don't hear Sam complaining.'

She looked away. I knew it! Something wasn't right. She'd been here almost a week now, and whenever I brought him up, she changed the subject.

'Lee?'

'What? You know I hate my chest.'

She walked off in front, hurrying to join the group, and I traipsed after her. I'd get it out of her if it killed me. I couldn't demand total honesty, though. What if she demanded the same from me? My mate was far from stupid.

Steampunk was actually quite witty and bawdy, as she chatted to the group, warming us up and playing her part. I could imagine her as a serving wench in an old tavern or something. We stopped in front of another small church, this one tiny.

She pointed to some flats next to the church. I didn't even know there were any flats this close to the centre. This one was an ugly seventies block, totally out of kilter with the rest of York city centre.

'The bodies of at least twenty children were found when excavating the foundations to these flats,' she said.

I shuddered. How horrible. It was creepy, listening to that at this time of night. Something rustled in the inside pocket of my coat, and I pulled it out, wondering what it was. When I saw it, I slammed it back inside before Lee clocked it and started asking questions. The envelope was marked HMP Wakefield. It came last week, and I'd forgotten all about it, with Lee coming to visit. I should have hidden it with all the others, at the back of my sock drawer.

I wondered what it said. What did he want? Chris wrote to me every single week and I was on tenterhooks every day when the post was due, in case there was something from him. Mum wouldn't miss that; not in an instant. I still wasn't sure she believed that Zac's father was an anonymous sperm donor, but she'd kept quiet about it, at least for now. If the whole story ever came out, though, I had no idea how she or Dad would react.

Next to me, Lee was weeping into a tissue. 'It's just awful. The poor little things,' she wailed. I sighed. She was always over-emotional when she'd had a bit to drink. I nudged her too hard.

'Stop it! Everyone's looking.'

She blinked and looked around, sniffing. 'It's a tragic story though, don't you think?'

How would I know? I hadn't been paying attention. I just hoped there wasn't going to be a test later.

'Which pub are we going to?' Lee asked too loudly.

Somebody behind us tutted in an over-irritated way, and we shut up. Then Steampunk was off again, with us, her little group of lapdogs, in tow.

Lee and I had somehow ended up right at the front of the group, next to her. I'd preferred skulking at the back.

'Are you enjoying the tour?' she asked.

'Oh, yeah. I'm loving it. It's a bit macabre though, isn't it?' I shivered.

She laughed. 'It's supposed to be. You'll love this next bit. It's about someone being bricked up alive behind a wall. With a baby, too.'

My stomach turned over at the thought. 'Really? I was expecting more along the lines of Caspar or Ghostbusters.'

'But that's not real life, is it?'

I blinked in disbelief as she put a spurt on, probably tired of talking to the idiot. Real life? And what she did for a living was?

Despite it starting to rain, the rest of the tour went by quickly. Steampunk was entertaining, and I only tuned her out in the grisliest bits. Who knew York had such dark stories? I supposed most places did, though. For the last twenty minutes, Lee never uttered a word, but listened to the woman with a spellbound look on her face. I hoped she'd sobered up a bit. I had. Roll on the pub.

***

'How come you always want to go the Slug and Lettuce?' I complained. 'There are better places, you know.'

'I love their fish pie,' Lee said, as went through the door.

'But we've already eaten.'

'Oh, yeah,' she said. 'Well, we'll just have a quick drink while we're here. I bet my hair's a real mess now. Is it? Has it gone all frizzy?'

I smiled at the red curls standing out around her face. They seemed to have multiplied in the hour we've been out. 'Only a little bit,' I said. 'You look fine.'

She pulled a face, and we found a vacant table. Steampunk had been as good as her word and, exactly sixty minutes after the tour began, she'd strode off into the night like some gothic vision. At fifteen quid each, it wasn't a bad way to make a living for an hour's work. If she got bigger groups in the summer, and she probably would, she'd be raking it in.

Lee took off her coat and pulled her hair back, twisting it into a low bun to tame it before releasing it. 'What are you having to drink? Ooh, look; they do cocktails.'

I watched her as she ran a finger over the drinks menu, her lips moving as she read the words.

'Are you going to tell me what's really going on? With you and Sam?'

She sat up straight with her shoulders back, and fixed me with surprisingly clear eyes for someone who'd been drunk not long ago. 'I'll tell you my secrets if you tell me yours.'

Oh, shit! Here it comes.

'I don't know what you mean.'

She pursed her lips and narrowed her eyes. 'Okay, I'll spell it out. How come your six-month-old kid is the spitting image of Chris?'

2

Chris

CHRIS, SITTING ON HIS bed, pressed his back into the cold stone wall and listened as the footsteps outside grew louder and louder. They stopped right outside his cell. In this place, sounds echoed and bounced around the cavernous space so badly it was deafening at times. A key turned in his door. Then the footsteps resumed, fading as the officer went to the next cell on the wing.

Chris breathed out, his eyes sliding away from the door, which would remain unlocked for the next hour: association. Time for either a shower or to use the phone, but not both. It could take most of the hour just to reach the front of the phone line. No wonder some of the inmates had illicit mobiles smuggled into the place, although they still used the regular phones, to keep up the pretence. Not that it fooled anyone.

He shifted his hand on the bed, and it landed in a bit of breakfast he hadn't known he'd dropped. Breakfast was doled out with the evening meal the day before. Some of the prisoners ate theirs the night before, complaining loudly the next morning there was nothing to eat, and they were starving. He'd gladly give them his.

The congealed cereal and milk clung to his hand. He could smell it. It was revolting. Everything in here tasted bad. He fought down the revulsion, got off the bed and washed the mess off his hand in the small sink. His OCD had been on overdrive since he'd arrived here, ramped up by the filth and squalor of the place: mould in the bathrooms, grime coating every surface and, no doubt, bacteria swarming over everything he put in his mouth. In the time he'd been here, it was a wonder he hadn't keeled over with some life-threatening virus or other.

Before being sent down, Chris had considered himself tough. Strong. Untouchable. But he'd soon found out he wasn't any of those things. He'd spent the first few weeks in a bone-deep dread, afraid every time the door opened. Eventually, the dread had left, giving way to an empty shell of nothingness. A void. He was no longer afraid of most of the other prisoners. He was afraid of the endless years ahead, waiting to die in here, and what it might do to him. It was in his head where the trouble now lay; that was where the weakness was. More than once, he'd thought that the only way out of this purgatory would be to do himself in. He felt like a caged animal in here. Imagining the feeling lasting the rest of his life terrified him.

He sat back on the bed and slammed his head back against the wall, then did it again, harder this time. Then harder still, over and over, until his vision went cloudy and his head hurt. He didn't care. At least it made him feel something. He rubbed the back of his head, annoyed his fingers didn't come away smeared with blood. A spell in the hospital would at least have got him out of this cell, away from the men on this landing. He had nothing in common with any of the prisoners, most of whom were scum. Some of them even called him 'Posh Boy', which he had to laugh at. With his background? Maybe his transformation from council estate Leeds-lad to middle-class, high-earning Londoner had been more successful than he'd realized, despite how Sarah used to tease him about his 'by 'eck' Yorkshire accent.

He put his head in his hands at the thought of her. She used to find his accent sexy, she said, even though he'd thought he'd culled all traces of it. Since he'd been in Wakefield, detained at her Majesty's pleasure, most of it had returned, despite the others thinking him posh. But, really, he wasn't any better than them. Just being here was proof of that. Weren't all killers the same under the skin? Monsters? Animals? That's what he was now. All he was. Maybe, despite the ladder he'd climbed and the pit of his childhood he'd clawed his way out of, it was all he was ever destined to be. Perhaps you couldn't outrun your destiny, no matter how hard you tried.

And it looked like it was his destiny to be here. They might never let him out. Maybe if he'd only killed once, it would be different. But he'd been put away for killing three people. At least they didn't know about the fourth, his own sister. Whether or not he'd killed her was debatable. True, he'd supplied the money for heroin she'd overdosed on, but he hadn't stuck the needle in her. She'd done that on her own. Her choice. It didn't matter anyway. No one knew and no one would ever find out, but it didn't change a thing. The main thing was she was gone, and that was what he'd wanted. For what she'd done. Served the stupid bitch right.

His eyes found the corkboard on the wall, where dog-Leanne's photo was sellotaped. It was the only decoration in the cell. She stared back at him, her tongue lolling out, her lips stretched back in a doggy grin. The sight of her made his eyes well up. He missed her so much it was a physical pain. They'd been through so much together.

He rested his elbows on his knees and cradled his head, rubbing the sore bit at the back. It was a pity he couldn't bang it so hard it would finish him off once and for all. But he couldn't. He'd tried enough times, yet here he still was.

He glanced at his watch, the one he'd told them he wanted to keep when he first arrived here. He'd thought wearing it would make him feel like himself, but it hadn't. At least no one had tried to take it from him. In here, he didn't really want to fight. Might get shanked, you never knew. More than once, he'd seen men hiding something that looked like a plastic toothbrush, filed to a nasty point, up their sleeves. Not a knife, but a weapon nonetheless. It'd still do some damage on its way in. His fingers traced the soft tissue of his throat as he thought about it. That's where he'd target, if he was attacking someone. In and out in a second.

He grabbed his washbag and towel and stood up. Might as well get his shower over with, even if he normally came back feeling no cleaner. The rush for it would have died down now, and he'd be in and out in minutes, and back here. He had no one to ring so wouldn't be queuing for the phone. He never rang anyone. Couldn't think of a single person he wanted to talk to. Talking was now something he did as little as possible of.

He wasn't a good mixer. Most of the inmates in here just irritated him. Yet there was no doubting the fact that a few of them, despite their horrific crimes, had decent enough educations. Not that it made a difference. Whatever made them notorious was in their DNA, it seemed to him. A foregone conclusion. Some of the serial killers that walked about this place as if they owned it weren't the dumb shits he'd thought they'd be.

He'd wanted to be sent anywhere but Wakefield, dubbed 'Monster Mansion', with its reputation for housing serial killers and kiddie-fiddlers. The reputation was true; he'd seen lots of them. He'd been surprised at first, expecting the sex offenders would be locked up separately, for their own safety. But they weren't. What they were, though, was fair game, and he'd witnessed numerous attacks on them by other monsters who obviously deemed themselves to have a higher moral code. He avoided all of them. He had no friends in here, nor did he want any.

He opened the door to his cell, closed it behind him, and made his way quickly down the landing on A Wing to the shower block at the far end, ignoring everyone he met along the way. Not that many of them noticed him. It was easy to be invisible in here. He was still powerfully built, even though nowhere near what he had been, and that probably kept most of them away. If anyone attacked him, he'd have to defend himself. If he killed them, what were they gonna do? Lock him the fuck up?

The shower block was almost empty, the floor wet and slippery from the earlier rush. Black mould lined the bottom edge of the tiles where the wall met the floor, and he tried not to look at it as he stripped off his ill-fitting sweatshirt and joggers. He kept his flip-flops on, washing one foot at a time and slipping it straight back in so it only touched foam. He also kept his boxer shorts on, just shoving his hand down the front to wash what he'd always thought of as his crown jewels. Another man entered, his skinny, white body angled away from Chris as he hung up his towel, a small square of rough cotton fabric barely bigger than a hand towel. He, too, showered in his boxers. Chris had seen the man before, but they'd never spoken. He reminded him of some weedy bloke off the telly, whose name escaped him. One of the Doctor Who's, maybe? He looked like a paedo, but for some reason, Chris thought he was in for armed robbery. Maybe the gun had made him feel like a big man. Loser!

He grabbed his towel, rubbed it quickly down his body, and got dressed again. His wet boxers showed damp patches straight away, but he'd put clean ones on when he got back to his cell. Most of the men didn't hang around in here, and most didn't get naked. He'd made that mistake on his first visit, stripping off and suddenly realizing all the others had kept their underwear on.

He dried his feet and flip-flops carefully, gathered his things, and made his way back to his cell, acknowledging nobody on the way. He closed the door behind him, wishing he could lock himself in, rather than it being locked from the outside by the prison staff for endless hours a day. A clothing catalogue was on his bed. It hadn't been there earlier. An officer must have placed it there.

Now he had enhanced prisoner status, he could buy his own clothes and get out of these rags. If anyone ever visited him, they could bring him clothes in, or have some sent through the post. No one had been since Sarah's one and only visit. That was about to change, though.

He flipped through the catalogue. The jeans and T-shirts in there were basic, but seemed designer compared to the prison-issue stuff. He had just enough in his account to buy two T-shirts and some jeans. Nothing resembling a uniform was in the catalogue. No black trousers and white shirts, lest he passed himself off as a screw.

He chose and filled out his order, then took out a pad of paper and a pen. He wrote to Sarah, never knowing if prison staff would read every word before posting. When he'd asked about it, they'd said some letters would be read, others not. It was just random. They didn't have time to read all correspondence into and out of the prison. That in itself would be a full-time job. Unless, of course, he was in for terrorism. Then it was different. Every word would be scrutinised.

He pictured Sarah in her little cafe, snatching his letter from the postman, slicing open the envelope and unfolding the sheets. Did she pull them out eagerly, unable to stop herself from reading what he'd put? Or would she slide them out slowly with cautious fingers, her still-bruised heart dampening any enthusiasm she might have had? He liked to imagine her locking the door and sitting down to read his words while tears spilled from her beautiful, expressive eyes at their predicament, their love, their separation. Occasionally, he wondered if she read them at all. Maybe she shoved them unopened in a drawer. Or straight into a shredder to be chopped into bits before she could change her mind. He only knew one thing for sure; she'd never once written back.

3

Sarah

'FULL DISCLOSURE,' LEE SAID.

Shit! She wasn't asking; she was telling. I'd seen that look on her face plenty of times over the years, and it didn't pay to argue with it. But she wasn't going to like it. She hadn't liked Chris from the moment she'd met him, finding his bullishness and overconfidence brash. She'd never seen his charming side, and when he'd hacked both our computers, it only confirmed he was as bad as she thought he was. Finding out he'd killed people hadn't done anything to win her over, either.

I watched her as she sat down across from me and put a tray on the table containing two Porn Star Martinis and two shots of sparkling wine. We'd relocated from the Slug and Lettuce to a quieter pub. As it was a Monday night, it wasn't busy. The only other people in were two couples at the far end and a table of four in the middle. I glanced around the place, stalling for time, but couldn't help thinking how nice it was in here. I really liked the flooring and the decor. It was modern, grey panelling, and stylish with—

'Sarah! Are you listening?'

'Um… yep.'

'No, you weren't.' She nailed me with her stare. 'I can go first, if you like, but I've got a feeling that what you have to say is far more interesting.'

'Alright then. You go first.' I was trying desperately to think of the best way to tell her that Chris had tracked me down and not only had I recognised him immediately, I'd deliberately conceived a child with him. And kept it all from her my best and oldest friend. My eyes slid to the clock on my phone.

'I know, I know,' she said. 'You can only have one drink and you have to be up at five, blah blah.'

'Are you getting up to help me again?'

She nodded. 'Yeah. I enjoyed it the other day, despite the ungodly hour. I actually had a good time. What shall we do tomorrow when you've finished?'

'I don't know. It's up to you. Anything you really want to do before you go back to London?'

'Not fussed. Just chill.'

I picked up my glass and clinked it with hers. 'Cheers. And thanks in advance for helping me tomorrow. It takes some of the pressure off when you're my lackey.'

She smiled. 'No problem. You know how much I love cleaning up the devastation you cause.'

Despite her flippant remark, she was staring at me. Her eyes seemed to go right into the centre of me, like she could see everything. I made a decision: I was going to tell her the truth. I trusted her completely. She had never let me down. It might actually feel good to share it with someone else. But I needed to hear what was up with her first.

'Ready?' she asked, pointing at our glasses.

I nodded, and we both ate the passion fruit garnishing the martinis, then gulped down the sparkling wine shots in one. I took a sip of the cocktail and spluttered. By God, it was strong! 'How much vodka is in here?'

She sipped her own. 'Dunno. However much they put in.'

When I finally stopped coughing, I jumped straight in.

'So, come on. What's wrong? Is it Sam? And don't lie to me. I'll know.'

She smiled, but it was tinged with sadness. 'Alright. But the same rules apply when it's your turn.'

'Deal.' I was going to have to tell her.

She put her glass down but kept hold of the stem and leaned towards me. We both looked around as a loud peal of laughter emanated from another table. They seemed to be having a good time. Not spilling their guts, like we we're about to.

Leanne sighed. 'I feel awful saying it, and you're going to think I'm mad, but…'

'What's he done?'

'That's just it, he hasn't done anything. You know him; he's a really nice guy. He's attentive and loving and goes out of his way to please me.'

'Sounds like a dream. So what's the 'but'?'

'Do you think someone can be too nice?'

'In what way, too nice?'

'In a nutshell, I'm bored. There's no excitement there for me.'

Had she just called her boyfriend boring? Sam the perfect man? The dishy young hospital doctor that had set her pulse racing when they first got together?

Her eyes were anxious, and she bit down on her lower lip. 'Do I sound like a spoilt brat? With first world problems?'

'Um… at first, yeah, a bit. But deep down, no, I suppose not. If that's how you feel…'

'I can't marry him, can I? Feeling this way?'

I blew out a massive breath and my fringe flopped up, then settled again. 'I dunno. There's only you can decide that. But if it's excitement you're after, remember Craig? Was that any better?'

She shuddered. 'Urgh, no! Definitely not. But maybe I was attracted to Sam's easygoing qualities because of Craig being the total opposite. Sam was the first bloke I went out with after Craig, wasn't he?'

We both lapsed into silence, thinking about Craig. A convicted rapist, he was now in jail, and still Leanne couldn't get over the fact that when she was engaged to him, she'd suspected nothing. But I reckoned it was testament to how good a liar and an actor he was. Like Chris. She was going to be so shocked when she found out he was in prison? What a weird bond we'd share. Our exes, the cons.

She twirled her engagement ring on her finger, the small diamond in the centre catching the light and bouncing it around on every revolution.

'How certain are you that it's not what you want?' I asked her.

She took a larger swig of her cocktail. 'I've been asking myself that for a while now. Trying to work out how I really feel. And I don't think it's fair to either of us to pretend it's what I want. I could spend our married life resenting him and regretting it, and he'd spend it trying to please me. And what a thankless task that would be for him.'

She really had thought about it. I should have known she would. If nothing else, Leanne always knew her own mind and didn't take crap from anyone. But if she finished with him, he'd be heartbroken. The poor man! None of this was his fault.

I sipped my drink, the vodka making my mouth feel numb. But it was so nice to be out like this; free, with no ties for the next hour. No dirty nappies or crying babies to soothe. Across from me, Lee's face was taut and drawn, and I felt guilty for thinking of my own pleasure.

'What are you going to do?' I asked.

'Nothing, for the moment. Wait and see if it passes, and it's just me panicking or being stupid. I'll go home and give myself a good talking to. So you don't think I'm being stupid, then?'

I thought about what I'd had with Chris: the near-constant buzzing in my body whenever we were together, the way I loved not knowing what he was thinking or what he was going to come out with, and the way I was never, ever bored being with him. On the contrary; he was like a drug I could never get enough of. I could understand what Lee was thinking, that she couldn't live with the steady, the boring, the lack of excitement. I wouldn't want to.

'No, I don't think you're being stupid. But remember, when you first met him, you were buzzing. You were absolutely smitten with each other. That's what you said, anyway. And I saw it. You were telling the truth.'

'I know.' She sighed and swirled her drink around in the glass so forcefully a bit slopped over the sides. 'And I wasn't making it up. But it's like, when the chase was over and we got together, it's almost as if he changed into someone else. He'd got his prize. He was happy to stay in and do nothing. Watch whatever I wanted on the TV, sit and chat about our days, especially mine. I've never known a bloke so interested in women's clothes.'

I side-eyed her.

'No, not like that! I don't mean he wants to wear them. It's just like, if I wanted to try a new food, he'd go over the top about it. Like he's desperate to have things in common with me. Am I making sense?'

'About the food? No. But in a general sense, yes, I think so.'

She put her head in her hands. 'It's just so stifling. He never disagrees with me on anything. If I complain about his clothes lying around, he'll apologise and pick them up.'

'What an absolute bastard! Chuck him immediately!'

She snorted. 'I knew you'd understand.'

'Look, if he's boring, don't marry him.'

She chewed her lip. 'I'm not saying he's boring. I'm saying I'm bored. It's not the same thing, is it?'

'Isn't it? Maybe not. But I think you're right not to do anything rash when you get back. Be really sure before you make a decision there's no going back from.'

She nodded. 'I will be. I'm hoping it's just a phase. Maybe when I get back, he'll do something really exciting and out of character.'

'What, like give you a good wallop? I don't think that's what you're after.'

'Definitely not that, no. But I think he's more afraid of me doing that to him. You did tell him I whacked Craig, if you remember.'

'A right belter, that was.' I did a quick uppercut through the air.

'My knuckles were killing me. I thought I'd broken them. Look, thanks for dragging it out of me. It's been good to talk.'

I drank some more, my senses dulled now by the alcohol. It no longer made me shudder. And I felt relaxed enough to let down my guard.

'So, your turn,' she said, settling back in her seat and folding her arms. 'Is Zac Chris's?'

I took a deep breath. Then I nodded. Leanne's face, reddened by the warmth of the pub, actually turned pale.

'I knew it! How? What the hell? Where is he? When did you manage that?'

'Alright, slow down! I'll tell you. But you can't breathe one word of this to anyone, ever. I bloody mean it, Leanne.'

'Course I won't. But tell me.'

So I did. The whole sordid lot. And it was as bad as I thought it would be. The emotions on her face ranged from shock, anger, fear to complete disbelief.

'I can't believe you recognised him right at the beginning! Weren't you scared?' Her eyes were wide as she shook her head.

'Of him? No, I wasn't. I think I'd been half-expecting him to find me, anyway.'

When I told her I'd slept with him deliberately to get pregnant and then gone to the police and shopped him, she went even whiter.

'It was the only way to identify him without any doubt,' I explained. 'You know what I mean…'

'My God…' she breathed. 'And you never breathed a word of it.' Her hand crept towards her glass, but it was empty. She'd finished it on auto-pilot, halfway through the story. 'So, what do your mum and dad think?'

'I told them I used a sperm donor. Like I told everyone. If they don't believe me, they haven't said. They know I was really cut up about the ectopic pregnancy, so I suppose it was feasible.'

'I can't see your mum buying that, though. Not really. Are you ever going to tell her?'

'I don't know. What's the point? He's in prison and he'll be there for years, maybe forever.'

Her mouth tightened and she narrowed her eyes at me. 'I knew he was bad, right at the beginning. Then we found out he was a hacker and a killer. And now this. It's just ridiculous.'

Her comment cut me, even though I knew she didn't mean it like that.

'Oh, ridiculous, is it? Is that what you think I am?'

'No, I didn't mean that. It's just… well, wow. I'm struggling to take it in.' She cleared her throat and sat up straighter. 'Sarah, you took a killer down on your own. You're one kick-ass chick!'

I crossed my arms tightly over my chest while she backpedalled. She was trying to make me feel better after putting her foot in it but it wasn't working. I didn't 'kick ass'. I wasn't even scared of him. In the end, I used him to get what I wanted and then left him to the wolves. To get what he deserved. And I didn't feel good about it, but every time I looked at Zac, I didn't feel particularly bad, either.

'Does he know? That he has a son?' Some of the colour had now returned to her cheeks.

'No. And he won't, either. Not from me.'

She nodded. 'I agree. He doesn't deserve either of you. Have you visited him at all?'

'Um… yeah. Once. Not long ago. When Zac was three months. I considered telling him, but it was so awful, Lee, at the prison. There were children there, visiting their fathers. It was horrible, and I decided I'd never do that to Zac. And I won't be going back to see him, so it won't be a problem.'

She was silent. I could almost hear the cogs in her brain turning, the neurons firing off in every direction as she tried to process everything I'd just said.

'So, you aren't in contact with him anymore?'

'No.'

'I can't believe all this has gone on and I didn't know a thing.' She looked at me with accusatory eyes, but I couldn't feel guilty for that.

I shrugged. 'I never told anyone. And you're the only one that knows now.'

Her eyes narrowed. 'You haven't told Claire, your new bestie?'

I laughed and so did she. I knew she was jealous of my friendship with Claire, the woman who works for me. She'd admitted it, and we'd had a good laugh about it.

'Yeah, Claire knows everything. With her being my new BFF and all.'

Lee raised her middle finger up at me and I stuck my tongue out at her. Our glasses were empty. It was time to get back.

'Come on,' I said. 'The fun's over. Let's get going.'

We left the pub, zipping our coats up. We'd be back at the flat in under ten minutes. The chilly air stung my face, and we sped up.

'What's your mum and dad's long term plans?' Lee asked.

'The money from the sale of their house has come through and they keep talking about buying a little ground-floor flat in York, walkable to the city centre. Dad's more keen to move out than Mum is. He keeps telling her me and Zac need our own space. I suppose he's right, but I don't want them to go.'

'The baby sitting certainly is handy,' she said cynically.

'I agree, but I can't imagine them not being there. I love it. And Mum's arthritis is only going to get worse.'

'I know, but come on, Sarah—it was always a short-term option at best. Even if you don't meet someone, Zac will need his own room, one day.'

I shivered as we turned a corner straight into a biting wind. 'Nah! I don't think I want to meet anyone.'

We were on Low Petergate. I loved this street: with its quirky shops and cobbled road, it oozed character and charm.

'Can I ask you something?' She hooked her arm through mine.

'Might as well. You know all my darkest secrets,' I said.

She bit her bottom lip. 'What was it like with Chris? I mean, how did he make you feel? Despite the fact I didn't like him, I could see how gorgeous he was and how he could turn on the charm. And it was obvious how in love with you he was.'

I swallowed hard as a lump filled my throat. How had he made me feel? I didn't even know if I could put it into words.

'He was my world.' I stopped and cleared my throat, my voice husky and breaking. My eyes fixed on a shop window display. It was easier to look at that and speak, than at her. 'He was my everything. From the moment I woke up to the moment I went to sleep, I ached for him if he wasn't there. Sorry, I know it sounds corny, but it's true. I would have done anything for him, gone anywhere with him. When we were together, I felt complete. Whole. Happy. Loved.' I glanced at her. Her face was flushed, and she looked enthralled. 'Does Sam make you feel like that?'

Her shoulders drooped, and she shook her head. 'No. Nothing like that. More like a comfy pair of old slippers you know will be waiting when you need them.'

'Ouch! That's harsh.'

'I know. Are you saying you still love Chris, then?'

'Yeah. I think a part of me always will. But it doesn't mean that another part of me doesn't hate him too. The evil things he was capable of. I don't love that part of him. But I have Zac, so I have the best bits.'

'Are you happy, then? You don't regret anything?'

'I don't regret anything I did. I regret the things he did, but those weren't mine to change. So, yeah, I guess I'm happy.'

Inside my coat, my arm rested snugly over the latest unopened letter he wrote me. I never mentioned the letter to Leanne, or all the others lying unopened at the back of a drawer in my bedroom. So much for full disclosure.

4

Joe

WHEN THE ALARM SHRIEKED, Joe groaned and reached a hand out from under the blanket, groping in the direction of the noise. As every other morning, the clock ended up on the floor but continued its incessant racket. Covering his head with the pillow wouldn't blot it out enough, so he hauled himself upright and opened his eyes. A pale, pencil-thin beam of light showed around the edges of the curtain, but not enough to illuminate the room.

'Turn the damn thing off!' came a yell through the wall, from the adjacent room.

Joe swung his legs out of bed, located the clock by the luminescent digits, picked it up, and shut it off, barely managing to resist the urge to smash the thing into a million pieces. If he did that, he'd sleep in for sure, and his job would be consigned to the past. He couldn't risk that, much as he would have liked to—it had been hard enough getting it. It had only been thanks to the supermarket having a policy where they employed ex-cons that he'd got it in the first place. So the do-gooders had actually done some good, for once.

When he'd been released from prison, he'd expected zero help to get his life turned around. The small amount that had come his way had been gratefully received, but if it hadn't been for Gerry, God only knew where he would have ended up. Probably back inside, knowing him. Instead, Gerry had been as good as his word, and here Joe still was, months later, bunking down in his mate's spare room, above the pawnbroker's Gerry owned. Okay, so it wasn't much of a room, more a cupboard rammed with clutter, but at least there was a bed. It beat the streets or someone's floor. But whose floor could he have slept on, anyway? He had no friends, a dead ex-wife, a now-dead junkie of a daughter, and his no-good son was in the slammer. You had to laugh. For all his son's efforts to drag himself out of the gutter and better himself, he'd ended up worse than his old man. He'd even changed his name when he'd shucked off his family. Chris, he went by now. Well, no way would Joe ever refer to him by that name. Colin was his birth name, and that's who Joe still thought of him as.

Joe chuckled to himself about his son's plight and ran a hand over his bristly chin. He had an hour before his shift at the supermarket was due to start, and he could walk it in twenty minutes. Fifteen at a push. Plenty of time.

He got out of bed, wincing at the pain in the small of his back from another night on the plank of a mattress, and was at the door in one step. He opened it quietly and, after another two, was in the bathroom. It only took a few seconds for the shower to run nice and hot. Having the bathroom to himself and being able to stay in the shower as long as he liked was a luxury he vowed never to take for granted. Again another chuckle, as he thought about Chris running the daily shower gauntlet inside. What was it like in Wakefield? Must be far worse than anything he himself had been forced to endure. He was never in a Cat A prison for convicted murderers. He still couldn't believe that his own flesh and blood had committed stone-cold murder.

He stripped off his pyjamas and climbed over the side of the bath, standing at the plughole end under the spray, revelling in the near-scalding water that cascaded over his head and shoulders, and down his body. The first few times Gerry had stepped into the shower after Joe, he'd screamed at the scalding he'd received. Now, before he got in, Gerry always triple-checked the setting Joe had left it on. Joe, after the verbal bashings, now remembered to turn it back to the lukewarm setting Gerry preferred. How he stood it, Joe would never know. After all those years together in the same nick, and all those stone-cold showers, Joe thought his mate would have liked the water hot. Instead, Gerry said his skin couldn't stand it anymore, and that Joe 'must have hide like a bleeding rhino'.

It didn't take Joe long to wash the lather out of his hair; these days, there wasn't much left. It seemed the fifteen years he spent inside actually were the ones he was at his peak. He was now on the wrong side of sixty and feeling every year of it. And pushing the wobbly conga-line of trolleys in the supermarket car park didn't make him feel any younger. No matter how hot or cold the weather, or how wet or dry, he was out there, forty hours a week, corralling the trolleys back into their pens, only to have to start again as soon as he turned around. It was never ending, like painting the Humber Bridge: get to the end and start all over again. And the abuse he was got. The school kids were the worst, cheeky young pups like Colin used to be. In his day, you could give them the back of your hand or take your belt off to them and nothing was said. Colin had felt it often enough, and worse besides. Much worse, to be honest. In those days, if the kid had a black eye off his dad, he just had a couple of days off school until it had gone. There were only so many times you could use the 'just walked into a door' line. But Colin had always brought it on himself. Never knew when to keep his trap shut, that one. Right gobby little shite, and what good had it done him in the end?

Joe turned off the shower, adjusted the setting for Gerry, and got out, knocking his foot on the edge of the bath and almost losing his footing. Steady! Gerry wouldn't be happy with all the banging about, not after the alarm had woken him again. Gerry would get up at tea-time every day if it wasn't for the shop.

He towelled himself down and pulled on his black supermarket trousers and polo shirt, then a fleece, a revolting, bright green thing. He looked like a radioactive giant mushy pea! In case he didn't stick out enough already, the ageing man pushing trolleys for a living. Most days, if it wasn't for the high-vis jacket, he felt invisible. Anyone could do what he did. Skill level—low, it had said in the job-centre. Low? Non-existent, more like. Although on the days when the wind was fierce and whipped across the car park with the savagery of a desert tornado, the skill level wasn't low. It took all his strength to stop the great line of massive wire-baskets-on-wheels from smashing into the cars in the parking bays.

As for the ones who didn't think the parking bays applied to them, and who just abandoned their vehicles along the sides of the entrance to the shop, it served them right if their cars did get scratched. They drastically narrowed down the space he needed to manoeuvre the trolleys. One such idiot had actually snapped 'Careful, mate,' at Joe, as he fought to keep the line from running down the slight incline towards his BMW.

'Well, don't park like a twat, then,' Joe had remarked, then instantly worried about losing his job as the ponce in a suit had bristled. Joe had stood his ground and eyeballed the man, who had eyed up Joe's height, and thought better of it, hurrying over to his car and quickly driving off without giving Joe a backward glance.

Joe knew he had an air about him that said 'Don't mess with me'. It wasn't even to do with being banged up; he'd always had it. On the estate, when he'd been married to Jane and living in purgatory with her and their two brats, most people had avoided him, knowing his reputation for reacting first, then thinking later. That had suited him just fine. If people kept out of his way, then even better. They could do whatever they wanted if they let him do the same.

After a quick cup of coffee and some toast, Joe pulled on his high-vis jacket and boots, and left Gerry's place. He walked to work, dreading another day of the mind-numbing tedium. How long he could keep this up was anyone's guess. The streets in this part of Leeds were no better than the Granford Towers area he used to live in before his son took his car joyriding, killed a kid, and let *him* get banged up for a long stretch. With that, and prison, it seemed he was destined to always live in shit holes. Probably no more than he deserved, he knew that. In another life, in another time, he might have been somebody. Really been somebody, instead of the nobody he'd always been. Not that he'd tried too hard.

As he neared his place of work, the second-hand phone one of Gerry's lads had given him beeped in his pocket. Joe sighed. He couldn't get to grips with these new-fangled bloody things. Text messages with his clumsy sausage-fingers took him forever. He took the glasses he'd been given in prison out of his trouser pocket, put them on, and squinted at the screen after unlocking it. There was a tiny envelope icon at the bottom. An email. Hardly anyone had his email address. Before he'd been sent down, he'd not even had an email address, preferring to leave such things to geeks. Like his son. Colin had drank in information of all kinds since being small. And from what he was now in prison for, it seemed that hadn't changed. Hacking some bloody woman's computer and camera so he could watch her? What possessed him? Joe hadn't even known such a thing was possible. Still, it smacked of being a pervert, and of all the things Colin was, he'd never had him pegged as one of those. Mind you, he'd never dreamed his boy could be a cold-blooded killer, either, and how much worse was that?

He tapped the screen and opened his email. When he saw the sender, his heart skittered. It was the one he'd been waiting for.

He opened it, and his eyes fixed on the first line. VISIT APPROVED. He couldn't stop the grin that was spreading across his face. Yes! He'd finally get to see the bastard face to face!

It had taken weeks to be checked out and verified that he could visit Colin in prison. Not to mention that Colin had to agree in the first place. He hadn't been sure Colin would agree. In fact, he'd been convinced he wouldn't. What'd made him agree to it, Joe couldn't fathom. Although, he himself would have done, had their roles been reversed. Curiosity would have got the better of him, and he'd have had to find out why. Colin was different, though. All his life, his son had been afraid of him. No surprise, really. Joe had been more than handy with his fists and it hadn't always been deserved.

When he walked into the supermarket, the elation he'd felt at reading the email disappeared. It was this damn place. The bloody job was demeaning. Everyone knew collecting trolleys was for the unqualified, the ones who couldn't get anything else, but he had no choice. Maybe today would be a better day, though. He could spend it deciding what he'd say to Colin when he saw him. Starting with what the hell had he been thinking, letting his old man go to prison for a crime he didn't commit? For fifteen bastard years!

5

Sarah

'I WISH YOU DIDN'T have to go. I've loved having you here. Although I bet you can't wait to sleep in a proper bed after my sofa.' I closed the door to the cafe behind me and wrapped Lulu's lead around my hand. After five on a Sunday, the streets of York were quiet, the shoppers having all gone home.

Leanne sighed and her knuckles were white as she gripped the handles of Zac's buggy. 'Your sofa's quite comfy. But I wish I didn't have to go, too. Do you know, I keep wishing I could move up here and start a new life, like you have.'

She bumped the pushchair down a kerb, jolting Zac and making him grunt. Normally, the more bumpy the pram ride, the better he liked it. Not today, though. To demonstrate his displeasure, he flung his green teddy out onto the damp pavement. I stooped to pick it up and handed it back to him. He looked directly at me and threatened to throw it again.

'Don't you dare,' I warned him. 'I'm not picking it up again.'

I grabbed it and pushed it down between his legs, under his cover. Thankfully, he left it there and gave a loud, high-pitched shriek that pierced my brain.

'Zac, stop doing that!' I snapped, rubbing my temples. 'It's his new favourite thing,' I told Lee. 'He keeps doing it, no matter what I say. '

She glanced at me, then down at him. 'His dad wasn't too good at doing as he was told, either, was he?'

If anyone else had said that, I'd have thought they were having a dig, but I knew she wasn't.

'True,' I said. 'So, have you thought any more about your predicament?'

The buggy got stuck on a raised cobblestone, causing the wheel to spin round. She shoved at it, but it didn't budge.

'You need L-plates for that thing,' I said, jumping out of the way as Lulu squatted down to pee.

'I'll get better. You've had more practise with it than I have,' she said, attempting to free the wheel, then giving up and tipping the pushchair back on its rear wheels and up the kerb. She huffed and puffed. 'It's damn hard work, this pushchair lark. And yeah, I've thought of nothing else.'

She looked at me, anxiety stamped on her face. 'Sarah, what am I going to do?'

'I think you'll do whatever's for the best, ultimately. For both of you. You know your own mind. You always have. But one thing I will say is that you're a long time married with the rest of your life to regret it. Don't make that mistake. Not if you're not sure, and especially not to spare his feelings. That wouldn't be right for either of you.'

We turned at the end of the road and sped up a bit. Her train was due to leave in twenty minutes. We were late, thanks to Zac filling his nappy just as we were about to leave.

'Come on,' I said, going faster still. Lulu was loving it, her little pink tongue lolling out. How come her legs were only about five or six inches long, yet she could beat us in a race every time?

'I need to get fit,' I panted.

'Me too,' she said, although she was leaving me behind.

Zac grizzled, fractious at being jolted up and down so much. Please don't cry, I thought. Instead, his eyelids grew heavy and started to droop. We reached the train station with twelve minutes to spare.

'What platform?' I asked.

'Three. Look, I'd better get going. I can't miss it.'

We hugged briefly. 'Keep in touch. Let me know what you decide and everything.'

'I will,' she said, her eyes already scanning the entrance to the throngs inside.

'You'd better.'

She tried to extract her holdall out from under the buggy, but it got stuck, and Zac woke up.

'Bye Zac. Be good for your mummy,' Lee said, giving him a quick kiss. He screwed up his face and blew her a raspberry. I must tell Dad to stop teaching him these things, but they both think it's funny.

'Bye, Lulu, you cutie,' she said, after patting her head. 'I still can't believe she was Chris's dog.'

'Text me to let me know you get back okay,' I called after her and she gave me a thumbs up before disappearing into the train station. I felt a pang of sadness watching her go.

'Alright, Mister,' I said, bending down to pull Zac's blanket over his legs. 'Let's get going.'

He looked up at me with eyes astonishingly like his dad's; how they expressed what he was feeling and how they seemed to look right into you, whether in a loving or accusatory way.

I dug into the hood of the pushchair and pulled out a homemade fruit bar. It was mainly apple and normally he loved them, but not today. He'd barely eaten a thing since last night.

'Here.' I squatted down in front of him and he stretched out a chubby hand to take it, then changed his mind as I handed it over. It dropped on the pavement between us.

'Zac! I'm going to have to bin it now.'

Before I could pick it up, Lulu was on it, and it was gone. Zac's behaviour was bothering me. I didn't like his loss of appetite. He usually ate whatever you put in front of him. I'd had to wean him early as I couldn't seem to fill him on breast milk alone, even though the health visitors wanted me to get to six months before trying him on other things. No chance of that, if any of us wanted to get any sleep ever again. And what do you tell your child when he's hungry and crying? 'You have to go hungry because the health visitor says so?' Since weaning him, I'd tried a massive range of foods, and the only thing he really hadn't liked was broccoli. He'd pulled a face like I was trying to poison him and had actually gagged. I didn't blame him.

I hooked the dog lead onto the pushchair and started to walk back, Lulu prancing along beside us; our little family of three. I didn't know why, but I always felt safe in York, even after dark, in a way I never did in London. Zac seemed mesmerised by the lights of the taxis entering and leaving the station. He kicked the covers off again, and I left them, just tucking them down beside him so they didn't fall out. In his padded snowsuit, he wouldn't be cold. As I pulled down his zip a little way, I noticed his face had gone beet-red. I hoped he wasn't building up to a full-blown crying session.

Lately, he'd started to wake in the night, and just didn't seem to want to go back to sleep. Mum was great, but I couldn't expect her to be up at three with him. I was grateful enough for all the help she and Dad gave me. It reminded me of when he was first born. I hadn't expected it to be as hard as it was, juggling a new baby and a business. God knows what I had been expecting, but it certainly wasn't feeling as if I'd been run over by a bus for the first few weeks. With the tiredness, early starts, and feeding him myself, I'd thought that things could only get easier. And surely, one day they would. But not for one second had I ever regretted my decision to go it alone and have him. In the deepest part of the night, with him snuggled up to my breast and feeding, it felt like one of the few things in my life I'd ever done right. I was never the best academically, but I know I was born to this—to be Zac's mum.

I sang to him as we neared Lendal Bridge, over the River Ouse. He was grizzling again. At the prospect of a disturbed night, I was glad the cafe would be closed tomorrow, and we could lie in bed together and sleep late, if we needed to.

Before long, a sob escaped him. I walked faster. Lulu glanced up at me as she broke into a trot. Another sob, and before long, he was screaming, and people were looking. I stopped the buggy and lifted him out.

'Hey, what's going on?' I jiggled him up and down, and he rested his red face on mine. He was burning up. Mum said I'd put too many layers on him. I took his arms out of his snowsuit and pulled it down to his waist as we set off again, me carrying him and steering the buggy with one hand. He quietened but was snuffly. Maybe he hadn't wanted his Aunty Leanne to go home.

'Is that it? Aunty Lee's gone?' I murmured into his ear. He turned his head away by way of response. 'Okay, fine. Have it your way.'

At least he was settling a bit now. Better not to put him back in the buggy and have him start again. As plain as day, I had an image of Chris, laughing, and holding his son under the armpits, Zac's legs kicking in the air, face to face.

'No wonder he's grizzly,' he was saying. 'He's just like me—happiest when he's got his face in your naked breasts. Nice one, kiddo.'

I went hot. Where had that come from? It was exactly like something he would have said. It was so real, as if he actually had said it. And then, he was all I could think about. His face filled my mind, and the familiar ache of longing to be near him started up. I tried to breathe slowly, in and out. It would pass; I just had to ride it out. I pushed away the certainty that I would never see him again, and just kept walking, one foot in front of the other, until our street came into view.

I unlocked the door to the cafe, once again shunning the metal steps round the back that led up to the first floor, and my kitchen door. Zac grumbled and shifted in my arms, nodding off now. I flicked the lights on in the cafe. The large sign Chris had painted for me still hung on the wall, and I stood, just looking at it. The sight of it made me think of Lulu, and I unclipped her lead. 'Do you miss him?' I asked her out loud. 'You must do. What's your history with him? I wish you could tell me.'

Lulu sat down, and I gazed at the plaque on the wall again. 'Life's too short to not eat the brownie,' it proclaimed. But was it, really? When I'd gone to visit Chris in prison, he'd said something like 'it would be a long, slow slide towards his grave'. He meant because I'd put him in there. His words had cut me deeply. Still blaming everyone but himself, in true Chris fashion, he'd then done a U-turn and apologised for everything he'd done to me. I couldn't imagine really what his days must be like in prison, but, like he said, his days were anything but short now. With his quick brain and intelligent mind, how did he keep occupied, and how was he really coping? It was an existence I couldn't really picture. More than once, I'd thought about taking the sign down, but I couldn't. I didn't want to.

I pushed the buggy to the back of the cafe, where I left it, and carried Zac upstairs.

Mum was in a chair, watching Antiques Roadshow. Lulu jumped into her lap, and Mum absently began stroking her.

'He looks hot,' she said, frowning, as I pulled off Zac's shoes and snowsuit.

'He is. He's just had a screaming fit, and made himself even hotter.'

I sat him on her knee, shoving Lulu aside, and unbuttoned his cardigan.

'No wonder. He's trussed up like a chicken. Poor little lamb. He's stifling,' Mum remarked.

I let her go on, tuning her out as my thoughts slid back to Chris and the night Zac was conceived. The night I stole life from him in more ways than one. While he gave me Zac, I had his taken away. But he'd left me no choice. The very minute he'd gone looking for me and found me, the writing had been on the wall for him.

'Shall I run his bath?' Mum said. 'Your dad says he can do it. He's bought a new book to read to him.'

'Okay,' I said, relieved to hand the chore to someone else. Tiredness crashed over me, and I stretched out on the sofa as my dad came in.

'Hi, love. You okay?'

'Yeah. Just tired.'

'Bath's running,' he said. 'We've got a new story to start.'

'So Mum tells me,' I said, my eyes closing. Before I drifted off, I heard Mum and Dad leave the room, closing the door behind them.

I woke abruptly to Mum screaming my name. What time was it? I was still on the sofa, and it was fully dark outside.

'Sarah! You need to come, quick,' Mum shouted.

I had never in my life heard her sound so scared.

Before I knew it, I was off the sofa and running towards the sound of her voice, almost tripping on Lulu, who was cavorting under my feet. Then my dad was yelling for me, too.

'Sarah!' my mum screamed. 'Call an ambulance!'

6

Chris

THE DOOR OPENED WITH such force it hit the wall. Chris almost leaped off the bed. The officer standing in the doorway narrowed his eyes and barked, 'Out!' at him.

Chris got slowly to his feet, the noise from the landing outside deafening through the open doorway. With the prisoners all out for association, it sounded like a battleground out there.

'Cell inspection,' said the screw. 'Wait outside.'

Chris didn't know the name of this particular officer, but always thought of him as Shortie. The guy couldn't be much over five-six or -seven, but his vile personality more than made up for his lack of stature. His officer number on his epaulette was 251. Some of the other officers would banter with the prisoners, and the odd one even seemed to have some semblance of caring, but not this one. None of the cons liked him, and they had multiple names for him, none of them complimentary, and most relating to his lack of height, bad teeth, and bottle-bottom glasses.

As Chris pushed past him in the doorway, trying to avoid brushing against Shortie's protruding gut, his hands bunched into fists. He could wrap one hand around his fleshy neck, lift him off his feet, and crush his windpipe in one easy move. How he'd love to smash him right in his face, but it just wouldn't be worth it. Instead, if he kept his nose clean and served his time, he had a smidgen of hope that he'd get out one day. Others had. If he didn't have that hope, then there was no point. Although, admittedly, that hope deserted him often, and was not very much in evidence today.

He stood on the landing, trying not to breathe in the stench of sweat, piss, and mould that always seemed to be present, and looked back over his shoulder. The screw had thrown the thin mattress onto the floor to shove his hand down the side of the bed. He was probably hoping to find an illicit mobile phone or some drugs. This place was rife with stuff like that, but the screw wouldn't find anything in his cell. He hadn't interacted with anyone enough to get anything, and it was going to stay that way. He was not after making any friends in here. Increasingly, though, he'd begun to think the time might pass more quickly if he found could find someone here on his wavelength. But who could you trust in a place like this? The irony wasn't lost on him.

His jaw clenched as he watched Shortie taking way too much pride in his work. The new bedding he'd ordered, along with his new clothes, was now in a crumpled heap on the floor. The sight of his few meagre possessions—toaster, kettle, underwear, washbag, and writing paper—in Shortie's damp hands, turned his stomach. It was a mess. The screws always made some attempt to put it back together, but he hated the fact they'd had their fingers all over his stuff. And he always had to rearrange everything back to the way he liked it.

The bloke in the cell next door, Norman, had once complained about having to put everything back properly.

'Why, got something better to do with your time?' Chris had heard Shortie say.

Norman was late-fifties and in for some kind of extortion and violence, though he wouldn't specify what exactly. Chris was surprised. Norman looked more like a nonce. He'd wanted to know all about what Chris was in for but hadn't been too keen on elaborating about his own misdemeanours. As a result, Chris had told him jack-shit. Norman was a nosy bastard alright. Chris couldn't stand him and always went the other way to avoid him.

He thrust his hands in his pockets of his new jeans and turned away from his cell. Might as well stretch his legs. Not enough time to go to the gym, if indeed it was even open. Half the time, it was locked when he went. Not enough staff, the usual excuse. Instead, he'd taken to exercising in his cell, in the tiny bit of available floor space. He could do sit-ups, press-ups, star jumps, squats, and lunges no bother, so he did, several times a day. Those who said prison was soft had obviously never been in this one. He'd expected it to be hard but absolutely hadn't been prepared to be locked up for twenty-three hours some days. 'Staff shortages' was what they put it down to when anyone asked. If they answered you at all. Compared to some, he'd hardly been there any time at all, but he now knew how an animal felt in a zoo.

As he walked down the landing, he looked up at the rounded ceiling high above. The old Victorian building was in a terrible state. Paint hung off the walls in great damp patches, the source of the ever-present fusty, acrid smell. He took shallow breaths so as not to breathe it in, but that only left him lightheaded.

At the far end of the landing, he paused outside the recreation room. The first thing he heard was the soft clunk of balls hitting each other on the pool table. He hated pool. At first, he'd been surprised they even had a pool table. Weren't the cues capable of being used as weapons? Then again, wasn't anything, if you put your mind to it? A vision of someone being beaten to death with a pool cue was now filling his mind again. He'd seen it on some crime thing on Netflix a few years ago, and it had stuck with him. Couldn't remember for the life of him what it had been called. A shout went up from the other side of the wall; sounded like someone had won the game of pool. As he straightened up, one thing struck him: he'd had more violent thoughts since he'd been here than in his whole life, and he hadn't been short of them before. Rehabilitation? What a joke! He could learn more about crime in here than anywhere: breaking and entering, robbing places, embezzlement, how to kill someone in ways he would never have thought of. And he could write the book on cybercrime if he felt like it. There again, he supposed, none of them were criminal masterminds were they, including himself, or they wouldn't be in here?

'What you doing, loitering out here?' A paper-thin voice that was more whisper came from behind and had him spinning round. First rule of prison was you didn't creep up on people.

Norman was grinning, and Chris turned away. 'Fuck off,' he said, and strode into the rec room.

The area was large, dingy, and stank of unwashed bodies. Men stood or sat in clusters, some around a TV at the far end. Some soap or other was on, but no one was watching it. He made for the far side of the area, where several empty chairs were arranged around a low table littered with dog-eared magazines. No one else was there. He sat down and picked up one of the magazines, flicking through it. Page after page of flowers and vegetables. My God! What the hell was it? He flipped to the front cover. Amateur Gardening? He resisted the urge to throw it back down and instead buried his face in it, keeping his head low whilst scoping out the room. The gang by the pool table was the most dominant. If you wanted anything, they were the ones to go to. But then you'd owe them a favour, and that had to be a bad idea. He'd heard stories of what some of them were in for, and it wasn't pretty. It mostly involved murder, often of their female partners. Hard as he tried, he just couldn't envisage killing your own partner. He would never, ever have harmed even one hair on Sarah's head. And she knew that. So, when she'd shopped him, it hadn't been because she'd been in fear of her life. It was just her gauge for right and wrong wasn't defunct, like his was. Hers worked on overdrive. He knew that now. And, for her, there were no exceptions.

He tilted his head towards the TV area. From the body language of two of the cons there, it looked like a fight was brewing. He scanned the room from one end to the other. Some of the guys in here looked evil; there was just no getting away from it. Shaven heads, scars, tattoos, cold and dead eyes. His hand instinctively moved up to trace the line of his own scar, the slash under his eye. He looked the same as them. But it was more than the way they looked. It was what they exuded, the dangerous vibes coming off them. He knew fine well they'd have no qualms about gutting him like a fish; in fact, they'd probably enjoy it. And there was a massive drug problem in here, which only made things worse.

His mind slipped back to the terror he'd felt when he'd first landed in here. He'd barely slept, being thankful that it was single cells and he wasn't sharing. Hideous wails, screams and moans punctuated the nights, along with cries of *Shut the fuck up!* as other cons beat and kicked their doors, demanding to be let out. It was as if he'd descended into hell but without the dying part first. He'd trusted and talked to no one (that hadn't changed), but gradually he'd began to stick up for himself on the occasions he'd been challenged. His sheer size had steered a lot of people away from him, and he was no stranger to exuding menace himself when he needed to. Now, although not terrified, he was still wary. You'd be a fool not to be. And he loathed every second in the place.

He sat up straighter, throwing the magazine down. Amateur Gardening! Were they having a laugh? Where was the bloody garden here to be an amateur in? Or maybe there was, and he just didn't know about it. He smirked at the thought of there being a lovely kitchen garden within the prison boundaries. It could sell produce to the local area. Convict veg. Yeah, that'd sell. One of those fancy telly chefs could make a programme about it and get even richer. Teach the cons the error of their ways, and they could repay their debt to society by growing lettuce. He shook his head.

A bloke he'd never seen before strode into the room as if he owned the place. He had a bloated moon-face, like a hamster with overstuffed cheeks. Mid-brown curly hair coiled on his head like springs, and he looked sort of...

personable. Innocuous enough. Maybe somewhere between thirty-five and forty-five. The chatter in the room seemed to dim slightly before starting up again. A group of hangers-on surrounded him, like moths to a flame. Or flies buzzing around shit. Chris surveyed the bloke more closely. He must be somebody around here. Maybe he'd been here before. The air around this guy seemed to ripple with an undercurrent of expectation.

He selected a new magazine, not bothering to look what it was. Interestingly, the new guy had walked to the pool table and just taken over. The others had surrendered and just left him to it. No, in fact, they all looked like one big happy gang. He was nothing special to look at, and Chris had definitely not seen his face before. He didn't recognise him from outside, either. If he'd been wanted for something and his face had been on the news, Chris hadn't seen it. He still watched the news most days. The guy's eyes were everywhere, and Chris didn't flinch or avert his gaze when he found himself the object, briefly, of the man's attention. The man looked away again, taking a keen interest in the rest of the room. One guy, a mean-looking, slicked-back dude who reminded Chris of one of the Krays, shouted, 'Hey, Tommy!', got up from the TV, went over to him and slapped him on the back in some sort of greeting. Hugs all round followed. The new guy handed him the other pool cue, and they started to play.

Chris was intrigued. Just who the hell was Tommy?

7

Sarah

'SHOULDN'T THE AMBULANCE HAVE been here by now?' Mum's voice was thick with tears.

Dad was already out on the street, pacing up and down, waiting for it.

Zac, in my arms, was horribly stiff, and I couldn't stop shaking at the sight of him. He was burning hot, and his muscles were hard and unyielding. He had stopped the crying, the most gut-wrenching, high-pitched sound I'd ever heard. And the soft spot on his head was bulging horribly. I couldn't tear my eyes away from it.

When I woke to Mum shouting me, I ran into the bedroom, dazed and not fully awake. Mum was holding Zac, sitting on my bed, and he just looked... wrong. I'd flicked the overhead light on to see better, and Zac had blinked and screwed up his face before crying again, turning away from the light. My first thought had been meningitis, the dislike of bright lights springing immediately to mind. All those hours on Mumsnet, pretending I was a new mother before I fell pregnant and had Zac, had finally come in useful for something. Dad was talking to the emergency services operator, after calling 999.

'Take his clothes off,' I'd told Mum as I ran to the kitchen cupboard for a glass. He was in his nappy when I returned and I snatched him from Mum, examining every inch of his skin for the telltale rash. Thankfully, there was nothing, and the tight band crushing my chest loosened the tiniest fraction.

'What are you doing?' Mum cried, looking at the glass in my hand. My knuckles were white as I gripped it.

'Checking for a rash. For meningitis. If you press a glass against it, it doesn't go. Can you see anything anywhere?'

She leaned in next to me and we both examined him.

'Nothing,' she said. 'He's a bit blotchy, but I wouldn't call it a rash.'

It had done little to alleviate my panic or slow my racing heart. Now, the glass was abandoned on the bed next to me. His skin still looked okay, but not everyone got the rash, if I remembered right.

'What else could be wrong with him, Mum?' I clutched him to me, frantic to feel him move, for the stiffness in his neck and limbs to go. His breathing was erratic, shallow, and way too fast. 'Please, Zac, come on. Breathe properly for Mummy.' But he was breathing even faster, if anything. My mind spooled back again to the Mumsnet posts. Parents posted tragic tales of babies dying from all manner of things, warning of the things to look for. Blotchy? Had anyone ever mentioned that? It didn't sound good. A splintered sound of panic escaped from my lips and Mum gripped my arm. What did blotchy mean?

I grabbed the blanket from his cot, and the babygro Mum took off him. When he was wrapped in the thick blanket, I rammed my feet into my shoes and took the stairs two at a time to where Dad was waiting in the street. He turned to look at me, and his face was grey under the streetlights. I almost fainted with relief when I heard a siren, and it seemed only seconds later before an ambulance turned into the street.

'We'll follow in the car,' Dad said as I handed Zac over to a paramedic.

'Get in,' the paramedic said, and I clambered up, my heart beating so fast and hard I felt lightheaded.

And then, thankfully, we were off, rushing through the streets of York towards the hospital. I was dimly aware of the shrill wail of the siren and the fast, bumpy ride as a numbness took control of my limbs. All I could do was watch the paramedic work on Zac, answering her questions as best I could.

'He's been out of sorts for a day or so, but mainly today. And it's not like him. He's usually such a happy baby.' I was gabbling and couldn't stop. 'I took him to the train station with my friend, she was going back to London, and he was grumpy and grouchy. I never thought…'

She nodded at me to continue as I tailed off, not taking her eyes off Zac and what she was doing. 'Anyway, I dropped to sleep, and my parents were giving him a bath. Next thing I know, Mum was screaming and telling me to call an ambulance. Zac was floppy, she said, and unresponsive. Like meningitis symptoms I've read about. And he seemed to have a temperature, too. We rang you straight away. Do you think it could be meningitis?'

The paramedic didn't look up from what she was doing with Zac. 'We'll know better when we get him to hospital and the doctors have examined him. He's going to be in the best place, and you were very quick to call us. That's all good.'

I knew she was trying to say the right thing, but tears clogged up my throat. He looked so helpless and tiny on the stretcher.

'I checked for a rash, but I couldn't see one. But they don't always get the rash, do they?' I sobbed, desperate to touch him but scared of getting in her way. She had unwrapped the blanket and was listening to his chest. His little foot, normally kicking the air, was still. It terrified me. His whole body was still, but his chest was rising and falling at an alarming speed.

'Also, he's hardly eaten a thing all day. Is that significant?'

'It could be.'

'How will they find out if it is meningitis?'

'The doctor will go through everything with you and take blood samples and cerebrospinal fluid if they think it is meningitis. It will help to identify which antibiotics to give him. But let's wait and see.'

I fell silent, thanking God that the hospital was only a few minutes away. Better to let the paramedic concentrate. Her calmness was helping me to stop panicking, at least a bit. As she bent down, obscuring him from my view, I was knocked off balance as the ambulance pulled into the hospital and came to an abrupt stop. Then everything happened so fast. The doors opened, and Zac was whisked away out of my sight. I didn't know what to do or where to go, so I just stood there for what seemed like an age until a nurse came over to me, touched my elbow and led me to a row of plastic chairs lined up against a scuffed green wall.

Her smile was tight and tense, and my stomach knotted further.

'Please,' I said. 'What's happening?'

'The doctors are with Zac. As soon as we have some news, you'll be the first to know. I'm sorry, I know how hard this must be for you."

Doctors? More than one? The sharp fingernail of my left thumb gouged into my right palm.

She went on to ask many of the same questions the paramedic had. I answered everything, despite my throat being so tight I could hardly speak. After she'd finished, she disappeared, leaving me on my own again, feeling more helpless and lost than ever.

Sick with worry, I lost all track of time until two people came rushing up the corridor towards me. Mum and Dad. At the sight of them, I burst into tears. We stood huddled together, our arms around each other, gripping and holding on.

'I can't lose him, Mum. I just can't.'

Her arms tightened around me. 'I know. And we won't. We're not going to lose him,' she said. 'The doctors here will save him.'

I untangled myself and sat down before my legs could give way, almost dragging my mum with me. The tremors started again, and I couldn't sit still. Every bit of me longed to hold Zac, to be with him, and all I could picture was how he was in the ambulance: still, stiff, and semi-conscious. The speed at which all this had happened was mind-blowing.

'Do you want a cup of tea?' My dad's voice broke into my thoughts.

'Oh, yeah. Thanks.'

I didn't really, but I knew my dad had the same need my mum and I did: to just do something useful.

He walked off to the vending machine, and I watched him go. His shoulders were stooped and he seemed to be withering away in front of me.

For the first time, I wondered if the medical staff would ask me about Zac's father in front of my mum or dad. What would I say? I couldn't lie to the doctors, but if I told the truth, my parents would know I lied to them about Zac's father being an anonymous sperm donor. Yet again, I wondered why I'd said that in the first place. I hadn't thought it through. It had kind of been a spur-of-the-moment thing, and I'd thought it would be easier than telling the truth—and, yes, I was also ashamed. Ashamed of Chris and what he was capable of. What he'd done to me. And ashamed I could love someone like that. But there was no point in agonising over that now. Why would they ask about his father, anyway? I couldn't worry about it. My focus had to be on Zac and nothing else.

Dad came back with a vending machine cup of tea for me. His hand shook as he handed it to me with a fake, bright smile.

'We left Lulu in the living room. She can get into the kitchen for her water bowl,' he said. 'I put a few biscuits down. You know, in case we're here a long time…'

I squeezed his hand. 'Thank you.'

What would I do without him and his practicality? We sat in a row, the three of us, barely speaking. What could we say?

We didn't know anything. All around us, the corridor was busy, with medical staff rushing about. No one approached us.

In the end, we waited for three hours before a doctor came to see us. We'd asked a couple of different nurses what was happening, and they'd told us that Zac was still alive and 'fighting'.

I stood up as the doctor walked towards us, trying to read his expression, but his face was giving nothing away. He stood in front of us, a young, harassed-looking man with dark-ringed, but not defeated, eyes. Then he smiled and my heart lifted. Just a bit.

'Hello, I'm Doctor Dawson. I've been treating Zac. You can see him. Just Mum for now, please.' He glanced at my parents apologetically. 'We can talk on the way.'

I looked at them. They were holding hands, leaning on each other for support. Their love for their grandchild, my son, overflowed from every pore.

'Go,' said Dad. 'We'll be right here.'

I stood up, not sure my legs would hold me up, but they did. It was all I could do to stop myself running to wherever Zac was. But that was the problem; I didn't know where he was.

'So, he's stabilised for now and the signs are looking positive. But we can't rest on our laurels. Zac is a very ill little boy.' The doctor paused for breath. I didn't interrupt, just kept putting one foot in front of the other down the corridor, letting him lead me. 'Thanks to your prompt action,' he continued. 'It could have been much worse.' His voice and face softened, and he slowed down. 'Zac has indeed contracted bacterial meningitis.'

I took in a big gulp of air as it became real. No longer me speculating from online posts. Zac had meningitis. He could still die. *He could die.* Then the steel band was back around my chest, squeezing the air out of my lungs.

'He's on antibiotics, and we have to wait and see how he responds to them.'

The floor beneath my feet grew blurred as my eyes clouded with tears again. I blinked them away and swallowed hard. Zac needed me to be strong, not a wreck who was incapable of functioning. I needed every ounce of my strength to get through this.

We stopped outside a door.

'Ready?' asked the doctor. 'Do you need a minute?'

'No. No. Please, take me to see him.'

He pointed to a bottle of hand sanitising gel fixed to the wall, and we both applied liberal amounts before he tapped in a number on a keypad to unlock the door. I'd never been so eager and yet so scared to get anywhere. I gazed at Doctor Dawson's back as we went right to the end of the ward. Before we went through another door, I saw Zac's name on a hand-written card in a slot on the wall. ZAC HAVERLAND. For some reason, it put the fear of God into me.

Somehow, my feet moved independently of my brain telling them to, and I walked to an incubator over near a large window. My darling baby was lying there, with wires and tubes coming out of him. His eyes were closed, and he wasn't moving. My blood felt like ice in my veins.

'We've sedated him. That's why he's so still,' said Doctor Dawson.

A nurse, bent over my child, looked up and smiled at me. 'Hello,' she said. 'You must be Mum.'

I tried to answer her, but I had no voice. I couldn't take my eyes from my baby. If I was scared before, it was nothing to the way I felt now.

8

Joe

WHEN JOE ENTERED THE prison visiting room, his son was already sitting there, waiting for him. Joe spotted him immediately and suppressed a grin. Look at the smug bastard now, in his grubby prison sweats. Was this Chris, then—the grand reincarnation? No, it was definitely Colin. Where were his fancy clothes, his swagger, his arrogance, and his fancy job now? All gone. Joe slowed his steps, studying him. His boy was slumped over in a plastic chair, not quite a shrivelled shell but certainly smaller, and shrunken in many ways.

He recognised it. It was this place. It took everything from you, even when you had no more to give. It would take and take, and suck and suck. Even in the prison he'd been in, a much lower category than Wakefield, there'd been a high incidence of suicide. Some of the men he'd been banged up with had seen it as the only escape. He'd lost some good friends that way over the years. He couldn't imagine the mental problems that would be in this place. It would be rife. He could almost smell the stress and the misery, and for a brief second, it tugged at him.

'Keep moving,' ordered a prison officer, off to the side. He was staring straight at him. Joe gave himself a mental shake and got going. It wasn't really his problem anymore. His problem was here and now, sitting right in front of him. Up until now, he'd never thought it was possible to hate someone so much, especially your own kid. But that was what he was feeling. He was going to have to pull off the acting job of his life right now. The good thing was, after fifteen years' incarceration, adapting and changing was something he'd become adept at. He was nothing like the person who first went inside.

Colin didn't look up as he approached, instead just rubbed repeatedly at the skin on one palm.

'Hello.'

Colin looked up at him and stopped rubbing, enabling Joe to bask in the surprise of what Colin was seeing.

'Dad?' Colin blinked. His mouth dropped open.

'The one and only,' Joe said, taking a seat. Before he dropped into it, he hitched up his trouser legs just above the knee, like he'd seen in the old movies, exposing his shiny, black shoes. He settled himself then undid the button holding his jacket closed, all his movements measured and slow for maximum effect. He glanced around him at the other visitors, well aware he was the only one in a suit. The room was full of polyester and denim. Nylon trainers. Blank stares in slack faces. No one else had dressed up for visiting. Well, that was fine by him. Made him stand out for the right reason. A well-groomed gentleman in a suit, visiting his son in prison? Oh, the poor man!

Colin's mouth dropped open further when Joe winked at him. The confusion on his face almost made Joe laugh out loud, and he bit the inside of his cheek hard to stop it. Immediately, he saw Colin as a child, cowering behind the sofa as Joe rampaged around the flat in a drunken rage. It was never a good hiding place, and Joe always found him. Afterwards, his rage spent, he'd feel better. The same couldn't be said of the boy.

'So,' Joe began jovially, throwing his arms upwards. 'Fancy seeing you in here.' His insides twisted at the thought of the years he'd spent inside thanks to Colin's lies. But he smiled and rested his hands gently in his lap after smoothing imaginary creases out of his trouser legs.

Colin's Adam's apple bobbed up and down as he swallowed. Joe watched as his mouth moved soundlessly. Colin sat up straighter but couldn't sustain it and slumped back in his seat as if slipping in oil. Then he cleared his throat but still didn't speak.

'Nothing to say to your old man after all this time?'

A brief look of defiance flashed across Colin's eyes before disappearing. Was the child once again coming to the fore? Too ingrained to be defeated?

'Hello,' said Colin, his eyes meeting Joe's before skidding away to look anywhere but. They eventually settled somewhere beyond Joe's right shoulder. His voice was barely a whisper. 'Hello, Dad.'

Joe crossed his arms. 'I've come all this way for a conversation so let's have one.'

'What's to talk about?' Colin pulled back his shoulders a fraction and straightened his spine.

Did the wimp have a backbone, then? Come on, let's see it, Joe thought. He poked the snake a bit harder.

'About where I've been for the past fifteen years. Thanks to you.' His voice was soft, barely projecting, but there was steel in it. His son couldn't fail to hear it.

Colin scratched his earlobe and finally met Joe's eyes. He shrugged, his mouth thinning. He was switching back and forth from the little boy to defiant, grown man so fast it was hard to keep up. It was quite unsettling. Or it would be if Joe cared.

'Saying sorry might be a good place to start, don't you think?'

To his surprise, Colin shook his head. 'Apologise? To you? No way.'

'Dear, dear,' Joe said, raising his eyebrows. 'You do surprise me, son.'

'Do I? Why?'

Joe let out a long, slow sigh. 'You sent your innocent old dad to jail. *Fifteen* years. I never had you pegged for a child killer. Lots of other things, but never that.'

Colin's hands trembled, and he rammed them under his thighs, but not before Joe saw. He was nervous. How long could he keep up the bravado? His mouth twisted and Joe thought, here it comes.

'Innocent? What about you was ever innocent? Why don't you apologise for knocking seven bells out of me, Shay, and Mum on a regular basis? Why don't you apologise for that?' Colin's eyes flashed with anger and darkened. This time, they didn't leave Joe's.

'Now we're getting somewhere,' Joe said, leaning forward. 'Come on, lad, carry on.'

Colin snarled then bit down hard on his lower lip, glaring at him. Joe wondered how much his straight, white teeth had cost. He ran his tongue over his own broken ones. Tombstone teeth. Not quite gnarled, blackened stumps, but more than halfway there. They didn't quite go with the suit, but hey, he could always keep his mouth shut.

Joe gestured at Colin to continue. Every bit of him itched to light up a cig.

Colin had slid down in his seat again, spent by his outburst, and was staring out of the window at a wall beyond. Joe was disappointed. His son could do better than that.

'Okay,' he said. 'You're right. I'm sorry. I did things when you were small that I should never have done. I wasn't the best father, I know that. Me and your mum, we should never have got married. We were bad for each other.'

Colin dragged his eyes back and was looking at him now, his jaw slack. They had never, ever talked like this before.

'You know Shay is dead, yeah? They tell you that in prison?' Colin asked.

Joe nodded. 'Course. They let me go to the funeral.'

Colin pushed his body back in his seat, as if a strong wind was pinning him there. 'You went?' His voice was barely audible.

'Yeah. Why wouldn't I? She was my daughter.'

'You never gave a shit about either of us. Was it just a change, to get out of prison for the day?'

Joe shrugged. 'Maybe. Alright yeah, it was a nice change.' He held out his hands in a *you got me* gesture. 'But the weather was crap. Fair threw it down.' He pulled a sad face.

Colin shook his head and crossed his arms. 'You haven't really changed at all, have you? Despite your time inside and your fancy suit. Which looks cheap, by the way. Shiny suits are out. They've been out for decades.'

Joe smiled and ran his hands over his thighs. 'You'd know. From what I hear, you were quite the fashion icon and ladies' man before. You could have given me lessons on grooming, but you're stuck in here now.' He cast his eye over Colin's prison issue clothing and felt his son wither under his gaze. That was the best kick in the cojones so far. 'So what happened there?'

He made a circling motion with his forefinger towards Colin's scar.

'Glass in the face. What does it look like?'

Joe nodded. 'It's really spoiled your looks, if you don't mind me saying.'

'What do you care?'

Joe paused. Was Colin fishing? Did he want him to care or not? He dug deep into himself, to see if he could dredge up any positive feelings for his son at all. Nope. He couldn't. But he could pretend.

'Would I be here if I didn't care?'

Colin blinked twice, then his eyes narrowed. 'Probably. I think you've come to rub it in. I've crashed and you want to see me burn. That's what I really think. You've never cared for me for five minutes. My life growing up was hell. Because of you.'

Joe watched as Colin's spark burned out as quickly as it ignited. The despair was plain to see as Colin looked around the room and remembered where he was. Joe could remember that feeling well, how it sapped the life out of you. But he didn't want Colin to demand to be taken back to his cell, not yet. He was enjoying himself far too much.

'Look,' he said, all conciliatory. 'You and me? We're all that's left of our family now your mother and sister are dead. I know it might sound strange, but perhaps I'm here to talk about forgiveness. I'm sorry for what I've done, for the shit father I've been, and you're sorry for lying about the accident and getting me sent down. Sounds fair enough to me. Let bygones be bygones?'

Colin was staring at him intently. 'Forgiveness? I would have chosen anyone else in the world to be my father but you. And yet, it's you I got. And you want to talk about forgiveness? The only thing I'm sorry for is getting caught and being in here.'

'So you're not sorry for running that kid over, then? It's what started all this off. If you hadn't taken my car—'

'Of course I'm sorry for that. I am. I always have been. I'd have given anything to be able to turn the clock back.'

'So let's talk about that. About what you did.'

'Which bit?'

'All of it.'

Colin clamped his jaws shut. 'I'm not into confessions. And you're hardly a priest.'

'Come on; I wanna know. Apparently you beat a man to death—'

'That was an accident. There was no beating.'

'... strangled an innocent woman—'

'What's the point of this?' Colin glared at him. Joe could feel the hate, and it fed his own.

'... and ran over that girl. Anything else I should know about?'

'You don't need to know anything. You haven't exactly been there for me in my life.'

'Ah, now, see—that's it. Blame Daddy,' Joe snapped, leaning forward.

Something in his voice stopped Colin short. He looked scared. Joe remembered the little boy he'd once been, shaking and shivering in his shoes. But it didn't last for long. Colin drew himself up.

'Alright, you want to talk?' Colin asked. 'Tell me, why were you such a vicious bastard? Did you get a kick out of people, your own family, being terrified of you?'

'Do you know, I probably did.' Joe stopped and relaxed his shoulders down. Took a long, steady breath in. 'Look, I said I was sorry earlier.'

'What's the point of this? Have you just come to antagonise me? Because there's not much left you can do to me now, is there? In case you haven't noticed, I'm fucked.'

Colin raised his hands and gestured around the room. Joe hadn't had this much fun in ages. His son, the arrogant son of a bitch, was suffering enough as it was. Probably best not to push it too far. He took a deep, calming breath.

'I told you why I came. I want us to start over. Like I said, we're all we've got now. I'd like to visit you again. If you want me to.'

Colin shook his head and pushed himself further back into his chair. 'I don't even know why I agreed to this visit in the first place, to tell you the truth. What do you and me have to say to each other?'

'And yet you did agree. Why? Curiosity?'

'I just said, I don't know why. Maybe it was. To see what effect you'd have on me after all these years. But I'm not a kid now and you can't really do anything to me, can you? I'm realizing that. I'm not scared of you anymore.'

Joe reached a hand out towards him, and Colin flinched back. It appeared his words weren't entirely truthful. Joe drew back.

'Look, have you got anything better to do with your time? Are people beating down the door to visit you? I think not. But I'd like to get to know you. I've already told you that. What have you got to lose?'

Colin stood up. 'I'll think about it.'

'That's all I can ask,' said Joe. He reached into his pocket and pulled out a post-it note he'd written on earlier. 'Take this. It's my mobile number.'

Colin looked at it but didn't touch it. There was no embrace or handshake. Joe knew his son would rather die than touch him.

'I'm done here,' he heard Colin say to a prison officer.

Joe watched Colin go then stood up slowly, his body creaking painfully. He blamed all those years of lying on a hard prison bed. He smiled at a woman at a nearby table as he walked past. All things considered, today had been a good day. It had gone better than he thought it would. He hoped he'd be coming back. And it hopefully wouldn't be too long, either.

9

Chris

HE DIDN'T LOOK BACK as he left the visitors' room. As he walked back to his cell, his knees were still shaking with shock. He'd hardly recognised his dad; he looked nothing like the man he'd last seen half his lifetime ago. When his dad had got sent down, he'd resembled an old tramp, with his shaggy, unkempt hair, all knotted and stringy. Chris had never seen him in anything other than filthy, torn clothes, with his fingers clutching a can of lager. There'd always been a cigarette hanging out of his mouth too, burning its disgustingness all over the place.

Yet today, he'd been confronted with a tall man, straight-backed and clean, with a neatly trimmed beard, and even neater fingernails. The biggest change was the hair, which was mostly gone.

And what was with the suit? Chris had been expecting his dad to look exactly the same, he realized, and not even have aged. Whatever prison had done to him, it hadn't been all bad.

Yet, after the initial shock of seeing him, Chris had felt the fear that had gripped him all his childhood come rushing back. It was as if it had never left, and he hated his father even more for that. How did that man have the power to send him scuttling back through time and dominate him so completely? Yet he'd fought back and finally showed some spirit. And it had felt so good. Amazing, even, for being so long overdue.

Apart from visiting, the prison was locked down once more, and the landings were deserted. He could breathe for once, without the confines of the space and all the other inmates crowding him. It was far from quiet, though, as several cons were yelling and kicking the shit out of their doors. Chris blew out a heavy breath laced with despair; it was just another day in paradise.

'Gillespie!' called out one of the prison officers, a hulk of a man Chris called 'Squeaky', on account of the laughably and unexpectedly high-pitched voice that emanated from his bulk. Chris couldn't remember his name or what the other cons called him. His officer number was 192.

Squeaky was leaning against the handrail of the walkway. He had a sheaf of papers in his meaty hand and began shuffling through them. Chris walked over to him, with no idea whether it was good or bad.

'Yeah?' Chris asked.

Squeaky was leaning over the railing now, peering through the net at something far below. He held a finger up, signalling him to wait. Chris tried not to rise to it; it was just another way to subjugate prisoners and reinforce the 'us and them' mentality that was prevalent in this place. The cons and the screws. Yet Chris would be willing to bet that at least half the screws in this place were bent. He'd learned a lot of the stuff that went on in this place happened with the full knowledge of the officers, and they turned a blind eye to it. He just didn't know which ones.

He glanced at his watch. Once he was back in his cell, he wouldn't get out again until tomorrow. As usual, the muck they called breakfast would be given to him later, for tomorrow morning.

Squeaky straightened up and handed him a slip of paper. 'Interview with the chef tomorrow morning, eight o'clock. Don't be late.'

Chris looked down at the paper. It was for a job in the prison kitchen. Kitchen jobs were like gold dust: long hours out of the cells and the best paid. It wasn't lost on him that he was actually looking at a prison kitchen job as a good thing; when you compared it to his lucrative IT career in his former life, it was laughable. He wanted that job, even if it was for some menial, mindless task. At the interview, he'd be the model interviewee.

'Okay,' he said.

Squeaky turned away, his attention already on something in the far distance.

'Back to your cell,' he said before lumbering off, his rubber-soled shoes making high-pitched noises on the floor, not unlike his voice.

Chris muttered, 'Where else am I gonna go?' under his breath, shoved the paper in his pocket and ambled towards his cell. On the way, he passed the phones. His phone card was in his cell. If he'd had it on him, he could have rung Sarah's number and found out if she'd changed it since he'd been in here. But what would be the point? She'd told him in no uncertain terms when she'd visited him that she wanted nothing more to do with him.

He went back to his cell and closed the door. The caged animal inside him awoke once more. He lay back on his bed and closed his eyes, wishing more than anything he was still in Brazil and had never returned. He and dog-Leanne could have had a good life there, but he'd had to fuck it up and come back to find Sarah. What had he been thinking? It had been by far the stupidest idea he'd ever had, doomed to failure, and now he'd wrecked the rest of his life because of it.

Panic engulfed him as the enormity of his situation loomed large, as it did several times a day, each time as severe as the last. It wasn't getting any better. He wouldn't last in here. This wasn't living. It was definitely a life sentence, whichever way he looked at it. Death would be better than this existence. His chest was rising and falling fast now, as his breath came in shallow pants. He couldn't take in enough oxygen and felt like he might faint. All he could do was ride it out and try to breathe more deeply, but it wasn't working.

He scrambled off the bed onto his hands and knees, gulping in air and sobbing, as the remainder of his life was laid before him in his mind's eye. The rest of his life was here in this cramped room, with its dark walls and tiny window.

He flipped over onto his back and tried to recall the azure sky of Brazil, the endless stretches of sand, and how the searing heat of the sun had beaten down on him. The vast, roaring ocean and shrieking sea birds. The vibrations of Miguel's tattooing pen on his arms, even the smashing of the glass into his face by his own hand. Anything to distract him from this room. The only thing he could successfully block from his mind was York, and his fleeting time with Sarah after he got there. If he thought of that now, of her, he'd truly go insane.

He saw Leanne almost drowning in the sea as he took her to England with him. How 'Lulu' was the first name that had come into his mind when Sarah had asked him what the dog was called. The kick it had given him back in Brazil to name the dog no one wanted after Sarah's best friend, the human bitch Leanne. He was thankful Sarah was looking after the dog now, but bitterly regretted leaving Brazil. Should have stayed there. At least he'd been free.

Later, after the storm raging inside him had passed, he got wearily up from the floor and read the note about the kitchen job again. Tomorrow morning, his door would unlock. It would remain locked until then.

He used the toilet and washed his hands before sitting back down on his bed. A small TV with a remote sat silently in the corner and he turned it on for company, and also to drown out the ranting and banging of the cons in their cells. The channels available were severely restricted, and he ended up on BBC1 again, some dumb game show that was playing. His mind snapped back to his dad's visit earlier.

When he'd got the visiting request from him, he hadn't been able to believe it. At first, he'd wondered if someone was playing a joke on him. Maybe that was why he'd agreed to it. He'd never actually thought that his old man would ever turn up. He'd never been there for him once during his childhood, so why now? All those missed school meetings with teachers, concerts, and trips his parents had never shown any interest in. He'd been known for being the kid whose folks never showed up to anything. His dad hadn't bothered to get out of bed for anything to do with his son, yet had practically broken his neck to rush to see him in prison.

He'd been right about one thing, though: that Chris didn't have anything better to do with his time, so why not see him again? And, on the plus side, his dad had actually said sorry for being a shit father, so that was a turn up. He'd never in a million years expected that to happen. But in the past, everything that came from that slimeball's mouth had been a lie. What made this any different? No, his dad wasn't sorry. He didn't know how to be sorry, so why say it? Was his dad up to something? But, if so, what?

Chris's greatest strength had always been his analytical, probing mind, but try as he might this time, his analysing turned up nothing. One of his favoured theories was the one where you eliminate everything implausible, and what you are left with must be the truth. So, the truth must be, then, that there was something else going on with his dad. Chris needed to see him again to try to find out what it was.

But first, he had to get this interview over with. Yes, he'd been pinning his hopes on getting out of this cell, but he realized that if he got the job, he was going to have to spend hours and hours with people he was probably going to hate. Would that really be better? He closed his eyes again and slumped back on the bed, willing sleep to come and for it never to leave.

10

Joe

'HOW WAS IT?' GERRY was barely visible at his pine kitchen table, flanked on all sides with piles of old magazines, newspapers, and general clutter when Joe walked in. Balanced on top of a stack of old mail was a half-drunk cup of what looked like tea. Next to it, a cigarette burned in an ashtray atop some magazines, causing Joe's heart to lurch.

Good God! Had the man never heard of a fire hazard?

Joe removed the magazines from under the ashtray and cleared some space, noting that it was only three in the afternoon and the shop downstairs was already closed. Maybe Gerry hadn't bothered to open it at all today. Wouldn't be the first time. He eyed the burning cigarette. 'You'll burn the bleeding place down if you're not careful.'

Gerry waved a dismissive hand. 'Hasn't happened yet.' He pulled off the filthy, stained flat cap that Joe sometimes thought must be glued to his head, revealing a bald, shiny pate, only disturbed by the odd white hair. He scratched a flaky patch of skin and replaced the cap. Joe wondered what colour it used to be when it was young, hundreds of years ago. Of all the germs crawling around the place, that cap was the one thing Joe wouldn't want to touch. Gerry reached for the half-empty cup of tea and sipped it.

'Urgh!' He pulled a face. 'Cold.'

'I'll make some more.'

Joe squeezed the kettle in under the tap, above a mountain of dirty pots, filled it and placed it back on its stand. His hand felt greasy, either from the tap or the kettle itself, and he wiped it on his jeans, glad he'd changed out of his suit as soon as he got back. It was now hanging in one of those suit cover things, mainly to keep cat hairs off it. He scanned around for clean cups and gave in. It was hard sometimes to even locate the sink in this place. Not that any of this mess bothered Joe in the slightest. Compared to how he'd lived years ago, both with his ex-wife Jane, and afterwards when he'd pissed off and got his own flat, this place was a palace. And in prison, things like that didn't matter. You didn't have enough possessions to constitute clutter. The cell he'd shared with Gerry when he'd been moved to HMP Lindholme at Doncaster had been littered with Gerry's detritus, but nothing on this scale. Gerry never needed a bin when there was a floor.

A ginger cat strolled through the door, over to a litter tray in the far corner, where it proceeded to take a huge dump. Joe wrinkled his nose. The damn cat was the worst thing about this place. Or rather, the litter tray was. Gerry only emptied it twice a week. The cat jumped onto Gerry's knee. It was a hefty thing; probably weighed two stone, by the look of it. It was a wonder it could even jump that high.

Joe sat down opposite Gerry, who was looking at him expectantly.

'So, are you gonna tell me or just keep me hanging?' Gerry's hand ruffled the cat's fur, and it purred loudly, arching its back.

Joe grinned. 'It was good. So nice to see my kid. Know what I mean?'

Gerry burst out laughing, knowing every bit of the history between Joe and his family. 'I'll bet. Was he surprised to see you looking so scrubbed up?'

'He damn nearly fell clean off his chair. I've been replaying it in my head ever since.' He mimed Colin's shock when he'd seen him and Gerry cackled louder.

'Wish I could've been there to see it. What did he say?'

'For a while, nothing at all. His mouth was moving, but no words came out.' He mimed again, exaggerating for effect. Gerry slammed his hand down on his thigh, unable to contain his mirth.

'The little bastard had it coming, alright. Fifteen years he took from you, Joe. Fifteen long years.'

'Ha, I know. I thought he was going to shit himself when I turned up. He probably didn't think I'd actually go. Turns out he has a bit of backbone after all. Told me he wouldn't apologise for letting me go down, and I should be the one saying sorry for being a shit father. Fair cracked me up, that did.'

'So, what did you do?'

'I apologised. To keep him on his toes.'

Gerry nodded and stood up as the kettle started to boil. After quickly swilling two mugs under the tap, he dropped teabags in, gave them a good dunking, added sugar and loads of milk, and returned with them to the table. Joe took a good swig and smacked his lips together. Gerry sure made a great cuppa. He glanced around, and Gerry plonked a half-empty packet of digestives in front of him. Joe fished out two to dunk.

'Are you going again?' Gerry asked.

'Yeah. I don't think he'll refuse. He'll want to know what I'm up to.' He dunked the first biscuit and popped it in his mouth whole, savouring the sweet hit on his tongue.

Gerry nodded. 'He's got no chance of ever guessing.'

'No chance at all. I'm going to play the doting father, just 'cos it pleases me. I can feel the hate coming off of him, though. He can't disguise it.' The second digestive got the same fate.

Gerry tutted loudly. 'Little bastard. Who does he think he is?'

Joe took an unopened pack of cigarettes from his pocket and Gerry nodded his approval; it was his favourite brand. Joe proffered the packet to him.

'Don't mind if I do. Are you partaking?'

'Damn right I am,' Joe said, lighting one up. He inhaled hard and settled back in his chair before blowing out a smoke ring. He sighed at the simple pleasure.

'This came for you.' Gerry passed him an envelope.

Joe ripped it open. 'Ah, good.' He removed his renewed driving licence, with its new photo ID. 'Christ, how old do I look in it?'

Gerry picked it up and scrutinised it. 'It's a good likeness. You're an ugly bleeder alright.'

Joe chuckled and took another drag. 'Have you got your Daz to look on that marketplace thing yet?'

'Yeah. He's already started. What would you prefer? A Fiesta? A Mini?'

He indicated his long legs. 'Oh aye! Me in a Mini? I'd never get out of the bleeding thing.'

'You would. They make 'em quite big, these days. Should rename 'em 'Not-Minis' or something.'

'I'm not that fussed about the make. Fiesta would be fine. Whatever five hundred quid will get me. It's all I've got.'

'Our Daz will find something half-decent for that. He can fix it up a bit, if it needs it. Always been good with cars, our Daz.'

Joe nodded, satisfied. Having his own set of wheels would be so much better. He thought back to the tan cavalier, the last car he owned, when Chris went joyriding. When Joe got sent down for it, he had no idea what happened to the car. It was going to be weird, though, driving again after all this time.

'Any preference on colour?' Gerry asked. 'I'll ring him later.'

''Yeah, okay. Anything but shit-brown. Maybe a nice red or blue.'

'Noted.'

Joe knocked back the rest of his tea then set the cup down. 'You sort that other thing yet?'

Gerry tapped the side of his nose. 'I told you to leave it with me. Don't worry about it. It's all in hand.'

'Okay.' Joe was more than happy to hand over responsibility to Gerry. His friend knew what he was doing. And if there was one person he could trust in this world, it was his mate, Gerry.

11

Chris

AT FIVE O'CLOCK, CHRIS awoke. He lay in the dark, blinking. This was his favourite time of every day. Not the dawn itself, but the brief moments upon waking when he forgot where he was. For those few seconds, life was normal, and he could be anywhere: his flat in Fulham, back in the motel in Brazil, his tiny flat in York. Several times, before he'd been fully awake, he'd reached out for Sarah next to him, feeling for her warm shoulder and instead touching the cold, hard wall of his cell inches away, jolting himself back to reality in an instant.

This time, he was under no illusions as to where he was, as booted feet and jangling keys echoed on the landing just outside his door. The sound passed. Today was his first day working in the kitchens. The interview had gone well, and the job was his. He blinked again, his eyes adjusting to the gloom of the cell. He struggled to turn over on the narrow bed, almost rolling off before scooting back to the middle to lie on his side. Now he was wide awake, his mind full of going to work in the kitchen today. Not for the first time, he wondered how it had got to this, from a successful IT career and his dream woman to life in a few feet of suffocating prison cell. No more working on IT security, the job that was so engrossing and enjoyable it never felt like work at all. To what? Washing pots? Sweeping the floor? Avoiding getting a kicking?

An overwhelming urge to punch the wall broke over him and he squeezed his eyes tight, willing it to pass. Instead, he clawed his hands into the thin sheet covering him, grasping it hard until his muscles spasmed. Everything that had happened to him had been his own doing. Every last little thing. All his life, he'd blamed other people for the things he was responsible for; Sarah had said as much when she'd visited him in there. His lips stretched into a grin, and a bubble of hysterical laughter burst from him. What a time to realise the truth. Another laugh exploded. He'd lost it. He was actually going insane. Caught somewhere between laughing and raging, a sob escaped, and before long, all he could do was cry. Soundlessly, because to make a noise crying in here would be a mistake and, at this time in the morning, the prison was the quietest it ever got, the kicks and screams of the night before having died down as exhausted prisoners gave in and went to sleep. It never seemed to be deadly silent in here, though. There was always someone shouting abuse or thumping a door, not to mention the early morning raids when the screws searched cells, looking for drugs, mobile phones or other contraband that was forever getting smuggled in. As fast as the officers discovered and confiscated it, the smugglers found new and more ingenious ways to bring more in. From dead birds and footballs stuffed with drugs thrown over the walls to visitors hiding contraband inside their own bodies, it was a war that had no end. None of it interested him.

He curled up on his side and let the tears wash out of him, leaving him spent. At six o'clock, when a prison officer unlocked his door, he was dressed in his new jeans, and waiting. The screw was youngish, maybe early to mid-twenties. A neat goatee with a hint of red. Chris couldn't remember if he'd seen him before or not.

'Are you ready?' he asked in a Liverpudlian twang. 'I'll be collecting you every morning for the kitchens. You can call me Phil. You're first pick up. We'll be getting some others along the way.'

Chris nodded. A small smile pulled at Phil's mouth, and they headed off, Chris falling into step behind him. They called to pick up another four men, all on his floor (the threes), and they walked along in silence. The sounds of stirring, shouting and doors being hit were beginning to escalate.

They left A Wing and the threes, and went down to the main prison kitchen on the ground floor. Chris had never been here before, his hot meal being delivered to the Wing serving kitchen every evening, along with all the other inmates on the threes. Phil held the door open for them and pointed to another officer standing at the back, talking to a small group of prisoners. Most of them looked bored to tears and barely seemed to be listening, but one was nodding and trying to look enthusiastic. Chris decided the forced enthusiasm approach might be best and arranged his features accordingly. Might as well get involved and attempt to get something out of the day.

'Over there. He'll take you through what you're going to be doing and I'll see you later to take you back.' Phil pointed the way.

As the others shuffled over the kitchen as instructed, Chris hung back.

'What time, roughly?' he asked, adding, 'Not that it matters. I haven't got any place else to be. I was just wondering.'

The screw smiled, properly this time, and Chris was taken aback at how genuine it was. Phil seemed to see a person, not just a con, when he looked at him, and that hadn't happened in a long time. It felt good.

'Around three.'

He disappeared off back through the door, and Chris stood for a second, surveying the group. There were eight now, all standing around awkwardly, as if they were new, like him. Other prisoners were already working at their stations, obviously having been there for a while. Banter filled the air, and the atmosphere seemed lighter in here than the rest of the prison. Chris was surprised to see Tommy, the guy they were fawning over near the pool table, emptying bags of carrots onto a stainless steel surface, which looked surprisingly clean given the state of the rest of the prison. A pleasing smell of bleach tainted the air, and he breathed in deeply. Bleach was good. It represented sterility beyond a normal clean, therefore zero germs.

'Oi, over here.' The officer spotted him and beckoned him over. 'Come on, we haven't got all day.'

Great! Another smart arse. All day was exactly what Chris did have. He walked over but didn't hurry.

'Name?' the officer said, looking down at his clipboard. 'No, don't tell me. Gillespie?'

'Yeah.' Chris looked at the screw's number. 31. If he had a name, he wasn't telling them what it was. Probably scared someone would find out where he lived and sort out his missus, one way or another.

The screw struck a pencil through writing Chris couldn't see and put the clipboard face down on the stainless steel bench next to him.

Had he seen this screw before? Didn't think so. Must have come from a different wing. They were always swapping about. Probably to stop them forming attachments and seeing the cons as real people. There again, some of the officers were decent blokes he could have a laugh with. They weren't all bad. But a handful really got his back up. 31 could well turn out to be another.

31 adjusted his bottle-bottom glasses and addressed the group. 'Right then, now all you newbies are here, we can get started.' He went around the group, pointing at each one in turn. 'Rowan, over there. Pot washing.' He gestured towards an area with two massive sinks and a towering pile of crockery. 'Same for you, Washington.' A lanky black kid scowled at the sight but said, 'Okay.' A blonde man with a

face full of decades-old acne scars who must have been Rowan showed no reaction other than the briefest of nods.

'Off you go, then,' the officer said, dismissing them condescendingly.

Chris watched as they slouched off, neither looking at nor speaking to the other. The screw sighed and Chris tried to not let it bother him. What was his problem? At least he'd be getting paid more than the few pounds a week Chris would be earning. Plus, he got to go home at the end of each day, the lucky bastard. Being here was his choice. Chris never chose to come to this shit hole. Or, he supposed in a way he did, when he chose to do what landed him here. See?—taking responsibility.

'Gillespie, you're on spuds.' He gestured vaguely to where Tommy was still messing about with carrots, his head down. 'Over there. Tommy will show you what to do.'

Chris wandered off. Where were the knives in this place? With all the food prep going on, there must be some damn sharp ones. Who got to handle them? Surely not just anybody, not with half the prison probably being in for some violent crime or other. He made a mental note to watch his back.

A huge sack of potatoes stood open on the floor. You had to be fucking kidding! A whole sack? A small, sharp knife lay on a chopping board. Chris picked it up.

'Yours is forty-two.'

Chris started at Tommy's voice. He'd been expecting to be ignored. Tommy had stopped arranging carrots in long lines and was now appraising him.

'Sorry?' Chris asked.

Tommy gestured to a large board on the wall, over near the door. 'Your knife. It's number forty-two.'

Chris stared at the board. It was massive, empty but for drawn outlines of utensils. He frowned.

'Shadow board,' Tommy said. 'Each knife, fork or whatever has a number, and they write down who has it. So they always know where everything is. This…' he held up a mean-looking chopping knife about six or seven inches long, 'Is number twenty-nine.' He looked at it affectionately. 'We've had some great time, twenty-nine and me. Oh, the things we've done together.'

Chris looked at him closely. Was he completely barmy? Tommy burst out laughing.

'Just shitting yer. They all go back on the board by the end of the shift.'

'Oh, right.' Chris nodded at the overflowing sack of spuds. 'They mine, then?'

'Yeah. But they'll muck in as well when they've done their jobs.' Tommy pointed with his knife to two other prisoners doing something Chris couldn't see around a work station.

'I'd best get started then.' Chris took a potato out of the sack. It was going to be a long day.

'Just chuck them in there for washing and peeling,' Tommy said, pointing to an industrial-sized machine Chris hadn't even noticed. Tommy chopped the ends off the carrots and threw them into a similar machine.

Chris rolled the potato over in his hands. It had seen better days—half of it was soft and coated in a white fur. It stank. He went to put it into the machine.

'Whoa!' Tommy said. 'You need to chop the bad bit off first. Are you trying to give us all food poisoning?'

Chris looked down at the thing. He couldn't remember preparing a spud in his life. His parents had never bought fresh fruit and veg, and when he'd left home and shopped for himself, he'd always got things ready prepared. And at uni, he'd lived on junk food. He'd once bought a peeler on impulse, and it had remained attached by a plastic tie to the cardboard label until he'd thrown it out. And when he'd been with Sarah, she was only too happy to take over preparing what they ate. The only thing he'd ever made from scratch had been a chocolate cake he'd done to impress her. He could see it now, standing on a wire rack, a bit wonky, but still—

He jumped as the potato was snatched out of his hand.

'Give it here, for God's sake!' Tommy slammed it down onto the side and chopped it in half, dropping the mouldy bit into a large bin next to him. Then he passed it back to Chris and said, 'Get a load more and look them over. They send us all the shit ones.'

Chris just gawped at him. The speed of Tommy with that knife…

Tommy burst out laughing. 'God, your face. Not a natural at this, are you?'

'Nope. I've only just realized.'

'Well, you'll get plenty of practise in here. You'll be a dab hand at it in no time.'

Chris grabbed another potato and checked it for signs of decay. It looked alright. He put it next to the one Tommy had cut. The third one was also mouldy at one end. As he chopped it off, he caught the skin on his finger.

'Ow!' He glared at the cut that had opened up. A dribble of blood came out of it.

Tommy dug into his pocket and brought out a fistful of bright blue plasters. He trapped one under his forefinger and pushed it over to Chris.

'Wash your hands, then put that on. I cut myself all the time. Don't worry about it.'

When Chris resumed peeling, with a new plaster covering the cut, his mind wandered, specifically to wondering about Tommy. With the way Tommy strutted about the prison, he'd been expecting some gangland arsehole who wouldn't give him the time of day. Instead, Tommy was personable and friendly. Chris was dying to know what the other man was in for. Maybe he could ask around, discreetly, of course. Norman next door seemed to know everyone and everything, so he could start there.

Tommy lined up carrots and chopped both ends off before putting them into the peeling machine. He was much faster than Chris. Chris got a rhythm going and soon the potatoes were piling up.

'How long have you been working in the kitchen, then?' Chris asked. 'You're a bit of a dab hand at that, if you don't mind me saying.'

Tommy shrugged. 'On and off, twenty years.'

'Twenty years?' He only looked mid to late thirties.

'Yep.'

'You like it in here, then?'

'What, the kitchen or the prison?'

'Um... both.'

Tommy just shrugged.

Chris watched as Tommy started the potato peeling machine. Jets of water cascaded onto the potatoes, washing the skin off by force. It didn't do a great job.

'Just be glad it's working and you're not doing them all by hand,' Tommy said, raising his voice over the racket of the machine.

'Does that happen?' Chris asked, aghast.

'Sometimes, while they're waiting to get it fixed.'

Chris shuddered. Twenty years of this and he'd be in the nuthouse. He glanced up to find Tommy looking him over. What was he thinking? A ripple of unease ran through Chris's insides, and he realised he was scared of this man, this stranger, with his apparent fondness for knives. Whoever he was, people seemed equally intimidated by him or in awe of him, all bar the screws. Thankfully, they didn't kowtow to him. He'd thought the idea of certain prisoners being looked up to in jail had been the stuff of movies, but it didn't appear that way now. Whoever Tommy was, he was someone you didn't cross. He shuddered inwardly, thinking what Tommy may have done to earn respect like that. Better not to make an enemy of him. He started a fresh pile of spuds.

'What are we making, anyway?'

'Mash. For Shepherd's pie tonight. One of the few things chef does that tastes half decent.'

The chef that had interviewed Chris was standing in the middle of the kitchen in chef's whites, chopping some kind of meat. Looked like beef. Could have been anything.

'He not a prisoner?' Chris asked.

'No. Him and some of the other kitchen staff aren't. How long have you been inside?' Tommy asked.

'Ten months.'

'You a lifer?'

'Yeah. But I intend to get out one day. I'm just gonna keep my nose clean.' He grabbed two handfuls of spuds and began checking them over.

'Drugs?'

'Nah.'

'Who'd you kill, then?'

Seemed Tommy had no problem asking that question. Who should he say he'd killed? Maybe just go with Luisa for now, the woman he strangled. It wasn't like Tommy could get his records and find out the truth. Was it?

'My neighbour.'

If Tommy wanted more information, he'd have to ask.

'What'd you do?'

He was hit by the memory of the smell of Luisa and her flat. Old, spicy cooking smells and her strong deodorant. The deodorant hadn't worked; the sweat stains on her shirt under her armpits had been pronounced. No deodorant would have been strong enough to mask the stink of her, especially not with his hands around her throat.

'I said what did you do?'

'To the neighbour?'

'Yeah.' Tommy's eyes seemed brighter and, after glancing around the room, he leaned forward. He tilted his head down, his eyes locked on Chris's.

Chris swallowed. 'I strangled her.'

Tommy pursed his lips and inclined his head in what could be taken as approval.

'Why?'

Why indeed? If he told him why, he'd have to mention Sarah and no way was he doing that. He wouldn't utter her name in this filthy place. He dredged the bottom of his brain, but the silt blocking it was thick and sludgy. This was more thinking than he'd done since he got here. What could he say? Tommy was waiting. Half the truth would do.

'She was a maniac. Found out she was stalking me. Taking my picture and bugging me all the time. Waiting to ambush me. Got right on my nerves. I told her to stop, and she didn't.'

Tommy laughed out loud. 'So you made her? Classic!'

'I guess so. It kind of all happened so fast. And it landed me in here.'

'Is that all you're in for?'

'Well… no. I got into a fight with a man and hit him. He ended up in hospital and died days later.'

'That weren't your fault, then,' Tommy said. 'Sounds like an accident.'

'That's what I said, but they pinned it on me, anyway. So…' He shrugged.

'That's what the bastards do.' Tommy barked out a laugh. 'Same thing's happened to me.' He winked at Chris. 'Several times. If you know what I mean.'

Chris didn't but laughed regardless. He knew, suddenly and without a doubt, that Tommy had no qualms about killing people. Or maybe he had them killed and let someone else do the grunt work, although Chris got the feeling Tommy would enjoy doing it himself. He wanted to know how many and how he'd done it, but didn't dare ask. You didn't ask blokes like Tommy stuff like that. You waited for them to tell you.

He didn't have to wait long. By the end of the afternoon, he knew more about Tommy than he ever wanted to. The man was basically a psychopath running a drugs empire from prison, and Chris had never been as scared of anyone in his life. Not even his dad. But Tommy seemed to have taken a shine to him, and was acting like a friend. If that was what it took to keep him safe, Chris would be his friend.

12

Sarah

IN THE INCUBATOR, ZAC was barely moving. His eyes were closed, and his breathing was shallow and rapid, causing his naked chest to thrust out and in alarmingly. Through gritty, sore eyes, I tried to focus on his gorgeous face, but all I could see was the tube trailing out of his nose, another leaving his mouth, and a mass of trailing wires attached to his chest.

I rubbed his tiny hand and willed him to wake up, but he didn't. The doctor had just left after another discussion about how bad things were, and I was so frightened I could barely breathe. We knew it was definitely bacterial meningitis now. We knew my little boy might die. They'd done a lumbar puncture because of the way the soft spot on the top of his head was bulging; apparently, it's a classic sign. The doctors were pumping him full of antibiotics. After all I went through to get him, the thought that I might not be able to hold on to him was killing me.

Mum came back into the room with yet another canteen sandwich, and a cup of tea, and once again I thanked God that the doctors had let her stay with me. She passed me the sandwich and I put it on the windowsill. I didn't know why she insisted on getting them when they would only go in the bin. The lump permanently lodged in my throat and chest that was stopping me from swallowing felt the size of a beach ball. The last thing I wanted to do was eat.

Mum's eyes flicked to Zac and then back to me. 'What did the doctor say?'

'No change. But, also, he's no worse, and he said that can be a good thing. It means the antibiotics are kicking in.'

She sat down heavily. All the sitting she'd been doing, in a hard, plastic chair, wasn't doing her arthritis any good. I could see from her grimace she was in pain.

'What time is Dad coming back?'

'He'll be a couple of hours. He's going to whizz Lulu around the park and have a quick shower. I've told him to get some rest if he can. He never closed his eyes all night again, you know. He was up and pacing around the flat half the night.'

I could imagine. Every night, they went home to my flat, and I stayed here with Zac. I practically had to shove them out of the door. If it wasn't for the stern nurse who came on shift most evenings, I didn't think they would leave. But they didn't argue with her. She was only telling them to go home and rest for their own sake. There was nothing they could do for Zac. There wasn't really much anyone could do for Zac. The doctor had more or less said it was up to Zac's own body now, but I wasn't going to tell Mum that.

'I got you this,' Mum said, holding up the sandwich.

'Thanks.' I turned back to Zac. 'I'll have it later.'

For a horrible minute, I thought she was going to say I 'have to eat and keep my strength up', for the millionth time. Thankfully, she didn't. Instead, she just gripped my hand, willing her strength into me that way. And, despite her being in such pain every day, she was surprisingly strong.

'You should have gone home with Dad. You're exhausted, too.' I squeezed her hand. In the four days Zac had been here, none of us had slept.

She fixed me with a look. That steeliness I knew so well was back in her eyes, having replaced the fear that had been there lately. 'You're staying with your baby and I'm staying with mine,' she declared.

I'd always loved her fierceness, her feistiness. It's where I got mine from. But her stubbornness was either her best strength or her worst weakness, depending which side of it you were on. At times, it made her her own worst enemy, like now. She looked dead on her feet.

'Mum, I'm okay. If you're here all the time, I just worry about both of you,' I told her. 'So it's twice over.'

'I'm not going. You can say what you like.'

There was no point arguing. But I really wanted to be on my own for a while. There were so many people in this room sometimes it was claustrophobic, and I felt there was no space to breathe.

'Why don't you go for a walk around the hospital grounds? It'll do you good to get out of this place. I'll ring if… I need to,' Mum said.

'Alright. I'll do that if you go home and rest as soon as I get back.'

'Deal.' She smiled at me and her love bolstered me. I could and would get through this. We all would. And so would Zac. I could feel it. He was going to get better, and we'd all walk out of here and resume our lives. Put it all behind us. I had to believe that.

By the time I'd put my coat on and left the room, the resolve I felt had melted away to nothing once more. But the fresh air and solitude was calling me, and I got the lift to the ground floor. There was a small garden where patients and families could go at the back of the hospital, and it was there I made my way towards. It was peaceful; there were colourful flowers and plants in pots placed around wooden benches. I pulled my hood up against the chill, the sight of the bright yellow daffodils and tulips lifting my spirits a fraction. I took my phone out of my pocket and switched it on. If there was a problem Mum would ring, and I'd be back upstairs in minutes.

The garden was empty, and I sat down on one of the benches, the dampness leaching out of the wood and into my jeans. I still couldn't believe what had happened in such a short time. Zac had been a little out of sorts and then everything went wrong at a frightening speed. Ever since then, it was like I'd been wading through treacle with a brain full of mush.

I couldn't even think about the cafe properly, so I was just trusting my staff to run it. By all accounts, they were managing without me, but I suspected only just, seeing it was me who made more than half of the stuff we sell. Martin, the new boy, had been thrown in at the deep end and was struggling to keep up with the cake-making, but he was doing an admirable job. We were doing a much-reduced range overall. Ellie was still on the pastries and trying to oversee Martin too. Claire texted or rung me every night after work to keep me updated. She tried to sound upbeat, but I could always hear in her voice how stressed she was with the increased workload. Plus, she was worried about Zac, too. They all were. Never once did any of them complain. I couldn't get better staff but right now, the cafe could fall down and I wouldn't care. Zac occupied my every thought.

After ten minutes, I was just brooding. I turned my phone off and retraced my steps back up to the ward to find Mum dozing off in the armchair. She jerked awake when I came through the door.

'Come on,' I said to her. 'Off home with you. And I don't want to see you back here until tomorrow.'

She blinked as my words sunk in. 'But it's only six o'clock.'

'I know exactly what time it is. Don't come back tonight. Stay with Dad. You're both worn out. Look, if you come back in the morning, I'll nip home for a couple of hours. Okay?'

She stood up and pulled on her coat. 'Yes,' she said meekly.

Wow! That was a first, her doing as she was told. Good, because I had no strength to argue with her. She kissed me and stroked Zac's cheek. He stirred but remained asleep.

'Ring Dad. He'll come get you.'

'No, no. He might be asleep. The bus will have me home in a jiffy.'

I knew she wouldn't ring him. 'Bye, Mum. See you tomorrow.'

It wouldn't take her long to get home, with the good bus service York had.

When she'd gone, I felt more alone than ever. The nurses here were lovely, but they were here to work, not chat with me. I looked around the room at all the monitors and machines keeping Zac alive. He was the only patient in here and I was glad. I didn't think I could sit here making small talk with other parents. At least this way I didn't have to bother.

The beeps and buzzes of the various machines faded into the background as I settled into the chair. The door opened, and a nurse came in, smiling at me as he performed Zac's hourly checks. He jotted down things I didn't understand on his notes.

'All good,' he said, before going out again.

I slumped back in the chair. I couldn't work here, in this place. They did a fantastic job and they were so dedicated, but I don't have the mental fortitude it must take. Thinking about what they did made my baking and my job seem unimportant. Cake? Desserts? It's all just fluff.

What must it feel like to save a life and really make a difference when you go home at the end of the day? As I gazed at Zac and thought how grateful I was that there were people who did this job, my mind started to tick over. Maybe I could do this job. I wasn't too old to retrain. But the thought of all those hours of studying, getting into debt and having no income—I couldn't possibly make it work, and look after Zac, too. Maybe making cake was all I was good for. All I was good at.

Zac shuffled around and whimpered. I got up and leaned over him, running my finger over his face, tracing the curves of his doughy features. He didn't open his eyes, no matter how hard I willed him to, but he responded to my touch, I was sure of it.

I stood stroking him until my back ached, and I had to sit down again. Time passed so slowly in this room. Every minute was like an hour, every hour a day. To think it had only been four days. Felt like forever. One of the worst things was I had no idea how long it would take Zac to get better. Were we talking days or weeks or months? The doctors hadn't been very forthcoming on that score. All they would commit to saying was that it was early days. As if I didn't know that.

I tried to nap in the chair, feeling better for being as close to Zac as possible. I longed to hold him, to nurse him better, but I wasn't allowed to even pick him up, he was so ill. The one thing I could do was to express milk for him and I did, several times a day. Any embarrassment I felt about it was long gone now, and I just got on with it.

After expressing and dozing and clock-watching, I read a few chapters of a book Leanne had lent me. I wasn't a big reader, preferring to leaf through magazines and things that didn't tax my short attention span, but since I'd been in here I'd found reading a good way to get lost in another world.

I picked up a crossword puzzle book Mum had left behind, even though I hated puzzles. They frustrated me. But at least it was something to occupy me. As I hunted around for a pen, the door opened and the nurse from earlier stuck his head into the room.

'Your mum is on the phone,' he said.

I frowned. It must be important if she was ringing. Not for the first time, I wished I could use my phone in here.

I followed him to the nurses' station, hoping nothing bad had happened at home. The nurse handed me the receiver then tactfully turned away.

'Mum? Are you okay?' Oh my God, was she crying? 'Mum. What's wrong?'

'It's your dad, love. He's collapsed. I've rung for an ambulance, but I don't know what else to do. He's not moving.'

My throat went dry, and I stared at the polished floor. This wasn't happening. It couldn't be. Not now.

'What happened?'

'He was fine when I got here. He'd taken Lulu to the park. Her feet were still wet. I told him off for not drying them. He told me to go and have a soak in the bath, so I did. When I got out, he was lying on the floor. Sarah, I don't know what to do. I don't know any first aid.'

Me neither. 'Er, try not to panic. You've done the best thing, ringing for the ambulance. Mum, is he breathing?' The floor seemed to ripple beneath my feet. I closed my eyes.

'I… I don't know. His chest doesn't seem to be moving.'

She couldn't speak as her sobs increased. She must be so scared and I couldn't do anything from here. The ambulance would get there before me if I went home.

'Go down and wait for the ambulance, like Dad did when we rang for Zac.'

'Alright. I'll… I'll do that.'

She put the phone down and the line cut off. I didn't mean for her to hang up. I stared at the phone in my hand, unable to think straight. My dad, my lovely dad, lying unconscious on the floor. What if he'd had a heart attack or a stroke or something? What if he was already dead?

'Are you alright?' The nurse was looking at me with concern.

I shook my head. 'No. My mum says my dad has collapsed. She's phoned for an ambulance.' I stopped as my throat clogged up and tears cascaded down my face.

'Sit down a sec. Are they bringing him here?'

'I don't know. I expect so, though. My mum's hung up. If they come as quickly as they did for Zac, they won't be long.'

'Leave it with me. I'll try and find out what I can. What's your dad's name?'

'Peter. Peter Haverland.' I wiped my face on my sleeve, tears spreading over my cheeks.

He scribbled it down on a pad. 'Go back to sit with Zac, and I'll find you the second I know anything.'

I nodded, unable to speak, grateful someone else was taking charge. My legs trembled badly as I walked back to Zac's room, not sure I would make it. But I did, and I sank into the same chair I was in a few minutes ago. When I'd thought life couldn't get much worse. But of course it could. It just had. It could always get worse.

13

Chris

CHRIS STEPPED INTO THE shower after his first week in the kitchen was finally over. He would have given anything to spend an hour in the shower of his Fulham flat and let the powerful jets massage away his exhaustion, but that luxury was gone forever. Instead, he was surrounded by mould and grime, and a flow of water that had bad days and good days. Today was a bad day, and the flow was weak and lukewarm. It didn't improve his mood any as he thought back over his kitchen work. At times, it had dragged, but so did sitting in his cell hour after hour. And he never wanted to see another potato as long as he lived. When chips or mash were served up from the spuds he had spent half the day doing, he could have thrown up.

He soaped his body in large, sweeping movements, anxious to be away. The thought that he could still be here in twenty years or more, showering in his underwear, entered his mind, but he refused to acknowledge it. Today was all he could process; the here and now. If he thought any further ahead than that, his brain would probably explode. Most days, he wished it would anyway, and that would put an end to the daily misery.

He wasn't alone; two other cons were in here, both wearing underwear and looking as eager to get out as him.

They were drying themselves, their backs turned to each other. No conversation between any of them.

He washed his face, hating how the disfiguring scar beneath his eye felt under his fingers, the raised edge interrupting the otherwise smooth contours of his face. Sometimes, especially in the dead of night as he lay awake, sweating and blinking in the darkness, the scar burned red hot—a reminder of his own stupidity and recklessness, from pushing a glass into his own face. He'd never used to be reckless, in fact, he'd always been the opposite. The consummate planner and organiser, obsessing over the smallest detail. Pernickity and finicky, that's how work colleagues had described him. It had driven a few of them mad. But with his old job in IT, looking for ways in to secure networks to test their resilience, those qualities had been what had made him stand out and rise to the top so quickly, In here, however, those same traits were character flaws and would single you out for worse, not better. In here, they'd be perceived as weakness, and used against you to gain others' advantage.

The other two cons left together, along with a screw who had been standing by the door. He turned off the tap and began to towel himself down. A laugh sounded in the distance, voices getting closer. Shit! He stiffened. He would never get used to the total lack of privacy in this place. Even when locked in your cell, an officer could open the door and barge right in at any moment.

As he was pulling on his joggers, three men entered the bathroom. Chris eyed them as dried himself faster. Could be Hispanic, could be Asian; it was hard to tell under the mops of hair and beards. They weren't speaking English, though. Sounded more like Spanish. During his first month here, a con had been badly beaten in the showers. Chris hurriedly pulled his T-shirt over his head and gathered up his things. If something was going to go down here, he wanted no part of it. A chill ran the length of his spine as he realised these three were together, a gang, and the outsider was… him.

One of them addressed him, saying something he couldn't understand. He'd heard them speak English before; why weren't they now?

'Look, I don't want any trouble,' he said, tucking his towel and washbag under his arm and holding his hands up. 'I was just going.'

He eyed them, one at a time. Could he fight them? At one time he would have attempted it, but he wasn't in peak condition. He was a long way off it. Plus, he wanted to stay out of trouble and not add a single day to his sentence. That wouldn't happen if he'd been fighting.

His eyes slid between the men, back and forth. They had formed a solid line between him and the exit, and there wasn't a single screw to be seen or heard. He could shout, but it would only further show his fear, and these guys would show no mercy. And he was scared. These guys weren't big, but they were mean. Wiry but muscly too. They were lifers, like him, but seemed to have long since given up hope of freedom. So they had nothing at all to lose. Maybe they didn't care if they never got out.

His heart was galloping now, as all three advanced without a word, huge grins splitting their faces. They were going to take pleasure in killing him. He took a step back, but there was nowhere to go. The tiled shower wall butted up against his back as a cry rose and died in his throat. He tried not to imagine what a razor blade would feel like slicing through first his skin and muscle, then pushing deeper.

The first blow, when it came, was worse than he expected, the force of a fist hitting him at what felt like a hundred miles an hour. Black dots grew into pinpricks of bright light that exploded in front of his eyes as his head smashed back into the wall. His jaws snapped together hard with the impact, biting into his tongue, and a scream died in his throat as blood spurted from his mouth. Tears sprung to his eyes and his knees buckled with the second punch, a slam to his guts. Then another to his head as he curled into a ball, wrapping his arms around his skull to protect his brain. He'd never known pain like it.

Punches and kicks rained down on him, each one more painful than the last. How long it went on for, he couldn't say. Time ceased to exist outside his world of agony. His ribs must have been broken, surely. He couldn't breathe. He tried to draw in a breath but his lungs wouldn't inflate. He imagined his lungs punctured with razor-sharp shards of rib bone. The blows suddenly stopped, along with the voices of the assailants. The quiet was somehow worse than the racket a second earlier. Chris forced his eyes open, wincing at how much even blinking hurt. The men were backing away now and he could see feet. More pairs of feet than just three. There were shouts and raised voices. He tried to lift his head and Tommy's face swam into view before going foggy and turning black once more as his eyelids closed.

'Chris?' Tommy's voice. 'Are you okay?'

He attempted to lift his head, but nothing happened. Then a loud scream emanated from him when someone touched his torso. That made him move his head.

Someone was yelling for an officer and a doctor when his head sank back onto the floor. When the room went black again, this time it stayed dark.

14

Sarah

IT WAS GONE TWO in the morning, and I was beside myself with worry about Dad. Zac was peaceful, still asleep, which only left me more time to think about what might be happening to Dad. I hadn't heard anything in ages, other than he'd arrived at the hospital and been whisked away. With me not being able to have my phone on, I hadn't even been able to contact Mum.

I was just checking Zac's nappy for the millionth time when Mum came in. She was white-faced and looked exhausted. The red rings around her eyes probably mirrored my own. I rushed to her and hugged her like I was never going to let her go.

'What's happening? No one's told me anything. I'm going stir crazy in here.' I burst into tears and released my grip on her.

'I don't know much, either. They took him away and hours later, told me he was stable. They were 'doing tests'. Well, of course they are. It's what they always say while they're trying to find out. What else can they say?'

'So they haven't said he's had a heart attack or a stroke or something like that?'

She shook her head. 'No.'

'That's good news then, in my book.'

She sagged against me.

'Come and sit down. You're done in. So much for going home to rest.'

'I know. I had a bath and then that was it. I found your dad on the floor and everything went berserk again. It was like a rerun of Zac coming in here.'

She was crying softly. I handed her some tissues. The nurses here kept topping them up. I couldn't even hazard a guess at how many boxes I'd got through since I'd been in here.

'He's alive, Mum. That's the main thing. Anything else, we can get through. Right?' My voice was much stronger than I felt inside. It gave me a bit of hope and courage. I didn't want to think about my dad not being here. I knew one day he wouldn't be, but not yet. He was much too young, and he had way too much to live for.

I knew, deep down, that thinking like that was stupid; none of us were infallible or immortal, but I couldn't help it. It made me feel better, so I was going to do it.

Mum nodded. 'Yes. You're right, love. We can.' She tried to smile at me through her tears, but it was watery and weak and barely there. She gazed at Zac. 'I don't know what's happening, Sarah. How much more can we take? It's like we're being punished or something. We must have been really bad in a past life, and this is karma.'

'Don't think like that. It isn't true. And there are lots more people worse off than us. These things happen. No one knows why.'

It wasn't like her to be self-pitying, so it was an indication of how bad she must be feeling. Usually, she kept me strong by being strong herself. I hugged her again.

'We'll get through all of this and it'll just be a bad memory.'

'I know. I'm sorry. I just can't remember ever feeling this worn down.'

'It's understandable. First Zac and now this.'

'It wasn't first Zac. It was first you. We thought we'd lost you when they rushed you in with the ectopic. I still can't get out of my head that you could have died.'

'Well, if it's true that things come in threes, then this is our last one, isn't it?'

'I suppose it is. Anyway, your dad and Zac need us, don't they, so enough of all this.' She sniffed and straightened her back. When she looked at me, some of the old resolve was coming back into her eyes.

I squeezed her shoulder. 'You are allowed to fall apart, you know. And get depressed. Especially at times like this. It's perfectly normal.'

She didn't answer, but I could see her ruminating on what I'd said. We sat side by side on hard plastic chairs, through the remainder of the early hours and into the dawn, disturbed only by medical staff coming in to see to Zac. I was so tired I thought I was bound to fall asleep, but I didn't. If Zac or Dad took a turn for the worse, I wanted to be the first to know.

At seven in the morning, stiff and aching all over, I stood up and stretched.

Mum blinked. I don't think she'd slept either.

'I might go and see if I can find out anything about Dad,' I said.

'They know I'm here. They said they'd send word.'

'But they'll be busy. And I'm sick of hanging around here.' My stomach gave a loud growl. When did I last eat? I couldn't even remember, but I was feeling a bit hungry, at last. 'I don't want that sandwich for breakfast. I might go grab something from the canteen. Do you want anything bringing back?'

'Okay, yes. A croissant or something like that, if they've got any.'

'Alright. I'll ring Claire, too, give her an update. She'll be wondering why she took this bloody job. I don't know what I'd do without her.'

'She's a treasure for sure, that one.'

I checked I had got my phone, kissed Zac, and pulled my coat on.

'I'll ask at reception if they've admitted him onto a ward.'

Mum nodded, her face anxious and drawn at the mention of Dad.

The door closed silently behind me, and I walked quickly away from the ward and down the corridor. I shunned the lifts and instead went down three flights of stairs to the reception desk, where I was informed my dad had been admitted. The woman on the desk told me where he was and, after getting lost and taking wrong turns twice, I eventually got there. It wasn't open for visiting, so I pressed the intercom.

'Hello,' a woman's voice said.

'I'm Peter Haverland's daughter. He was admitted last night. Would you be able to give me any information on his condition, please?'

'I'll be right out,' she said over the crackly line, her voice tinny and thin. Then it went dead, and I hugged myself while I waited.

Please don't let the news be bad. What if he was in a coma or had sustained brain damage or something. I never thought of that. I hadn't thought past a heart attack. I didn't even know what ward this was. The receptionist had only told me what number. A vision of him lying there like an empty shell filled my head. He might never talk, or walk, or smile, or play with Zac or Lulu again. The horror was unimaginable.

Just then, the door opened, and a nurse stepped out. She smiled. 'I can't let you in, I'm afraid. It's not visiting.'

'I know. I haven't come to visit. He was brought in last night and my baby is here, with meningitis. I've just come down to see what happened with him. My mum doesn't know anything, and she's worried sick.'

'I'm so sorry to hear that. Let me check the doctor's latest notes. I'll be right back.'

She closed the door again but was back before too long, holding a clipboard and reading some notes.

'The doctor was going to contact your mum when he gets back in. It says here that she's with you, in the paediatric intensive care unit.'

'That's right.'

'We're still doing tests on your dad, waiting for blood results to come back. But he's stable. You can visit him later today.'

'Oh. Is he conscious? I mean, can he speak?'

'He's sleeping right now. But he's conscious, yes. Were you told he wasn't?'

'Only because Mum found him on the floor. He was unresponsive. No one's told her anything. She was in A and E for hours with hardly any information, then she came up to find me. She's been there ever since.'

'Yes, that's not unusual, I'm afraid. These things take time.'

'Oh, I wasn't complaining. I know he's in good hands.'

She nodded. 'Come back at midday. We should know more then.'

'Thank you. We will.'

She went back inside, and I stood there outside the ward door. It didn't sound too bad. She hadn't said anything to make me worry. She hadn't sounded worried herself. But they did that, didn't they? Kept quiet about things they weren't sure about, so you didn't sue them for misinformation.

Before I got to the canteen, I went outside and rang Claire. She answered on the first ring.

'I've been wondering whether to ring you. There's no one here and Lulu is on her own upstairs. I can hear her barking. What shall I do?'

'Have you got your key to my flat?'

'Yeah.'

'Can you just let her out to go to the toilet? She's been on her own all night.'

'Of course. What's happened?'

I could hear her unlocking the door to my flat, then the noise of her running up the stairs.

'Hang on,' she said. 'I'm just getting her now.'

'Could you pop her to the park, just for five minutes?'

'Yeah, course. Olwyn will be here soon. She'll take her out for longer.'

'Ring me back when she's running around and I'll fill you in. Thanks again; you're the best.'

'No problem.' She cut the call and called me back a few minutes later.

I brought her up to date, and she was stunned. 'Is there anything I can do? I can't believe it, Sarah.'

'Just knowing the cafe is okay is a massive weight off my mind. Is everything alright there?'

'Yes, all good. You don't need to worry about a thing. Just concentrate on getting your dad and Zac better.'

Like I could make it happen. I would if I could. I know what she meant, though.

'I thought I'd come by tonight around seven, if they'll let me in,' she said. What do you think?'

'I'll ask them. And if they won't, I'll meet you outside. I'd love to see you. I'm going mad in here just looking at the same walls.'

She paused. 'What's the latest on Zac? Any change?'

'He's no worse, and the doctors have said that's good, so…' There was nothing more to add to the exchange we now had every day.

'Alright. I'll see you tonight then,' she said before hanging up.

For a moment, I wanted to be back at the cafe so badly I could cry. The days at work were long, but I loved every damn second of them. I'd taken it for granted that it would always be there. My cosy little life, full of people I loved, who cared about me and helped me more than I deserved. I had no idea how long Zac might be in hospital and that, along with any possible lasting damage from his illness, was the worst part. That was if he survived, obviously. I couldn't go there. He would survive because no way was I letting him go.

At midday on the dot, Mum and I were waiting outside Dad's ward. A nurse let us in and led us to Dad's bay. She hadn't said a word, and that was making me even more nervous. She stopped halfway down the corridor and gestured to a bay on our left. I gasped when I saw Dad. I stopped dead, and Mum bumped into me.

'What?' she said, clutching at the collar of her jacket. She peered past me and gasped, too.

Dad was sitting up in bed, wearing a thin hospital gown. He waved when he saw us and gave us a grin. A bit of a sheepish one.

'Hello,' he said. 'Fancy seeing you here!'

Mum just gawped at him.

'Pull up a chair each and I'll bring you up to date.' He pointed back into the corridor, where towers of plastic chairs were stacked up. There was an armchair by the side of the bed.

'You sit there and I'll just get another chair,' I said to her, before going to the stack outside. What was going on? Dad looked fine. I hurried back and waited for him to talk.

'It was just a scare. My blood pressure took a dive, what with the tiredness and stress of everything. I've had a full MOT and service, and I've got a clean bill of health.

Trust him to play it down like he was a bloody car.

'So I'm getting out.'

'When?' asked Mum.

'In two hours.' He ripped off a strip of tape that was stuck to the back of his hand. 'I'm just waiting for the paperwork to be done and dusted.'

He flung back the covers and swung his legs out of bed. They looked pale and thin under the dark hairs. 'My clothes are in that locker there. If you want to pull the curtains, you know, preserve my modesty. I can't have those nurses out there all after my body, now, can I?'

Mum smiled. Her eyes were moist. 'I should think those poor nurses know much more about your body than they'd like. I shudder to think.'

I pulled the curtains and waited outside while Mum helped him dress. The relief was overwhelming, and I sagged back against the wall. Then the curtain was whipped back, and he was sitting on the bed, looking like... himself.

'I've just got to wait here for a couple of hours. The doctor says I'm fine. But I want to look in on Zac before I go. I wonder if they'd let me pop up there now.' He glanced down at where his watch should be and tutted in annoyance to find it not there.

'No. You need to go home. Zac is asleep. There's no change.'

Dad frowned, but I folded my arms. 'You need to pay attention to yourself, Dad. This is a scare. A warning sign, or whatever. It's serious.'

He was quiet. 'I know. And you're right. I will take better care of myself.'

'Shall I ring for a taxi for you for later?'

'No. I'll do it. It'll give me something to do.'

I sat with them until his discharge paperwork was done. It was ready by half-past one, and we left the ward with him bantering with the nurses. I think he was enjoying himself. I watched him from the corner of my eye. He was walking fine, and he had a bit of colour back in his cheeks. I looped my arm through his and Mum did the same on the other side.

'I'll make sure he doesn't do anything stupid,' she said.

By the time we got outside, some of the tension in my body had eased. If he was okay, then I could concentrate on being with Zac. A taxi arrived in minutes and I waved them off before going back inside to spend the afternoon feeling useless.

When Claire arrived, I'd never been so glad to see anyone. I hadn't been sure they'd allow her on the ward, but I'd begged them, and they'd agreed she could visit if she kept it short.

'Hi,' she said as she entered.

'It's great to see you.'

She hugged me then reached for her handbag. 'Before I forget, I brought these for you, in case there's anything important.'

She handed me a stack of mail. Right on the top was another letter from Chris. I shoved everything into my bag. Claire immediately bent over Zac and started cooing.

'Hello, little man. Remember your Aunty Claire?'

It was the first time she'd seen him in here. If she was shocked at the sight of him, she hid it well. As I sat back in the chair, a wave of exhaustion hit me. My eye lingered on the letter from Chris, nestled at the top of my bag. He wasn't giving up. Still every week, without fail.

Every day, around mid-morning, the postman would leave any mail in a little locked box on the wall outside. I'd slip out, unlock it, get the mail and pocket anything from Chris, then slide the key back under the tray in the till. I hadn't realised Claire even knew where the key was.

I zipped up my bag, and the letter disappeared from view. I would shove it in the drawer with the others when I got home. Maybe one day, I'd open them and read them all. But not today.

'So,' Claire said. 'How is Zac?'

Instead of answering, I burst into tears.

15

Joe

JOE BREATHED IN DEEPLY as satisfaction at the view before him coursed through his veins. Colin was hunched over in his chair, waiting for him in the visitor centre, just like before. Once again, he was looking down at the floor, paying no attention to anyone or anything else in the room. He was rubbing one palm with the other thumb, up and down, round and round. Like he was distracted or anxious. Even from this angle, Joe could see Colin's face was swollen and battered.

When he reached him, Joe stood in front of him, demanding to be noticed. Nothing happened. He narrowed his eyes in irritation.

'Hello, *son*,' he said.

Colin looked up slowly, blinking. His right eye was so badly puffed up it wouldn't open. His face was all shades of yellow, purple and black, even striated with green, and his bottom lip was twice the size it should be.

'What the hell happened to you?' Joe hitched up his trouser legs before dropping into the chair.

Colin shrugged. 'Walked into a door.' He folded his arms across his body and hugged his ribs, wincing.

Joe folded his own arms and deadpanned, 'Really?'

'Fell down the stairs, then.'

Joe rolled his eyes.

'Why did you want to come again, anyway?' Colin asked, even though it plainly hurt him to move his mouth. Or any part of his face. 'At this rate, I'll be seeing more of you than I saw in all the years I was growing up.'

Joe tried not to rise to the slight but failed. 'Always did have a smart mouth on you, didn't you? Is that how you got that?' He nodded at his face.

Colin sat up straighter and lifted his chin. 'What? I did? With you? Are you fucking kidding me?' he winced and prodded at his mouth.

Joe considered this and nodded. 'Alright. Maybe not with me you didn't, no.'

'You would have taken my head off. I hardly dared to say a word to you. You were always like a grenade about to go off. You were a nasty bastard then, and you probably still are. Despite your…' Colin gestured to Joe's suit, currently on its second outing. It had taken him ages to get the damn cat hairs off, despite it being in the bag thing.

Joe swallowed a chuckle. Needling Colin was more fun than he'd thought it would be. 'Maybe I've changed. Maybe I'm not that man anymore.'

'No,' Colin spat out. 'Maybe you're Father of the Year material. Shall I nominate you for a Pride Of Britain award for services to parenthood?'

This time, Joe's throaty laugh broke free. 'How did it come to this? I only asked what had happened to your face. So, anyway, what did happen?'

Colin deflated, his anger dissipating as fast as it had exploded. Joe watched his son, who was once again looking at the floor between his feet. His hands were bunched into fists by his sides, and his shoulders were somewhere up around his ears. Misery, anger and fear oozed out of every pore. Joe placed his hands on the table in front of him, interlocking his fingers. He cocked his head and looked at his son. How long would Colin last in here? There was no way to tell.

He was jolted out of his thoughts when Colin mumbled, 'I was jumped in the showers. They took a dislike to me for some reason.'

'What happened?'

'I was in there on my own. Three bastards decided to use me as a punchbag. Not much else to say.'

'No screws around?'

'What do you think?'

'What made them stop?'

'Someone else came in.'

'A screw?'

'No, another prisoner. He's got a lot of respect around here. Nobody seems to cross him. He's got a lot of clout.'

Joe raised an eyebrow. 'The screws are scared of him?'

'No, the screws aren't. But they aren't on his case all the time, either. It's like an uneasy truce, it seems to me.'

'A mate of yours now, is he?'

'I suppose. I've got a job in the kitchen and he works in there, as well.'

'What's he called, this other prisoner?'

'Tommy.'

A bead of blood forced its way through one of the splits in his lip. He dabbed at it with a finger and grimaced at the sight of the blood.

Joe tried hard to imagine his son working in a prison kitchen. Him with his fancy A-Levels and degrees and whatever. Pity he couldn't picture it. But he did find it funny. He wanted to say, 'Dear, oh dear, how the mighty have fallen!' but Colin was just opening up nicely, and he'd hate to spoil the flow. Besides, they were 'bonding'. They'd never done it before. It was lovely. He swallowed down another desire to laugh, coughing it away instead.

'So he comes into the bathroom. What then? What did he do to stop them?'

Colin frowned as best he could and stared at him out of his one open eye. Joe tried to read what was behind it, but he couldn't tell. Maybe it was because of his injuries, the bruising and the swelling everywhere, or maybe it was because there was nothing behind them to see. If Joe thought of himself as cold, perhaps his son had taken it to a whole new level. Certainly his crimes, the very reason he was in here, were shocking. He'd done things far worse than Joe, things Joe wouldn't even have thought of.

'What's with all the questions?' Colin asked. 'Why do you care so much all of a sudden?'

Joe watched as Colin tried to push himself back in his chair and sit up straighter, but gave up, clutching his side again. 'Just showing some concern, that's all.' He stared pointedly at Colin's ribs.

Colin's mouth contorted as he laughed and then grimaced as his swollen lips stretched. 'What's the real answer?'

Joe held up his hands. 'Fine. Don't tell me. What else shall we talk about? All the wonderful things you've been doing in here?' The words were out before he could take them back.

Colin's eye narrowed as his head jerked back. A dull flame there burned brighter. 'You can put on all the fancy clothes you want, but don't try and kid people that that monster inside you isn't still there.'

Joe bristled, sick now of the way Colin still managed to try to claim the high ground. Yeah, so he hadn't been the best father. He'd apologised for that, despite not really being sorry. He had no issues with himself.

'Wow! Monster? You're the killer. If I'm a monster, what the hell does that make you?'

Colin glared at him, and slowly and painfully stood up. Joe recognised the look on Colin's face. Hatred. He should know.

'Do us both a favour; fuck off and don't come back,' Colin said as he began to shuffle away.

'Fine by me,' he muttered under his breath.

He didn't look back. But he did smile.

***

He stood in the prison car park, by the old banger Gerry's son Daz had got him, a battered Golf that was more rust than bodywork. And it was bloody lurid yellow. Gerry referred to it as 'the custard car', and thought himself hilarious. The sight of it made Joe scowl every time, but beggars couldn't be choosers, and he was certainly that. He stamped his feet, partly to keep out the cold seeping up from the ground and partly to contain the anger that that little gobshite in there still thought he was better than him. Within minutes, he was marching up and down, smoking fast, taking quick, hard drags deep inside before blowing them out.

Joe looked at the austere building, happy at the knowledge he wouldn't be coming back. He'd seen the inside of enough prisons to last him a lifetime. Although, it had to be said, this place was worse than any he'd been banged up in.

He glanced at his watch. How long was Gerry going to be in there? Although, the visit hadn't even been a quarter of the way through when Colin had limped off in a sulk. Gerry could be ages yet. Joe sighed and leaned on the roof of the car.

At last, Gerry came out, looked around, and waved when he spotted Joe, which wouldn't have been hard seeing as he was standing next to something akin to a massive canary. Gerry lit up a cigarette on the way over.

They both held their breath as Joe turned the ignition key. After a splutter and a noisy bang it caught, and they pulled away. Joe glanced at Gerry. He could wait no more. He'd learned practically nothing from Colin.

'Well?' he said, as Gerry grappled with the window winding handle before giving up.

Gerry twisted round to look at him. 'It's all in hand. Absolutely nothing to worry about.'

'What did Tommy say? Does Colin suspect anything?'

'Not at all. Why would he? I told you our Tommy knows what he's doing.'

'Okay. Good. Colin hardly told me anything. We fell out instead.'

'I saw. All not well in paradise, then?'

Joe laughed out loud. 'You could say that. He basically threw me out and told me not to come back.' He hung his head in mock sadness. 'It was very unpleasant.'

'Right. Well, that's you told, then.'

'So it's up to Tommy now. What if—?'

'He won't let us down. Stop panicking. He knows what he's doing.'

'Does he think Colin trusts him?'

'Seems to. And he's working on it every day. Them being in the kitchens together is a massive bonus. A right turn up for the books, that. Even our Tommy couldn't have engineered that one.' He raised his eyes as if he could see right through the car's dirty roof. 'Seems there is a God.'

Joe nodded, breathing easier now.

'Colin certainly doesn't suspect our Tommy put those guys up to it,' Gerry said. 'Tommy would have picked up on that. Very intuitive, he is. Full of sensitivity.'

They both chortled at that.

Joe slowed down for a stop sign. 'How close to him does Tommy think he'll be able to get, now he's Colin's saviour?'

'He said he's practically got him eating out of his hand already. Said your boy has no other friends in there. In fact, he told me your lad actively avoids people and stays on his own. Or he did. But now he's got a new best friend…'

Joe changed gear, and the engine stuttered alarmingly. For a horrible moment, he thought it might stall and not start again. He floored it hard to compensate, and it roared back into life, kangarooing forward several times in the process.

'Careful,' snapped Gerry, as his head hit the headrest and careened off. 'Or I'll be having a whiplash claim in.'

'Sorry.' Joe eased off the juice, not sure if Gerry was joking or not.

As they drove, Joe thought back to the visiting room. As he'd left, he'd seen Gerry and Tommy at a table together.

They looked natural with each other, at ease and relaxed. For a fleeting second, Joe had been jealous. They were closer than him and Colin had ever been (not that that was hard), but they weren't even father and son. Over whisky one night, Joe and Gerry had had the idea when Gerry had mentioned his nephew was in Wakefield nick. Tommy was Gerry's sister Maureen's lad, but Gerry had just about brought him up, taking him in when Maureen died and absorbing him into the family. With such a big family to start with, Gerry hadn't batted an eyelid about one more, and neither, it seemed, had his long-suffering wife, Maggie. Although she had eventually left him during one of his stints inside. Gerry never mentioned Tommy's father, but Joe got the feeling he'd never been around from the get-go. Gerry and Joe had sat up half that night, and Joe had marvelled at the difference between what family meant to them. To Gerry, it was everything. To Joe, barely anything at all.

He relaxed back into the car seat. All in all, it had been a good day. Tommy had it under control, and would keep working on it. And when the time came, Colin wouldn't know what had hit him. Joe's only regret was that he wouldn't be there to see his face.

16

Chris

JUST THE VERY ACT of smoothing out a sheet of paper hurt his ribs. Chris grimaced, waited for the stabbing pain to pass then picked up the pen. As he considered what to write, he scratched his nose, forgetting for a second the state of it. A sharp sting made him wince as he knocked the scab off. It immediately started to bleed.

'Shit!'

The deep cut had happened during the beating and, with other, more severe, injuries he hadn't noticed it at first. It looked to him like maybe one of his attackers had hidden something between his fingers, a piece of metal perhaps, just enough for a sharp end to protrude and cut him.

He shuffled off the bed and went over to the sink to dab water onto the cut. After the fight, he'd been taken to see the doctor, who'd checked out his ribs by poking and prodding them in a most excruciating way, then rocked back on his heels and announced, 'Yep. Three broken,' before leaving a male nurse to explain that they couldn't do anything, and it was just a matter of time. Chris would have to be careful, he'd said, but they would heal in their own time. Chris had almost said, 'Are you kidding? How can I be careful? If this happened once, what's to stop it happening again?' But he hadn't said anything. There was no point. As it was clear, though, that he'd been the victim and not the perpetrator, no action would be taken against him, therefore, more importantly, no time would be added to his already unbearably long sentence.

As he leaned over the sink, he took shallow breaths, washing his face as quickly as he could, then dabbing it lightly with a scratchy towel, barely touching his skin in case he made something else bleed. He lifted his sweatshirt and looked at his body; the bruising on his torso was still spectacular, being all shades from purple and indigo, to yellow and grey. They'd done a real number on him, alright.

Being under doctors' orders to rest had put paid to him working in the kitchens. He'd been given two weeks off and now spent all day in his cell again, only getting out for association. Even shuffling around the exercise yard was out of the question, and he had no idea when he'd be able to do sit-ups again. Just the thought of it was painful.

He returned to the bed, sat down, and picked up the pen, sucking the end of it; he knew the start: *Dear Sarah*. That bit was easy. In past attempts, he'd started with *my darling Sarah*, *my dearest Sarah*, and *my beautiful Sarah*, each time striking a line through it and going back to 'dear'. The others had made him feel like some ponce in a ruffled shirt from a period drama, and he'd never gone in for that shit. Even 'dear' sounded so formal, but what else was he supposed to put? Y*o, bitch?*

He wrote *Dear Sarah* then stopped.

It was getting harder to know what to put. Wish you were here? Guess what I did today? Let me tell you about my day? Instead, as usual, he poured his heart onto the page. The first time he ever did it he'd felt stupid and clumsy, but by the end, he'd experienced a cathartic release like never before, and hadn't realised he'd been in tears by the end until he'd wondered what was tickling his face. He'd put his hand up and discovered the wetness on his cheeks.

He needed this release again now and hoped it would come.

Dear Sarah, I don't know if you'll ever read this but if you do, I just want you to know how sorry I am for what I did to you. Truly sorry. I've never met anyone like you, and I screwed up what we had so badly. The thought of what I did to you is even worse than the punishment of being in here, and I now have to live with the shame. Knowing I hurt you is killing me. If there was something I could do to make amends and make you forgive me, I would, like a shot. I'm a stupid, selfish, thoughtless bastard who didn't know a good thing when he saw it. In you, I had everything I ever wanted, and I threw it all away.

It's been a hard lesson I've learned. Most people don't screw up so bad that they don't get a second chance, but I've never been one to do anything by halves, have I? Every day without you, every day in here, is torture. Don't get me wrong, I know I deserve to be here, but I really have learned my lesson. According to the great British justice system though, there's no way for me to prove that. When the judge sentencing me declared me to be 'a danger to society' I could have laughed. I so am not. Of course it was wrong but I only did what I did trying to protect you. To protect us and keep the rest of the world out.

If I never see you again, I hope for one thing for you. I hope you can be happy. No one will ever love you like I did. Like I still do. But please, my darling, be happy. You deserve that more than anything.

If you do ever read this, can I ask one thing of you? If you could find it in your heart to visit. I have no visitors. Without visitors, the days are long and without colour or definition. They have no shape but an endless circle, going round and round. Every week, I see others going off to see their families who visit. I can see the joy in their faces and the way they perk up at the thought. And afterwards, I see how they are bolstered, and how it sustains them until the next time. Some lucky bastards even have kids that visit. That must be the most amazing thing ever. Some days, all I can think about is you and the baby of ours that wasn't to be. I don't suppose I'll ever have a family of my own now. Do you remember how we used to talk about it, a baby of our own one day, when we used to snuggle up on the sofa or lie in bed, thinking about it. Of all the losses, that one is without a doubt the worst.

Anyway, there's no point me going on about it. What's done is done, and we have to get on with it. I love you. I miss you. You are my world.

Love forever, Chris.

He lay the pen down, folded the paper over, placed it in an envelope, and sealed it. Hopefully, it wouldn't be read before posting by prison staff. And if it was, so what? It might make them see him as a person rather than just another no-good con. Once he'd addressed the envelope, he put it to one side, next to his pillow. Then he lay down and placed his head next to it, letting out a groan as his broken ribs protested at the movement. He thought back to his dad's last visit, when he'd lost his temper. He had no desire to see him ever again, and if he asked to come again, he'd refuse. No way. All that was there was hate, and it was on both sides. The relationship was just too damaged to ever be put back together. He turned onto one side, slowly and carefully placing his bruised face onto the hard, thin pillow. In his mind, he relived the beating every day. When it had happened, he'd been filled with a fear he'd not known since his childhood run-ins with his dad. Was that what Adam had felt as he crumpled after Chris had elbowed him in the head? Or had his concussion wiped out anything after?

He clenched his fists at the thought of Adam. If it hadn't been for that stupid twat, none of this would have happened, and he wouldn't be spending eternity in here. He'd be with Sarah, living their life together. Adam had changed everything. If he'd not stuck his nose in, everything would have been alright. He certainly wouldn't be calling blokes like Tommy Evans a friend.

A deep sigh left him as he closed his eyes. Tommy was something of an enigma. A murderous bully to some, and a caring best friend to others. Someone you could rely on. It struck him that that's how Sarah would probably describe him. Not that different to Tommy, then?

He was very different to Tommy in one way, though. Tommy had happily admitted in the kitchen one day that when in prison, he became what he called 'gay for the stay', forming relationships with others for sexual gratification, then returning to women when on the outside. Chris's fingernails dug into his palms as he thought about it. Tommy had better not try anything with him. He most definitely wasn't gay for the stay. He couldn't imagine anything worse.

He had no idea when Tommy was last on the outside, despite trying to find out. People were tight-lipped where Tommy was concerned, tending to fall into two camps: either loyal or scared shitless. He reckoned it must have been ages ago. Tommy just wouldn't stop with his drug dealing ways. Chris thought it couldn't be worth it, to keep re-offending and getting sent back to the slammer. If he ever got the slightest chance that he could get out of here, he would grab it with both hands and fight like hell to keep it.

17

Sarah

DOCTOR ZAHIR CAME IN as I was fastening Zac's clean nappy.

'Hello,' he said. 'How is Mum doing today?'

At first, it seemed weird when the staff referred to me as 'Mum' and not 'you', as if that's what defined me. In here, I suppose it was. It still seemed odd, but it'd become easier to just respond to it.

'I'm okay, thanks. And you?' I eyed him, warily. Doctors scared me. They had the power to make or break things with just a few words.

Doctor Zahir nodded, preoccupied by the clipboard of Zac's notes he had just picked up. Another thing I'd learned from being in here for two weeks was that they weren't really being rude when they seemed distant. The patient's welfare was what mattered most to them, and everything else was just fluff. White noise. I wondered what it was like to have your brain constantly stuffed full of responsibility, information, and big Latin words.

Instead of speaking, I stepped back, stayed quiet, and let Doctor Zahir do his job. He placed the clipboard back and glanced at the machines with their various patterns of lines, doing whatever it was they did to keep Zac alive. When he seemed satisfied, he gave me his full attention.

He was a striking-looking man. The first time I'd met him, I'd thought 'Wow!' I'd put him around thirty-five to forty-ish, and in great physical shape. The one word that sprung to mind about him was 'masculine'. Also 'handsome'. Another was 'capable'. I just trusted he knew what he was talking about. I trusted him with Zac. And he was fabulous with babies and children; he just had a way about him. I'd noticed some of the other mums tidy their hair and pull their stomachs in when he came onto the ward. The nurses seemed to like him, too. I liked him a lot, but not in that way. Just as well, with the wedding ring on his finger.

He removed his glasses and rolled up his shirt sleeves. Just the action of him folding the cuffs over and over was like a slam in the guts. That's what Chris used to do all the time. So much so that I'd asked him why he didn't just buy short-sleeved shirts. He'd pulled a face and told me he couldn't stand them.

'Wankers wear them,' he'd said.

At a loss for words, I'd left it at that. Another of Chris's weird but strangely endearing foibles.

Doctor Zahir breathed in. I cleared my throat, the hair standing up on my arms. It felt like he was building up to say something. I hoped to God it wasn't more bad news. I didn't think I could take it. One of the other babies on the ward had arrested and died yesterday, and the mood of the place had been different ever since. The staff might be used to it, but we parents weren't. We'd all been exchanging terrified looks ever since whenever we'd passed in the corridors.

'Have a seat,' he said, leaning against the windowsill. Was his voice neutral or ominous? I couldn't tell. My legs began to shake, and I sat before they could give way.

'What?' I said. 'Is it bad news?'

He smiled. 'No. The opposite. I just wanted to be absolutely sure before we had this talk.'

'Sure of what?'

'That Zac's recent improvements weren't just temporary. Sometimes they can be, and parents get their hopes up before baby then takes a turn for the worse.'

I blinked. 'What are you saying?'

'I'm saying Zac is going to be alright. He's over the worst. All the signs are there that he's going to make a good recovery.'

My heart nearly stopped as the words I'd waited so long to hear finally sank in.

'He's going to be alright?' I whispered. 'Really?'

'Really. He's a little fighter, that one. He's responded well to the antibiotics and fought off the infection.'

'And no signs of sepsis?'

'No. None. The antibiotics stopped it getting that far.'

I'd had terrible images in my head of babies with amputated limbs; I'd seen them every time I closed my eyes. Now, they might go, in time. We were lucky. Zac was going to be alright. He'd be well again. It felt like the crushing weight that had been pressing down on me for the last two weeks had just gone, leaving a massive urge to cry in its place. I put my hands over my eyes to will it away.

The door opened, and Mum returned from her trip to the toilet. Her eyes shot from the doctor to me, then to Zac.

'What?' she said. 'What's happened? I've only been gone five minutes.' She clutched at her throat, her cubic zirconia rings glinting. She saw the tears in my eyes and rushed over. 'Sarah? What is it?'

I forced words out of my constricted throat. 'Zac's going to be alright. The doctor just said.'

Her whole body sagged in relief. 'Oh, thank God'"

She hugged me, and we were both sobbing. Doctor Zahir straightened and pushed away from the windowsill.

'We'll keep him under observation for a bit longer, then we'll be thinking about you taking him home.'

As he walked to the door, I could see his mind had already moved on to his next patient. I hoped it was good news for those parents.

''I'll leave you to it, and see you soon,' he said. 'The nurse will be in shortly to remove some of this gubbins,' he said, giving us a smile.

He must mean the tubes and wires. It would mean I could pick Zac up without worrying about anything being pulled out. Every time I picked him up, I felt it would hurt him if they snagged.

'Thank you for everything you've done. Thank you so much,' I said, reaching for the tissues yet again.

He stopped, his hand on the door. 'My pleasure,' he said. 'It's the sort of day I like.' Then he turned and was gone.

'He's coming home,' I said to Mum. 'Just like I said he would.'

'You did.' She squeezed my hand. ' I can't wait to tell your dad.'

'He'll be here in half an hour. Why don't we wait for him to get here instead of ringing him? I want to see his face when we tell him.'

'So do I. Although I'm not sure I can hang on that long.'

I bent over Zac and finished fastening the poppers on his vest, stretching it over his nappy. The wires attached to his chest ran like veins, only on the surface of his skin instead of underneath. I preferred when they were hidden under his vest, rather than when he only had a nappy on and you could see them all. I hoped it wouldn't hurt him when they pulled off the sticky pads that attached them to his skin. No more heart monitor. No more drawing of blood, where I had to close my eyes rather than watch the red come streaming out. He'd had so many needles stuck in him, I worried he'd leak like a colander when I bathed him. I must have developed this morbid sense of humour as a coping mechanism. I would never have had a thought like that before all this happened.

'You're coming home,' I told him. 'Granddad will be there. And Grandma. And Mummy. And Lulu.'

His eyes were open and blinking. He'd been awake more for a few days now, but I didn't blame the doctors for being overly cautious. I couldn't imagine how I'd feel if they'd told me he was going to be alright and then he relapsed. It was unthinkable, yet, like Doctor Zahir said, it can happen.

Mum was smiling from ear to ear.

'You're like The Cheshire Cat,' I said.

'I know. My mouth is hurting. Oh, Sarah; I'd hardly dared hope this day would come in case I jinxed it.'

'Me too. Now life can get back to normal.'

'Yes.' She hesitated. 'I think we'll go back to looking for our own place, though.'

'I know. I'll help you. Some of the ones you liked before all this happened might still be for sale, if you're lucky. You can finally go and see them.'

It was the right thing for them, even more so now after Dad's scare. They weren't young and fit anymore, and they needed some time to themselves. Ultimately, Zac was my responsibility, not theirs, and they'd helped me so much already.

Ten minutes later, Bea, my favourite nurse, came in, a huge smile lighting up her face.

'I can't tell you how much I've been wanting to do this,' she said. 'Let's get him unhooked from all this lot.'

Within seconds, Zac was free from everything, the only unpleasant thing the choking sound he made as the tube up his nose was removed. He looked strangely bare.

'Can I pick him up?' I asked.

'You certainly can,' said Bea, stepping back.

I slipped one hand under his head and the other under his body, then scooped him up and hugged him to me, burying my face deeply in his hair. He grizzled a bit, reached up, and grabbed my hair, pulling it tightly. Just like his old self.

'Ow! That hurts.'

He gurgled as I disentangled my hair from his little fingers, and then he grabbed again, a different section this time. He yanked at it hard. Even though my scalp was burning, I couldn't stop laughing.

'He's a monster,' I told Mum, after finally breaking free. 'Look at that.' Zac had a fistful of my hair and was examining it closely. 'You're a monster,' I told him, squeezing him tight and blowing a raspberry into his neck. He giggled more.

'I think I'll go down and meet your dad, get some fresh air first. Do you want a cup of coffee bringing back?' Mum stood and put on her coat.

'No, I'm okay. Just make sure you don't tell him. We agreed.'

She made a zipping motion over her mouth as she left. Whether she'd keep to it, I didn't know. She was the worst keeper of secrets I'd ever known.

There was one thing I'd been longing to do, something I'd wondered if I'd ever get the chance to do again. I put him to my breast and it felt so perfect. I watched him as he fed, and knew without a doubt I was the luckiest woman in the world. Before long, his eyes began to flutter before remaining shut.

I shuffled him into a sitting position, and he let out a long burp without waking. When Mum and Dad came, Zac was asleep over my shoulder, with his arms wrapped around my neck. Dad stopped dead when he saw us.

'Oh, he's out of the cot? His tubes are gone.' His eyebrows shot up.

Amazingly, Mum had managed not to blurt it out. She smiled at me, a knowing look in her eyes.

'Hi Dad. We've got some good news. Your grandson is coming home.'

Dad sat down heavily in a chair. Mum stood next to him and rested her hand on his back.

And that was it. Now it was back to business, in every way. Back to my cafe and my little flat. A new start with just Zac and me. And I couldn't wait. Everything would be fine. Surely, our run of bad luck must be over. There was nothing else left to happen.

18

Chris

CHRIS MADE HIS WAY through the corridors to the kitchen, trailing after Officer Phil. It was just gone six in the morning, and it was his first day back since he'd been jumped in the showers. His nerves were jangling, he ached all over, and his ribs were still sore, but as long as he could avoid anyone coming into contact with them, he should be alright.

Phil slowed down for him to catch up. 'You okay, Chris?'

'Still a bit tender.' He held a protective hand over his side where the bruising had been at its worst. 'Those blokes who jumped me. I haven't seen them since. Are they in the seg? I'd just rather not run into them, that's all.'

'You won't. Two of them have been moved to different wings, and the other has been transferred to another prison.'

Chris breathed out slowly, still walking. He'd barely been out of his cell since the attack, and when he had been he'd looked over his shoulder the entire time. Thankfully, Tommy had made sure Chris knew he had his back. He'd never been so grateful to anyone in his life. Knowing Tommy was looking out for him definitely made him feel safer.

As they reached the kitchen door, Chris's anxiety spiked. What if Tommy wasn't there? Chatting to him had been the only thing that kept him sane when he was working in the kitchen before.

Phil held the door for him. Some of the other screws would have just let it go, right in his face, just for the hell of it.

'Thanks.' Chris followed him inside.

'You'll be back in the swing of things in no time,' the officer said.

By the swing of things, Phil no doubt meant the overflowing sack of spuds that was waiting just for him. He hadn't missed that part. He looked across to where he and Tommy worked. Tommy was there. Thank God. His muscles unclenched a little.

'Alright, mate?' Tommy grinned. 'Good to have you back. The bloke they've had in your place—right wanker. Thank God he's gone. He never stopped going on. Yap, yap, yap.' His extended fingers opened and closed, mimicking a flapping mouth. 'I nearly picked up a knife a few times and stuck him with it, just to get him to shut up.'

Chris glanced at him. He must be joking, surely. A nervous laugh escaped him. 'Well, don't be stabbing me, will you, if I say something you don't like?'

'Hmm, I can't promise. Just don't be a tosser.'

'I'll try not to.' Chris picked up a potato and eyed it like an enemy. 'I wish I could say I've missed you, but I can't.'

An officer keeping tabs from over the other side of the room made a 'get on with it' gesture at him.

'For God's sake,' muttered Chris.

'What?' Tommy asked.

'I only just got here and that idiot's on at me for not having chips ready yet.'

Tommy snorted. 'What I want to know is, seeing as they use fresh stuff like this every day,'—he pointed to the carrots and parsnips laid out in front of him—'Why does everything that comes out of this place taste like crap?'

'I dunno. One of life's great mysteries, eh?'

Chris began to sort the potatoes, now remembering how he got cramp in his hand so much from having his fingers in the same position all day. Several rolled onto the floor.

'Fuck's sake!' He stooped to pick them up, his ribs protesting at the movement.

Tommy narrowed his eyes. 'Not in the best of moods today, are you? I'd have thought you'd be glad to get back. Least it passes the day on. There's loads that would kill to get in here, you know. It's classed as a cushy number, this is.' He indicated the room with a flourish, like a TV weather presenter with a weather map. 'What's not to like?'

Chris grunted. 'I'm still pissed off at getting jumped. My ribs are sore and look at this.' He drew an imaginary circle around his still-bruised face. 'Look what they did. When I was training every day, I'd have kicked the shit out of them, alone or not. And I'd have won.' Just saying it made his spirits rise, and he felt some of the old fight flood into him like a welcome old friend.

'You used to train?' Tommy looked him up and down. 'You don't look like it.'

Chris bristled at the insult but let it go. 'I trained all the time. Had a right body on me. I lost a lot of weight recently but I'm working to get it back.'

Tommy's eyebrows shot up. 'I haven't seen you in the gym here. How come?'

'I've been a few times, but I've mainly just been doing bits in my cell. And now, after the kicking, it's all I can do to even stand, let alone lift weights.'

'I go all the time. There's not much else to do, is there?' Tommy said, tipping carrots into the machine and starting on a fresh pile.

'No, I guess not.' The memory of how training used to make him feel was coming back; the chemicals and hormones, and the rush of heady energy through his body. And the exhilaration and exhaustion after a good session that you just couldn't beat. He missed it so much. And if Tommy was in the gym, why not? He could bulk right up again with not so much effort.

'Get back to it, mate. We'll see what we can do with you.'

'What are you, some crack-shot personal trainer?'

'If you like. I can probably sort you out.'

Tommy was looking Chris up and down. Chris hoped he wasn't being checked out for some 'adult' fun. No way.

'I can see, actually, from your body type, that you'd build muscle fast.'

'I do, yeah. Had a home gym at my flat in Fulham. Spent a fortune on it.'

'Oh, nice. What happened to it?'

'Fuck knows. Went the way of everything else when I did a runner from the cops.'

He paused. Tommy knew some of his background, the bits he'd told him, but by no means everything.

'Them bastards'll take it, every time. All this confiscated stuff, I mean, where does it go? Who gets the dough from flogging it, that's what I wanna know? They say they sell it off to the public, but who believes that? And they say we're the scumbags.' Tommy shook his head and viciously chopped the end off a carrot, the knife thwacking onto the wooden board. 'What did they take of yours?'

'Christ, let's see.' Chris screwed up his face, remembering. 'Everything in my flat. Thank God it was rented, or they'd have had that as well. Expensive suits, my good clothes, watches, my gym stuff. Massive smart TV, gadgets and devices. But the thing that hurt the most was losing my car.'

Tommy looked up. 'What was it?'

'Mazda MX-5 soft-top. Bloody beautiful, she were. And new. I almost cried.' He put the first load of potatoes into the machine and set it going, watching the water as it jetted down.

'That would have hurt, them taking your car.'

'Oh, no; they didn't take it. I sold it to get me out of the country fast. For my safe passage on a private flight.'

Tommy nodded. 'Probably worth it at the time. Why did you come back here then, if you'd got away? Bit stupid, wasn't it?' He shook his head. 'Not sure I would've.'

Chris debated how much to tell him. He longed to talk about Sarah, but to mention her name in here would be to soil it somehow. There again, talking about her would be the next best thing to seeing her, and what would it hurt, really? He was aching now to talk about her; it would feel like she was still in his life. And Tommy didn't know her. He glanced across. Tommy was looking at him quizzically.

With no preformed lie springing to mind, he said, 'A woman; what else?' He felt a headlong rush of something warm, just saying the words. Pleasure? Guilt? Anticipation? What the hell was it?

'Oh, aye? What woman?'

He smiled, staring down at the sack of spuds but seeing only Sarah. 'The type you can't stay away from, even though you know you really should.'

'Ah, the best type! I'm all ears, mate.' Tommy looked at him with a lascivious grin. 'What's she like?' He ran his hands through the air in the shape of a curvy woman, then checked his machine.

Chris hesitated. Tommy wanted smut, and he wasn't going to talk about Sarah like that.

'Oh God,' Tommy said. 'Uh-oh!'

'What?'

'By the look on your face, you really had it bad for this girl, didn't you?'

Chris briefly closed his eyes. He would have thought, just by the admission that he was willing to come out of hiding and risk his freedom to find her, that it was obvious she wasn't some casual thing. Was Tommy really that dumb?

'Okay, hit me with it. It's not like we have anything better to do, is it?'

Chris inhaled deeply. He had to make sure Tommy knew how special Sarah was. Suddenly, it was the most important thing in the world. He glanced all around, but none of the other cons or screws were close enough to earwig. Where to start? Tommy nodded at him, his hands feeling for the next carrot while his eyes never left Chris's.

'Come on, don't leave me hanging! Spill.'

Chris told Tommy about Sarah, beginning in the only place he could. Right at the start, meeting her in the solicitors' firm where they both worked. He omitted the part where he hacked her laptop and webcam, and spent many hours watching her and snooping through her computer. He didn't think it would make him look good. And half the truth was better than none of it. Tommy looked rapt. The more he listened, the more Chris divulged. It was therapeutic, and his soul was soaring. He paused only when officers wandered by. The sack of spuds wasn't going down fast enough, and he sped up when one officer looked pointedly at the peeled pile that had come out of the machine. It was woefully small.

'On a go-slow, are we?' he said.

Chris would have loved to smack him but went faster, instead, willing him to go away so he could carry on talking about Sarah. This was the best he'd felt in the entire time he'd been in prison.

Chris edited as he went along, leaving out the bit about the joyriding that put his dad in jail. Tommy already knew about Chris killing Adam and Luisa, and Chris engineered the story to make it sound like he and Sarah were forced to spilt up when he fled the police and the country. One thing he did notice was that Tommy kept steering the conversation back to Sarah. What must Tommy's own love life have been like if he was that invested in his? Then, he remembered; what he and Sarah had was special. Tommy must be jealous to death not to have found his life partner, with his string of failed relationships, including three marriages. But Tommy did have one thing that Chris was envious of: four kids. When he got to the part where Sarah lost the baby, he'd been surprised, after all this time, to find himself misty-eyed.

'That must have been tough, man,' Tommy said, with a low whistle.

'It was. Losing both of them…' Chris gathered himself together. This was the last place on earth you'd show weakness of any kind. He cleared his throat.

'Look, let's change the subject,' Tommy said, leaving Chris grateful for his insightfulness. 'Tell me about your family growing up.'

'Huh!' Chris said. 'That lot of sad losers? Not much to tell. My ma was a lush, my dad also liked a drink, and lots of other things besides, and my sister—well, she was a right waste of space.'

'Was? She no longer around, then?'

'No. She died of an overdose last year. My ma's dead and my dad… I don't care where he is. I don't want anything to do with him. I don't think he'll be visiting me here again.'

Tommy nodded along. 'Sounds like you did much better than any of them, though, with your fancy place in London.'

'Yeah. I did.'

'So, did you make contact with Sarah when you got back?'

Not talking about Sarah hadn't lasted long. 'Yeah.'

'Where did you find her?'

'In York. By the time I returned from Brazil, she'd moved there and was running her own cafe. I found her through Facebook. She's still there. There's no way she'll ever give that place up. It's her life.'

'A cafe? What's it called?'

'Delish. Same as the two in London. It's a nice little place.' The thought of the cakes they served there made his mouth water.

'What does she do?'

'She's a baker. Cakes and shit.'

'I like cake. Maybe if I ever get out, I might go there for a bite to eat,' Tommy said, wiggling his eyebrows. 'Look her up. See if she's as good as you say.'

Chris suppressed a shudder and hoped for Sarah's sake Tommy would never, ever get out. He also hoped he hadn't divulged too much. He stole a glance at Tommy from the corner of his eye. Thankfully, Tommy seemed to have had enough of talking and had lapsed into a deep silence. Chris was glad. He'd spoken so much his throat was hurting. But, for once, he felt good.

19

Joe

JOE WAS PRIMED, WAITING for Gerry to come back from visiting Tommy. He was pacing around the living room in Gerry's flat, up and down, interspersing it with peering down the street out of the bay window that had seen better days. It was hard to even get to the window for clutter, but he squeezed through, just. The paint on the inside was only marginally better than on the outside. Joe hadn't thought it was possible for paint to weather inside, but it seemed it was. He pulled at a loose strip of it and it flaked off, revealing the dry, split wood beneath. It fell to the carpet, landing atop a pile of similar debris in the gap between an old vacuum cleaner and a broken portable TV. He shoved it to one side with his shoe and went into the kitchen.

He surveyed the towering pile of dirty pots. Washing them would pass some time, as would cleaning the place. His eyes flicked to the pans heaped in the washing-up bowl in the sink, crusted with days-old baked beans and God knows what else. It would take him longer to clear enough space to have room to start than it would to wash up. Nah! He'd leave it.

Back in the living room, he lit up a cigarette. He'd started rolling his own; uneven, skinny little things. Not as good as his favourite brand, but cheaper. A deep lungful of smoke calmed him. How much longer was Gerry going to be? Joe had to wait until visiting time for any information to get passed between them thanks to Gerry's inability to use a mobile phone. Tommy could get contraband mobiles in prison no problem, but Gerry wouldn't know how to text if his life depended on it. Admittedly, Joe wasn't great at that sort of stuff, but he was at least willing to learn. With Gerry, it was a flat 'no'. 'What do I need to do that bollocks for?' was the response when Joe had suggested it. Joe hoped that this time, Tommy would be able to persuade him of the benefits.

Joe took an old mobile out of his pocket and thumbed down the contacts list. It wasn't time-consuming. There was only one number in it; Gerry's. He started to type a text message to Gerry, hoping that by some miracle he might get one back. His fingers constantly tapped two keys at a time and the words came out all wrong. It took longer to correct the message to the point where it made any sense at all than it did to type it in the first place.

Hows it goin? he texted. That was all. He wasn't expecting a reply and wasn't disappointed when, half an hour later, there hadn't been one.

He turned on the TV. Afternoon racing from Chepstow. He settled back in the threadbare armchair to watch it. He'd enjoyed the racing at one time. Hadn't minded a flutter, not that he'd ever won anything. A glance at the clock told him he'd got an hour until his next trolley-collecting shift started; the shift no one else wanted—four while midnight. They'd more or less told him he'd been working it permanently from now on. Surely Gerry would have returned by four. He closed his eyes and began to drift, as the commentator's ever-more-frantic voice faded into the background.

He awoke with a jump when the door from downstairs banged loudly. Gerry's heavy footsteps thumped on every stair. Joe looked at the clock on the wall and subtracted the thirty-seven minutes it was fast by. He needed to leave for work in fifteen minutes. That should be enough time.

He stood as Gerry came through the door, accompanied by the fat ginger cat. Its fur was slick with rain, as was Gerry's coat. Gerry dropped the coat on the floor, but his moth-eaten cap stayed on.

'Tea?' Joe asked, knowing Gerry wouldn't say no. He never refused a hot beverage.

'Aye, go on then. That traffic was murder. Thought I was never going to get here.'

Joe hurried to put the kettle on, followed by the cat, and called back, 'I've got to go to work soon. Any news?'

He returned to find Gerry making himself comfortable in the chair he had just vacated, looking mighty pleased with himself.

'I got news, alright. Our Tommy's done well. Your lad is fair eating out of his hand.'

Joe nodded, willing him to go on without voicing it. Gerry liked to get round to things in his own time. This time, though, the excitement was proving too great.

'Apparently, there's a lady on the scene. From before he went inside. Someone Colin is still smitten by. Our Tommy thinks that she could be your Colin's Achilles heel.'

Joe was stunned. He'd never thought of that, yet it was so obvious. 'A woman? Does she visit him?'

'I don't think so. Tommy said there's lots Colin is holding back. He diverts when he doesn't want to answer the question. But Tommy's patient. He has time. The more Colin trusts him, the more he talks.'

'So, this woman? Does she have a name?'

'Sure does.' Gerry looked pleased with himself again and extracted a pack of cigarettes out of his pocket, slowly and carefully, before placing one between his lips and putting it away again. Joe thought he might scream. In his mind's eye, he saw himself beating the shit out of Gerry until he talked. He blinked the vision away. The cat meowed for food.

The kettle switched itself off. Gerry made no move to leave the chair. Joe waited out the silence.

Gerry's eyes fixed on the ceiling as he thought. 'Susie. No, wait… Sharon.'

Joe leaned forward. 'Which is it? Susie or Sharon?'

'Hang on.' Gerry frowned, looking troubled. 'Um, no, it's Sally.'

'Sally.'

'Sarah,' Gerry shouted, throwing a jubilant punch into the air. 'Sarah. That's it. Hundred per cent.'

Joe stared at him doubtfully.

'Definitely Sarah. And, she used to live in London but now resides in York.' He grunted to himself, satisfied, as if he'd just revealed the secret of world peace or something.

Joe left the room to put his work clothes on, his interest more than piqued. 'Carry on. I can still hear you,' he called back.

In a raised voice, Gerry said, 'She runs a cafe in the centre. Summat to do with cakes.'

'Cakes?'

'Aye. She makes them herself.'

A cafe in the centre of York. Joe frowned as the cat came through the door. He removed his jeans and put his black, thirty-two-inch-waist work trousers on. When he started the job, he couldn't believe he wasn't allowed to wear his own jeans for pushing trolleys, but they'd insisted. 'Company policy,' they'd said. Joe hated the words 'company policy', generally coming, as they did, before some utter shite or other. The trousers were too tight and dug in around his waist throughout his shift, and it wasn't as if his waist was big. He was a thirty-three, like he'd always been.

'Any idea what this cafe in York is called?'

'Something like 'delicious' or is it 'tasty'? Um, 'yummy'? Something ridiculous; one of them names that don't make any sense. Trendy, like. Give me a minute. It'll come back to me.'

'Whereabouts in York is it?'

'I told you. In the centre.'

Joe took off his T-shirt and put on his polo shirt. He eyed the lime-green fleece and put it on, trying not to catch sight of himself in the mirror. That wasn't hard in this room. There was only one mirror, all pock-marked and scratched, and it was peeping out from behind a tower of boxes, all full of junk. Still, even a single glimpse would set him off. He turned his back on it and called out to Gerry.

'Any idea what road it's on? Did Tommy say?'

There was no answer. Joe took a couple of backward steps into the hallway, almost tripping over the damn cat. It had been twirling around his legs and he hadn't noticed. Ginger hairs were now clinging to his trousers, from the shins down.

'Piss off!' he hissed at the cat, shoving it away with his foot. It sat down, lifted its hind leg, and began to lick its privates.

He could see into the living room: Gerry's chin was on his chest, and he was snoring. He blew out an irritated breath. If Gerry wanted to sleep, there was no way you would stop him, and he could be out for hours. Still, on the bright side, he had much more information than he had ten minutes ago. And there would be more coming. Yep, Tommy had done well.

He brushed his trousers down, put his black shoes on and pulled at his waistband. Every time he asked for a bigger size, they said they were 'sorting it out'. He popped the top button open and pulled the polo shirt over the top to conceal it. Last thing he wanted was to be accused of flashing. He'd be straight back inside.

He left the flat, closing the door quietly behind him, whilst pulling his coat on. Drizzle immediately settled on his hair and face as he zipped his coat right up. He should have got one with a hood. Maybe he should get a hat. All he could think of was that he'd be walking around in this for the next eight hours. He'd be piss wet through before he even got there at this rate. To put him in a better mood, he let his mind wander back to what Gerry had told him. A woman. Sarah.

Runs a cafe in York. Shouldn't be too hard to find out who and where she is, not these days. If he could get Gerry to text Tommy the street or the cafe name, it should be plain sailing.

He walked faster, having to step into the road to pass a bus stop crowded with people waiting. Why the hell couldn't they queue so they didn't force people into traffic? He could be mown down because of their stupidity. What was wrong with people? Everyone was an idiot these days, it seemed to him. He got back onto the pavement, thinking now about Colin. He was still smarting from their last exchange, where Colin had more or less banned him from visiting again. How that little turd could try and claim the moral high ground and expect to get away with it was beyond him. The sheer nerve of him! The blood in his veins heated up as he thought of all the time he'd spent in prison because of his son. There was no love lost there on either side. None whatsoever. He'd never thought it possible to hate your own flesh and blood as much as he did now. Sure, he could take or leave his wife and daughter while they were still alive, but his son was something else. He shook his head as he ran through the last conversation he'd had with Colin. This woman was Colin's Achilles Heel, was she? Well, then; he didn't have to look too far where to strike.

20

Sarah

IT WAS SO GOOD to be back home and at work. At first, when I'd come home, I was so fearful Zac would fall ill again, I barely slept. That, coupled with the lack of sleep while he was in hospital, had left me feeling like a zombie, unable to function. Mum had given me a good talking to, in her usual blunt fashion.

'What good is it going to do anyone if you make yourself ill?' she'd said. 'How is that going to help Zac?'

'I know. It isn't, but I just can't help it. I'm scared to close my eyes in case he gets ill when I'm asleep, and I don't wake up. You know what the doctors said—it was touch and go, and the only reason he wasn't worse is because we got him to the hospital so quick.'

She'd given me a look from under her fringe. 'I'm well aware of that, and I fully understand, but he isn't sick now. Look at him; he's fine. But you're not.'

I'd looked to where Zac was sitting in his bouncy chair, waving his arms and legs around to make it bounce harder. Lulu was next to him, her tail wagging harder with each of his ear-piercing squeals. True, he did look a picture of health, but the speed at which he'd got ill before was truly frightening. Sometimes, I didn't think I'd ever forget the raw, gut-wrenching terror of that day. But, somehow, as the days passed, the fingers of anxiety that had wrapped around my heart lessened their grip and we got back into a rhythm again, me getting up early to work while Mum saw to Zac when he woke up.

It'd been three weeks now, and I was enjoying the solitude of being in the kitchen at seven in the morning, trying out a new recipe, when Mum walked in carrying Zac. He immediately held out his hands to me. His face and chest were covered in what looked like chocolate Ready Brek. Not an appealing sight. Liberal amounts of it were also sticking up his hair.

I recoiled. 'Mummy can't pick you up. She needs to stay clean.' I glanced down at the fresh apron I'd put on not long ago. 'And you, little urchin, look like you've just done a day down the pit.'

Mum laughed. 'I'll clean him up when I get back upstairs. I just wanted to share some news. Your dad and I have decided to put an offer in on that one-bed apartment on Verne Street. At the top of Micklegate.'

I spooned flour into the weighing scale pan. 'The ground floor one? Yeah, that one did look nice but are you sure it's big enough, just the one bedroom? And the garden's tiny. Why not consider a two-bed?'

'Why would we need more than one bedroom? I'd rather save a bit.'

She was concerned about spending too much of their nest egg on a property but she'd been focusing on the tiniest places, where there wouldn't be room to swing a cat. This place, though, was one of the better ones, being well designed with lots of storage to compensate for the lack of square footage. But I'd kind of thought they'd prefer a house with a decent-size garden.

'Aren't you going to miss doing a bit in the garden? You liked pottering in London. So did Dad.'

She adjusted Zac on her hip as he shuffled about. 'It got harder and harder. Now, I just don't think I could do it anymore, and a bigger place is just more to clean. So, no.'

Zac cried out and leaned forward, reaching out for something. She picked up a clean wooden spoon and gave it to him. He studied it closely, as if it was the most amazing, intriguing thing he'd ever seen. He gave it a tentative chew with his still-toothless gums. I thought he would have had some teeth by now, but the health visitor said it wasn't unusual at seven months. I think she was implying I didn't need to worry about it, like I constantly worried about everything else. Maybe she was right.

I tipped the sieved flour into the cake batter and started to fold it in slowly, careful not to knock out the air I'd just spent five minutes whisking in.

'What are you making?' Mum asked, dodging as Zac tried to bash her on the head with the spoon.

'Chocolate and peanut butter layer cake. It has honeycomb, toffee popcorn and chocolate shards on top. It's one of those showstopper-type cakes. I thought it would look good in the centre of the counter.'

'Sounds yummy. Not so good for the waistline, though, I imagine.'

'Is anything I make?'

'No. Ow! Stop it, Zac.'

Zac dropped the spoon on the floor.

'I'll get it,' I said, before Mum could bend down and hurt herself. She found it hard to carry Zac for long periods and she'd be struggling soon enough. I eyeballed Zac. 'Don't hit Grandma. It's naughty.'

Zac just grinned at me and chortled.

'I'd better take him back upstairs and get him cleaned up.'

'Alright. I'll be up soon for a break when Claire gets here.' I thought about giving him a kiss, but the brown stuff smeared everywhere made me think again.

'I'll put the kettle on. Say bye-bye to Mummy,' she said as she left the kitchen.

I gave him a little wave, and he pouted, reaching out to me. Before long, he was wailing. I could still hear his cries as Mum carried him back upstairs. He'd been so clingy since we got back from the hospital. Some days he didn't want to let me out of his sight and was giving Mum and Dad a right headache. Dad had been whipping him off to the park and taking him for extra walks more and more to give Mum a break. I wondered if Zac would be worse or better when it was just him and me in the flat, when Mum and Dad had moved out. When they weren't there at night, would he cling to me more than ever? At least the spare room could be his nursery, although whether he'd want to sleep in it was another thing.

I heard someone unlocking the cafe door, and I poked my head out of the kitchen.

'Hi,' Ellie called, jumping out of the way as Claire appeared behind her, stopping her from closing the door.

My shoulders relaxed down at the sight of them. I don't know what I would have done without them when Zac was ill. They'd become like sisters to me now.

Half an hour later, I nipped upstairs to where Mum was lifting Zac out of the bath. I sat on the toilet seat while she wrapped him in a towel, then handed him to me. Zac chuckled as I lay him on the floor, tickled his belly and put his nappy on.

'What's Dad doing today?' I asked Mum.

She sat down on the edge of the bath and pulled out the plug. 'We're going to go to the estate agents to put the offer in. You know how he hates doing these things over the phone.'

I lowered my head so she couldn't see me smile. Dad thought phones were 'new-fangled' things, especially mobiles. He couldn't grasp anything to do with the internet, and all the devices you could get these days, nor did he want to. Mum, on the other hand, was a whizz at it. She had her own tablet, read eBooks, and surfed the internet like a pro. She was also great at online shopping, but knew when to reign it in, unlike I did in the years before Chris. She humoured Dad and his dinosaur ways, rolling her eyes at him when he wasn't looking. I knew she could easily have emailed an offer to the estate agents, but was letting Dad have his way.

'I hope you get it, if it's the one you really want.'

She chewed at her lip. 'Me too.'

After living in the same house in London for over thirty years, they weren't pros at the property game, and they were both nervous about the buying process. The horror stories about the gazumping that used to go on years ago still haunted them. Me? I hadn't even known what it meant. If I could ever afford my own place it'd be a miracle.

'Are you offering under the asking price?'

'Do you think we should?'

'Don't most people? They do on the TV programmes, anyway.'

'Won't it seem a bit cheeky, though?'

'Mum! It's not cheeky. It's how the game is played. Besides, not doing that could cost you thousands more, couldn't it?'

She shrugged, looking blank. 'But I'd hate to lose it now. I'm sure it's the right one. I like everything about it.'

I picked Zac up and cuddled him, loving the way his pudgy little body felt so right in my arms. 'Come on, mister, let's get you dressed.'

Mum followed me into my bedroom, still talking. 'Are you sure you'll be alright when we move out?'

No, I thought. 'Yes, of course I will. You'll only be a few minutes away, won't you? But this place won't be the same without you both. I'll miss you so much.'

'You need the room, really, for Zac. I keep picturing him toddling around the flat and having all his toys in his own room. He's going to love it. And the park at the end is so handy for you to go whenever you like.' She hesitated. 'And you won't want us living here when you meet someone.'

'I'm off men. I don't want to meet anyone.'

'No, you don't now. But you don't want to be on your own forever. It'll be a lonely life, Sarah. Don't let one bad apple put you off.'

I kept my head down, reaching for Zac's clean clothes. Chris was more than a bad apple.

She wasn't done. 'I know that last one was a bad 'un, but they're not all like that. Look at your father—he's a good man.'

I hoped she wasn't gearing up for a long tirade. I needed to nip it in the bud.

'Mum, I'm fine. It'll happen if it's meant to be, won't it?'

She apparently couldn't argue with that, and I dressed Zac, having to hurry as he got bored so quickly. 'I've got time for a quick cuppa before I have to go back downstairs. As long as you're not going to go on about me getting fixed up.' I eyed her, and she shrugged.

'Deal. I've said my bit, anyway.'

We went into the kitchen to find Dad already in there, boiling the kettle. Lulu was almost sitting on his slippers, her eyes never leaving him. I had a feeling he'd been slipping her biscuits again. She licked her chops, a dead giveaway. Since Dad had got out of hospital, his recovery had been amazing, especially after Zac had been pronounced well. He seemed back to normal, if a bit quiet at times.

'We were just going to make some tea,' I said. 'Looks like you beat us to it.'

'Ah, great minds think alike,' he said, taking three cups out of the cupboard. As he turned to get the milk from the fridge, he caught one of the cups with his sleeve and swept it onto the floor. It hit the tile with an almighty crash, making Mum and me jump. Zac, however, didn't flinch. They didn't notice, but I did. It wasn't the first time it had happened since we'd got back from the hospital. With a sinking dread, I'd been starting to wonder if Zac wasn't as fully recovered as we'd thought. I was thinking the meningitis had affected his hearing, even though the doctors hadn't said it had after all the tests they'd done.

Another thing on my to-do list today. Ring the doctor.

21

Chris

CHRIS LOOKED UP FROM the TV in surprise when his unlocked cell door was pushed open. Tommy stood in the doorway, his corkscrew curls wilder than ever.

'Okay if I come in, mate?'

Chris sat up. 'Er, yeah. Sure. In fact, be my guest.' His first thought was to wonder why the King was gracing him with a royal visit. He picked up the remote, muted the rerun of Family Fortunes then thought again and turned it off.

Tommy pushed the door to behind him but didn't close it fully. The screws didn't like it. The prisoners were allowed to associate in each other's cells but only with the doors open. Everyone knew the reason why: years ago, a nonce had been held hostage, tortured and killed by another two cons. One of them, Robert Maudsley, was still in a box-like cell of his own on F-Wing. The custom-built glass-fronted cell was thought to have inspired the makers of Silence of the Lambs to copy it for Hannibal 'The Cannibal' Lecter to reside in. The most macabre bit of the Maudsley tale was about the victim having a spoon pushed through his ear and into his brain, not something Chris ever wanted to dwell on. Whether or not it was true, it did nothing to dispel the 'Cannibal' stories. And here he was, locked up with these lunatics.

He waved towards a small desk and chair, mere inches from his bed.

'Have a seat. You alright?'

'Yeah,' Tommy said, pulling out the chair and sitting in it, crossing one foot over the other knee. With his legs spread wide, there was no space in the cell. Chris's throat tightened with the claustrophobic feelings he'd started to have lately. If only the window would open. If only it wasn't so high up, and he could see out of it properly.

'To what do I owe the pleasure?' Chris asked, smiling to show he wasn't being sarcastic.

'Just visiting a friend. Nothing wrong with that, is there? You seem to be hiding in here quite a bit. Something wrong?'

'No. Nothing's wrong. It's just…'

'Just what? Aren't we good enough for you?'

'Don't be daft.' Was he being serious? 'Sometimes I'd just rather be on my own, that's all. Always been that way, I guess.'

'I know what you mean. Look, why don't you come for a walk around? Get yourself out for a bit? It's got to be better than being cooped up in here.'

'Alright. Sounds good.' He stood up, straightening carefully.

'How are the ribs doing?'

'Getting there. Each day's better than the one before, put it that way.'

'Those men who jumped you, I can fuck them up for you, if you want. Payback.'

Chris didn't doubt it. 'No, it's alright. Thanks anyway.'

'Offer's there, mate, if you change your mind.'

'Cheers. Phil told me they've been moved, anyway. Probably better that way.'

'Whatever you want. They've only gone to D Wing.'

'Nah, just leave it.'

They left Chris's cell and took a slow lap around the landing. Chris's eyes went immediately to the net strung over the vast space. Had prisoners leaped off the landings in prisons before? They must have. Or, more like, some could have been thrown over. That net wouldn't be there for no reason. A shiver went up his spine at the thought of the drop below, onto solid concrete, if the net wasn't there. It would split a head wide open. No coming back from that one.

'Long way down, yeah?' Tommy said.

'It's horrible. Did people really jump off?'

Tommy shrugged. 'Must have done. Mad bastards. I hate heights.'

'I'm not keen, either.'

'I thought you said you lived in a tower block growing up?'

'I did. Always kept right away from the edge, though. Never looked over it like this.' He stuck his head over and pulled it back when he caught a glimpse of the floor below.

'I've never lived in a tower block,' Tommy said. 'Lived in a flat in Manchester, but it wasn't a tall building. Two storeys. Don't know why the council didn't build them higher.'

'Is that where you lived with your folks?'

Tommy didn't say anything, but cleared his throat. 'Yeah,' he said finally.

'What did they do, your folks?' asked Chris, aware he might be encroaching on territory Tommy wasn't happy with. They veered around a group of men clustered on a corner, speaking in hushed voices. An officer down the far end was watching them. Whatever they were plotting, Chris didn't think it would be good. As long as it didn't involve him, he wasn't bothered.

'Dunno really,' Tommy said. 'Didn't really have a dad, and my mum died young, so I went to live with my uncle and cousins.'

'They took you in? That was good of them.'

Tommy looked at him and frowned. 'Why was it? It's what families do. They look out for each other.'

'Maybe in yours. Not in mine.'

Tommy's eyes narrowed. 'Well, they should.'

Chris huffed out a laugh. 'Never met my old man, did you? Well, I wouldn't bother if I were you. I wish I'd never met him, either.'

'What about your sister, though? I'd have loved real brothers and sisters. Kind of felt like I'd missed out on that, growing up.'

Chris twisted his head to look at him. 'What about my sister?'

'What was she like? Were you close?'

Chris spluttered. 'No. She was horrible. She was a filthy druggie.'

Too late, he remembered that Tommy ran a drugs empire, although he'd mainly found out about Tommy's business through other people.

'Was there a lot of drugs on your estate, then?' Tommy asked.

'Loads. They were rife.'

'Did you never dabble?'

'Bit of weed and coke here and there. Never anything stronger. And never heroin. That's for losers.'

'You got that right,' said Tommy.

But it's made you rich.

'You said before that your sister died of an overdose.'

'She did, yeah.'

'What of?'

'Heroin, most likely.'

'Ooh, bad. How long had she been using?'

'For years. I knew it would kill her in the end.'

'Did you?'

'Yeah. But it would have been her ideal way to go.'

They turned another corner. Chris was aware of eyes on him, probably because he was with Tommy. If he was walking on his own, he'd have been hassled, bumped into and jeered at, but now—nothing. People were keeping a wide berth.

'Ideal? How do you mean?'

Chris put on a high-pitched, silly voice. 'She died doing the thing she loved the most.'

'Maybe. You don't sound sorry.'

'I'm not. Maybe someone did her a favour.'

'Like what?'

Chris knew then he was going to blurt it out. And what did it matter? Supplying money and means was way different to him sticking the needle in her. He wanted to tell someone. To get it off his chest.

'When I got back from Brazil, I had a bit of spare cash. So I gave it to her. Not my problem what she did with it. She could have spent it on anything.'

Tommy was side-eying him now. 'If I'm hearing this right, though, you knew she'd buy gear with it.'

Chris shrugged. 'No one could ever know that. She could have used it to get clean, for all I knew.'

'Was that likely?'

Chris was suddenly defensive. Was he being judged by a man who actually supplied the stuff? The worst kind of predator except for sex pests, some would say.

'Alright then, no. But she was a parasite, leeching off society, and I did society a favour. It's not like I stuck the needle in.'

'What did she say when you gave her the money?'

'Say? She didn't say anything. I shoved it through the letterbox and left it to fate.'

Tommy pulled a face. 'So she didn't know it was from you? Are you telling me you killed your own sister?'

Chris backtracked, remembering Tommy's stance on the importance of family. It was a bit rich though; Tommy seemed to have no problem killing members of other people's families.

'Nope. I've told you, I gave her money and walked away.'

'Wow!' Tommy said. 'And some people call me cold.'

Despite being scared of Tommy, Chris's hackles were rising fast.

'You're judging me? From what I've heard, you're the one bringing drugs into the country. How many people do your drugs kill? I kill one, and I'm the worst person ever?'

Tommy held his hands up. 'Whoa, I never said that. I'm not judging you. And like you said, she's the one stuck the needle in, not you. Calm down, man; Jesus!'

Chris breathed out, long and slow. He wanted to get back to his cell, away from prying eyes and Tommy's questioning. 'Sorry. It's just hit a nerve, that's all.'

'I get it, man. I really do. Let's just forget it, eh?'

'Agreed.'

'Anyway, I have a favour to ask.'

Chris's head jerked up. That must be why Tommy came to find him today. He should have known.

'Erm, what favour?'

'I need you to hide something in your cell for me.'

'What? Oh, no. Look, I don't think it's a good idea. It's not drugs, is it?'

'No, course not.'

'What is it, then?'

'A phone.'

Chris wiped a hand over his face. Burners were rife in prison, but if his cell got spun and they found it…

'I can show you where to hide it, so they won't find it.'

'Like where? The cell's barely two metres wide. There is nowhere.'

'It's just for one night, okay?'

'One night? And that's all?'

Tommy nodded. 'Look, when did your cell last get spun?'

'Um, a few days ago.'

'So they won't do it again for a while.'

'Probably not, but I don't know. They hardly give advance warning, do they? I don't want any bother. I want to get out of here, not stay for longer. And why now?'

'I've had a tip off that mine's going to get done tonight.'

The alarm bells in his head ramped up. 'Tonight? You want to do it tonight?'

Tommy grasped Chris's sleeve and stopped him walking. 'It's not a big deal. It's for one night. And you owe me.' There was an edge to his voice.

It was true; he did owe him, and Tommy wouldn't let it go. He pulled away, his sleeve slipping out of Tommy's grasp.

'I know. But this… man, I don't know.'

Tommy's voice dropped back to soothing. 'It'll be fine, Chris. And then we'll be even. No more favours on either side. How 'bout that?'

What choice did he have? And the chances his cell would get searched on the one night he was hiding something for Tommy were minimal. And if he wanted to keep his limbs attached to his body, then…

'Okay. Fine.'

Tommy clapped him on the back. 'Good man. We don't have long left until lock up. Might as well get it over with now.' He gestured for Chris to lead the way back to his cell. 'After you.'

Chris walked on leaden legs, every bit of him thinking this was a bad idea. But if he wanted to keep Tommy on his side, then better to just get it over with.

On the way back to his cell, an uneasy feeling started up in his bowels. He shouldn't have told Tommy about his sister. Had he just given him more ammunition? Where Tommy was concerned, he needed to start keeping his mouth shut a bit more. That urge to offload he kept having needed to be reined in a bit. He wouldn't be spilling again. Not that there was anything much left to spill. He cursed his own stupidity.

When they reached his cell, Tommy sprang into action.

'Stand near the door,' he barked, removing the cistern lid on Chris's toilet.

He reached into his sleeve and took out a mobile wrapped in a plastic bag and a small roll of duct tape, which he taped it to the underside of the lid in about five seconds flat. It was like a Formula One pitstop. Chris watched with mounting horror. It was like a place a five-year-old would hide something, for God's sake! If he got spun tonight, they'd find it in about ten seconds flat. His anxiety grew as he watched, and he swallowed it down. One night. It was just for one night. They wouldn't toss his cell again so soon. Or they might, if he was acting shifty.

'Bring it with you to the kitchen tomorrow and give it me back.'

'Alright.'

He tried not to think of the risk of getting caught with it on him, but the walk to the kitchen was relatively short. Much shorter than the hours it would spend in his cell.

After that, Tommy disappeared without a word, no doubt to offload all the other contraband he'd been stashing.

In the end, Chris needn't have worried, although he spent the night awake, listening for booted feet coming to his door and stopping outside. The sound of keys jangling. But any footsteps passed right by.

The next morning, he walked to the kitchen on tenterhooks, his nerves in shreds and the skin on his stomach burning where the phone touched it.

'Hey,' Tommy said when he saw him.

He slipped the phone out of the waistband of his joggers, his jeans being in the laundry system somewhere, and handed it back to Tommy when no officers were watching. Tommy deposited it back up his sleeve.

'See. Told you there was nothing to worry about, didn't I?'

Chris had to admit he was right, but he wasn't keen to repeat the exercise anytime soon.

'Did you get spun last night?'

Tommy nodded. 'Yep.'

'I suppose they didn't find anything.'

'Nope.'

Chris wondered which of the officers fed Tommy the information. No one else could have known. Which one was in Tommy's pocket? But, there again, there might be more than one. Tommy wouldn't be telling. Didn't really matter. Chris didn't trust any of them.

22

Sarah

ZAC WAS WAILING LOUDLY when I was locking up the cafe after work. I could hear him all the way through the shop. I flew up the stairs to the flat to find him sitting on Mum's knee in the living room. When he saw me, he held his arms out and shoved his head back into Mum, lifting his bottom in the air.

'What's the matter? Is he okay?'

I picked him up, and he wrapped his arms around my neck, sniffling hard.

'It was my fault. I'm sorry. I just stood on his hand. I didn't realise his fingers were in the way. He threw a toy, and I just got up to get it for him and… '

I breathed a sigh of relief. 'He's alright otherwise, though?'

Mum put a hand on my shoulder. 'Yes. He's fine.'

'Thank God! It's just he was so miserable last night. He was shuffling about in my bed all night, whining.'

'I think I know why. I can feel a tooth coming through. His first one.'

'Really? Where?'

I tried to see in his mouth, but he turned away.

'On the top about halfway back on the left. There's a little hard white bump. I put some of that teething gel on that you bought. It seemed to do the trick.'

I laid him on the floor on his back and put my finger in his mouth, feeling all around. Mum was right. It was there, a tiny lump. I could—

'Ow! He just bit me! My God, he's only got one tooth coming through and he got me right there. Zac! That's naughty. You don't bite Mummy!' I didn't know why I was telling him off. What if he couldn't hear me? I was still waiting for an appointment to come from the hospital to see a specialist and get his hearing checked out. Something else to worry about and stop me sleeping. I just wished it would hurry up.

I examined my finger closely. On the first knuckle of my index finger was a red mark. Zac chortled. The little sod!

'When he gets teeth top and bottom, we're going to be in trouble. If he knows it gets a reaction, he'll do it all the more. You know what he's like,' I said.

'I know. I'm not putting my fingers anywhere near him or I'll have none left.'

'Let me see your hand.' I picked up Zac's hands. Couldn't see anything.

'Which one did you stand on?'

'The right one. He wouldn't let me look at it. Does it look alright?'

'I think so.'

I bent his fingers and his thumb gently, keeping well away from his mouth. No reaction.

'Nothing's broken. Panic over.'

I kissed his fingers, and he scowled at Mum. I hope she hadn't become Public Enemy Number One in his eyes. Sometimes he had a way about him, a willingness to do anything to get his own way and an absolute refusal to give in. Like his dad.

I smiled at Mum. 'Aw, he's getting teeth. I've been a bit worried—'

'I know. You worry too much. I told you he'll get them when he's ready.'

I watched as Zac rolled over onto his stomach and began to pull himself onto his hands and knees. He steadied himself and then rocked backwards and forwards.

'Did you worry all the time over me, or am I just being over the top?' I asked Mum.

'Are you kidding? I was a nervous wreck. I used to check all the time you were still breathing.'

'I do that with him.'

'Yes, but you were ten!'

I laughed. 'So I'm not overreacting, then?'

'I don't think so. Especially now, with what you've just been through with him. Course not.'

'That's good. When does it stop?'

Mum gave me a strange look. 'Stop? It never stops. I worry about you all the time. Every day.'

'Do you?'

'Of course I do, you silly girl! Maybe I was worse than most, though, you know, being so much older than the other mums when I had you. The other miscarriages…'

She tailed off, thinking, I'm sure, of the four pregnancies she lost before I came along. She'd never kept the fact from me, and we'd always talked openly about who my brothers or sisters might have been. And I was also aware that if they had survived, then I might never have been born. Somehow, I didn't think she and Dad would have wanted five kids.

I leaned my back against the sofa, still sitting on the floor, and closed my eyes. I really needed an early night.

'Sarah! Look,' Mum said. Her voice sounded urgent.

I opened my eyes to find Zac a foot away from where he was a moment ago, with a look of immense concentration on his face, and he was studiously moving forward, one hand, one knee at a time.

'Oh my God, he's crawling!' I said. 'Quick, where's my phone?'

'Over there.' Mum nodded at the coffee table and I grabbed it, turning the video on. Zac ignored me as I started filming his progress forward. He looked so cute, with his hair sticking up at the back and dribble on his chin, every bit of him focused on his task. In his head, he was probably conquering Everest.

'When he gets going properly, we're really going to have to watch him. He'll be down those stairs in a jiffy,' Mum said.

I groaned at the thought. 'We're going to have to lock him in.'

Zac kept going, his balance improving all the time until he got tired and fell onto his side. He looked shocked, but he was okay. I didn't need to rush to him all the time. I kept filming.

He didn't cry. Instead, he rolled back to his starting position, rocked in place, and was off again until Dad opened the door Zac was right behind and bumped him on the head. The screaming started, and I turned the video off. The place erupted in chaos. Lulu was running around in circles, barking madly at all the noise.

'Have you had her round the park again?' I asked him, jiggling Zac up and down.

'Yes. What happened? What did I do?'

'He was crawling. You opened the door and bumped his head.'

Dad looked like he might cry himself, and he ruffled Zac's hair. 'Really? Wow! I'll read you an extra bedtime story later to make up for it; how about that?'

That would probably be a bigger treat for him than for Zac. I'd often peeked through the crack in the door and seen Dad reading long after Zac had dropped off, doing funny voices and making animal noises. He always claimed he hadn't realised Zac was asleep, but I didn't believe him. Fingers of panic clutched at me; could Zac hear his grandad reading to him and giving it everything he'd got? I imagined my dad's voice sounding muffled, like cotton wool had been stuffed in his mouth, and shook myself. No point dwelling on things we didn't know yet.

'Watch,' I told Dad.

I sat Zac back on the floor, and he threw himself forward onto his hands and knees. After rocking backwards and forwards a few times, he was off again, a look of fierce concentration on his face. Dad let out a gasp then laughed. 'Go on lad,' he said.

'I'd better check the casserole,' Mum said, hauling herself off the sofa.

I sniffed the air. It smelled delicious. 'Brilliant. You spoil me. Who's going to cook my dinner when you've moved out?'

'Oh, that's another thing I forgot to tell you. Our offer—it's been accepted.'

'That's great. If it's the one you really want. I'm glad. Well done.'

'Got it a bit under the asking price,' Mum said proudly. 'I played hard ball. We were by far the ones in the strongest position, what with not being in a chain and having cash, so I didn't cave in. Five thousand under.' .

I smiled at the look of smug satisfaction on her face. 'Wow! Look at you go. You'll be getting a job in an estate agents' next.'

A spark of interest ignited in her eyes. Why did I have to say that and put ideas in her head?

'I can just see it. Me in a power suit with eighties shoulder pads—I read they were back in—and those power heels. Oh, but who'd look after Zac while I was earning a crust? We couldn't trust your dad to do it.'

'Oi! I am here, you know,' Dad chipped in.

'I know you are,' she said. 'I'll just go and check the dinner. Should be about ten minutes.'

She went into the kitchen and the air was filled with the clattering and banging that was normal when she was cooking.

I wandered into the bedroom to get my laptop, leaving Zac with his eagle-eyed grandad watching him crawl. I sat at my little desk and powered it up. As I waited for it to come on, I ran my finger over the tape I'd stuck to the webcam, checking it was secure. It was. Good!

There were five unread emails, four to do with nothing noteworthy and one from Ben.

Hi Sarah, I know it's short notice but we're taking Sofia to Legoland on the nineteenth, and could stop off and see you on our way back up, the twenty-third. Let me know if it's okay xx

Mum popped her head around the door. 'It's ready now. Are you coming?'

'Yes. I've just had an email from Ben. They might visit this weekend. That would be nice.'

Mum looked blank for a second. 'Oh, Homeless Ben, you mean? The soldier one.'

'Yes. Stop calling him that. He's not homeless.'

'Well, it just helps me remember who he is. You know I have to assign tags to things, or I wouldn't have a clue.'

'I'll just be a minute,' I told her, shutting my laptop down.

She closed the door as she went out. I stood up, dug around in my pocket and pulled out yet another letter from Chris. As I opened the drawer to put it in with the rest, I glanced over at the door. Instead of putting the letter in, I scooped the others all out and placed them on the bed in an untidy pile. I counted them. Forty-one. What the hell could he think to say all the time, given where he was?

For the past few weeks, curiosity had been pulling at me more and more. He was obviously not going to stop. Soon, I was going to break and read them. Like maybe tonight. I'd planned to wait until Mum and Dad had moved out, but really, what was the point? If I read them, did it matter when? He wouldn't know because I was never going to write back.

I made a snap decision. At bed time, I was going to sort them into the order they arrived, according to the dates on the postmarks. And then, if Zac was sleeping, I was going to read the lot of them. Every word.

23

Chris

AFTER FINISHING THE LATEST letter to Sarah, he dropped the pen onto the bed. What was she doing right now? What did she do when the cafe was closed and she was on her own? While he was stuck in this place, she'd find someone new soon enough. All he'd be doing was rotting and vegetating. Despair welled up in him and overflowed.

He lay back onto the bed and slammed his foot onto the wall, once, twice, three times, then again until his ankle and heel hurt. With the physical pain in his body greater than the emotional pain in his head, he sat up and rubbed his foot, trying not to notice the way it felt like the walls were closing in on him. Although the cell felt like a refuge at times, at others it was more like a straitjacket. At what point did things become an issue in prisoners? If he ended up with full-blown claustrophobia, would there be any help at all available? With all the other issues facing prisons, he doubted it somehow.

It was association, and men were grouping together for their precious time out of their cells. Chris got off his bed and tested his foot out. He could stand on it, but it hurt. Shouldn't have kicked the wall. The wall always, always won.

He limped to the door and opened it, stopping to look outside before going any further. This prison was a tinder box of violence, which could explode at any time. Fights were commonplace and often brutal, and the screws could only do so much to keep people safe. If prisoners were determined to act like animals to the degree some of the ones in here did, then it was a downhill battle all the way. He'd thought that stuff about there being a hierarchy in prisons was just a myth, but it so wasn't. Drug kingpins (Tommy), serial killers, and armed robbers were at the top, filtering down to sex offenders and child rapists, considered the lowest of the low. He didn't know where he fitted in, but at this stage in his sentence, his best hope was to get moved to a lower category prison for good behaviour as soon as possible.

Tommy would probably be dominating the pool table again. Might as well have a walk down to see. He passed familiar faces on the way, but only vaguely knew the names. A few bothered with him, but after the briefest of acknowledgments, he carried on his way, ignoring the throbbing in his foot. He didn't feel safe out in the open like this anymore, and checked all the time for danger or threats coming from every possible direction.

He was right. Tommy was playing pool.

'Hey, man,' Tommy announced on seeing him. He took a pool cue from the man he was playing and held it out. 'Game?'

Chris glanced at the man who'd lost his cue. He was glaring at him, steam practically blowing out of his nostrils. Saying he looked unstable was putting it mildly. Chris couldn't remember his name but knew it wasn't someone whose bad side he wanted to get on.

'No, I'm good. You two carry on.'

He gestured for the man to take his cue back and sat off to the side. Now his ribs weren't as bad, he wanted to start at the gym, but Tommy hadn't mentioned it again. When he asked about it, Tommy just made non-committal noises. Tomorrow he'd go on his own, a regular thing, regardless of whether Tommy went or not.

Over the other side of the landing, Officer Phil stood talking to another screw. Chris got back up and made his way over, standing back until Phil spotted him.

'Hello, Chris. Can I help you?'

'I'd like to run something by you. Have you got a minute?'

'Yeah. Sure. Go ahead.'

Phil turned so his whole body faced Chris square on.

'I've had an idea. You know how helping others in this place goes a long way towards your rehabilitation?'

'Yeah.'

'I have skills that maybe I could put to good use. IT skills.'

Phil pursed his lips, nodded. 'Go on.'

'I can teach others, beginning with the basics. What do you think?'

Phil plucked at his bottom lip with a thumb and forefinger, thinking. 'It sounds good to me. I can certainly put it forward and, if it came off, it would look favourable for you.'

'It would be good for me, too, to do something for others. It's so boring. I think the boredom is going to be the thing that gets me in the end.'

Phil put his hands on his hips. 'But you know things don't move fast in here, don't you? It could be days, weeks, or months before anything came of it. If it did, I mean. The wheels in prison have almost ground to a halt in some ways. It's as frustrating for us as it is for you guys. They come up with yet more reform plans that come to nothing and often make things worse.'

The woes of the prison service? Tell him about it!

'I really would like to do it. I don't know if I'm a good teacher. I've never tried. But I do know IT. Be a shame for me to vegetate in here and not pass any of it on. Give others skills for when or if they get out'

'The internet would be out, though. They'd never go for that; you lot watching porn and hacking into stuff. Can't blame them, really.'

Chris's face felt hot at the mention of hacking. Was Phil aware of what he did? Course he would be. It was all in his records.

'Okay, leave it with me. I'll give you some paperwork to fill out.'

Chris nodded, but his spirits were sinking. Of course. More paperwork that would probably never get read or looked at, same as all the other forms he'd filled in since he'd been here.

Phil's attention went to another prisoner hovering nearby, and Chris turned away. From out on the landing, he could hear Tommy's deep rumble of laughter, others following it with their own. If Tommy laughed, they laughed. If Tommy looked angry, they looked angry. Chris halted. Was that what Tommy wanted him to become, one of his sheep? He'd never been a sheep in his life. He'd always tried to blaze his own trail and follow no one else's. But it was different in here. In here, the wrong thing could get you killed. He was under the same roof as some of the country's worst serial killers and sex offenders, for God's sake. How the hell he got lumped in with them, he'd never know. He was nothing like them. But you had to watch your back all the same. Men like innocuous, odious Norman, for example—couldn't trust him; not even for a second. In here, if someone stabbed you, the others would gather round to watch. They'd enjoy it, feed off it. It would be the highlight of their day to watch another man bleed to death in front of them. A bit of entertainment. No, Chris was under no illusions that this place was anything other than hell, no matter how many friends or acquaintances he made.

But, when all was said and done, at that moment he needed Tommy more than Tommy needed him. In here, it seemed Tommy could get most things, no questions asked. You wanted drugs, Tommy could get you them. Mobile phone, no problem. Even a weapon, if you were willing to pay the high price. It had to involve bent screws. For some items, there would just be no other way.

So, yes, Tommy's price was high. It only took one thing, and you'd be in his debt forever. Chris wasn't sure it was worth it. But there was one thing he wanted. Was he willing to be in hock to Tommy for it, though, given how dangerous he was?

He walked back over to the pool table and sat back down, purportedly watching the game, laughing in all the right places. Tommy was winning, of course. Not that the other bloke was letting him, but Tommy was genuinely really good at pool. Probably because he'd spent so much time inside playing it. A smile twisted Chris's lips at that thought and he tugged his mouth back down. Stay on his good side. Play the part. But he knew deep down that he was in it alone. Whatever happened from now, he'd consider himself first in everything he did.

24

Sarah

ZAC HAD COMPLETELY WORN himself out crawling. For the past few days, it was all he'd wanted to do. Every inch of the flat had now been thoroughly explored by him; not difficult considering the size of it. Lulu thought it was marvellous and followed him around on her belly, scooting forward whenever he did. They were like a Britain's Got Talent comedy duo. It was so funny to watch. I had hours of video of them together, but now I no longer went on Facebook or Insta, they just stayed on my phone. I'd sent some to Emma, in America. What started out as a six-month job for her over there had turned into something much longer term. I missed her awfully. Again today she sent me a message begging Leanne and me to go visit her. What she thought I'd do with Zac, I wasn't sure. Despite me sending her pictures and videos of him all the time, it was like she hadn't considered him at all. She certainly was clueless as to what life as a single parent was like. She was busy living the party life over there, Sex and the City-style, and I didn't blame her. Yet I wouldn't swap her life for mine, not for one second.

It was nine-thirty on a Friday evening. Zac was asleep in his cot over by the window, Mum and Dad were watching TV, and I was crashed out on the bed, worn out as per usual. Zac shuffled and began to snore. In front of me were the letters, spread out on top of the duvet. I'd meant to read them a week ago, but when it came to it, I couldn't do it. Every night this week, I'd barricaded the door with my small chest of drawers and laid out the letters in a line, just like they were now. Also on the bed was a letter from the hospital with an appointment for Zac to have a hearing test with a specialist. It was three weeks away.

I put it to one side and picked up the first letter, weighing it in my palm. I turned it over and sniffed it, not sure why. It smelled of nothing. Did I expect to smell prison on it? Or his aftershave? Did he even use aftershave in prison? If he did, I couldn't see it being that fancy, expensive stuff he'd worn when we were together.

I turned it back over and placed my finger on the flap, searching for an unglued bit, a way in. It was stuck down firmly. I tore it open before I could change my mind, ripping half the envelope in the process. Three sheets of paper were folded inside and I slid them out. His writing caused me to suck in a breath. He'd once apologised for being a dick by writing the words I'M SORRY on a sheet of notepaper, photographing it and sending it to me. It was personal, funny and meaningful all at the same time. I hadn't expected just the sight of his handwriting to get to me. My eyes blurred, and I blinked hard. I hadn't read anything yet and already I was gone.

I settled back on the bed, glancing at the door, and began to read. For three pages, he told me how sorry he was and how much he loved me, over and over again. Words of contrition. How he hated himself. How he wished he could turn back the clock and put right the wrongs he'd done. He'd handle the situation with Adam differently, and he'd walk away from Luisa (instead of losing his temper and throttling her? Good to know!). How all he thought about was having a life with me. How he wished he'd never taken his dad's car and caused the accident all those years ago.

He went on about the baby I'd lost and how it would have changed both our lives. How we could have been one big happy family, with lots more kids along the way. My eyes slid to Zac. If only he knew.

I put the letter back down on the bed, having reached the end. I felt strangely calm and emotionless. After the initial reaction, the expected floods of tears never came. All this time, I'd been telling people Zac's father was a sperm donor, and it hit me now that that was still the truth. Chris had donated his sperm; he just never realised it. So next time I said that, I wasn't going to feel guilty, like I always had. Did I have anything to feel guilty about? No, I didn't think so anymore.

I glanced at the door and listened. All I could hear was the TV. Mum and Dad had probably fallen asleep, like they did every night. Zac wore us all out. The second letter was right under my fingers. I folded up the first one and placed it back in the envelope. Then I put it to the other side of me and opened the second one, read it, then reached for the third.

For the next hour, I read each one. After the last one, I folded the paper and put it on top of the pile. Each one said much the same thing. Variations on a theme. Some went into his childhood a bit more and told me things I hadn't known, like him leaving home at fifteen and working part time in a computer shop. He'd lived above the flat and told his boss he was sixteen. At that point, I admit I did cry for him. His family life was truly terrible. Maybe it's why he turned out like he did. He had no direction or guidance at all, just two parents who preferred alcohol to their own children. It made me so mad. Parents like his not only didn't deserve to have kids but, more importantly, they didn't deserve to keep them. If Chris had been with a different family, he might have been a different person. He might have been beside me in this bed now, with our son between us.

He also told me about his time in Brazil, after he fled the country, and the lengths he'd gone to to change his appearance so he could get close to me. Me. I was the reason for every single thing he'd done. By far the best bit was him detailing how he found Lulu, and how she sort of adopted him as her own. At that point, I put down the letter and picked her up from where she was sleeping curled up next to me. I looked at her with fresh eyes, trying to imagine her almost drowning in the sea as Chris sneaked back into the country. When he described her lifeless body, along with his panic and despair, I squeezed her tight and wept. I'd known she was precious, but not to that extent.

I sat up, picked up the letters, and placed them back in the drawer, hiding them under a tangled heap of knickers. I hadn't been sure what I'd feel on finishing his words, but I hadn't expected this: I just felt numb and kind of drained. There was nothing I could do to help him. Each letter ended with him begging and pleading for me to visit him, but it wouldn't be a good idea. I'd needed to say a final goodbye to him, and I'd done that when I visited him. No need to rake over all that again.

I turned the light off, placed my head on the pillow, and barely closed my eyes all night. Zac, for once, didn't stir.

***

After work the next night, Kate, Ben, and Sofia arrived. I met them at the train station, waiting with Lulu and Zac. When Sofia saw Lulu, she let out the loudest shriek and ran full pelt towards us, leaving her parents way behind. I could hear Kate shouting her name, and Ben set off after her. Just before she reached us, he scooped her up and tucked her, still wriggling, firmly under his arm.

'Hi,' he said in his Scottish lilt, ignoring Sofia's yowling. He bent from his lofty height to kiss me on the cheek and pull me into a one-armed hug. Kate caught him up, red in the face, and hugged me tightly. Sofia, all this time, remained trapped, squirming to get down.

'Doggy,' she screamed. 'I want the doggy.'

'Hello,' I said, laughing. 'You all look really well. Fighting fit, even.'

Ben put Sofia down but didn't let her go. 'Be careful not to hurt the doggy, okay?'

Sofia ignored him completely and threw her arms around Lulu's neck. Lulu lapped it up, bending double trying to lick Sofia's face.

'And this must be Zac,' Kate said, bending down in front of his buggy. She held out a small, bright red bunny rabbit, dressed in a green coat and a yellow hat. 'This is for you,' she said.

Zac took it, then solemnly blew her a big fat raspberry of thanks.

Kate laughed and straightened. 'You must have been so worried when he was in hospital. Is he better now?'

I glanced down at him. His eyes were fixed on Sofia and he was gazing at her wondrously, the rabbit clutched to his chest.

'To be honest, we don't fully know. We thought he was when they sent him home, but I'm waiting to see a specialist. He isn't reacting to noise, and meningitis can cause deafness, so…'

Ben and Kate gawped at me. 'Oh, no,' Ben said. 'I hope the little fella is alright. I don't know what to say.'

'I know. It's just another thing to contend with. We'll just have to wait and see how bad it is. Best hope is that there is some hearing there, and it's not total deafness.' My throat tightened; were we destined for a life of hearing aids and sign language? Ben put an arm around my shoulders. 'Anyway, other than that, he's fine, so let's have a lovely weekend,' I said.

'Looks like that cafe has been the making of you,' Ben said. 'You look so happy. And it's so nice to meet this little one. I still can't believe you've got a baby. Last time we saw you, you weren't even pregnant.'

No, I thought. Because Chris hadn't found me then. 'I can't believe how long ago that was. I feel like I've been living here forever.'

I turned the buggy, and they followed me out of the station, Sofia now carrying a struggling Lulu and almost dropping her.

'I think she'd rather walk,' I told her.

Sofia scowled. 'She asked me to carry her. She's heavy.'

'Put her on the floor, please,' Kate said.

She huffed and puffed and put Lulu down, almost falling over herself.

'But you can hold her lead, if you want. It's a very important job. Just make sure you hold it tightly, and wrap it around your wrist like this.' I bent down and wrapped it around her arm several times. She looked smug and satisfied. Ben held her other hand.

'Do you want to go to the hotel first and drop off your bags?' I asked Kate.

'Sounds good to me,' she said, looking all around. 'I love York. Came here on a school trip once and we had such a good time.' She frowned. 'I have no idea where our hotel is, though.'

'It's the Coach House, isn't it? It's right in the centre of the shopping part. I've booked a restaurant for us for tonight so we can have a good catch up. Mum is looking after Zac, and she's offered to have Sofia too, if you want to have a break. Somehow, I don't think Sofia will mind, if Lulu is there. She'll hardly know you're gone.'

'You're right. I think that would be lovely, if she doesn't mind,' Kate said, throwing Ben a hopeful glance.

Ben shrugged. 'Fine by me. But she has no idea what she's letting herself in for.'

'That's sorted then. I'll tell Mum and Dad there'll be two kids this evening. I actually think it will be good for Zac to have another child to play with, although I don't know how he'll be. With a bit of luck, he won't bite her with his one tooth.'

Kate laughed. 'Don't worry. It'll be fine. And we have so much to catch up on. I want to know everything about your life here.'

I sneaked a quick look at Ben. He was looking relaxed and happy. I wasn't sure how he'd be, although he emailed me all the time. His depression and his urge to escape his responsibilities looked to be in the past. But you can never tell.

'So how are you doing, Ben?' I asked.

'I'm doing great.' He smiled at Kate. 'Aren't I?'

'Yes,' she said. 'You are.' She turned to me. 'He is. His demons are still there, but he's keeping them at bay.'

Ben nodded. 'Aye, I feel so much better. I kept up with the counselling and the other PTSD treatments.' He mimed taking tablets. 'And they're really helping. Like Kate said, I fight the odd demon, but I'm winning. So it's all good, yeah.'

'How is your work going, Kate? Still conquering the business world up there?'

'Yep. In fact, it's been so good, I've had to take on two staff members. I'm trying to not let it grow too quickly and get out of hand.'

'Well, if anyone knows about that sort of thing, it's you.'

'Although,' she paused and glanced at Ben. 'I am going to have to step away from it for a while.' She patted her tummy.

'Really? Oh, brilliant. Congratulations! When are you due?'

'I'm five months now. The bump's rather small, though, so with a coat on, you can't tell.'

'I bet Sofia can't wait.'

'Oh. No. Sofia has reliably informed us she doesn't want a brother or a sister. She wants a dog. And Lulu here hasn't helped. I didn't know you had a dog.'

We all looked down to where Sofia was gazing fixedly at Lulu and singing softly to herself. She'd walked into the buggy three times already.

'Sorry. I thought I'd told Ben about her. Anyway, Sofia will change her mind when it's born. Do you know what you're having?'

'A boy. And she definitely doesn't want a brother, under any circumstances. Uh-huh.'

'Oh dear.'

'Yeah. Boys are dirty and rude, apparently.'

I looked down at Zac. 'Pretty much, yeah.'

We stopped to cross the road, waiting for the traffic lights to change. Kate paused and looked at me with concern.

'But what about you? I'm going to have to ask about that Chris bloke. I've been wondering ever since you told me about him. Have there been any developments? Is he still on the run?'

Ben turned his head to catch the answer. I could tell them some of the truth. Might as well get it over with.

The lights turned red, and we hurried across, Lulu trying to streak ahead and dragging at Sofia's arm. She, in turn, pulled at Ben's hand.

Once we'd crossed, I said. 'There have been some developments. He's in prison.'

Kate gasped. 'What? How do you know that?'

'Because he's been writing to me from there.'

Ben looked at me, frowning. 'Where? Which prison?'

'Wakefield.'

'How does he know where you live?' Kate asked.

'Through Facebook. My bosses kindly blabbed everything on there, even posting pictures of me and the cafe; although they didn't know what it would lead to. They didn't know they were doing anything wrong; they were just promoting the new cafe. I wasn't aware they'd done it. Thing was, though, they made it easy for him, so he probably found me in under five minutes.'

'So, he's in prison, then,' Ben said. 'How long did he get?'

'Life. He killed three people, didn't he?'

'Will he ever get out?' Kate asked.

'I don't know. No one knows that.'

'Have you seen him?' Ben asked. 'In prison?'

I hesitated. I hadn't thought this bit through. What should I say?

'You have, haven't you?' Ben asked.

I bit my lip. 'Just once, and I'm never going back. It's done. Finished. Time to move on. So, end of story.'

They got the hint that I'd said all I wanted to, but I could still feel the shock waves rippling through them for the rest of the walk to their hotel. We changed the subject to more pleasant things instead, but it all felt a bit superficial and forced.

Before they disappeared into the hotel, I said, 'I'll come back for you in an hour, and we can drop Sofia off at mine. You can come in and meet Mum and Dad, and make sure you're alright about leaving her with them.'

'We'll be alright. You could do with the break. You're exhausted,' Ben said to Kate.

She nodded. 'True.'

'I'll see you in an hour, then.'

As expected, Sofia kicked off when she had to leave Lulu.

'I want her to come to my room,' she said with a giant pout.

'She's not allowed in the hotel,' I said. 'Anyway, you'll see her again in an hour.'

That pacified her, and she went into the hotel after kissing Lulu. I pushed the buggy back to my flat, looking forward to a nice meal out with my friends.

***

In the end, it wasn't great. I mean, the company was, but the food was awful.

'I'm so sorry. I had no idea it was like this. It's the first time I've been here,' I said, after we'd chewed our way through overcooked, leathery steaks that we'd waited ages for.

'At least my teeth have had a good workout.' Ben poked at something in his mouth with his tongue. 'What's left of them, anyway? Are we having dessert?'

'Are you kidding? I'm not paying good money here for their rubbish. We can get something much better at mine.'

'Sounds good to me. I've got backache sitting here, so I don't mind moving,' Kate said.

We left the restaurant and walked up Stonegate, looking in lit-up shop windows. Dusk was falling, and the pubs were overflowing with Saturday night drinkers. The May evening was warm and pleasant.

'We could go for a drink first, if you like,' I suggested. 'We don't have to hurry back. The kids will be fine with Mum.'

'Yeah. Okay.'

We lost a couple of hours just drinking and chatting more. It was nice. I told them about the ghost walk I went on with Leanne and regaled them with some of the more gory stories from it I could remember. Eventually, Kate yawned, and I realised how tired she must be.

'Come on, let's call it a night. You look done in. Early pregnancy—I remember it well.'

She looked grateful as she stood and put her jacket on. 'I am, but it's been a lovely night.'

'We'll have more time after work tomorrow. The cafe closes early on Sundays.'

We left the pub and were almost back at my flat when we passed Betty's Bloody Tea Rooms.

'Ooh, look,' said Kate. 'Betty's. We could go there tomorrow.'

She caught the sight of my lip curling.

'Oops, sorry, I forgot. Let's go somewhere good instead.'

I laughed and linked my arm through hers. A minute later, we were at the flat. I unlocked the shop, and we went inside.

'This does look great. I absolutely love it,' Kate said, looking around. 'Especially that. It's so unique and quirky.' Her eye had gone to the *Life's Too Short Not To Eat The Brownie* artwork.

I just smiled and said, 'Thanks.'

Ben mooched along behind us. I think his three beers had mellowed him as his eyes were half-closed.

At the top of the stairs, I opened the door to find Sofia and Lulu playing on the floor. Zac was crawling around after them as if his life depended on it.

'Hello,' said Mum. She was sitting next to Dad on the sofa. Her face looked weird; kind of tight.

'Aunty Sarah!' shrieked Sofia. Everyone jumped, except Zac. 'Who's the bad man in jail who kills people and writes you letters? Is he your friend? Does he play with you? I'm playing with Zac. He wants me to be his best friend, but I don't know. He's a bit young, and he's a boy. I don't really like boys.'

She sprawled on the carpet and tickled Lulu's belly while I stood there, my feet frozen to the floor. When Mum picked up the remote and turned off the TV, the silence hurt my ears.

'Um, I think we'd better be off,' Kate mumbled.

I nodded as she grabbed Sofia, who immediately started kicking off about leaving Lulu. Kate was having none of it, and Ben gave my arm a quick squeeze as he went by.

'See you tomorrow,' he mouthed.

Then they were gone. Mum and Dad's eyes were on me. Mum's were like chips of ice. She raised her eyebrows.

'Well?' she said.

She was smiling, but it didn't reach her eyes. It barely reached her mouth.

25

Sarah

I STOOD THERE, FEELING the panic rise .

'Erm... um...' I said, desperate to escape; I'd never, ever felt so trapped.

'Well, we're listening,' Mum said, her eyes fixed firmly on mine.

My bowels churned. I'd been well and truly caught out, all because of a child listening to a grown-up conversation. I hadn't felt this way since I was six, and I burnt Mum's best dress with an iron I shouldn't have been using.

'So, this man who kills people—the one who writes those letters every week—you know, the ones you hide away? Who is he? Does this have anything to do with what happened back in London? And don't lie to us; we're not stupid,' Mum snapped.

My dad put a hand over hers but didn't speak. The look on his face was enough. It said 'the game is up'.

I closed the living room door behind me, and took off my coat, then my shoes, for something to do. Stalling. I had never seen Mum like this before, ever. I scoured her face for anything good, but there was nothing. Dad's was a mask of disappointment. I didn't know which was worse.

'It seems there's a lot has happened that we don't know,' he said. 'You need to start talking.'

I sat down. 'Okay. But first, you have to understand why I kept it from you.'

'Huh!' muttered Mum. 'This is going to be good.'

'I was ashamed. The more time that passed and the more things that happened, the harder it got to tell you.' I blinked back tears, determined they wouldn't fall. They already probably thought I was weak. I wasn't about to make myself look weaker. 'Alright. I'll tell you everything.'

And so I did, the whole damn sordid lot, up to the point Chris was jailed. But not about him being Zac's father. There was so much to tell, it took ages, and Zac was fast asleep on the carpet long before I'd finished. When I got to the end, Mum was aghast.

'So hang on, he came here on an evening, when you were alone, and painted that sign downstairs? You told me an Irish man did it, when I asked about it.'

'Yes, but you asked about it in front of Claire, who believed he was. What was I supposed to say? But no, he was never Irish. It was part of his disguise. He was stupid enough to think I wouldn't recognise him. That was his mistake.'

Her eyes slid to Lulu and then to me.

'It's not the dog's fault,' I said.

'No, I know.'

Dad frowned. 'Hang on. We're talking about the same one whose baby you lost in that ectopic pregnancy?'

I could see his cogs turning, but I just said, 'Yes.'

'You had a killer under this roof? A wanted man?' Mum was shaking her head, unable to believe it. 'You put Ellie and Claire at risk, as well as yourself.'

'How did I put them at risk? They were hardly here when he was.'

'He shouldn't have been here at all,' she snapped.

'But he was. Why are you making it sound like my fault? He came back, and I did everything I could to catch him. I made sure it was him and then called the police the second I was sure. I got his DNA and fingerprints on a cup and handed it over. And yes, I put myself at risk to do it. But he was never a danger to me. He could have killed me back then in London, remember, but instead he saved my life. I did the right thing in the end.'

'The right thing? He was here for weeks and you did nothing.'

Was Mum even trying to understand? All she was doing was blaming me. I took a long breath in to calm down. It didn't work.

'I didn't do nothing. How did I do nothing?'

I stood up and started pacing, walking around Zac. He'd woken up again. Wouldn't a normal kid be crying by now, with all the shouting? Instead, he was lying on his front, gripping Lulu's fur. The dog, though, was cowering from our angry voices. I gave her a quick pat on the head.

'Don't pull Lulu's fur, Zac.' I picked him up and checked to see if his nappy was clean. It was.

My dad stared at me, then Zac. A look passed between him and Mum, and her mouth twisted.

'Sarah…' he began. He looked at Mum in a helpless kind of way and my stomach dropped. I could see both of them putting the pieces together. Mum's face was white.

'Is he the sperm donor you used?' She made air quotes with her fingers. 'Oh, God! It's all making sense now. And the timing is right.' She put her head in her hands, mumbling something I couldn't make out.

I clamped my lips shut and bit down on them. I wouldn't need to answer. They knew. All the fight went out of me and I slumped back down in a chair, clutching Zac tightly to me.

'Do you know what, I'm actually relieved it's all out in the open. Now there's nothing you don't know. Yes, Chris is Zac's dad, and yes, he's the one who's been writing to me from prison, when I obviously did such a bad job of hiding his letters. But I don't answer them. I only just read them, for the first time. And that's the truth, whether you believe it or not.'

Mum made a dismissive noise.

'It is. I did. Believe me if you want, or don't—it's up to you.'

The atmosphere was so bad it was toxic.

'I can't believe you slept with him. That's the bit I can't get my head around,' she whispered.

This was truly excruciating. I looked at Dad, but he wouldn't look at me. Couldn't they see why I did it? Did I really have to spell it out?

My leg was jiggling up and down as I considered telling them the last bit. The kicker. They hadn't really left me a choice.

'Alright, it was the only way to be one hundred percent sure it was him. There was no other way. If you know what I mean. He'd changed everything else but he couldn't change that.'

Mum's face flushed. She knew what I meant, alright. 'I can't believe how you could have been so stupid as to get pregnant,' Mum said. 'And I don't understand how you could keep things of this magnitude from us. Why didn't you tell us?'

Stupid? Her words cut me deeply. My voice rose again. 'You want to know why I didn't tell you? Maybe because I knew you'd react like this.'

'Maybe I'm reacting like this because you've kept so much from us. Lying by omission. Have you considered that?' Mum's voice began to rise, and she was trembling. It was awful. 'We sold our house in London and moved here to be with you, and you couldn't even be honest with us.'

'And what would you have said if I had? I didn't want us to be in this position now, fighting about it.'

Mum struggled to stand up.

'Stella, please, sit down. You'll make yourself ill,' Dad said.

'I'm not the one making me ill,' she said, glaring at me. 'Our daughter is.' She finally managed to get to her feet.

My blood was starting to boil. So her arthritis was my fault as well, then? How ridiculous!

'I've already said, if I knew your reaction wouldn't be this bad, perhaps I would have told you. But I knew you'd start yelling at me.'

'No, you wouldn't have told us. Because you knew what you were doing was wrong. You knew he was bad, and you wanted to see him, and that's all there was to it. What's wrong with you? We didn't teach you to hang around with men like him. I thought we'd done a better job than that.'

She paused, breathing hard. I was doing the same.

'So maybe it's your fault, then.' I snapped. 'Maybe you didn't do such a good job of bringing me up.'

'Why don't you both sit down before one of you says something you'll regret?' said Dad. 'This isn't getting us anywhere.'

Instead, Mum looked at me and shook her head, slowly. 'I'm shocked you can be so deceitful. I just don't know what to say. I feel like I don't know you anymore.'

Her words were like blades, each one slicing me to shreds.

Out of the blue, Dad asked, 'Sarah, was Zac an accident?'

There it was, out in the open: ugly and raw.

I lifted my chin and rested it on Zac's head. 'No, he wasn't. Zac is the best thing that's ever happened to me, and I don't regret it.' The childish, silent 'so there' remained unsaid.

'He wasn't an accident?' Mum repeated.

'No. I planned him. I wanted him and I love him.'

Dad's mouth dropped open now. 'I don't understand.'

The only sound in the room was Zac gurgling away to himself.

Then Mum said, 'I think I do.'

I raised my eyes to hers. There was still no warmth in them, but the hard lines in her face had softened. I no longer felt I needed forgiving, though. I stood by my choices one hundred percent, and I had to stick up for myself to have any self-respect left at all.

'So, what? It affects how you feel about Zac, does it? You're going to disown him because he has bad blood? And let's kick the dog out while we're at it, eh? Shall I just open the door and chuck her into the street?'

I knew they didn't think that, but hurtful words were all I had.

Mum's face crumpled. 'Don't be stupid! I love that little boy with everything I have. He's the innocent in this. And the poor dog.'

'Because I don't regret him, Mum. He's my world.'

'Of course he is. I think I get it now.'

'I wish I did,' Dad chimed in.

We ignored him, Mum and I, but our eyes remained locked on each other.

'You love him, don't you, this man? He's 'The One'.'

'He was, yeah. He isn't now. I've moved on.'

Mum sat down next to me and went to take Zac, but I held him tight and wouldn't let her have him. Tears spilled down her face as she spoke.

'You poor thing. You've been through hell, haven't you? I'm sorry, love. I didn't mean those things I said just now.'

Determined not to cry, I swallowed hard. 'Yes you did. You meant every word. And so did I.' I stood up. 'It's been a long day. I'm taking my son to bed.'

'Sarah…' she began.

But I closed the door behind me, went to my bedroom and lay Zac in his cot. Then I cried.

26

Sarah

THE MORNING AFTER THE row, I got up earlier than ever, leaving Zac sleeping soundly, and went downstairs to the kitchen. Not wanting to see either of my parents, I decided to get cracking on my day's baking. I knew I'd have to see them sooner or later, but I just wanted to put it off for a bit longer.

Yesterday was so awful I didn't think I'd sleep much. Surprisingly though, despite waking early, I slept better than I had in ages. Maybe because my guilty conscience had been appeased. They say confession is good for the soul. I certainly felt better than I had in a long time. No more sneaking about collecting and hiding letters, or lying to the people who meant the most to me. It was refreshing, despite the bad things that were said last night.

Normally, I would decide the night before what I was going to bake the next day, but last night had imploded so spectacularly I couldn't even think about it. I had to think about it now, though. I needed an easy, stress-free day so I'd go with the things I could make in my sleep; brownies, cupcakes, and caramel shortcakes. No hassle, even given the huge quantities I had to make. Sunday was always a busy day in the café, so I needed loads of everything.

Just as I got started, Mum appeared in her dressing gown and slippers. I stiffened at the sight of her. She looked awful, as probably did I. Her hair was all over the place, her eyes puffy, and her face drawn. For a split second, I didn't know how to play this. She said some horrible things to me last night, and I couldn't just ignore that fact. But we had to live together for a while longer, and I still needed her on my side for the foreseeable future. But, more importantly than anything, she was still my mum, and I loved her to bits. I didn't want us to fight.

'Morning,' I said, as pleasantly as I could, continuing to collect all my paraphernalia together. At least when I was bending down to reach for stuff, I didn't have to look her in the eye.

She just stood there, and I could almost feel her agony. Should she apologise or skirt around it? She didn't know what to do any more than I did. We hardly ever fell out, and never this bad, so this was all new.

She took a tentative step into the kitchen, then stopped again. She was wringing her hands in a repeated washing motion, over and over, round and round. But I couldn't intervene. She had to decide on her own what she wanted to do.

Another step.

'I'm sorry,' she said.

I waited, fiddling with some wire cooling racks.

'Those things I said last night. And what you said. I haven't slept for thinking about them. You were right when you said we both meant them. We did, at the time. But what I really, truly think, deep down, is that you are the bravest person I know.'

I stopped fiddling and looked at her. 'Brave? Me?'

'Yes. I don't think I would have had the courage to do what you did. Yes, you took a risk, but it landed him behind bars, didn't it? You actually got a killer locked up.'

'Well, that was the idea, yeah.'

'It's just a lot to take in. Most of all, though, I'm sorry you didn't feel you could talk to me back then. That means I'm the failure, not you. I thought we could talk about anything.'

I sighed. 'You're not a failure, Mum. Neither of us are. We're strong women, doing what we have to do to get by. I am strong because you made me that way.'

She dragged a stool over and sat down on it. 'Can you ever forgive me?' Her eyes were wet, and full of pain.

'Look, people fall out. It's natural. We had an extremely horrible row, yes, but we can clear the air and get over it. It's what families do.'

She looked so miserable I had to go over and give her a hug.

'And I really am glad it's all out in the open,' I told her. 'It's been horrible keeping secrets from you. I've hated it, but the more it went on, the harder it became to tell you, until I just didn't know where to start.'

She sniffed, and I squeezed her tighter.

'Don't cry, Mum. Everything's okay. The only thing we have to worry about now is Zac's appointment. That's going to take all our focus.'

'What will you say to Ben and Kate? I humiliated you in front of your friends. What must they think of me? I'm so sorry,' she sobbed.

Her tears were threatening to set mine off. 'I'll sort it out. Don't worry. They won't judge.'

'But that's what I did. I judged you and I had no right.' She pulled a tissue from up her sleeve and mopped her eyes with it. When she tried to speak again, I hushed her, but she shook her head.

'No, no, I need to say this. You're a grown woman. Your life is your business, and however you choose to live it is up to you. I can't tell you what to do, and I don't want to.'

'Look, I just want to forget the whole thing ever happened. I'm not proud of any of it. Things escalated beyond my control, and I thought I could handle it, so that's what I tried to do. There was never any intention on my behalf of hurting you, or lying to you, or anything like that, I swear.'

'I know. When I said last night I didn't know you anymore, I was being stupid. Of course I know you.'

'You weren't being stupid. We were in the heat of the moment, and both of us felt under attack. That's all it was. We need to move on. I, for one, am happy to never ever mention it again. I hated every second of it.'

'So, just one more thing—is this episode over? I mean this man? Everything to do with him is in the past?'

'Yes. Dead and buried. Good riddance to him.'

Footsteps sounded on the stairs, along with Zac burbling.

'Dry your eyes,' I said to Mum, wiping my own.

Dad poked his head around the door and then swiftly retracted it, as if he was under enemy fire. It made me laugh, and that set Mum off.

'We alright in here?' he asked. 'Or should I go back for my hard hat?'

'We're fine. Just clearing the air,' I said.

'No, that's not quite it. I'm having my breakfast here,' Mum said.

Both Dad and I said, 'What?' at the same time.

She mimed eating. 'A large slice of humble pie.'

Dad's eyebrows shot up. 'Oh, I see. So I'll be getting my own breakfast today, will I, if you've already stuffed your face down here?'

'Yes. Same as you do every day. Now get on, you daft bat. Zac needs feeding. And changing, no doubt. And our Sarah's got work to do.'

She shooed him out of the kitchen and back upstairs, and I heaved a sigh of relief. She'd called me 'Our Sarah'. Everything was alright. It would be a relief to be able to talk openly about Chris, especially as Zac's dad. Hopefully, things might start looking up now.

27

Joe

'I HOPE YOU KNOW what you're doing. If I was you, I'd just put it behind me and get on with my life,' Gerry said, knocking back the rest of his tea.

'No, you wouldn't. You'd be out for blood. Me? I'm just fancying a bit of good old-fashioned revenge, to show him he won't get away with any of it,' said Joe, crossing his arms in front of him and leaning back in the hard, pine kitchen chair.

Gerry thought for a bit. 'Ah, maybe you're right. Yeah. I'd have a distant family member bump him off for me.' A braying laugh escaped him. 'Well,' he said, standing up. 'No rest for the wicked. And no prizes for guessing what you're doing today.'

Joe held up his car keys. 'Yep. That's if the old girl gets me there and back in one piece.'

'Course she will. Old custard won't let you down.'

Gerry went downstairs, on one of the rare occasions he was running his own shop. Joe followed him down into the pawnbrokers, stopped, and sniffed hard. He loved pawn shops. There was just something about them. They were like treasure troves from the past. Dust floated in the air, illuminated in a shaft of sunlight that was managing to battle its way through the dirty front windows and onto the cat, busy languishing in an old armchair. His eye snagged on a beautiful old grandfather clock in the corner and he made his way over to it, to trail his fingers on the rich wood surface. It was even still going, its tick loud, although the time was ten hours slow.

'Nice that, isn't it?' remarked Gerry. 'I'll sell it to you if they don't come back for it.'

'I'd have it if I had my own place. There's nowhere in yours to put it.'

Gerry grunted in agreement. If he was tiring of having him as a house guest, then he wasn't letting on. On the contrary, he seemed more than happy to have Joe around.

'I'll see you later, then. Fish and chips tonight, if you like.'

'Sounds good to me,' Joe said, as he went out to the sound of an old-fashioned clanging bell on the door.

As it was Sunday and the store closed at four, he wasn't working today, so he'd be home for tea. Home. He twisted round to look back at the shop. Was this really his home? If he could afford it, he would move out and get his own place. He was a scruffy git, but Gerry took it to another level, and Joe felt claustrophobic every time he set foot in the place. But on his shitty wages, he couldn't afford a place of his own, and that was that. And, above all else, he was immensely grateful to Gerry for taking him in at all.

The yellow heap of rust was parked at the kerb, waiting for him. He put the key in the driver's side door (the central locking having long since given up the ghost), and hauled himself inside. He patted the steering wheel, looked around, and settled into the seat. The old girl may be dropping to bits, but he was actually quite fond of her now. Ladies her age should be loved, cherished, and cared for. And, being a car, she didn't have the gob a woman would have. It was funny really, he thought, starting her up and waiting until her smoker's cough had cleared a little; when he'd got out of prison, he'd thought he'd want to find a woman as quickly as possible, but it turned out he just wasn't that bothered with the hassle it would bring. They just wanted money or attention. The ones you paid for it wanted the money and the free ones the attention. Nah. He was fine as he was.

As he headed for the motorway, his jovial mood turned sombre as he reflected on what Tommy had told Gerry on his last visit. Apparently, Colin had implied that Shay's death was because he'd given her money for an overdose, being sure she would take one. And it had worked. So, not only had Colin been responsible for his dad getting sent down, he was also the reason Joe's daughter was now dead.

He had no love for Shay, it was true, but he had no love for anyone when it came down to it. It was the principle, however. Yet another thing he had to begrudge that little piss-head son of his for. Yes, he was in prison, getting punished for what he'd done, but the best way to get at him would be to strike at him from outside. And, if Shay had still been alive, he could have bunked down there, in their old family home. She would have been compliant. She would have looked after him, made him meals and done his shopping. And because of Colin, that would never happen now. So, in a way, it was Colin's fault Joe couldn't move out of Gerry's.

His thoughts of both his children turned in his mind all the way to York, and before he knew it, he was parking up near the Barbican. On his first visit, the cost of parking had absolutely staggered him. He'd thought he'd be bankrupt at this rate. There again, he realised, he could go without other things, if it came down to it. He needed very little money to survive. Now, these visits were bringing him so much pleasure they were worth every penny. His job meant he always had a little extra, even if it was going on fuel and parking, as the money Gerry took from him for his keep was more than fair.

He got a ticket from the machine at the barrier, parked up, grabbed yesterday's Daily Mirror from the passenger seat, and left through the heavy security gate. The car would be safe here, but he doubted if he left it on the street with the engine running and the door open that anyone would make off with it.

Outside, he took in a deep lungful of ring road air, and eyed the open space around him. Would he ever get used to it? After the confines of prison, space was the one thing that unnerved him. Along with decision-making. The simplest things could throw him off, no matter how much of a display of confidence he put on in front of Gerry. But it was early days. It would get better. He lit up one of the roll-ups he rationed and inhaled hard, closing his eyes. He had all afternoon here, no trolleys to collect at four, and he was a free man. Apart from the anxiety that niggled away in the pit of his stomach, life was good. He squared his shoulders and set off.

This was his fourth visit. It hadn't been hard to find the cafe, based on the information Tommy supplied. Tommy had remembered the name, and passed it on. A quick scan of Facebook by one of Gerry's sons had given them the address, and working the four until midnight shift actually now fell in Joe's favour, as it gave him the day free.

The first time he saw the place, he'd stood outside, taking it all in. He'd been impressed. The signage was black and pink, with 'Delish' written on it in fancy lettering. There were four small metal tables outside, arranged neatly in front of the immaculately painted pink shop door. A froth of pink, yellow, and purple plants spilled over from two silver window boxes, in front of sparklingly clean windows. The whole set-up was pleasing to the eye. It certainly had more kerb appeal than Gerry's shop front, with its peeling paintwork, littered doorway, and, often, stale vomit.

From his vantage point across the road and just off to one side, Joe had watched the comings and goings for a long time. Three different women seemed to work there, all of them coming out regularly to serve customers at the outside tables. Of course, he didn't know which one, if any, was Sarah. One was pretty, tall, with wavy blonde hair; one had weird blue hair and a face full of piercings; and the last one—well, she was simply stunning. It couldn't be her, could it? She was like a model or actress or something. Surely she wouldn't give his Colin the time of day, although, it had to be said, Colin was far from ugly. Usually, though, when he pictured his son, he saw either a gap-toothed, snot-encrusted little boy, or an awkward gorilla of a teenager. The adult Colin was handsome, though Joe had missed the transformation from ugly duckling, so it could be her.

Today, though, he knew exactly which one she was. He straightened his shoulders, tucked the newspaper under his arm, adjusted his new fedora-type hat to just the right angle (some might say rakish, some might say jaunty), and ventured inside. The hat had one purpose only: doffability. He liked the idea of doffing a hat to the ladies. Made a man seem much more approachable and charming. Plus, it covered up the lack of hair, at least until he took it off. Seeing Colin's thick head of hair had made him more conscious about his own lack of it. But he wasn't one of those men to get too hung up about it. No point.

The blonde one behind the counter smiled at him as he went in.

'Hello,' she called out in a friendly voice.

He nodded at her, before going a spare table at the back, under a massive, painted sign, trying to see if Sarah was in the kitchen as he passed. So, Sarah was the dark, gorgeous one. Who knew! He would have mentally congratulated his son for getting one in the back of the net with her, but when he'd realised, he'd experienced a real stab of jealousy. He had never, ever, scored with a woman of that calibre. She was quality he'd never even paid for. He wouldn't have been able to afford it.

On his second visit, he'd heard someone call her name, and she'd appeared out of the kitchen like some vision, to sort out some problem at the till. He'd been dazzled by her; she was even better close up. Even now, when he saw her, he had to tell himself not to stare.

He removed his jacket and laid his hat on the seat, staking claim to his table. With a practised move, he brushed imaginary dust off the front of his second-hand slacks, then walked over to the counter.

'Hello, again,' said the blonde one.

If he knew her name, he'd forgotten it now. All he knew was it wasn't Sarah.

'How are you today?' she asked with a bright smile.

'Very good, thank you. And yourself?' If he had been wearing his hat, he'd have doffed it.

'Oh, I'm just dandy, thanks. And what can I get you?'

He glanced down at the menu still clutched in his hand. 'Oh, yes, um, let me see—I'll have a large cappuccino and a sausage roll, please.'

'Coming right up,' the blonde said. Her eyes flicked to where he was sitting. 'Table seven. That'll be six ninety, please.'

This time when he handed the money over, he didn't flinch. At first, he'd thought the prices in here were ridiculous, then he'd realised it was the same everywhere. Prices had gone up while he'd stayed the same. Fifteen years' worth of inflation! At least the sausage roll was a jumbo. Good job, because it was all he'd be having until his fish and chip supper with Gerry later.

'I'll bring them right over,' the blonde said, looking down and sorting the cash he'd given her. Then she looked up and smiled at him again.

Joe didn't remember the world being such a smiley place in his younger days. Or perhaps it was just his part of the world. Where he'd lived in Leeds, no one seemed this nice and smiley. Perhaps they bred them different in York, he thought, making his way back to his table.

When he was seated, he opened the newspaper and unfolded it on the table, pretending to read it. Where was Sarah? She must be in. She owned the place, didn't she? He hoped he hadn't driven all this way to find she wasn't here. He turned a page, not seeing a damn thing that was printed on it. Then another. His ears were attuned to everything around him, but he couldn't hear her either. That didn't necessarily mean anything, though.

Before long, the blonde delivered his order. The sausage roll was nice. Good job: it cost enough. The flaky, buttery pastry was lovely. He really could eat another. He eyed the crumbs on his plate, and when no one was looking he licked a finger and collected them up, sucking off every last bit. The tendency to still gobble his food down was one thing he couldn't seem to get out of since he'd left prison.

Half the cappuccino was gone in one gulp. That was the trouble with it. It was all froth. The actual coffee was way down, like buried treasure. But he liked cappuccinos, with their chocolatey dusting on the top adding to the sweetness; they were just so nice, like little cups of luxury. The coffee in prison—well, the very thought of it made him shudder.

He looked up as a man possibly around his own age, and a woman came through a door to the side of him. He caught a glimpse of stairs. Looked like it led to a flat above. The man was carrying a buggy, and the woman was holding a baby of indeterminate age. Joe was no good at guessing that sort of thing, and besides, all he could see was the back of its head. Before the door closed, Joe heard howls and whines coming from upstairs. The man tutted and leaned the folded buggy against the wall.

'I'm going to have to go back for her,' he said, before disappearing through the door again.

Joe watched as the woman flicked a stray piece of hair behind her ear and hitched the baby further up on her hip. Before long, the man appeared again, this time with a small white dog tucked under his arm. He stooped to pick up the buggy with his other hand. The three didn't look his way before they got to the counter. Sarah appeared out of the kitchen and said something to them. It was then the baby turned around, and Joe caught sight of a face that sent him hurtling back through time. The floor seemed to drop away with the years, and his mouth hung open as all the air was sucked out of his lungs.

All he could do was stare. The child! Colin's child! It had to be. They were like carbon copies of each other at the same age. If anyone had asked Joe what his kids looked like as babies, he would have shrugged and said, 'Dunno. They all look the same, don't they?' He wouldn't have imagined he could pick his own out in a line-up, but, by God, he would have been wrong.

Sarah bent and kissed the child, and it was then Joe saw the resemblance between her and the older woman. It must be her mother. She had the same bone structure and delicate features. The same shape and colour eyes. The same slim build.

Joe, finally able to breathe, snapped his mouth shut and dipped his head, pretending to scan his paper again. He lifted his cup with a shaky hand. All the time, he was looking at the family from under his eyebrows. The couple with the baby were now leaving the shop, and Sarah was waving them off. He made a snap decision.

He wasn't sure his legs would hold him up but he drained his cup and got to his feet. Thankfully, they did, and he walked as nonchalantly as he could past the counter and out of the shop, leaving his newspaper behind. Everyone was busy. No one noticed him. He stood in the street, looking left and right. They couldn't have got far. Off to his right, he spotted them, the dog now on the ground, trotting beside the buggy with its tail high in the air. Joe let his shoulders relax down and his body soften, after the shock had made his system surge with adrenalin. He took a deep, calming breath in, then slowly released it. He didn't have to hurry. He had all afternoon, and they had no clue they were being followed.

He could hardly keep his face straight as he covered his mouth with his hand to keep the laugh in. This was better than anything he could have imagined. Gerry was going to love this snippet of information. This was pure gold. Or maybe he'd keep it to himself for now and savour it a while longer. It tasted much better than anything in that overpriced caff.

28

Sarah

WHEN THE CAFE CLOSED, I met Ben and Kate. What the hell was I going to say to them? Zac was in his buggy, burbling at the new bunny they'd bought him, and Lulu was trotting happily along beside us. From the outside, we probably looked a picture of cuteness and harmony. But I knew the reality.

I was meeting them outside the Minster, and we were just going to mooch around for a couple of hours until it was time for dinner. I saw Sofia first; she was running along behind a pigeon, with her hands out. Instead of flying away, the dumb thing just tried to walk faster, its head going back and forth like a wind-up toy.

Ben waved and nudged Kate when he saw me. Sofia spotted us and rushed over, the pigeon long forgotten, and with Kate hurrying behind. She bypassed me and went straight to Lulu, who promptly squatted down and peed on some grass.

'Her party piece,' I said to Kate, trying to make a joke.

She gave me a weak smile. 'Are you alright? What Sofia said… I should have known she'd be earwigging. She's always bloody doing it, like some silent assassin, waiting to take you down.'

I laughed. 'I won't lie. At first, it was bad, yeah. We had a huge fight. Basically because they knew nothing. And I mean nothing. You knew far more than them. But, I mean, do you tell your parents everything?'

'Not a chance,' she said, and Ben shook his head, too. 'Nope,' he said. 'Does anyone?'

'I know they were pretty big things to keep, but the longer it went on, the harder it got.'

I just managed to stop myself from blurting out about Chris being Zac's dad when I remembered they didn't know that bit. This was getting so confusing and difficult to juggle. But Mum was right about one thing; it was my business at the end of the day who I told what to.

'Anyway, Sofia kind of did me a favour. It's all out in the open now, and that's a real relief.'

We all turned to look at Sofia, who was kneeling down and chatting away to Lulu. She couldn't drop me in it any more than she already had, but she didn't even appear to be listening. Maybe playing innocent was how she got away with it. Was she listening now and storing it all away to drop another bomb at the most inopportune time?

We started to walk away from the Minster when Sofia piped up. 'Did you argue with your Mummy and Daddy about the jail man?'

I bloody well knew it!

***

Later that evening, I got back to the flat to a much calmer scene than the night before. Ben and Kate were getting an early train back home the next morning, so we'd said our goodbyes. It wasn't the visit I'd envisaged, but it had turned out alright in the end. Now, the next big test was Zac's hearing appointment. I'd been watching him as much as possible to see how he reacted to loud noises. Most of the time, he didn't. I'd tried clapping and dropping things on the floor. Nothing. I'd slammed doors and even tested the smoke alarm, which freaked Lulu out big time. He reacted slightly to the alarm, so perhaps he could hear some frequencies and not others. The stress of waiting and not knowing was killing me.

'Hello, love,' said Mum from her position on the sofa. The same place as last night, but a world of difference. Lulu shot straight past me and leaped onto her knee. Mum stroked her as she curled up on her lap. For a horrible moment last night, I'd thought they were going to reject the poor dog, and I couldn't have stood that.

'Hello,' I said, putting Zac on the floor.

'Did you have a good time?' asked Dad.

'Yes. Lovely.' I just stopped myself from saying it had been an enjoyable weekend. Obviously, it hadn't all been good. If I'd said that, would they think I was lying again? Was this how it was going to be from now on, us tiptoeing around each other and watching every word that came out of our mouths? For the first time, the thought of them moving out came as a relief. I never thought I'd say that, and the fact it had just crossed my mind saddened me immensely.

Dad hadn't said a lot about the revelations of last night. He often did that, kept things close to his chest. He'd just clam up. It left you second guessing, much of the time. Whether that was the end of it from his point of view, I didn't know.

'Mum, can I borrow you for a minute?'

'What for?' She looked startled, and her hand went to her throat.

'Relax. It's nothing bad.'

I went to my bedroom, knowing that she would follow.

'Close the door,' I said when she entered.

'What?' She looked worried. Maybe she couldn't take any more revelations.

I sat on the bed and patted the duvet beside me. She sat. I slid open the drawer next to my bed, grabbed the letters, and tossed them onto the duvet.

'Read them.'

Her eyes widened. 'Oh, I… I don't think it's my place…'

'Why? I thought you wanted to know what they were about.'

'But they're private. I don't want to.'

I flicked back through my memory of reading them. There was nothing in there that was too personal. He didn't describe us going at it or anything. I found the first one and pushed it towards her.

'Please. I want you to read them. I want your opinion on something.'

She stared at the letter as if it might burn her or something.

'Look, you wanted to be in the know. Now you are. And this is the price of knowing.'

She still didn't move.

'You started it,' I said, moving the letter another inch closer to her.

She looked from the envelope to me. 'Are you sure? I mean, what do you think it's going to achieve?'

'Read them, and then we'll find out.'

She picked it up, took the paper out, unfolded it, and began to read.

She read them all in order, checking I still wanted her to before she read the next one. She cried in the places I did. What was she really thinking?

When she'd finished, she handed it back to me. I couldn't read her expression.

'I feel like I shouldn't have read them. They were addressed to you, not me.'

'Too late for that now.'

'I have a question. Does he know he has a son? Because it doesn't sound like it from these.'

'No. And he's never going to. It would make things way too complicated. It'd also give him a foothold back into my life, and I don't want that.'

'So, what did you want my opinion on?'

'Now you understand everything, do you think I should go and see him again one more time? Or just walk away for good?'

'I thought you said it was done. 'Dead and buried' your exact words were. Why would you visit him? What good would it do?'

'It might be the only way to get him to stop writing these damn letters. While ever he's writing to me, it's keeping that connection there.'

'Yes, I can see that. But what if it made you realise you still loved him and couldn't walk away?'

'I already know I still love him. And I could walk away.'

'You have a child together, Sarah. There's the connection right there.'

I sighed. There wasn't a simple answer. 'But he doesn't know that, does he? And he's never going to. So, what do you think I should do?'

She looked at me. 'To be honest, I don't know. Only you can decide. But whatever you decide to do, I'll support you. And so will your dad.'

29

Peter

'ARE YOU TAKING HER out again? You've only just come back,' Stella said, jiggling Zac up and down on her knee.

Peter's teeth ground together at Stella's tone. 'I haven't just come back. I've been back an hour. And the weather's alright; well, I mean, it's not raining. I just thought...'

He bent and clipped Lulu's lead on. Why did he have to explain himself all the time? He was supposed to be retired, not in ruddy prison. But some days, it felt like that.

'Alright, alright! I wasn't having a go. I was only saying.' Stella tutted and turned to look out of the window.

'Well, what else is there for me to do around here?' he snapped, before he could change his mind.

'For God's sake; not this again!' Stella said, not quite under her breath.

He picked up his jacket from the back of the chair and closed the living room door behind him, trying but failing not to slam it. He stood there, his hand resting on the doorknob, trying to massage away a developing headache, and his bad temper, by rubbing his temples. Lulu looked up at him, her tail wagging expectantly.

'Come on then, lass,' he said. 'Let's get out of here.'

He walked through Sarah's neat kitchen and out through the door at the end that led to the external metal fire escape.

He couldn't face going through the café. It was always rammed at this time. Sarah never used this door, said the steps weren't safe. She'd more than likely have a go at him if she knew he was using them now. Ah, well: he was past bloody caring.

He trudged down the steps, Lulu jumping lightly down each one after him. The sight of her little pink tongue lolling out made him almost smile. Almost. He sighed and turned for the park at the end. He'd be better finding other areas to walk instead of coming here all the time. That would relieve the mind-numbing tedium he found himself in most days.

He walked down the back alley to the end, which brought him opposite the park. After crossing, he made for the entrance, then suddenly swerved the same time as Lulu pulled on the lead to go in.

'Sorry,' he told her when she looked up at him accusingly. 'Let's go somewhere else for a change.'

He carried on walking, away from the Minster. It was mostly cloudy, the sun valiantly trying to break through the thinnest of the cover, but not quite managing it. He glanced down at the dog, thinking how little it took to make her happy. Just a warm bed, regular food and plentiful walks. That was something to envy, alright. His own life… today, it felt like nothing would satisfy him.

As he walked along, over a bridge to the other side of the river, his thoughts slid back to his old life in London. He was missing it more and more. Was it possible to be both busy and bored? Ever since Zac had come along, it was like he'd barely sat down, and the dog was forever needing walking, according to his wife. Yet, despite all that, he was bored, too.

Back in London, he had no shortage of friends to see and places to go. Until his retirement, he'd had a fulfilling work life as a middle manager. He'd earned respect from people. He'd made important decisions that affected people's lives and families. He'd sacked people, then locked himself away in toilet cubicles while the guilt lessened and he pulled himself together. When he'd spoken, people had listened, and taken on board what he'd said. He'd had knowledge. Experience. And now, he pushed buggies around and threw sticks and balls for a little dog that, strictly speaking, wasn't his. Although, there was no doubt he loved her: she brought him great joy. But where was the purpose in his life?

He walked past several hotels and carried on towards the train station, deep in thought. For one daft, brief moment, he thought about hopping onto a train and going back to London, back to his old life and his friends. As he neared the station, he stood outside, looking in. It was busy, as usual, and he felt a pang of something. He was being stupid. He made his feet move and didn't look back. Another sigh escaped him as he glanced up at the sky. Still thick clouds. The colour of them matched his mood. Grey. Dark. Gloomy. Outlook: bleak.

It wasn't that he didn't love his family, especially the new additions, but he'd used to be somebody. Now, he was little more than a bit player in his own life, no longer centre stage, but watching from the wings. He'd become the understudy without knowing when or why it happened. And when was the last time anyone had trusted him to make a decision without overriding it? Always two against one: Stella and Sarah against him. They won, mainly because they were women and, according to them, for some unknown reason, that meant they always knew best and were always right.

No. That wasn't fair. He was just feeling sorry for himself, that was all. This mindless walking was increasingly having that effect. It was giving him too much time to think, that's all it was. Too much time to brood and let the pity take hold. He hated thinking this way about his wife and daughter. It made him feel bad. It wasn't their fault. And, most of the time, they did know better than him when it came to childcare and domestic things. But there was one thing that had knocked him for six, and he doubted they knew best about that—it was the bombshell his daughter had dropped on them the other day. Not because she wanted to, but because she'd been found out. She'd had no intention of telling them any of it. She had been deceitful, and it wasn't sitting well with him. And she hadn't been brought up to run around with hooligans, like this man. He sounded just awful. Not the sort of person you wanted your daughter to go near, yet his had had a baby with him. Deliberately. He didn't understand any of it.

He stopped to cross the road, wondering where he was. The streets looked unfamiliar. It didn't matter. He'd find his way back over the river, eventually. The lights changed, and he hurried across, almost dragging Lulu, who'd stopped to sniff at a litter bin. He barely noticed. His mind was a million miles away. He'd never felt this conflicted. When Stella had first suggested they moved to York, he'd had his reservations alright. What about his friends down The Jacks? That pub had been almost a part of him. He'd drunk there twice a week for forty years, and not even Stella's reduced mobility and increasing pain had stopped him.

'You will not sit moping and blaming me. I don't need a nursemaid,' Stella had told him when he hadn't got ready for his first Thursday night session.

They'd been to the specialist's that day and had more or less been told there was very little that could be done to alleviate Stella's arthritis. It was a pain she was going to have to live with. Yes, she could have painkillers, but they might only make it more bearable. Yet, on that day, Stella had handed him his jacket and shooed him out of the door. 'Get to The Jacks, and don't come back before half-past eleven,' she'd said. And so he had.

Did his friends down The Jacks miss him like he missed them? They'd all promised to keep in touch with him, but it was very sporadic, and he was as bad as them; not one for picking up the phone or writing letters, and don't get him started on texting. So what other ways were there to communicate with people? Bloody email? Half the time, they'd sit in the Jacks, each nursing a pint, and barely utter a word, each comfortable in the presence of the others. There'd usually be some match or other on the large screen

TV on the wall opposite. Their silence was never awkward, more comforting. They had no need to be talking all the time.

And here, now, he had none of that. Yes, he'd joined a bridge night in the pub after seeing a hand-made sign in the window about it, but it wasn't the same. The men there were friendly, mostly, and they made an effort to include him, but the history he shared with his friends back in London wasn't there in York. How could it be? Perhaps if he went to more places and did more things, it would get better. Making new friendships at his age wasn't easy, though. It was also quite a daunting prospect, and not one he could handle now, with all the other stuff that was going on. Besides, with Stella and Zac to care for, where would he find the time? It just wasn't feasible.

A path on the left led back over the river, and he took it. There were almost as many bridges in this city as back home. Back home—would he ever think of this as home instead of London? The thought he might not gave him a jolt. It was everything, really: the shock and horror of Zac's illness that he was still trying to come to terms with, coupled with his own health scare; the endless house hunting and all the railroading that had gone with it; and now this: Sarah's bombshell. No wonder he felt anxious and depressed. How could he not?

He squared his shoulders as he made for the flat. Home. For now. But it didn't feel like it, and nor would that tiny place Stella had insisted they buy. It was little bigger than a damn rabbit hutch. He should have tried harder to make his feelings known, should have put his foot down. When had he become such a pushover? At one time, Stella had asked his advice, listened to it, and taken his feelings into account. But the offer had been accepted. It was too late. He was going to have to make the best of it.

He glanced down at the little dog, tiptoeing beside him. She brought a smile to his face for a second, but it fell away as a heavy weight settled in his chest. In his heart. And it wouldn't shift.

30

Chris

THE IT THING HAPPENED much more quickly than he was expecting. One day he was working in the kitchens, and the next, he was told to report to the library the following morning. As he walked there for the first session, lumbering after yet another new officer he'd never seen before, a stocky, short-haired woman who was more butch than he was, he couldn't help feeling glad that he'd be doing something different. After the monotony of his cell, the kitchen had started to feel like another jail. Also, it had put him off potatoes for life. How long did the top brass think people could do the same thing, day in, day out, before they cracked up? The parallels between prisoners here and the behaviour of animals in a zoo were staggering. So, yeah—going to the library today might just save his sanity.

As he walked with Butch to the library, they were in full sight of other officers the entire way. Chris was amazed they had female officers in here at all. Didn't seem the best idea, even if they were heavily outnumbered by male ones. There again, Butch was more manly than lots of the men. He smiled at the thought and dropped back a few paces.

She barely spoke, other than yes and no. After a few attempts at conversation, he gave up. All there was left to do was stare at her huge, gelatinous arse. He watched it moving from side to side; it was as if the thing had a mind of its own.

It was so low-slung it could double as a floor sweeper. His mind did its usual thing and, before he could stop it, it had proclaimed her to be a one out of ten. He snickered to himself behind her back. There was only a handful of women in his life that had come that low. Even Luisa had been a three. This woman—if she was the only woman on earth and he was the only man, he'd be perfectly happy to let the human race die out rather than jump in the sack with her.

When she stopped and opened the library door for him, he was dragged away from his thoughts. Not a bad thing, considering they weren't pleasant. What would she think if she knew he was thinking that the thought of shagging her would make him throw up?

He stepped into the library. It was not a place he'd been to very often since he'd been here. The range of books was chronically bad. Nothing to interest him. He wasn't a fiction reader, and other than that, this place had either memoirs or textbooks for the various courses you could learn in here. The emphasis in prison was supposed to be on rehabilitation and education, but that was a joke. How could you be rehabilitated and educated when you were locked up so many hours a day? Most of the books couldn't be removed from the library. Nicking them must have been an issue, then. But it wasn't like they could leave the building.

'Over here,' Butch barked.

She showed him to where some tables had been pushed together along one wall. Chris turned as he heard a cough. Another screw had stepped into the doorway behind them, no doubt to protect the female officer from the likes of him. He turned back. Some of the oldest PCs he'd ever clapped eyes on were lined up, ready for action. He eyed them, disgusted but not surprised. Why had he expected anything better? These damn things wouldn't look out of place in a museum. There were four, so he assumed the class would be him and three others. Or four others, and he wouldn't have a machine. That'd be more likely the case. HMP Wakefield liked to get its money's worth.

'Do these even work?' he asked Butch.

She looked at him like he was something nasty she'd stood in.

'Well, what do you think? Would there be much point in them being here if they didn't?'

He ground his teeth, then decided to let it go. Looked like someone had got out of the wrong side of the bed this morning. Not his problem.

He shrugged. 'I dunno. But everything else around here is shit. Why would these be an exception?'

She scowled at him. 'I've got to go. Your 'students' will be along soon.' She made quote marks in the air (something he couldn't abide), and he blinked away the vision of him smashing her head into the wall. Good job no one in here could read minds.

'Can't wait,' he said, giving her a bright smile, which only made her frown deepen. 'My very own little class. Just what I've always wanted.'

She looked about to say something, then thought better of it. With a slight curl of her lip, she strode out on her short legs, dragging her arse behind her, and left with the other screw.

Chris soaked in the solitude of being alone in all the space. He spread his arms out to the sides, breathed in deeply, and turned in a slow circle. Bliss! But it wouldn't last long. Whoever ran the library would surely be along soon, as well as his 'students'.

The machine nearest him snagged his interest. He just couldn't help it. No matter how old and shitty it was, it was still a computer. He was drawn to it like a moth to a flame. Or a fly around shit. As if controlled by an outside force, he pulled out the chair and sat down, all his attention focused on the dark screen. With a shake of the mouse, it flickered into life. Windows XP? For Christ's sake! What was he supposed to do with that? He sighed and checked what was installed. Student versions of Windows Office, early versions, all out of date. So he'd be teaching them word processing, spreadsheets and simple databases. It was better than nothing. And it definitely beat peeling spuds!

He walked around the other computers and checked them out. All set up the same. He peered at the nearest keyboard. Urgh! It was coated in a greasy film. The sight of it made his skin crawl. The others looked the same. Had they ever been cleaned? He wiped his hand on his jeans, but the sensation remained.

Just then, the door opened, and a different screw escorted four cons in. He'd never seen any of them before, including the screw. Mind you, there were over seven hundred men in the prison, so it wasn't surprising. The cons, two blacks and two whites, looked to be of ages ranging from probably teens to mid-fifties. None of them looked too pleased to be there.

The screw motioned for them to sit. They sat.

'All yours,' he said to Chris.

Then he sat down at the back of the room, put his feet up on a desk, and opened a newspaper. Nice easy day for him, then. Looked like the most taxing thing he'd be doing would be picking his teeth with his fingernail before extracting it and examining it. Chris looked away, mildly nauseated.

He was the teacher, so he supposed he'd better start acting like it. None of the men were looking at him or each other. One of the black guys, the youngest of the group by the look of things, wiped his nose on his sleeve, examined it, and sniffed twice. Chris swallowed back a bit of bile.

'Right. I'm Chris. Your teacher. Let's start by introducing ourselves.'

He looked at the guy nearest to him; the sniffer.

'AJ,' Sniffer said.

Great, Chris thought. Another thing he hated: people who seemed to think initials constituted a name.

'You?' The next guy's face was dotted with pus-filled spots all around his mouth. Brilliant. Another druggie, by the look of it.

The guy mumbled something which could be parrot or carrot. Alright. Parrot it was, then.

Chris pointed to the oldest of the group. His hair was like a grey Brillo pad, and by god, he stank. Chris leaned back a bit to get away, but the smell followed him like a heat-seeking missile. And he was the heat source.

'Charlie,' the guy said.

At last. A sensible name.

'Last but not least…' Chris raised his eyebrows at the last man. He looked mean. Mid-twenties, maybe. His angular face was hard and his eyes cold. Dead. Like a fish on a slab. The eyes of Putin or Hitler.

'Mickey,' said the guy in such a weak, high-pitched voice that Chris fought the urge to laugh. He must have taken several hammerings over the years for a voice that idiotic. It even beat Squeaky's.

'Alright, that's the preliminaries over,' Chris said.

Blank looks all round. Chris doubted these men could read above primary school level. He didn't want to be judgmental, but you could just tell. Miss school and this was what you got. He resolved to use only small words, where possible, preferably just the one syllable.

'Have any of you used a computer before?'

'A bit.' Sniffer.

'Not much.' Parrot.

'Some. A bit.' Mickey.

The old guy just shrugged.

This still surprised him, especially given how young some of them were. Probably no need to learn in the rat-infested drug dens they'd crawled out of. Their preferred method of communication would probably be young boys on bikes passing messages and small packages.

'Right then; let's get started.'

None of them looked particularly enamoured with the idea, he had to admit. This venture could be about to bomb in the first few minutes. But surely they knew what a mouse was, in this day and age. He was in luck; they did. Well, except for Charlie. But none of them were great with one. Where had they been living? Maybe when he'd had a phone or gadget in his hand, their gadget of choice was a gun or a knife. A ripple of unease went through him at the thought. He shook it off and moved on. It was still better than peeling potatoes.

Two hours later, and it was all he could do not to beat his head against the nearest wall. They'd got the machines switched on okay, and then it went tits up. He tried Word first, thinking it might be easier, but the reading and writing skills of all of them were negligible. It was a travesty, he thought, how people could drop through the system, like these had. Perhaps he should be teaching literacy first, then moving onto computer skills. He'd imagined the people they sent him would at least be able to write 'the cat sat on the mat.' He was further behind than when he started. These poor sods had clearly had no help in life, whatsoever. He'd have to request they send him prisoners who could at least write a sentence. This wasn't what he'd envisaged at all. He'd pictured men, focused and concentrating, hanging on his every word, eager to learn and listen. This bunch had the attention span of goldfish. In fact, he'd probably get further teaching actual goldfish. The men didn't listen to a thing he said, preferring to make daft jokes and sexist comments among themselves. Apart from the old guy, who stared into space and said nothing at all. Not one damn word.

By the end of the lesson, they'd learned nothing, and his patience had worn so thin it was transparent. Maybe they could send him different people next time. There was no point sending this lot again.

Butch returned to take him back to his cell. He took it all back: being locked up in his cell all day was preferable to what he'd just been subjected to. At this rate, he'd be begging to go back to the kitchen.

Back in his cell, after his evening meal and outside exercise, Chris ventured out for association. He made straight for the pool table, hoping to see Tommy. He was in luck. As usual, Tommy was holding court there. This time, he had an arm around a young lad's shoulders. The lad was gazing up at him, hanging on his every word.

Chris looked him up and down. Looked to be no older than eighteen or nineteen. Must be Tommy's new piece. They changed every few weeks. He suppressed an involuntary shudder at the thought of what might go on between the two; somehow, he didn't think Tommy would be the most caring or tender lover. Chris's eyes travelled the length of the boy's body. He was slight, whereas Tommy was powerfully built, tall and muscular. Horrible visions of the kid not being able to walk afterwards caused him to turn his head away and swallow hard. Yet, Tommy seemed to have no shortage of willing volunteers.

Tommy looked up, saw him, and walked over to meet him, leaving the lad looking after him longingly.

'Where you get to today?' Tommy asked.

'Didn't they tell you? I was sent to the library to teach people who can barely speak to use a computer.'

'No one told me that. I thought maybe something bad might have happened. You know, like before.'

'Nah, nothing like that. I think I might be doing it as a regular thing.'

Tommy narrowed his eyes. 'Every day?'

'No. I'll still be doing the kitchen as well. I think, anyway.'

'Good,' Tommy said. 'Not the same without you in there. The guy they sent in your place was a right dick.'

'No, I'll still be there some days.'

'Fancy a walk outside?' Tommy said, jabbing his thumb towards the door.

What for? 'Alright, yeah,' he said, after a moment's pause.

They walked to the exercise yard in silence, steering around men clustered together. Chris wondered if any of the screws he could see were in Tommy's pocket. The more he thought about it, the more sure he was that that was the way contraband was being smuggled into the prison. He'd also heard about drones being used. Tommy could probably set something like that up, but the drones were being blocked more and more by technology that jammed their onboard computers. That'd really piqued his interest. He wished they'd let him get involved in that sort of thing. It'd be right up his street. A thousand times better than trying to teach Sniffer, Parrot, and the rest.

Tommy finally spoke. 'You been to the gym yet?'

'No. My ribs feel better though, so I will do. If they bother to open it, that is,' he said, rolling his eyes.

'Sounds good. I'll oversee you getting back into shape, if you like. Think of me as your coach.'

Chris didn't need anyone's help in training, but he tamped down his pride and said, 'Thanks, mate. Appreciate it.'

They stepped outside and Chris squinted at the evening sun, a fiery orange ball, hanging low. He glanced around, still not sure what Tommy wanted.

They fell into step with each other as they started their first lap of the exercise yard. Maybe Chris had got it wrong and Tommy really just wanted to walk. His muscles relaxed some.

On the second lap, Tommy leaned in and said, 'I've got something for you.'

Chris tried not to turn his head too quick, aware of the screws watching from the perimeter.

'What is it?' What could Tommy have that he'd even want? Didn't gifts from him have a price tag that was much too high to pay?

Tommy pulled up the sleeve of his sweatshirt and Chris gawked at the sight of a mobile phone. Looked like a good one, too. Within a second, it was out of sight.

'I can't take that,' he said. 'What would I do with it?'

'Well, I thought you might send a message to that girl of yours. Sarah, was it?'

Chris's pulse ratcheted up at the thought. He wanted it. 'Where would I keep it?'

'What about the library, seeing as you'll be going there often? Next time you're in there, have a look around.

Enterprising guy like you, can't be that hard. I'll keep it for you until then.'

Chris swallowed. 'I can't afford it, though. What would you want in return?'

Tommy nudged him with his shoulder. 'Now, I'm offended. Can't a man just give a gift to a mate? No strings, I promise.'

Chris wanted to believe him. Why wouldn't it work this way? It wasn't as if he'd asked Tommy for the favour.

'Alright, mate, cheers.'

Just in time, he stopped himself from saying, 'I owe you one.'

For the rest of his time walking around the yard, all he could think about was whether he really could use the phone to get in touch with Sarah.

31

Joe

JOE STOOD AT THE entrance to the park, next to the sign that read *Museum Park Gardens*. He watched Sarah's dad throw a stick for the little white mutt to chase. The kid was nowhere to be seen, and nor was Sarah's mother. He couldn't say for sure they were Sarah's parents, but he was pretty certain.

Since he saw the kid's face three days ago, he'd barely stopped thinking about it. What an opportunity. He was a grandad, and Colin had never said a word. He couldn't if he didn't know, though, could he?

Joe took a few steps into the park, still watching the dog. It was a pretty little thing, if you liked dogs. He could take them or leave them. He liked them better than cats, especially the big fat thing at Gerry's, always waving its tail or arse in your face and twirling around your legs. Good kick up the arse would have stopped it, but Gerry would play hell with him. No cats in here though, just dogs, squirrels and people.

The park was handy for the cafe, he had to admit. Less than a minute's walk at the end of the street. The more he came here, the more he liked it. It had a nice feel, and the shops and Minster were close by too. There was no doubt York was lovely. If he was a man of more means, he'd like to move here, but the estate agents' windows he'd looked in had almost made him choke. Bloody ridiculous! Like London. He wouldn't be able to afford a shoebox here. Although, with some of the snooty shops in the centre, he wouldn't afford shoes either.

As he walked purposefully towards Sarah's dad, he ran through the story he had prepared in his mind, should he need it. With a bit of luck, he would. Names, places, people: all were fully formed and rounded in his head. Also, all completely non-existent. Maybe, if he thought about it, they were remnants from a life he'd never had but would have liked. He never thought about it.

32

Peter

'LULU! COME ON, GIRL. Fetch it back, for once.'

Peter sighed as the dog ran after the stick he'd lobbed and then raced past it, straight towards a black Labrador. What was wrong with this dog today? She wouldn't do a damn thing he told her.

The Labrador snatched up its ball when it saw Lulu approaching and belted off with it. Lulu looked back at Peter, then the other dog, clearly deciding what to do.

'Lulu! Come here!' he snapped.

He was relieved when her tail and ears went down. Her whole body language changed, and she slunk towards him, lowering her head as he clipped her lead on.

Peter spotted an empty bench at the far end of the path, in a prime spot in full sun. Sit in the sun or go back to the cafe? Some days, it was mayhem in there, and today would be no exception. With Sarah not being there, they would be short-staffed and running around like mad buggers. He chose the bench.

'Come on,' he said, tugging at the lead.

Lulu's head jerked up, and she trotted happily by his side until they reached the bench. Peter felt oddly lost without the buggy to push. He'd usually got both of them to look after, the dog and his grandson. But not today. He was missing the little guy.

Today, Sarah and Stella had taken Zac to the hospital for the appointment with the specialist. Today, they would be a step further down the road to finding out if Zac had hearing damage from his illness.

He sat down heavily on the bench. Zac's illness. Illness sounded too flippant. A brush with death, more like. Six months' old and dicing with death. He sighed again; it was all he seemed to do lately, sigh. He leaned back and crossed his legs. Although the May sun was warming, his insides were like ice. It was the same every time he thought about it: Zac could so easily have died. The thought filled him with terror then, and it still did. And now, the kid may face a lifetime of hardship and disability. Peter didn't know if he believed in God or not, but this whole thing was making him err on the side of not. What sort of God would do this to a small child and let the family suffer? There again, much worse things happened to other families all the time, and God did nothing.

Lulu sat down at his feet, her head jerking from left to right as she watched other dogs in the park. Peter patted her on the head. Why couldn't life be as simple for him as it was for her? It took next to nothing to please her; a bit of food, a walk in the park, a nice fluffy bed.

A man sat down next to him on the bench. Without acknowledging him, he shuffled up a bit. But Lulu spotted him and jumped up, raking a muddy paw down the man's trouser leg. Peter inhaled sharply.

'I'm so sorry,' he said, jerking at Lulu's lead until he pulled her away.

The man's trouser leg now had dark brown streaks smearing the navy material. Peter was horrified. Stella would have something to say about it if she'd been here. But she wasn't here, was she? She was off doing her family duty. He felt a stab of jealousy that the attention she used to lavish on him was now being lavished elsewhere. Knowing it was irrational to feel it didn't lessen it any.

'Naughty dog,' he said to Lulu, more to be seen reprimanding her than anything. 'Even when it's dry, she still manages to find some mud.' He turned his head to look at the man seated beside him.

He was of a similar build to himself; lanky, long and lean. He was smiling at him. Peter watched as he removed his hat and placed it on the bench next to him. Peter fleetingly wondered who wore a hat in this weather. It must be over twenty degrees today.

'It's not a problem,' the man said, brushing at a streak of dirt on his shin. He leaned forward and addressed the dog. 'It's only a bit of muck, isn't it? It'll all come out in the wash.'

Peter attempted a smile at the pun, not really in the mood. But he felt better for having made the effort.

The man nodded at Lulu. 'She's cute. What's her name?'

'Lulu,' said Peter, slightly embarrassed. 'Daft name, but nothing to do with me.'

'Ah. I understand.'

'Women and their daft ways,' Peter said, feeling the need to doubly clarify that he hadn't named the dog Lulu. 'Yet they expect me to stand in the park and shout it.'

The man laughed. 'Right enough. My missus had a cat called Bubbles. And I always had to take it to the vets and stand up when they called it.'

Peter winced. 'Ooh, now that is bad. Makes Lulu sound normal. Well, almost.'

The other man chuckled, seemingly enjoying reliving the memory.

'Does she have any ridiculously named pets now?' asked Peter. 'Like a pot-bellied pig called Fifi?'

His stomach sank when a sad look came over the man. 'Alas, no. She's dead. And so is Bubbles.'

Inside his brain, the sound of the Family Fortunes buzzer went off, an ear-splitting raspberry. He knew, he just knew, the moment he'd asked the question that he'd said the wrong thing.

'I'm so sorry,' he said, retreating back into his shell. And it had been good for the few seconds he'd emerged, poking his antennae back into the world.

'No, not at all. It's fine,' the man said, his eyes fixed on Lulu.

'Me and my big mouth,' said Peter.

'Never had a pot-bellied pig as a pet. Never fancied one. Have you?' The man twisted his torso to face him.

'Gosh, no. We never got much further than a hamster called Nibbler, and two cats called Treacle and Toffee. Toffee died not so long ago at the grand old age of nineteen.'

'Good age for a cat. Treacle and Toffee, eh? Who thought those up?'

'Oh, my daughter. She was still at school at the time. But despite their names, there was nothing sweet about them, especially with the way those two killed birds.' He shuddered, remembering.

'Urgh, I can imagine. Bubbles was too lazy to get off the settee to kill anything. Totally the opposite.'

Lulu whined and wagged her tail. Peter patted the bench, and she jumped up, sitting between the two. Then, to Peter's chagrin, she put her chin on the other man's thigh and gazed at him.

'Oi, feckless,' Peter said, poking her. 'Just remember who'll be feeding you later.'

The man laughed and stroked her head. 'Wandering allegiances, eh?' he said to the dog. 'We've got your number, alright.'

Peter relaxed into the bench as the sun came back out from behind the cloud. He lifted his face to it. He hadn't enjoyed talking to anyone so much in ages. The man reminded him of Dave, one of his friends back in London. Always good for a bit of banter, was Dave.

The man dug into the jacket pocket of his dark brown sport coat and Lulu went rigid, her whole body trembling with anticipation. She licked her lips and her tail wagged madly. Peter might as well be invisible. He put a hand on her collar to steady her, but even he was watching the man's hand, now slowly sliding back out. A small dog treat was wedged between finger and thumb. He held it up for Peter to see. Lulu's eyes were riveted to it.

'Can she have it?' the man asked.

'How could I say no? Look at her—she'd be heartbroken.' Peter grinned and eased up his hold on her, enough for her to snap the treat down in one.

'Whoa!' the man said, snatching his fingers back and performing a mock inspection of them. 'All still there.'

'I think she likes them,' Peter said. 'I'm curious; do you always carry dog treats when you're out, even though you don't have a dog?'

'Ah, well; I used to be a postman, and I always had a pocketful to appease the dogs on the round. Old habits die hard, I suppose.'

'It's worked today, so yes. Are you from around here? I haven't seen you in the park before, and I'm in several times.'

'Several times a week?'

'No. A day. My wife's always telling me Lulu needs a walk. Although I usually have my little grandson with me.'

'Oh, nice. How old?'

'Seven months.'

'Ah, really small, then. I didn't realise you meant he was a baby. What's his name?'

'Zac.'

'Any other grandchildren?'

'No. And we only have the one daughter, so if she doesn't have any more, he'll be it.'

'Must be nice only having one to spoil.'

'You sound like that's not the case for you?'

'It isn't. I have two daughters and two sons, and they've all reproduced like rabbits.'

Peter tried not to recoil at the word 'reproduce'. It conjured up images of Sarah he'd rather not think about.

'So, how many have you got?'

'Thirteen, at the last count.'

Peter was aghast. 'Thirteen? Wow! How do you keep up with them all?'

'Not all of them live around here. They're kind of scattered about now. I only have five I see regularly.'

'That's still a lot. I'm worn out with just Zac.'

'They keep me fit, I'll admit. All that rugby and football, and that's just the girls.'

Peter laughed along. He was all for girls doing male-dominated sports, and vice versa. Sarah once called him a 'new man', whatever that meant. He'd laughed along with her.

'So where is he today, your grandson?'

Peter paused. He didn't want to mention the illness and the hospital. This was the first time his nerves had settled in ages, and he'd rather reserve his strength for when his anxiety returned, which it would soon enough, along with his wife and daughter.

'He's out with his mum and grandma. I forget where they've taken him now. Some routine baby thing. They have so many, I can't keep track.'

The man nodded. 'They do.' He stuck his hand out. 'I'm Gerry, by the way.'

'Peter.'

They shook hands and Peter realised Gerry never answered the question of where he was from earlier.

'Where are you based?' he asked again.

'Oh, I used to live in Leeds, but now I'm much nearer to here. About three miles outside of York. Not been there long. And I'm also newly retired so I have more time on my hands. I've been at a bit of a loss as to what to do with myself some days. It's why I'm here now. Aimless wandering, I suppose you'd call it. I'm thinking of looking for a little job. Something undemanding, like collecting trolleys at the supermarket.'

'I know what you mean. I'm retired, too. Had to retire early when Stella, my wife, got ill. But I thought you'd be busy with all your grandkids.'

'They're all at school. Not much to do with them until after four o'clock.'

Peter nodded. He couldn’t imagine what Zac would be like in his school uniform on his first day. It’s seemed so far in the future.

'You don't sound like you're from around here,' Gerry said.

'Oh, no; I'm not. We've moved up from London to help my daughter run a cafe here. Just over the road down there.'

His phone burbled in his pocket, and he took it out. ‘Stella’ was flashing up.

He stood up. ‘Sorry, I need to take this. Lovely to have chatted to you, I’ve enjoyed it.’

Gerry slowly got to his feet. ‘Me too. Maybe see you around here again. Take care.’

Peter strode away with Lulu and answered the call.

‘Hello, love. How did it go?’

Stella was crying. She tried, but could hardly get any words out. It made Peter’s scalp prickle.

‘Stella? Put Sarah on. I can’t make out what you’re saying.’

He thought, but couldn’t be sure, he heard her say, ‘Peter, it isn’t good. It’s worse than we thought.’

The line went dead. She’d hung up. He left the park and walked on heavy legs back to the cafe, wishing more than ever he could go back to his happy, carefree life in London.

33

Sarah

I DIDN'T WANT TO walk through the cafe with Zac. It was heaving, and Claire, Ellie and Olwyn would see us. They'd come rushing over, wanting to know how it'd gone. And I would break. I'd been trying not to cry all the way back, and so had Mum.

Mum's supporting hand was on the small of my back as I was about to open the cafe door. I stopped and turned to look at her.

'You go straight up, and I'll handle things down here,' she said.

'Are you sure?'

'Yes. Go on. I'll be up in a minute.'

I pulled the door open, and the first person I saw was Dad, waiting for us. He gave me a brief smile as I lifted Zac out of the buggy. It almost set me off. My throat was tight and my eyes were stinging. I swallowed down the urge to cry.

'I'll bring the pushchair up,' he said.

I walked through the cafe, feeling eyes on me, while Dad folded it down and carried it behind me. Behind the counter, Claire stopped talking to her customer for a split second, then began again, turning the contactless card reader around for them to swipe in one practised move. She gave me the faintest eyebrow raise, and I shook my head. She bit her lip and turned her attention back to her customer. We didn't need words. She knew it was bad.

Then I was through the door and up the stairs, holding a wriggling Zac, with Dad right behind me. My tears were threatening to burst out before I could get into the living room.

'Sarah? I'm really worried. What your mum said...'

He was stomping up the stairs behind me, the buggy catching on the wall all the way. I would have talked to him, but I couldn't speak.

In the living room, I put Zac down. He crawled over to his toy box. Dad stood the buggy up in a corner at the top of the stairs and looked at me, just waiting.

'From what they can tell, he's totally deaf in his right ear and partially deaf in the left. Maybe only thirty percent hearing, they don't know yet. They'll know more when he's older. More tests, for years.'

It was surprising he could understand me with the words coming in between bouts of sobbing. I wished he could make it better, but of course he couldn't. No one could. I watched my son as he dragged random stuff out of the toy box. He'd never hear the fullness of an orchestra playing, or a rock band. Never properly experience a theatre play. Yes, he could have hearing aids, but it wouldn't be the same. He'd heard our voices for seven months; what would he hear now? A muffled, underwater dullness? I couldn't bear it. It made me realize how much we took our hearing for granted.

Dad still hadn't spoken. He was just standing there, looking totally shocked. He looked from me to Zac. Lulu came running out of my bedroom and sprang up into my arms in one bound, something she'd become good at lately. I caught her, hugged her, and buried my face in her fur before she could lick my salty tears. Then Dad finally moved.

He went to Zac and picked him up. Zac turned his attention from the little rabbit Kate had given him to his grandad. Then he slowly bit it with his lone back tooth and proffered it to Dad.

'Thanks very much,' Dad said as he took it. 'I'm honoured.' He looked at me. 'So we carry on as normal. What else can we do?'

He walked into the kitchen, still carrying Zac, and I heard sounds of him putting the kettle on and rattling cups about.

'Tea?' he called.

'Yes, please.'

Just then, Mum came in. 'I've explained briefly. They're going to come up later, when the cafe is closed. I've told them you won't be coming down today. They weren't expecting you to, anyway.'

'Good. Thanks. I don't think I could face it, not looking like this.' I pointed at my puffy, red eyes. Hers weren't much better. 'Dad's making a drink, if you want one.'

She sat on the sofa, and Lulu squirmed in my arms to get down. When I put her on the floor, she jumped onto Mum's knee.

'Are you alright?' Mum asked Dad when he came back in.

'Yes. Why?'

Mum looked at him for a long time, watching as he put Zac back down on the floor. Zac sat, stuffing the rabbit in his mouth. Dribble ran down his chin, and I wiped it off. Maybe another tooth was coming through.

'I just think you've been a bit quiet lately. It's understandable, with that business with your blood pressure, and all that. You'd tell me if you didn't feel right, wouldn't you?'

'Of course.'

Dad disappeared back into the kitchen. I knew what he was really doing, though. So did Mum. His usual avoidance of awkward situations. I still didn't know what he really thought of the row that had erupted about Chris. It was like he'd brushed it under the carpet instead of us discussing it. 'What good will it do?' was what he usually said when faced with talking about things he didn't like.

I looked at Mum and she looked at me, then shook her head and raised her eyebrows.

'I'm worried about him,' she said.

'In what way?'

'Don't you think he's moping about, like he's at a loose end all the time?'

Was he? I hadn't really noticed. There again, I did spend an awful lot of time downstairs in the cafe, while both of them were up here watching Zac.

'Do you think he doesn't want this life? What if it's been foisted on him? It's nothing like the life he was living back in London, is it? He had friends there, and things he liked doing,' I said, worried now.

'No, and that's what scares me. I feel like maybe I jumped into moving and just kind of dragged him along with me.'

It was a massive shock to hear her say it. And to think they'd sold the house they loved, all for me. It was an enormous sacrifice. The biggest. Maybe I never realised how big, and I should have done. I didn't want my dad to be unhappy because of me. And now there was the deafness to contend with, on top of everything else.

Dad came back in, holding three cups on a tray. If he heard what we were saying, he didn't let on. Of course, he wouldn't, would he?

'I was talking to a bloke in the park earlier. Fellow about my age, give or take. Not seen him around before. Nice bloke,' Dad said, sitting down.

Mum's antennae twitched. 'Oh, that's good. Maybe you'll bump into him again.

'I hope so. He said his name was Gerry. He's retired, like me. We had a lot in common.'

'Get his phone number next time. You could do with making some friends around here,' Mum said.

'Oh, yeah! I'm not asking him for his phone number. What if he thinks I'm getting a bit familiar, or something.'

'Dad! Don't be daft. Why would he think that?'

'I don't know. He might.'

Mum and I burst out laughing. It wasn't lost on me that Zac didn't notice or join in, like a normal kid would. I watched him, content in his own (silent?) world, busy chewing his rabbit. I hated that word 'normal'. It occurred to me that it might not apply to Zac anymore. Was he going to be different at school, and have all the other kids pick on him? Would he be able to go to a 'normal' school? Or would he be put in a school for deaf children? I had no clue. It wasn't that I thought there was a stigma to being deaf, it was more like life would be more difficult for him. Why was nothing straightforward?

'At least he's still here,' Mum said. 'That's enough to be thankful for.'

I looked at her, confused. 'What? Dad?'

'No. Him.'

She looked towards Zac, and I realised she had been watching me just now. She was right. He was still here. When I thought of how ill he'd been, I knew he was one of the fortunate ones. I should be more grateful.

After the cafe closed, Claire, Ellie, and Olwyn came up to the flat, full of anxiety and with serious faces. They loved Zac to bits and spoiled him rotten every chance they got.

It turned out Mum had only given them the bare bones, but there wasn't a lot more to add at this stage. We just didn't know enough yet. Apart from what the doctors said, all I knew was from Google and Mumsnet. Where else?

Ellie lifted him onto her knee and gave him a big cuddle. 'Do you know, my cousin is deaf? He was born like it. My aunty and uncle didn't know until he was two.'

'Really?' I'd never met anyone deaf. It was kind of something I'd never really considered, other than if an advert for a deaf charity came on the telly. 'And what's his life like?'

'He just gets on with it. He's in his thirties now, with two kids. Mainly gets by on sign language. I can't sign, myself. Always meant to get round to learning it, but I never have. It's made me think now, perhaps I should. At least make the effort. But he's really good at lip-reading, too, so he just does that with me.'

'Does he work?'

'Yeah, course he does. He tells me he doesn't consider it a disability or a setback. What you've never had, you never miss. His partner signs. She tells me what he's saying. I could introduce you, if you like. I'm sure he'd be happy to help.'

I shook my head. 'Thanks, but no. I need more time to get used to it myself. Maybe later, in a few weeks or months, I will. But not just yet.'

'Okay, it's no problem. Just know the offer's there.'

'Thank you. I appreciate it.'

Zac screeched as Ellie tickled his tummy. My own stomach sank. If he couldn't hear, would he then stop making noises of his own? Like that screech and his beautiful laugh? I knew everyone was saying the right things about being brave and looking to the future and such like, but deep down, in my bones, I didn't feel it.

34

Peter

PETER HAD BEEN NERVOUS about the house purchase, convincing himself it would take ages to complete and be fraught with problems. But he'd been wrong. The estate agent had been as good as her word, which had surprised him. He'd never heard anything good about estate agents, only that they were all in it for self-interest, to line their own pockets. But Kerry hadn't been anything like that. She was old enough to be experienced, but young enough to still have energy and enthusiasm for the job. She'd instilled confidence in him when he'd been unsure and had kept him informed on what to expect every step of the process. He couldn't help thinking how much she reminded him of Sarah, with her forthright opinions and drive. Not that Sarah saw herself like that, he was sure. Sarah, like Stella, were forces to be reckoned with, in everyone's eyes but their own, yet each recognised it in the other.

He was waiting now, with Stella and Zac, outside their new home, for Kerry to meet them and hand over the keys. Stella had said they could pop into the estate agent to pick them up, but Kerry had been adamant, informing them that this was the best, most rewarding, part of her job, and no way was she going to miss it. She was going to meet them there and accompany them when they walked inside. Peter hadn't wanted to deny her the joy he'd sensed it would bring her.

'She's coming,' Stella said, nudging him hard on the arm.

Peter grunted. He wasn't blind. He'd seen her ages ago; her bright pink dress and matching heels were hard to miss in the sunshine. Zac, in his pushchair, wriggled, whining to get out.

'Not long now,' he said to him, bending down to ruffle his hair. Even though he knew he couldn't hear him, Peter didn't think he'd ever be able to stop talking to Zac. Nor did he want to. It just broke his heart to think Zac might never have a normal conversation with him.

Kerry saw them waiting and put a spurt on, waving to them. Peter looked at her feet. How the hell women walked in those pointy shoes with the high, skinny heels, he'd never know. In the wrong hands, they could quite easily become a murder weapon. A stiletto in the eye had felled more than one character in the crime books he occasionally read.

'Hello. Have you been waiting long? I'm not late, am I?' Kerry huffed, as she stopped beside them, her cheeks as pink as her dress. Dark circles stained her underarms.

'No, love. We were early. Peter's eager to get in,' Stella said.

Peter side-eyed her and pointedly raised his eyebrows, which she ignored. He'd been halfway through putting some lobelia in Sarah's window boxes when Stella had wanted to leave. He'd had to rush it and bung them in any old how. The window boxes had been his little project when they'd first moved here. Ellie had suggested it, and he'd got the job. They'd since become his to look after, and he took pride in it, deadheading, watering and feeding them. He looked forward to it, and it had made him miss his old garden a little bit less. And everyone said how eye-catching they were.

Kerry pulled the keys out of her bag and made a big song and dance about ceremoniously handing them over. Peter thought she'd have placed them on a silk cushion if she'd had one. Better not suggest it. She might go for the idea.

'Ta-da,' she said with a flourish at the end. 'I wish you the best of luck. I hope you'll be happy in your new home.'

Stella took the keys from her, beaming, and turned to Peter.

'It feels so real now, doesn't it?'

'I hope so, with what it's cost,' he said. It came out more harshly than he'd intended, and Stella frowned, shaking her head. Kerry looked surprised, her eyes sliding to Stella's.

'Let's get inside then,' Stella said, brushing the moment aside and taking Peter's arm. She passed him the keys. 'You can do the honours.'

There wasn't much of a front path to the flat. As Peter turned, brandishing the key, Kerry said, 'What time is your furniture arriving?'

'They estimated around two-ish,' Stella said. 'It should have left the storage unit in London about an hour ago.'

Kerry clapped her hands as Peter got the door unlocked and pushed it open. She reminded him of a demented seal, and her exuberance was beginning to rub him up the wrong way. He took a single step inside. It smelled alien. Sterile. Not unpleasant, just different. Not like home. Not like theirs. It made him not want to go any further, and he hesitated on the threshold. It felt like the final nail in the coffin of ever moving back to London. It seemed this would be the place he'd be spending the rest of his days, whether he liked it or not.

Stella gave him a gentle push from behind. He stepped aside, his back against the door, and let her go first. She smiled as she passed him, mistaking his reticence for chivalry.

There was no entrance porch. Instead, it was straight onto the living room. Peter looked around. Where would they hang their coats and put their shoes? There wasn't even a small cupboard. If he kicked them off near the door, Stella wouldn't be happy. He could imagine the complaining already. He followed her in as Kerry overtook him and went to join Stella in the kitchen.

'So everything should be clean and ready for you…'

Peter could hear them opening and closing cupboard doors. With a sinking feeling, he realised he didn't want to live here, not in this flat. It was so small. It was like Sarah's student accommodation at uni. He was too old for student living.

A stiffness worked its way into his shoulders. He'd slept badly the night before, like most nights since the blood pressure fiasco. He rotated his neck, cracking it in the process, and freed Zac from the buggy. Stella seemed to have forgotten the pair of them, she was so engrossed in things. He lifted Zac out, enjoying his weight in his arms. The little lad was nicely solid; thriving. He was also dribbling again, and Peter wiped his mouth with a tissue.

'Peter! Can you come here a sec?' Stella shouted from the kitchen.

He straightened his shoulders and dug deep into himself to find a more positive attitude.

'Duty calls,' he said, hitching Zac higher. 'Coming,' he called back.

Stella was holding a bottle of wine, the fridge door open behind her. 'Look what Kerry and the estate agents have left for us? Isn't it nice of them?'

'Oh, yes. Thank you, Kerry. It's much appreciated,' he said, surprised. Did all estate agents do this, or just this one?

'You're most welcome. Enjoy it. Well, I must get back,' Kerry said. 'I hope your furniture arrives soon. I bet it will look lovely in here.'

She walked past Peter and went to the front door, Stella following, still clutching the wine. As the women stood talking at the door, Peter went into the bedroom. It didn't take long, being a metre or two at most away from the kitchen. He closed the door behind him and put Zac down to crawl on the carpet. The brand new, mid-grey carpet that was fitted everywhere but the kitchen and bathroom; he wasn't sure how he felt about it. What was wrong with a nice beige? None of their bedding would go with this grey one. At least there was a blind up, grey again, so they would have something to block out the light.

His phone rang, and he pulled it out of his pocket. It was Gerry.

'Hello,' he said.

'Hello. Are we still okay for tonight?'

It was going to be Gerry's first visit to Peter's bridge evening. When he'd arranged it, he'd forgotten it was the same day they would be moving in. Would Stella be annoyed if he went out tonight? If all the furniture was in place, he might get away with it. Should he nip and ask her?

'Peter, are you there?'

'I'll ring you back in two ticks,' he said.

He really ought to check with Stella. The last thing he wanted was to get on her bad side. He picked up Zac and went to find her. She was just closing the door after Kerry.

'Um, I've just had Gerry on the phone. About the bridge night. His first one...' He chewed his bottom lip as Stella narrowed her eyes.

'Oh, I'd forgotten about that. Is it tonight?'

He nodded. 'I can cancel, if you'd rather I stayed here with you.'

She looked thoughtful. 'No, you go. Sarah's coming over later to help me get things straight and plan the housewarming. You go and meet Gerry and enjoy yourself. We don't need you.'

He went back into the bedroom to ring Gerry back. That was exactly it, he thought—what Stella had just said. They didn't need him. He was surplus to requirements. An extra. And he didn't like how it felt.

35

Chris

THE IT LESSONS HAD been going better since the disaster that was the first one. Chris now did them three times a week in the library, on Mondays, Wednesdays and Fridays. On the days he wasn't teaching IT, he was in the kitchen, still sorting potatoes, still standing next to Tommy. The monotony of it was threatening to send him insane. Sometimes, he'd found himself hoping that if he ever got jumped again, this time they'd do the job properly and finish him off.

Thankfully, today was a library day. The officer he was following down the corridors to the library was Butch, the miserable little round bitch. In the weeks he'd been doing the job, she was no friendlier or eager to talk than that very first time he'd met her, so now he just didn't bother interacting with her at all.

She unlocked the door, let him in, and locked him inside without a word. He stood inside, listening to her footsteps fading away. This was the time he lived for. The library was deserted, and he would probably have ten minutes on his own at the most, before the librarian or his students arrived.

He glanced around, checking there was nobody hiding in the shadows. All seemed clear.

Under the librarian's desk was a computer tower. Not for the librarian an aging laptop on its last legs. The innocuous-looking tower was the best thing in Chris's life. He scooted over to it, crouched behind the desk and knelt on the floor. Two screws in the casing looked to be screwed in, but they were only finger-tight, so were easily undone without a screwdriver. It had taken him a few goes with several different-sized pilfered teaspoons with various ends to get them loose enough to unscrew in the first place. The only perk he'd found of working in the kitchen.

The front came off easily when he pulled out the screws. He didn't need to take it all off, only enough so the top came away from the unit. Once he could reach inside, he took out the mobile phone Tommy had given. Charging it would be a problem, but Tommy had said he'd see to that, if he smuggled it back to him.. And he didn't ask. Better not to know. So far, though, that hadn't happened. Luckily, it hadn't needed it yet.

He switched it on and once again fought with himself not to send Sarah a message. He wanted to, but what could he say? No, better to wait until he was desperate, but just having it and holding it gave him hope. And what was a man without hope? Dead, that was what. And he wasn't dead yet. This phone was his lifeline to the only thing worth having on the outside.

The phone started up quickly. Of course it wasn't the latest iPhone but it wasn't bad: an android. Galaxy. Even had a decent camera (not that there was anything worth taking a picture of in this place). Most of the contraband phones were tiny things, barely bigger than a two-pound coin, not a proper phone. A camera was the last thing he'd been expecting.

He listened and glanced around. Probably okay for another few minutes. He held it in his hand, a little plastic box of hope. Then he almost dropped it when it beeped. He peered at the screen. A text? But no one knew the number.

He clicked on the message icon.

Hello it read.

He almost dropped the phone. That was it. Nothing else.

Footsteps in the distance. Coming closer. He turned off the phone, placed it back inside the tower, replaced the front and was turning on the laptops by the time the door opened.

What the actual fuck? Was that message meant for him?

As an officer came in with his 'students' for the day, Chris thought about the message. It wasn't a new phone so it was probably meant for the previous owner. He put it to the back of his mind and tried to focus on the impossible task before him: teaching imbeciles.

36

Joe

JOE PARKED THE CUSTARD car in the Barbican car park again and hurried towards the centre of York. Peter had been on at him to come to one of his bridge nights, and Joe had finally relented. He'd been more bothered about getting to know Peter one on one, but Peter seemed so keen on including him, it was getting harder to refuse.

Normally, the bridge nights were on Mondays, and Joe would be working the tea time to midnight shift, but this one was on a Sunday. As one of the regulars couldn't make the Monday, they'd changed it. It suited Joe down to the ground, as it was the only night he could guarantee he wouldn't be collecting trolleys, looking at his watch, and wishing his life away.

Joe had agreed to come, but wasn't looking forward to it one bit. More petrol, more parking, more money spent, but he had to remember it was for the greater good. It hadn't taken long for Joe to realise Peter was a friendless, lonely man, desperate for company. It couldn't have worked out better, really.

Peter was waiting for him outside The Three Tuns pub, in his casual beige windcheater and black slacks. His hands were thrust into his pockets and he was glancing first one way up the street, then the other. Joe felt shabbily dressed in his jeans, T-shirt, and old jacket.

Peter broke out into a big smile when he spotted him. 'Gerry! I was beginning to think something had happened, and you couldn't make it.'

'No, no, nothing like that.' He thought fast. 'Our Jane was late picking her little 'un up, that's all. I'd had her for the afternoon.'

He followed Peter into the gloom of the pub, biting his tongue. Jane was the first name that had sprung to mind. It was also his ex-wife's name, so not one he'd prefer to think about. Some weeks, he was having trouble remembering what he'd told Peter his kids' names were. Gerry had suggested he put them in a spreadsheet, and they'd both had a good laugh at that, although neither of them really knew for sure what a spreadsheet was. He was now convinced Jane had been Kathy at first. If he'd noticed anything odd, Peter wasn't saying.

Peter led him through a half empty, old-fashioned pub, to a table in an alcove at the back. Three men were sitting there, one making a hash of shuffling cards, one drinking a pint, and the other doing something with his phone. They looked to range from around Peter's age, sixties, to nearer eighty. Joe suppressed an inward sigh. Was this it, the grand bridge night? He'd been expecting rows of tables, all laid out, and maybe twenty or thirty people. But not this! They looked boring as hell. He just knew he wouldn't have anything in common with them. None of them looked like they'd been anywhere near a clink, never mind done time in one.

The men all looked expectantly at Joe as they arrived at the table. Joe suddenly wondered if they bought rounds. He didn't have enough money. He'd just have to say he'd get his own.

'This is Gerry. Gerry, this is Brian, Lenny and Ollie,' Peter said, going around the table.

Brian, the card shuffler and the oldest, in a flat cap and what looked like a padded fishing waistcoat, nodded and said, 'How-do.'

Joe disliked Lenny on sight. Whether it was the know-all, smug expression, the obvious comb-over, or the excess nose hair, he wasn't sure. Probably a combination of all three.

Lenny put down his pint, looked him up and down, and just nodded. Not a word. Joe had the feeling he'd been judged and had fallen short in some way. He was going to have to watch that one. He'd met his sort before, people who thought they were better than everyone else.

Ollie put his brick-sized phone down on the table, stood up, reached over, and grasped Joe's hand, pumping it vigorously up and down. 'Good to have you on board, Gerry,' he said. 'The more the merrier.'

His palm was as sweaty as the top of his head, where a select few brown hairs clung gamely on. Behind magnifying lenses, his eyes bulged and boggled. Joe extricated his hand and wondered where he could wipe it.

Peter sat down and gestured for Joe to do the same.

'It's nice to meet you all,' he lied, thinking of all the things he'd rather be doing, like kicking Gerry's cat, or trying to send a text.

'Well, let's see what you're made of,' Lenny said. His competitive streak was bursting out of him. He took the pack from Brian.

Joe glanced at Peter, who immediately jumped in, like he was his knight in shining armour.

'Gerry hasn't played before, Lenny. It's his first time.'

Lenny's spine straightened, and his eyes gleamed. 'Oh. Well, in that case, we'll have to teach him.'

'I can just watch, if you like. I'm sure I'll pick it up as you lot play,' Joe said.

'No, no. I'll explain it to you. It's not that easy to pick up,' Lenny said.

Joe suppressed a sigh. He'd been right. The bloody know-all couldn't wait to give the novice a lecture.

'Lenny's the experienced one,' Ollie said, pushing his glasses further up his nose with a middle finger. 'He usually wins.'

Whoopie-do! What did he want—a medal?

'Before we get started, what are you drinking?' Peter asked.

'I'll come to the bar with you and see what beers they've got,' he said, getting ready to stand back up.

'Fosters, John Smith's, Guinness, and Carling,' Lenny reeled off, reshuffling the pack properly this time, while Ollie looked on. 'Craft beers are on the board up there.' He didn't look up as he flipped the cards from one hand to the other. Joe felt a stab of satisfaction as one fell out.

'I can't read it from here,' he said, walking off to the bar.

Peter caught him up as he got there. Might as well come clean.

'Thing is,' he said, 'I've got some cash flow problems at the minute. It'd be better if I just got my own.'

'That's what we do, anyway,' Peter said. 'It's just better that way. We don't do rounds.' He leaned closer and lowered his voice. 'Between you and me, I got the impression that Lenny never bought as many rounds as the others in the past, and it rankled with them a bit.'

'Ah. There's always one freeloader,' he said.

'Oh, I'm not sure he's a… er—'

'What can I get you?' the man behind the bar called from a few feet away, managing to tear his eyes from the big screen TV in the far corner, where Chelsea were losing to Tottenham.

'A pint of Foster's, please,' Joe said, hoping it was the cheapest thing on draught.

The man nodded and placed a dripping glass on a beer towel in front of him a minute later.

'Four-sixty,' he said.

Joe reluctantly handed over a fiver. He'd better make it last.

'I'll have a shandy, please,' Peter said.

Joe bit back a loud tut. Of course. What else would he have?

They took their drinks back to the table as Peter said, 'I'm looking forward to this. They're not a bad bunch. Not that I know them well, mind you. I've only met them a few times.'

Joe wished he could say he was looking forward to it, but he wasn't. Especially the lecture about gameplay he knew was coming from Lenny the moment they sat back down. As he suspected, Lenny didn't disappoint.

The man droned on for a full ten minutes, explaining the rules. Joe tuned out after somewhere around the two-minute mark. None of it made sense. It sounded like a stupid bloody game. Like all card games.

'I'll just watch,' he said, halfway through, but Lenny held his hand up for silence. Joe had the urge to kick the man's head in. Funny, he thought; the younger version of him wouldn't have thought twice about it. He clenched his jaw and took the tiniest sip of lager.

'Goes on a bit, doesn't he?' Brian said, rooting through the multiple pockets of his waistcoat. Joe half expected him to pull out a trout and was disappointed when he extracted a packet of cigarette papers and a tin of tobacco instead. 'I'm off for a smoke 'til he's done,' he said, squeezing past Peter and making for the exit.

Joe wished he could go with him, but, seeing as the lecture was solely for his benefit, stayed where he was. *Focus on why you are doing this. See the bigger picture.* He repeated it like a mantra. It helped him get through until Lenny finished droning on, and Brian had returned.

Two hours later, and it turned out he wasn't as bad at bridge as he'd expected to be. Although, to say he enjoyed it would be stretching the truth. After Lenny had finished explaining the rules, Joe had insisted that watching would benefit him most. And he wasn't wrong. They could have skipped the lecture and it wouldn't have made any difference. Just like he'd thought. He gained far more from watching a couple of games, and Peter explained things going along far better than Lenny had.

It wasn't even that hard. The crowning moment came when he almost beat Lenny. The Bridge King's crown had slipped and almost choked him, and it was a great shock to him. The look on his face made the whole thing worth it. Would he come again? It would have to depend on how things went from here.

After the last game had ended, and no one seemed in the mood for another, including Lenny, their talk turned to other things, and it went downhill further. They'd droned on about fishing and golf and football and Formula One for the next hour. At one point, Joe thought he might have to slap himself across the face to keep awake. He'd long since finished his pint. None of them had spent much. The pub wouldn't be keeping afloat based on their contribution.

As they got ready to leave, Joe's thoughts turned to driving back to Gerry's place. If Gerry asked him if it had been worth it, what would he say? He supposed it was a yes, as everything that brought him closer to Peter had to be a good thing, and Peter had acted like he'd found a true friend in Joe. Being as he was the one who'd found him and invited him along, it seemed they were a unit the others were slightly outside of. Or that's how it felt to Joe, anyway, and Peter seemed to like it that way.

Peter cleared his throat as they stood up to leave. 'We're having a housewarming in two weeks. Stella told me to invite you all along.'

Joe's ears pricked up. The family would be there. He'd really be getting his feet under the table. Spending some time with the lovely Stella, and Sarah, not to mention his grandson—well, that had to have made the evening worthwhile.

Yes, he thought as he bade them goodbye and went off; he could tell Gerry it had been a success on all fronts.

37

Chris

OFFICER PHIL HAD PICKED him up to take him to the library, and all he wanted to do was talk. Chris was desperate for him to get a move on. He wanted to see if there had been any more messages on the phone. Days had gone by with nothing, but the *hello* message from before still fascinated him.

'Your lessons are proving quite a hit with the higher ups,' Phil said.

Chris grunted. 'Sometimes I don't know whether I did the right thing suggesting it,' he said.

'Why not?' Phil slowed down. Chris badly wanted to shove him. He rammed his fists into his jean's pockets instead.

Chris walked faster, hoping to speed the other man up. 'It's like beating your head repeatedly against a wall for ten hours every other day. I'm getting better people, but some of them would still benefit from literacy lessons instead. I can't show people how to use Word if they can't read. I have to try to use words with only one syllable.'

Phil smiled and shrugged. 'I know, I know. Yet those people still need help.'

'Get them reading lessons, then.' Chris sighed at the prospect of another day spent in close proximity to a phone he couldn't touch. 'Well, better get a move on then, so I can make sure things are ready.'

He strode off. Phil, thankfully, matched his pace.

'You're keen for someone who doesn't want to do it,' he said. 'We'll be sprinting next.'

'Well, it sure beats the kitchen,' Chris said, forcing his lips into a smile. He didn't want Phil to think he was behaving any differently.

Two corners left, and they'd be there. But what if Phil stayed to talk until the students arrived? It had happened before.

Phil unlocked the door of the library and accompanied Chris inside. Instead of leaving, he took a seat right behind the librarian's desk. His left knee was inches from the tower Chris needed to get to. Chris cursed under his breath, averted his eyes, and set about powering up the laptops.

'I think there are some new ones coming in today. Hopefully, some might already know the basics,' Phil said.

Chris doubted it. It hadn't happened so far. Why should today be any different?

Phil was still in the chair when the students arrived, along with the librarian, accompanied by a different officer. He almost cried as his one chance to get to the phone disintegrated before his eyes. Whether he'd be on his own after class and get the chance then was debatable. Would it be a bad idea, if he did get two minutes alone, to grab the phone and take it back to his cell? Should he risk it? His cell hadn't been subjected to a search in a while and must surely be due one. There was nowhere in that tiny box that he could hide something so it wouldn't be found. The screws knew every trick in the book. Under the toilet cistern lid or up his own arse were the only possible places, and they'd look there first. The thought of shoving a phone up there made his bowels contract.

'I'll leave you to it,' Phil said to Chris, standing up and pushing the chair back.

Chris wanted to scream but instead turned his attention to the students. Another bunch of losers, by the look of them. They shuffled in and stood around, looking awkward. Every single one of them was new. So much for continuity. If they weren't going to bother sending some of the same people, he'd never get past lesson one—this is a mouse and it moves about like this. Christ Almighty!

The next few hours felt like the longest of his life. They broke for an hour at lunchtime, the students left, and a new bunch were ushered in. All of these had been at least once. Things were looking up. One of them, knowing what a word processor at least did, was streets ahead of the others. He was also keen to learn, wanting to take charge of an appeal he was launching. Chris spent the most time with him, but he wasn't relishing the challenge. His eyes went repeatedly to the librarian's desk, where the librarian, a lifer, sat, picking his nose in between fiddling about with books. It seemed he was just shunting them from one pile to another and back again. How he'd got the plum job of librarian, Chris would never know. It was one of the most sought after jobs in the place, and the arsehole didn't look as if he'd ever read a book in his life.

After the last session ended and the students left, Chris found himself alone. He was itching to get the phone. His fingers twitched and his whole body felt electrified. Did he have time? He took a step closer, his ears straining in the silence. The librarian had left before the students, and his chair was pushed out at a crooked angle. Chris went over to it and rested his hand on the back, still listening. Nothing. Phil had been late to collect him by up to ten or even fifteen minutes. Not knowing how long he had always annoyed him; all that space to luxuriate in and not being able to relax. It was like looking at a delicious cake and not being allowed to eat it.

Fuck it, he was doing it! He took a pencil eraser from the desk, dropped to his knees, and placed it on the floor. His fingers automatically went to the screws and began twisting them. He forced himself to slow down, scared he would drop one and not be able to get the cover back on.

He pushed his hand in through the small gap, committed now, and thumbed the phone on even as he was pulling it out. If Phil came through the door, he would shove the phone up his sleeve. Maybe he should do that, anyway.

The door remained shut. No officer came. Even the women, the quieter, slender ones, made some noise as they approached.

The phone screen remained black. What was wrong with it? Finally, it came on. No texts. The phone had WhatsApp on it, though, and the icon appeared on the screen. A message. He clicked on it, glancing at the door, then almost dropped the phone as a photograph filled the screen. It was Sarah, outside the cafe in York. The picture had been taken from across the street, from the shop opposite by the look of it. He drank in the sight of her, his pulse quickening and his breath held. A tidal wave of emotion threatened to burst as his eyes filled with tears. What did it mean? There were no words with the message.

Was that whistling? His head jerked up. Faint footsteps, becoming louder. He thumbed the phone off, thrust it back into the computer tower and did his pitstop turn again, replacing the phone in seconds.

The door opened.

'Chris?' Phil called.

He crawled out backwards from underneath the desk on his hands and knees.

'Here,' he said, standing up. He held up the eraser between thumb and finger. 'Dropped it.' He placed it on the desk.

Phil glanced at it, then turned to go. 'Ready?'

Chris nodded, unable to speak for fear his voice would give him away. Blood was rushing in his brain, sounding loud in his ears. He held out his hand to indicate for Phil to lead the way.

All the way back, he wondered what it meant. Was someone playing games? If so, who? Not Sarah. She hadn't taken the picture herself. He wished he had taken the phone now. He could have looked at her during the night. But it would only wear down the battery and if he gave it to Tommy to charge, he would see the messages. The text he could delete, but he was never deleting the picture of Sarah. His mind whirred and clicked, going into overdrive. He had a whole day to wait before he could see what happened next. He was sure there would be something more waiting for him the next time he turned it on. Someone was definitely playing games.

It was only when he got back to his cell that he remembered that, with all the excitement over the picture arriving, he hadn't checked the number. Didn't even know if it was from the same number that had sent the text. He got out the paper his dad had written his mobile number on, stared hard at it and memorised it. But he couldn't see it being him. None of it was making any sense.

38

Joe

THE CARRIER BAG HANDLES dug into his skin under the weight of the two bottles of wine inside. He winced at the red line that had cut deep into his fingers and swapped hands. It could hurt the other one for a bit; at least then he'd have a matching pair. The bottles clinked as he transferred the bag to the other hand. The wine, cheap as it was, was still more than he'd rather have spent, but you couldn't turn up to a housewarming party empty-handed, could you? It wasn't the done thing. Not that he had much idea of done things. He'd never really given a shit. But, oh, he gave one now, alright. Acting like a gentleman, blending in, was exactly what he needed. Ever since talking to Peter that first time in the park several weeks ago, he'd been worming his way in to the man's life. It had been much more enjoyable than he'd been expecting, with the endgame making it even more so.

He'd had to call in sick at work today, with the party not beginning until six. Would they dock his pay? Could they dock his pay? Hopefully not. It was the first time and people got sick, right? He needed the money as he'd be out of pocket otherwise, on tonight alone, with the petrol to get here, and then the parking, and the cost of the wine on top. Too late to worry about it now.

He squared his shoulders and stood at the end of the road. Was this the right address Peter had given him? He'd expected quaint little houses, but this was a newly built block of flats. There again, had Peter ever said it was a flat, or had he just assumed it was a house? Probably the latter. He needed to stop making assumptions.

He took in the place. The building was about four storeys high, so nothing like Granford Towers. But crikey, the flats must be small. He'd seen bigger rabbit hutches. A smile creased his face at the thought that the rooms must be like cells. A bit like the one Colin resided in at Her Maj's Pleasure.

He hadn't pictured Peter and Stella (who he hadn't yet formally met) living in a characterless place like this. She'd had style and flair when he'd seen her in the cafe. She deserved more than this. What had Peter been thinking, buying this place?

He marched up the road, adjusted the angle of his hat and knocked on the door. There wasn't much noise coming out. The parties they'd had on the Granford Towers estate had been nothing like this. If anyone had knocked on the door and complained about the music, you just laughed, offered them a beer, and cranked the music up. Mostly, people were trying to get in, not out.

The door swung open and Peter stood there, with his shirt buttoned right up and his tie nice and straight. Joe was wearing his prison suit, as he'd taken to calling it. Next to Peter's pressed clothes, it looked like he'd slept in it.

Peter beamed at the sight of him and opened the door wider. 'Hello, Gerry, good to see you. Thanks for coming. Please come in.'

Joe smiled, wishing Peter would take the stick out of his arse and loosen up. He was undoubtedly a nice man, but not much fun, it had to be said. If Joe hadn't had an ulterior motive, he wouldn't have bothered with someone like Peter at all. But needs must, so…

'Thank you for inviting me,' he said, stepping inside.

When Peter led him around the corner to the kitchen, Joe's first thought was that it was the worst party he had ever been to. He'd been at livelier funerals.

'Everyone, this is Gerry,' Peter said. 'This is Stella, my wife; Sarah, my daughter; Ellie and her partner; and Claire, who both work in the cafe.'

It was obvious Peter had either forgotten Ellie's partner's name, or plain didn't know it. He rushed on, continuing around the small gathering.

'This is Olwyn, who also works in the cafe, and these reprobates here you met at bridge the other night, of course.'

Joe doffed his hat to Stella, ignoring the rest for now. 'It's a pleasure. Peter has told me a lot about you.'

'Has he now? Oh!' Stella seemed startled as Joe took her hand, raised his knuckles to her fingers and went to brush them with his dry lips.

'All good, of course,' he said, dropping Stella's hand quickly, as he felt then saw the odd bend in the fingers, the swollen joints and misshapen bone. They were horrible, like crooked sticks. He'd never noticed that when he'd seen her in the shop. It definitely spoilt her.

'And Sarah,' he said. After Stella's reaction, he left Sarah's hand where it was, and his hat stayed firmly in place. Maybe he was overdoing it and ought to tone it down a notch or two. Didn't want to appear weird or strange, in any way.

He'd already forgotten two of the women's names from the cafe, although he'd seen them all in there. There was the old one with her twinset and pearls, and stiff back; the young one with the blue hair and odd make-up; and the pretty blonde one, Claire, who'd served him the most often. He liked Claire. If he was thirty years younger… or even twenty.

Just then, a small girl came in from another room, carrying the baby. She was older than a toddler, maybe at primary school. He was no good at guessing kids' ages. While he watched, Sarah bent down and scooped the baby out of the girl's arms. She turned to him.

'This is my son, Zac, and that's Darcey, Ellie's and Jeb's daughter.'

Peter nodded and muttered, 'Jeb,' under his breath, but Joe still caught it.

'Hello everyone. Nice to meet you. Oh, hello, again.' He nodded and smiled at Brian, Lenny, and Ollie, the men from the bridge club at the pub. He had no intention of spending any longer with them than he had to. Since the bridge night, he was now of the opinion that they were three of the most boring bastards he'd ever had the misfortune to meet. And here they were again, all three lined up on a small sofa that had seen better days. Joe couldn't work out if he was standing in the kitchen, the dining area or the living room—it seemed to be all the same space. This place was making Gerry's look like a penthouse in comparison.

'Can I get you a drink, Gerry? Ooh, thank you,' Stella said as he passed her the carrier bag of wine. 'Oh, lovely.' She pulled the bottles out with her twisted fingers. Gerry looked away. Maybe he'd have a beer instead.

'Beer? Wine? Whisky? Gin?' Peter asked, gesturing at a small corner table crammed with bottles with the flourish of a magician's assistant.

'A beer would be perfect, thanks,' he said, noting the almost-empty pint glass next to Peter.

On another table plates of sandwiches and other delights were covered in cling film. Joe's stomach rumbled. He hoped it wouldn't be long until the cling film came off and they could get stuck in. He hadn't eaten since breakfast that morning, having been saving himself for the freebies. Peter caught him eying the goodies.

'Sarah and Ellie have done it all.'

'It looks very tasty,' Joe said, meaning it.

The cakes had been spared the cling film, and his mouth watered at the sight of them. He was partial to a nice bit of cake, and wasn't too fussy about what sort. In prison, delicious, homemade cake was a long-distant memory.

He turned as Peter pulled the tab on a can of Fosters and handed it to him, not bothering with a glass.

'Ooh, that's just what the doctor ordered,' he said.

Peter picked up his own glass and drained the meagre contents. Joe watched. Would he have another? He seemed stone cold sober. At the Granford Towers parties, no one had been sober for long.

'You not having another?' he asked, as Peter rinsed his glass out under the tap then filled it with cold water.

'Having to pace myself. Issues with the old blood pressure; the medication they've put me on is making me feel a bit dicey at times. Besides, Stella's watching me like a hawk,' Peter said, sipping his water.

Joe briefly wondered what it was like to have a woman like Stella fussing over him. Apart from her hands, he'd like it. She was still a dusky beauty, despite her age. She was probably somewhere around his own age, but he'd always liked them younger. Although he still wasn't bothered about finding a woman since he'd got out of jail, he wouldn't say no to one like her. And definitely not her daughter.

Sarah was jiggling the baby up and down, over by the window, and making it laugh. He decided it was time to make his move. He walked over to her, clutching his pint.

'He's a bonny little lad. It's Zac, isn't it?'

39

Joe

JOE LOOKED AT HIS watch, then towards the park entrance. He'd been waiting twenty minutes now for Peter. It was rare for him to be late. It was gone half-past one, and he had to be in work at four.

He sighed. It was sad, but true, that he had so little going on in his life that this little game he was playing was the only thing that served as entertainment these days. Sometimes, he thought he'd had more fun in prison. He hadn't, of course, but everything there was simpler. You were told what to wear, what to do, how to behave, what to think. Yes, at the time it had been stifling, and he'd longed to escape the constrictions, but now—well, he was still finding it harder than he'd expected to run his own life and make his own decisions. Along with the pleasures of freedom, he struggled to manage his own affairs; from finances, paying bills, holding down a job, to even deciding what to eat. He could stand in front of the food fridges in Aldi and be paralysed with indecision about what to buy. It hadn't got easier, as he'd hoped. If anything, it had got worse, as had the anxiety and worry that went along with it all.

When he'd told Gerry about his struggles, Gerry had just nodded.

'Yep,' he'd said. 'It's got a name.' Gerry had nodded as if he were some wise old sage, and turned to the back pages of the newspaper to study the form at the races.

'What name?' Joe asked. He hated when Gerry started a conversation then just aborted it when he felt like it. It was like pulling teeth.

'It's called being institutionalised. It's a common thing for us ex-cons.'

'Oh. Right. What does that mean, then?'

'That it's easier to live in a controlling institution, like a prison, or nursing home, than fend for yourself. Some people lose the ability to make their own decisions. And they don't want to have to.'

Joe was stunned. Gerry had got it bang on. He'd hit the nail on the head. And now he'd gone back to reading his paper.

'So does it get better?'

Gerry had shrugged. 'Buggered if I know. I don't suffer from it, see? I'm fine. Wherever I am, I just adjust. I can decide whether I want tea or coffee, pie or fish for tea.'

He might be talking bollocks. Joe didn't know. But now, sitting in the park waiting for Peter to arrive, his anxiety was reaching a new peak. He should have arranged it for the morning but he'd wanted a lie-in. It had backfired, and now he'd be rushing to get back in time. A nagging voice in his head told him things would be easier if he just told Peter about the damn job. He'd said, when they first met, that a job pushing trolleys would suit him, but he'd come across as joking. The truth was he was embarrassed by it, in a way his prison sentence didn't embarrass him. It was stupid, really.

He checked his watch again; he was starving after yet another skipped lunch. The irony that there was enough food to feed a small country in Sarah's cafe wasn't lost on him. But it was expensive in there. He should have got a sausage roll from Gregg's or the supermarket. He didn't think well when he was hungry.

He'd give him another five minutes, then ring him. Half the time, though, Peter didn't think to have his phone on him, especially if his missus hadn't badgered him about taking it. Joe scuffed his feet on the tarmac path. Every minute dragged on.

At last, Peter strolled through the gate, pushing the buggy. The dog was trotting at his side, her lead looped over the buggy handles. Joe waved as Peter stopped and looked around. Peter waved back, unclipped the dog lead and sauntered over.

'Sorry I'm late,' he said. 'This little one's got a touch of tummy trouble. Just as I was about to leave, he filled his nappy, then wouldn't stop crying. I let Stella sort it out, but she insisted on calling Sarah upstairs. Then they spent ages talking about his toilet habits not being right. I think it's just a stomach bug, but you know how women fuss.'

'It's alright. I'm in no hurry,' Joe lied.

He tried to calm down and breathe slowly. He eyed the pushchair. Should he take a snap of the baby yet? His heart leaped at the thought. Peter didn't always bring the kiddie, so Joe would have to take his opportunities when they presented themselves. Like now.

Peter sat beside him on the bench and watched the little dog dashing about. Joe grabbed the buggy handles and swivelled it around so the child was facing him. If Peter thought it odd, he didn't say anything.

'Hello, Zac. How are you today?' he said, attempting to strike up a conversation.

Zac stared back at him, unblinking.

'Doesn't say much, does he?' he said to Peter.

Peter turned to look at him, and Joe noticed how drawn he looked.

'He's deaf,' Peter said flatly. 'I thought Sarah told you at the party last week.'

Joe sat back, stunned. 'Really? No, she didn't. Oh, I'm sorry. I didn't know.'

Peter sighed. It seemed to come right from his sensible shoes.

'No. It's been a bit of a shock. I haven't told you this, but Zac had meningitis recently. It was touch and go whether he'd pull through. It wasn't until after he'd been discharged that we began to notice he didn't respond to sounds. The tests they'd done in hospital… well, they didn't pick it up.'

Joe searched Peter's face. He felt genuinely sorry for the man, but this could play into his hands. He knew now how much Peter needed a male friend, a sounding board. Peter was a trusting soul. Too trusting by far.

'That must be so hard. The poor little fella. What did the doctors say?'

Peter's eyes settled on his grandson. Joe remembered with a jolt that he was the same to the lad. He'd just been looking at his own grandson. Although he knew what the kid was to him, he rarely felt anything when he looked at him. This time was the same, but he did feel a sense of sadness. His grandkid was deaf; how awful was that?

Peter unbuckled the straps keeping Zac in the buggy and lifted him onto his knee. The dog was back, sitting at Peter's feet, begging for something. Peter took a dog treat out of his pocket and gave it to her. He heaved a sigh before speaking.

'He said Zac is totally deaf in one ear, and they're not sure about the other one. Partial deafness, they said. He's got no end of tests and things to come.'

Joe shook his head and looked down at the grass. 'Crikey! It never rains but it pours, doesn't it?'

He reached across and put his finger into Zac's hand. Instead of snatching it away, Zac curled his fingers around it, like a newborn. Then he pulled it to his mouth and tried to bite it. Joe laughed.

'He's teething,' Peter said. 'Sarah said he's got seven now.'

He threw a stick for the dog, who went haring after it. They both watched as she tore straight past the stick and up to where a woman was throwing a tennis ball to a toddler. As the little boy dropped the ball, Lulu scooped it up without breaking stride, and shot off to the other side of the park, followed by sounds of wailing from the child.

'Great,' muttered Peter, standing up. 'She won't give it back. She's done this before.'

He went to put Zac back in the buggy, but Joe held out his hands.

'Give him here while you go get the dog,' he said.

Peter hesitated, and Joe reached out and took Zac, settling him onto his own lap.

'Young Zac and me, we'll be just fine until you get back.'

Peter nodded gratefully and looked over to where the white speck in the distance was still racing around with the fluorescent yellow ball clamped between her jaws. 'Back in a sec.'

Joe watched as Peter trudged off, calling Lulu's name. Zac was surprisingly heavy on his lap. He didn't have long. He whipped out his phone and thumbed the camera on. Thanks to one of Gerry's sons showing him all the shortcuts, he was getting expert at these things now. Well, almost. He reversed the camera so it captured Zac and himself perfectly. His eyes slid to Peter, who was trying to get the dog to return to him. Peter's annoyed voice carried, and the dog slunk back to him, dropping the ball along the way. Peter clipped her lead on and straightened up, looking the other way and speaking to the woman with the toddler, no doubt apologising.

Joe adjusted the camera slightly and snapped off three photos as quickly as he could, then pocketed the phone and jiggled the kid up and down on his knee. Was there any point in talking to the kid if he couldn't hear him? Maybe he would, just for Peter's benefit. It was what normal people would do. Peter was striding back over the grass now, Lulu trotting beside him. She didn't looked too chastised.

As Peter sat back down beside him, he was singing The Wheels On The Bus over and over.

'He seems perfectly happy with you. I think he likes you,' Peter said.

'Yeah. We're best buddies, aren't we, Zac, you and Uncle Gerry?'

Peter looked off into the far distance. Joe wondered what he was thinking. He looked so miserable. Only one way to find out.

'Are you alright? Only, you look like you've got the weight of the world on your shoulders.'

Peter sighed and ran a hand over his face. Joe was interested now. There could be some juicy stuff. When Peter began to talk, it was as if the sluice gates had opened. Peter's cosy, cushy life with his lovely wife and daughter wasn't all it was cracked up to be. Peter had deep reservations about moving, he said. He hadn't adjusted well to it, yet his family didn't seem to have noticed, especially his wife, other than her asking a couple of times if he was okay. Joe sensed a reluctance for Peter to talk about his woes. He wasn't a man to slag people off. He was far too nice. But with Joe's encouragement, it wasn't hard to get him to open up and say far more than he'd probably intended. Joe didn't normally like listening to people's moans, but this was great.

When Peter paused for breath after twenty minutes, Joe pointed at Zac and asked, 'So, what about this little one's dad then—is he in the picture? Only he's never been mentioned.'

Shutters came down over Peter's face. Interesting! He couldn't read his expression at all.

'No,' he said, finally. 'He's not around.'

Should he dig for more? Probably not but suddenly, he wanted to know what Peter knew about Zac's dad.

'Who is he?'

'Just some guy our Sarah knocked around with for a bit. A bit of a bad sort, as it turned out.'

Joe raised his eyebrows and gave Peter time.

'Anyway,' I'm going to have to go,' Peter said, with another huge sigh. 'I've got a doctor's appointment.'

'Oh. Not ill, I hope.'

Peter laughed, but there was no humour there.

'No. That's it. I'm not ill. It's stress. It landed me in the hospital, and Stella won't stop worrying. She's made me a check-up and is insisting I go. I'm sorry to cut this short but I didn't know she'd booked it until this morning. They fit me in at short notice.'

'It's not a problem, Joe said. Even though it was.

Zac had fallen asleep on Joe's lap, and Peter took him. Zac stayed asleep as Peter strapped him into the pushchair.

'Sorry to bend your ear and go on about stuff. I don't usually,' Peter said, looking embarrassed. 'I don't know what's come over me, just lately.'

Joe glanced at his watch, relieved at the time. At least he wouldn't have to rush now. 'Chin up, old boy. Things are never quite as bad as they seem,' he said, getting up.

Peter nodded. 'You're right. It's just me wallowing in it.'

'Don't be daft. You've got a lot on your plate.'

'Oh, while I remember, are you coming to another bridge night? The lads have been asking. Apparently, they really took to you.'

Joe's eyebrows shot up. 'Did they? I didn't feel the love coming from Lenny, I must say.'

Peter smiled. 'I think he's like that with everyone. So, how about it?'

Joe saw the opportunity and took it. Sod the embarrassment! 'I can't, mate. Not if they're on Mondays. I've got myself a job. In fact, I'm going there later. Starts at four.' He stared straight ahead but felt Peter twist to look at him.

'Job? What job?'

He cast him a sheepish glance. 'Promise you won't laugh?'

Peter stared at him, mystified. 'Why would I laugh?'

'It's collecting trolleys at Asda.'

'Oh! Nothing funny about that. Wouldn't mind doing a bit of something myself, actually.' He blew his lips out with a deep breath.

'You? Collecting trolleys?'

'Hmm. Well. No. But, you know; something.'

'I thought you were busy enough with the little one. I'm only working because I need the money.'

'Yes. I am busy enough. But, good for you, Gerry.'

As they walked to the park gates, Joe was relieved; at least he wouldn't get asked to any more bridge nights with that idiot, Lenny. He watched Peter walk away, back to the café; the man looked as if the woes of the world were on his shoulders. Joe couldn't stop grinning as he hurried back to his car. The pictures on his phone were priceless. He was more than satisfied with today's efforts. Next, to get a picture of Zac and Sarah together. Shouldn't be too hard. He'd more than ingratiated himself with the family now. Again, the only fly in the ointment was that he wouldn't be there to see Colin's face when he opened the picture. It had been the same with the *Hello* message he'd sent from Gerry's phone. He'd really wanted to put '*Hello Colin*' but that would have given the game away, and it was too early.

It turned out to be a dream of a day. He made it back in good time. No roadworks. No red lights. He walked into work with a smile on his face for the first time ever.

40

Sarah

'I'M WORRIED ABOUT DAD,' I said. 'Does he seem like himself to you?'

Mum shuffled back into the sofa, cradling her empty cup. I listened for any noise coming from Zac's baby monitor. Nothing.

'Is he okay?' I asked.

She sighed. 'I don't know. He's snappy and short-tempered sometimes. He never used to be like this.'

I chewed my bottom lip. 'Do you think he's happy? Living here, I mean?'

Her shoulders rose a fraction then fell. 'I don't know that, either. He tells me he is, but he doesn't seem to be. I worry that I rushed him into buying the flat. He says it's too small. What if he's right, and I should have listened to him?'

'What should we do?'

'What can we do? Our life is up here now. He'll have to get used to it.'

'I feel really guilty now. He moved up here because of me. And Zac.'

'I made him, not you. It was me who pushed for it.'

'Do you regret it?' My heart lurched at the thought they might do. Their decision had been a momentous one. To relocate at this time in their lives—what if they both regretted it, not just him?

'No. Well, I don't. I don't think he does, really. He's just at a bit of a loss. He hasn't made many friends around here, other than that Gerry. Those ones at that bridge club aren't true friends. He has nothing in common with any of them.'

'Maybe we should encourage him to spend more time with Gerry, then. They do get on well together. And less time looking after Zac. Maybe I could get a child-minder.'

She shot me a horrified look. 'I'm not having my grandson looked after by a child-minder when that's what I'm here for.'

'No, it's not what you're here for. I know you think that, but you and Dad should be spending quality time together now, not babysitting. It's worth a try. I'll look for one.'

'No, don't. Your dad's fine with Zac. He loves him. And Lulu.'

'Hmm. Yet you're here, and he's in that little flat on his own. Which means he prefers it there.'

'He doesn't. He would have come tonight, but he has a headache. You're reading too much into this. Anyway, I'd better get going and see if he's feeling any better.'

I stood up and took her cup. 'Do you want me to walk back with you?' I held out my hand and helped her out of the seat.

'No, don't be daft. It's still light out. And Zac's tucked up in bed. No need to wake him.'

'I'll see you tomorrow. We can talk some more then.'

I saw Mum down the stairs and out of the cafe. Although I'd have preferred to walk back with her, there was no point arguing.

Upstairs, I checked on Zac and wandered around the flat. It was far too early for bed and there was no cleaning to do, thanks to Mum running herself ragged all day as usual. I peered out of the window into the back alley. All was quiet enough. Just lately, I felt at such a loss in the evenings, now the nights were lighter. It seemed to highlight the fact I had nothing to do, and no one to do it with.

I picked up my laptop and sat back on the sofa. The last page loaded on Google was YouTube, full of sign language videos. No matter how many I watched, it wasn't going in. I was wasting my time. I'd never learn it enough to have conversations with Zac. Just the sight of the videos was becoming depressing.

I closed the lid again, not in the mood. Had I been right to bring up my concerns about Dad? For a while now, he hadn't seemed himself. It was since he'd had the anxiety attack and come home from the hospital. It had really shaken all of us. And I couldn't help feeling responsible that he'd moved his life to York to support me. This was supposed to be my fresh start, me proving to the world I could stand on my own two feet, and what had I done? Not stopped my parents from changing their entire lives to be near me. Was that even normal? Yet, realistically, how would I have coped with having a baby and working the hours I did without their support? I wouldn't. Which meant that I'd actually achieved nothing. It wasn't a good thought.

My phone rang, startling me. It was on the arm of the sofa right next to me. I picked it up.

'Hi, Leanne. I was going to call you later.'

'Beat you to it, then.'

'How are you?'

'Not bad. Just calling with a quick update.'

'Ah. Okay. So how is life after Sam, dare I ask?'

'Surprisingly good. You know, I think I made the right decision. I really did.'

'Good.'

Was she telling me the truth, though? She sounded convincing enough. When Leanne had told me that she'd ended things with Sam, I'd expected tears and endless heart-searching sessions, but there'd been none of that. So, maybe it was true.

'Have you heard from him at all?'

She paused. 'A few times, yeah. He wants us to get back together. And I feel bad for hurting him, but…'

'I know. He's a nice guy. But you shouldn't settle for second best, if that's how you feel.'

'I know. Anyway, I've started an advanced dress-making course.'

'What? What can anyone teach you about making clothes?'

'No, sorry, I mean I've started teaching one. At the local college. Kind of a night school-type thing.'

'Oh, that sounds right up your street.'

'It is. I love it. And the extra money comes in handy.' Did she mean now she had to meet the rent on her own since I'd left and now Sam had gone? 'How's your mum and dad doing, now they're in their own place?' she asked.

'Hmmm. I don't know. Mum just told me Dad doesn't like it. Thinks it's too small.'

'Oh God! And they've bought it now.'

'Yep. And, to be honest, I'm not finding it that easy in a morning. You know, with me getting up at five. Mum is getting here before seven but if Zac wakes early and cries, I can't get things done in the kitchen.'

'Is he sleeping better now, though? Surely as he gets older, he'll sleep for longer, won't he?'

'I think he is, overall, but it's a problem. There's no one upstairs with him. Sometimes I've had to have him with me in the kitchen, in his high chair, but he gets bored. And it's not a good environment for a baby, is it?'

'No, not really. What are you going to do?'

'I don't know. I don't want Mum to get up earlier. She's tired enough as it is. I'll just have to cope and hope he sleeps through more often. Maybe when he's finished teething, he will.'

'So, what's it like being there on your own?'

'A bit boring on an evening sometimes. But I do actually like us having the space to ourselves.'

'Yeah, I do here, too, but I'm going to have to advertise your room. I can't afford the rent on my own for much longer. Or I could look for a one-bed somewhere. I quite fancy that, actually. So, does your dad really hate the flat, then?'

'I don't think he hates it. But he's not doing great since his hospital stay, so it might have something to do with how he feels in general.'

'Really? What do you mean?'

I told her my worries, and what Mum and I had talked about. She listened and let out a low whistle when I'd finished.

'Oh no. Poor Peter. Is it really that bad? It sounds like he may have depression.'

'That's what I've been thinking. But you know what he's like. He won't tell the doctor that. Mum has a hard enough job getting him there for his routine heart checks.'

The baby monitor picked up Zac snuffling. He gave a little wail.

'Just hang on a sec,' I said.

It was fifty-fifty if he'd stay asleep or wake up and start screaming. Hopefully, he'd go back down. No more noises came. I breathed out slowly; I'd had a reprieve.

We chatted for a bit longer. Leanne was excited about her new teaching post, and I tried to sound interested. I was pleased for her, but just so tired, and my mind kept wandering to Dad By the time she rang off, I could barely keep my eyes open.

I shook off my tiredness and eyed my laptop. There was one thing. I picked it up again and opened a new window, then stared at the blank page. I'd been thinking about this for a while now. Should I, or would it open a whole new world of problems? I typed dating websites into the search bar. Just looking at them couldn't hurt any. I wasn't about to start swiping left. Or was it right? I had no idea. I'd never been on any before, and never thought I would. Adam and Chris had kind of both found me. All my previous boyfriends had.

The results loaded—pages and pages of them. The big names were first, of course. Maybe they were big for a reason. The smaller ones might not have good vetting procedures.

Just think of the weirdos you might get. There again, I'd found Chris without a dating app and look how that turned out! I clicked on the ones on the first page and looked at the happy, smiling faces. But to get any further into the websites, I'd have to create accounts on them. Still nothing to lose, so I did. eHarmony, Tinder, Plenty of Fish, and Match.com. I browsed for a long while and, although some of the men looked nice enough, none of them gave me the gut reaction, or the feels, that Chris had. But maybe looking for that again was the wrong thing to do. And I had to move on or I'd be stuck in this situation forever. That's when it struck me—I hadn't had a letter from Chris in a while now, and I hadn't even noticed. Perhaps he'd got the message and had decided not to write anymore. I was relieved but disappointed at the same time.

I set the laptop to one side. The truth was, I did get lonely on an evening, with just me and Zac in the flat. Ellie would go home to Jeb and Darcey after work, Claire was still playing the field and seemingly seeing someone new every month or so, and Olwyn had her husband of over fifty years, Jack, waiting for her. Even Mum and Dad had each other. Martyn, the young trainee in the cafe, said he was too busy with his mates, and too young, to look for love. But the thought of all the nights to come being just like this one had started to fill me with dread. If I wasn't careful, the rut I was in might get deeper and swallow me whole.

I sighed and picked up my laptop again, thinking back to the conversation with Mum earlier. This time, I typed in Child-minders, York, into the search bar.

41

Sarah

I TILTED MY HEAD in Mum's direction, and she followed me around the corner and into the kitchen. Away from where Dad could see us.

'How does he seem to you?' I asked her.

'Oh, not too bad. It was a good idea of yours, to suggest we invite Gerry for dinner. He agreed it would be something to look forward to.'

I peered around the corner to where Dad and Gerry were sitting too close together on the small sofa. I had no idea what Gerry was talking about but Dad was listening closely, leaning further in to catch what he was saying. I hadn't seen him look so happy in ages.

'Thanks for doing all this, love,' Mum said.

'It won't be long before it's done, and then I'll be off.'

I checked the time on the wall clock above the table. 'Five more minutes, and it'll be ready for serving.'

I'd been with Mum since the cafe closed, preparing a one-pot meal of lamb casserole. Dad had asked Gerry what he liked to eat when he'd invited him, and he'd said lamb. Dad ate just about anything and Mum wasn't too fussy, so lamb casserole it was.

The small table was laid for three. I wasn't staying. After I'd dished up, I was taking Zac home. Claire was coming round, and we were going to watch something on Netflix. I was really looking forward to it, an evening with my friend, a bottle of wine, and some laughs. And, with it being Sunday, I could lie in tomorrow as long as Zac would let me. We'd talked about opening the cafe on Mondays, but decided to leave things the way they were. Jenny had told us not to, too.

'You need at least one day off, if not two,' she said. 'You'll be getting me locked up for exploitation, or slavery or something, at this rate.'

'What would you like to drink, Gerry?' Mum asked.

'Ah, just a cup of tea, thanks. I'm driving. Dinner smells lovely, by the way. I could eat a scabby donkey.' He rubbed his stomach.

I laughed. 'Good. I hope it tastes better than one, though.'

I thought of the bottle of white wine and the cans of beer Dad had put in the fridge earlier.

'I thought I'd give him a choice,' he'd said.

And now he wasn't going to be drinking at all. I hoped, for Dad's sake, his friend wouldn't be running off too early. He was always so busy with his children and grandchildren. At least he kept himself active. It must be so hard for him since his wife had died. Dad had told me all about it, how she'd lost her battle with cancer a few years ago, before any of their grandchildren had been born. For Gerry to be telling him stuff like that, they must be close. Men hated talking about personal stuff, didn't they?

That made me wonder what Dad may have told him about us. Me. Mum. Zac. Oh God! I definitely wouldn't come out of it looking good. Surely Dad wouldn't tell a new friend all our family secrets, would he? I didn't want my dirty laundry airing, not with the amount of it I had.

I walked out of the kitchen area. Gerry was laughing at something Dad had said, Zac was crawling around all over the place, and Lulu was on Dad's knee. I watched them while Mum busied about doing something behind me. She was humming to herself. It had been a while since I'd heard her do that. She used to do it all the time when I was growing up.

It meant she was happy. So, now, she must be feeling happy that Dad had found a friend he trusted.

Mum didn't need new friends, she'd told me. She was happy with her family, thank you.

'But maybe you should make some,' I'd said. 'There are probably some clubs you could join.'

The look she'd given me had been enough. I'd never mentioned it again. But Dad was different to Mum. For as long as I could remember, he'd gone places and taken up new hobbies. Interests, he called them. Flash-in-the-pans, according to Mum. Some had lasted a few years, others barely weeks before he'd lost interest. But he never minded. *Variety is the spice of life* was one of his favourite phrases. Maybe he was right, and finding new friends was something he should focus on. For whatever reason, the time he spent with Gerry had brought a flush of colour back to his cheeks, so, for that alone, it was worth encouraging.

The oven timer went off, and I took the casserole out. As I straightened up, I heard Zac cry.

'What's happened?' I said, going to pick him up from where he was lying on the floor.

Dad had just been about to pick him up but sat down again as I scooped him up. He threw his arms around my neck and buried his face.

'He bumped his head, I think. On the corner of the TV unit,' Gerry said.

I kissed Zac and shushed him, whilst feeling his head for bumps. Nothing serious.

'He does that all the time, lately,' I said. 'He's not content with just crawling. He's trying to stand up every chance he gets, and he's constantly falling over.'

I walked over to the window and showed Zac the cars on the street below. His snuffling stopped, and he watched a woman walking a massive dog on the other side of the road.

'Doggy,' I said. Perhaps Zac would become proficient in lip-reading. Apparently, he could do.

Zac burbled.

'Say cheese,' said Gerry.

I turned around to find him pointing his phone at me.

'Oh, no. I don't like having my picture taken,' I said. 'I take an awful photo.'

'She always says that, but it isn't true,' said Dad. 'I mean; look at her. She's lovely.'

'Just a quick one. My granddaughter wanted me to take some snaps when I said I was coming here. She wanted to see Zac. So I said I would.'

I posed, smiling for the camera, and trying to get Zac to look at the lens. Miraculously he did, for a millisecond. I put him back down on the floor and Lulu followed me into the kitchen.

'It's no good you getting comfortable,' I told her as she eyed up the pot. 'We're not staying.'

I lifted the lid off the pot and turned to Mum.

'I'll get going and let you dish up,' I said. 'I want a shower before Claire arrives.'

'Okay. And thanks again, love.'

I strapped Zac into his buggy and left, waving at them all. Zac did the same.

On the walk back, I thought about Gerry. Dad said he lived a few miles outside York but hadn't said where. I felt sorry for him. Dad had told me Gerry had jumped at the dinner invitation when he'd asked him. He said that, despite Gerry's busy life and big family, he reckoned he was lonely at times. He might be right. In my experience, people often put on a front. Just look at Facebook. When I used to go on it, I was amazed at the stuff people put on there. Friends I knew to be thoroughly miserable, but you'd never know it from their profiles. Their happiness had been made up, and it was really common. I was glad I was off all that now. All that fakeness. Urgh! No thanks.

You had to laugh, though. With all the secrets in my past, I was probably covering up more than most. I wasn't doing it on Facebook, though.

Tonight, I was going to tell Claire I'd joined some dating sites. I didn't think she'd laugh. She'd used them herself. She told me. Maybe she and I could look through some of the profiles. I might even make the first move if there were any that looked promising. Nothing could be worse than what I'd already had, could it?

42

Chris

CHRIS WALKED BACK TO his cell with beads of sweat dotting his hairline. The phone was in the front pocket of his jeans, small, but it felt heavier than a house brick. And what if it was making his pocket bulge? He pulled his sweatshirt down over it for the hundredth time. The paranoia wasn't helping him sweat less.

Phil, thankfully, hadn't noticed Chris's stress. He unlocked his cell and Chris stepped inside, relieved to be back in his own space. After the door was locked, he slid the phone out and put it in his pillowcase. When he'd got to the library that morning, he'd had time to switch it on and see another WhatsApp message was waiting, but not had the chance to open it before the students arrived. In a panic, he'd shoved it inside his clothes, where it had remained all day.

He sat on the bed, wondering whether to wait until later, after lights out, or look at it now. He should wait, but could he? It was association soon, and they'd all be unlocked. Anyone could walk in. Tommy had taken to doing it, and it made Chris uneasy. No. Better to wait. He'd almost mentioned the message and photos to Tommy, but had thought better of it. He didn't trust him, and the phone had come from him, after all. He couldn't work out if Tommy was involved somehow and was playing games with him. Tommy hadn't given him any indication that he knew anything about it. Had he got someone on the outside to locate Sarah from what he'd told him, and take pictures of her to send to his phone? But why; what would be the point? But without the phone, he wouldn't have the picture of Sarah.

At that thought of the photo, his hand crept inside the pillowcase and powered the phone on, all without intervention from his brain. He stood with his back pressed firmly against the door. His sweating got worse, and he could hardly control the way his hand shook. He slid it out just enough to see the screen, while his heart banged so hard it made him feel woozy. But he had to look. Couldn't wait.

It started up and settled on the home screen. The green WhatsApp icon clearly showed a message. He hadn't been seeing things. He checked the battery: ninety percent. Okay there. But it needed powering off soon. For the want of something as simple as a charger, and most people had drawers full of the damn things, his whole world could be screwed if it ran out of juice. As soon as he gave it to Tommy to charge for him, he'd see what was on it.

It was time. He couldn't hold back any longer. He pressed the icon and WhatsApp opened. Chris gawped and almost dropped the phone at the picture that loaded. It was Sarah, and she was holding a toddler on her hip. They were standing next to a window, and bright sunlight was coming through the glass, lighting them up. She was smiling.

Adrenaline flooded through him as he fixed his eyes on the child. He swallowed hard. It couldn't be, could it? The kid was the spitting image of him. Absolutely. Without a doubt. There had been a photo in a drawer in the flat in Granford Towers of his dad at a few months old, and people had always remarked on how alike he and his dad were as babies. The shape of the chin and nose, the set of the eyes. The thick, curly dark hair. 'It could be the same kid,' everyone said. And it was true. As time went on, the similarities between him and his dad had become less prevalent, less defined, until they barely resembled each other as adults. He hadn't even thought about the photo in years. But now, it all came back to him with absolute certainty. That kid with Sarah was his. And she'd never said a thing. His thoughts went back to the one night they'd spent together. She'd been insatiable. Was this why?

He blinked and shook his head. All the messages and photos had come from the same phone number. He grabbed the paper his dad had scribbled his number on. It wasn't the same.

Who the hell was doing this to him? It made no sense. He turned the phone off and hid it in his pillow again. Even more now, he didn't trust Tommy. It must have something to do with him. There was no other explanation. He was going to have to watch his back.

43

Joe

JOE'S DAUGHTER, SHAY, HAD been on his mind a lot lately, and that wasn't usual. He felt robbed, cheated, by the fact he couldn't stay at her place and have her look after him. And it was Colin's fault.

At the thought of Colin, he changed gear savagely, then turned on the radio to rid himself of him. Some god-awful rap thing came on, an assault on his ears. He switched it off. On reflection, silence would be preferable. He rolled his shoulders back and down as best he could in the driver's seat and forced himself to relax. It was nice and early, just gone ten. He was spending most of the day with Peter, and had no worries about not getting back for his trolley shift, as he had plenty of time.

He peered up out of the windscreen. Not a cloud anywhere. It was warm and sunny; perfect.

Thoughts of Colin soon wormed their way back in, especially what his son had done to him. The injustice, the sheer damn cheek of him, was eating away at Joe. He could say without a doubt that he hated Colin with such ferocity it threatened to overtake him. Banged up for years, and all because of him. Joe's desire for revenge had grown and was the only thing that mattered now. Joe wasn't a planner. He couldn't plan to save his life, but what was wrong with being impulsive and taking risks? When the time was right, instinct would take over. He was convinced of it.

And, ultimately, if whatever he did landed him back in prison, he wouldn't be that bothered. When Gerry had said he was institutionalised, he was right. Inside, there were no worries. It wasn't easy or pleasant, but it was bearable, in a way that life on the outside sometimes wasn't, with all its decisions and worries. If Gerry kicked him out, he'd have nowhere, other than a park bench. He'd have sunk lower than ever before in his miserable life. At least in prison he had his own bed. So, if that was where he ended up, so be it.

He clenched his jaw and crunched through the gears as he entered York. He could park at Peter's for free if he used their visitor permit, Stella had insisted, with a warm smile. She certainly made him feel welcome. If only she knew who he was. Wouldn't be such a happy granny then, would she?

Ten minutes later, he rang the bell. Stella answered the door and handed him the permit, which he went to put on his dashboard. He was back within ten seconds.

'What have you two got planned for this morning?' Stella stood aside to let him in. 'Peter's just in the bathroom. He won't be long.'

'I'm not sure what we're doing, actually, Stella. We take it in turns to decide, and it's Peter's turn.' He hovered barely inside, still on the doormat, and pushed the door to behind him.

'Oh, God help you there, then.' Stella laughed. 'He can't make a decision to save his life.'

'And I'm not much better,' Joe said, chuckling, adjusting the cuffs on his shirt that peeked out from his jacket sleeves.

'Morning,' Peter said, emerging from the bathroom just ahead.

Joe didn't bother to repeat the conversation he'd just had with Stella. Peter would have heard every word, the bathroom being all of three feet away. His prison cell hadn't been much smaller than this.

'I have decided, thank you very much,' Peter said, giving Stella a stern look.

'Go on, then. What is it?' she said.

'The library.'

'The library?' Stella and Joe said together.

Good God! The library? What was wrong with the man? Joe swallowed. It was going to be a long day at this rate.

'What do you want to go there for?' Stella asked the question Joe couldn't.

'I want to research York. I'm thinking of doing a history on it. Gerry gave me the idea.'

Joe hid his surprise. He couldn't think what he'd said. He hated history. It was all old hat. Who cared about yesterday or yesteryear? A day in the library! Jesus! He had to get out of it somehow. He said the first thing that came into his head.

'What are you doing today, Stella?' he asked.

'Oh, you know. Just looking after the little one at Sarah's.'

'We can do that. You chill out and do your own thing. You deserve a rest.'

'No, don't be daft. You two can have the day to yourselves.'

'You could book yourself in for a manicure, a massage, or a nice facial,' Joe said. 'Treat yourself. Those nail things are everywhere these days, aren't they? You just turn up. My daughter goes to them all the time. Zac will be just fine with us.'

Stella looked undecided and surveyed her nails. 'They are a mess. I haven't had them done in ages.'

'That's settled then. And our Judy's been dying for her little one to meet Zac. They're around the same age. I could see if she's free and meet her in the park, so the kiddies could play together, then you could collect him, Stella, and take him back to Sarah's. How does that sound? Best of both worlds, eh?'

He could see she was tempted. He just needed to prod Peter a bit.

'What do you think, Peter? Our Judy's mad keen on history. It was her uni course. You two would get on like a house on fire.'

Peter thought about it. 'The library's not going anywhere, I don't suppose. Yes, okay then.'

'Zac not here?' Joe asked, looking around.

'Yes, he's out back, in the garden. If you can call that postage stamp of grass a garden. There isn't even room for a nice shed,' Peter said. The corners of his mouth turned down.

'It's perfect,' Stella said, nudging him. 'It's plenty big enough for the two of us. And the grass is cut in five minutes, with one of those push mower things that don't need electricity. Zac needs a place to play outside and there's nowhere at Sarah's.' She looked at Joe. 'It's what appealed to me about this place; being a ground floor, we get the garden to ourselves.'

'Well, you wouldn't fit anyone else in it,' grumbled Peter.

'He misses his garden back in London,' Stella said, talking over him. 'He had it lovely. But we can make this one lovely, too. Add a few tubs and a nice seating area. A little barbeque, maybe, with some climbers up the fence. Has he told you he does the window boxes at Sarah's shop? Everyone admires them, don't they, Peter?' She touched Peter gently on the arm, like someone calming a flighty stallion. 'And I actually think we could fit a small shed in the back corner, if you want one, love.'

Joe didn't know what was going on between the two of them, but something was. He just couldn't work it out. Stella was treating him like he was mentally unstable and could go off at any minute.

'Well, if you're sure. I'll go and get him then. And I might ring one of those nail places after all.' She went off, humming to herself.

Joe waited as Peter put his shoes on and faffed around doing the laces in double knots.

Stella was back, carrying Zac, in just a matter of minutes. Zac smiled and clapped his hands when he saw Joe. Joe looked at Zac's black hair and deep brown eyes. Did he feel anything at all for the kid? He considered for a moment. No, he didn't. Exactly the same as he'd felt for Colin and Shay all those years ago. It could be anybody's baby.

'He's really taken to you,' Stella said. 'He loves his Uncle Gerry, don't you?' she said in an irritating baby voice that set Joe's teeth on edge. And he wasn't a bloody uncle, was he? He was a grandad and should have rights as such.

Nevertheless he smiled at Peter. 'Where's the dog?' he asked.

'She's at home. She's hurt her foot, so Sarah said she had to stay there. We had to have her to the vets the day before yesterday. She jumped off the sofa and landed funny. The vet said she'd sprained it and had to rest.'

Stella handed Zac's cardigan to Peter, and he put it under the buggy.

'Lulu's not happy about it,' Stella said, strapping Zac into the pushchair. 'You should have seen her this morning when we picked Zac up, whining and crying. She hates being cooped up in that flat on her own all day.'

Joe was eager to get going before Stella changed her mind and kept Zac.

'Come on then, old feller,' he said to Peter. 'We've got new plans to make.'

Peter looked happy enough as he pulled on a thin jacket. 'Yes. Let's be impulsive for once. We'll see you later.'

He kissed Stella on the lips, grabbed the buggy, and followed Joe into the sunshine.

Joe looked up at the sun. 'It's a perfect day for impulsivity,' he said, grinning.

So Peter wanted impulsive, did he? Alright then. He'd see just how impulsive Joe could be.

44

Peter

'HAS JUDY GOT BACK to you yet?' Peter asked.

Gerry glanced at his phone. 'No. Sorry. Maybe another time. She must be busy.'

Peter nodded. 'Of course.'

He looked at Gerry. His friend seemed a bit off today, like he had something on his mind he was anxious about. Peter felt bad for his mate. For weeks now, all he'd done was use Gerry as a shoulder to cry on when he thought he and Stella had made the wrong decision in rushing up to York. It was about time he repaid Gerry's kindness and patience by being a good friend in return.

They'd been out for three hours now. They were down by the river next to the museum, standing in the dappled shade of a horse chestnut. After they'd scrapped their plans, Gerry had suggested they just mooch around some of the areas of York they were less familiar with. Peter had liked the sound of it, so had gone along with it. Neither of them were any good with maps on phones, so they'd got a paper fold-out map from a tourist shop, along with a walking guide book, and began following it randomly.

Peter had been surprised how good a time he'd had, just wandering on their tour of discovery. They'd chatted about their childhoods, their families, their jobs, hopes and dreams. Peter was amazed: he'd had no idea Gerry was so well travelled. Some of the jobs Gerry had done sounded interesting and exciting, especially his time in the military and working in Whitehall. Peter had longed to find out more, but Gerry had said he was only allowed to say so much and he'd said too much already.

'Official Secrets Act,' he'd said, tapping his nose.

Peter had understood and nodded. 'Of course. Forget I asked. I wouldn't want to compromise national security.'

After that, Gerry had gone quiet. From the corner of his eye, Peter saw him look at his watch. What if he was boring him? After all, his life hadn't been anything half so exotic. He had no interesting stories to tell.

'Um, are you alright?' You seem a bit…' He waved his hand in the air, his gesture as vague as his words.

Gerry blinked, as if coming out of some reverie. 'Oh, yeah. Sorry. Had a bit of bad news the other day at the doctors, that's all. It keeps coming back to me. Sorry if I seem a bit distracted.'

Peter was right. He'd known there was something wrong. His grip tightened on Zac's buggy. Zac had been fractious for the last two hours. Peter's nerves were now frazzled by Zac's screaming and crying. Turned out he'd needed his nappy changing. Stella normally did it; he was all fingers and thumbs, not to mention the way his stomach contracted at the sight and smell. He'd got through it, though. Thankfully, now Zac had gone to sleep, and the silence was blissful.

'Er, why, what's wrong?' Peter was even more alarmed to see Gerry's eyes had grown moist. Oh hell! What if he was dying? What did one say at times like this?

'It's my heart. I've been having problems. They've said I might have to have a bypass.'

Gerry grimaced and shook his head. Now he'd mentioned it, Peter noticed he was looking a bit peaky.

'It's knocked me for six, I can tell you. I've just got to take it easy until they know more.' Gerry clutched at his chest, gripping his shirt, then let the fabric go. 'I didn't say anything earlier because I didn't want to spoil our day.'

Peter's own heart thwacked against his ribs. He was touched that his friend hadn't wanted to bother him with it. Instantly, he felt bad.

'Of course, yes, you should take it easy. Um, do you want to sit down anywhere?' Peter looked about him. The few benches near the river were already occupied.

'No, no. I'm fine just wandering about. It's better for me than sitting, anyway. The doc told me to do gentle exercise, like walking. Look, why don't we head back to the shops and get something for dinner? I still need to eat.'

Peter nodded. 'Sounds good. Do you need salad or something like that?'

'I don't know. They never said anything about eating. One meat pie probably wouldn't hurt. I like that shop near the top of the Shambles. Could go there.'

Peter was doubtful the doctor would condone pies, but chose not to disagree. Instead, he turned the buggy around and set off slowly, not wishing to tax Gerry. If he had a heart attack right now, in the street, what would Peter do? Other than phone an ambulance, of course. It was about a ten-minute walk, fifteen at this pace, but that was alright. They had time. Stella had phoned half an hour ago, saying she was just going into the hairdressers. She'd be about an hour. She'd ring when she was finished and come and meet them.

Peter's heart slowed down a bit. Gerry seemed fine. He wasn't out of breath or anything. His thoughts slid back to his wife. He was looking forward to seeing her with her hair all done. He knew looking after herself made her feel good. She hadn't done so much of it since Zac had come along; she hadn't had time. It would do her good. All she did these days was worry about him, and that made him feel bad. Sometimes, it seemed to him, he felt bad about everything. He hadn't told her how he felt; didn't want to worry her. She had enough on her plate. Despite what he may have inferred in some of his conversations with Gerry, she did the lion's share of everything. A break would do her good.

When they reached the shop, Gerry reached into his jacket pocket for his wallet. Peter stopped him.

'What do you want? My treat,' he said, putting the brakes on the buggy after manoeuvring it into a little spot between the pie shop and the boutique next door. He had a brief flash of guilt at the thought of patronising another shop that sold pies when he could get them from Sarah's. But if Gerry wanted them from here, then that's what they'd do. Especially after his bad news and all. It might cheer him up a bit.

'Thanks, if you're sure,' said Gerry. 'I'll have a steak bake with some potato wedges, then I won't have to bother cooking later on.'

Peter went to lift Zac out of the buggy, but Gerry stopped him.

'Don't wake him up. Just leave him. I'll stay out here with him.'

Peter straightened up. 'Righto. Steak bake and wedges coming up.'

Peter went into the pie shop. He'd have loved to have the same, but Stella made them a hot meal every evening; he'd be better just having something light now.

He was too far from the counter to be able to read the board behind it. It was one of those blackboards with white chalk. He could never make out the damn letters. There was a fridge to his right, and he picked up two bottles of water. That was healthy, wasn't it? It might counteract the pie. He chuckled to himself at the thought. If only things could be that simple.

There were at least six people in front of him waiting to be served, and they weren't particularly speedy in this establishment. He'd been in once before and had waited over fifteen minutes for his apricot and custard pasty. It had definitely been worth the wait.

He sighed as a burst of steam hissed from the coffee machine. It was that damn thing that did it. It took forever.

Whenever someone wanted a cappuccino or some other-cino, it added five minutes on.

He frowned. Gerry hadn't mentioned a hot drink, and it wasn't like he'd asked for the water. He turned around. There were another four people behind him now. He couldn't see Gerry out of the window as he'd been standing to the other side. No way was he giving up his place in the queue. He shuffled forward as a woman left the counter, clutching a sandwich.

'What can I get you?' the woman in the funny little hat behind the counter asked the next person.

Peter wasn't sure, but he thought he heard the words 'four cappuccinos'. He groaned. Sweat pooled under his arms, and he took off his jacket. The shop was sweltering.

He'd heard right about the cappuccinos. It was a massive food order, too, with items that needed cooking. Those melt things in that foreign-sounding bread. It was another thirteen minutes when he eventually got out, two bottles of water in his pockets, Gerry's steak bake and wedges, and a tuna sandwich on wholemeal for himself wrapped in paper bags. The heat in the shop had got steadily worse and when he tumbled out onto the pavement, eager for some fresh air, he had a banging headache. He turned to where Gerry had been waiting with the buggy. The buggy had gone, and so had Gerry.

He scanned the street in both directions, looking for the bright red buggy. There was no sign of it. He gripped the steak bake bag tighter, his fingers becoming slippery with grease. His heart bumped in alarm as something on the floor, right where the buggy had been, caught his attention. The few yards it took to walk it felt like an age, his legs were so wobbly.

Right there, on the pavement, Zac's little red rabbit lay abandoned on the floor.

45

Chris

CHRIS FROZE AT THE sound of his cell door being unlocked. He was still in bed. He turned over and looked at the officer standing in the doorway. It was Squeaky, the massive one with the ridiculous voice. Squeaky sighed when he saw him.

'Kitchen,' he said. 'Why aren't you up?'

He groaned. 'I have a stomach bug. I can't go today. I've been puking half the night, and now I've got the shits.'

Squeaky sniffed the air. He wouldn't smell anything other than Chris's lie. But would he care?

He was silent. Then, 'When did you last throw up?'

'About an hour ago.'

'And go to the loo?'

'Maybe two hours. I don't remember exactly.'

'Mmm,' he said. Chris could practically hear the cogs turning in his brain. 'Do you need to see a doctor?'

'I don't think so. I think it's just a bug. But I can't be in the kitchen like this, can I?'

He pulled himself up in the bed a fraction, doing his best to look ill. He knew what the screw was thinking. It was a lot more work for him to get Chris looked at. And he couldn't prove he was lying. To go along with it would be easier.

'Alright,' he said. 'Someone will look in on you later. Holler if you feel worse in the meantime.'

'Okay.'

He backed out of the door and the sound of the key turning in the lock seemed extra loud. Squeaky's footsteps died away, and he lay back down. No kitchen duty today, then. Thank God. He couldn't face it. He needed a day here, alone, in his cell. Just him and the phone. With time to think. Although, being alone with his thoughts wasn't necessarily the best thing for him. He could end up going stir crazy.

Yesterday, when he'd opened the picture of Sarah and the child, he'd been gobsmacked. The shock had been physical, like he'd been punched in the gut. He hadn't been lying about feeling rough; he'd barely slept.

Last night, he'd opened the picture again. Before he'd shut the phone down, he'd sent a message back. *Who are you?*

No one had replied.

He thumbed the phone on, stuck it under the covers, and checked. Still no reply. He turned it back off again. Conserve the battery. But he longed to leave it on and just gaze at Sarah, both the picture of her alone, and the one with the child.

For the last few days, he hadn't seen Tommy at all. Tommy hadn't been in the kitchen, for some reason. Was he keeping a low profile? But why? All Tommy cared about was himself, so why would he bother? The man was so self-centred and arrogant, he wouldn't spare a thought for anyone else. And Tommy certainly wasn't afraid of anyone in here.

He stared up at the ceiling in the gloom. How long had it been since he wrote to Sarah? Must have been at least a month. He hadn't written since he'd started teaching the computer class. He didn't really know why he'd stopped. Maybe he could compose a letter today. Or maybe it was just a waste of time, although time was the one thing he had in abundance.

He wouldn't write. The lack of return letters, not a single one, must mean that she wasn't interested. It was about time he stopped chasing that particular dream and put it to rest.

He slid his watch out from under his pillow. It was early. He'd leave the phone off until midday and check again then. He needed to find out who the hell was playing games with him. And why. He lay, blinking at the grimy ceiling. He'd never felt so trapped and helpless. What did they want?

46

Joe

JOE'S LUNGS WERE BURNING from pushing the buggy and hurrying away. He needed to stop somewhere soon, and he had little idea where he was. He'd never been in this part of York before; it was mainly houses. Zac, however, seemed to think it was all a great adventure, and had laughed at being jiggled up and down so roughly as Joe hurried along. He wasn't laughing now, though. Instead, he was grizzling, squirming to get out of the buggy.

When Joe had grabbed the buggy, purely on impulse, he'd had no real idea of what he could do next. Or where he would go. No, he hadn't thought it through, but had still believed something would occur to him, or strike him as being the right thing to do. Instead, it hadn't. It had been forty-five minutes now; forty-five minutes of pushing the kid around with no plan. All he'd done was flee the city centre, or at least the shopping part where they'd been, and now he was lost. He needed to sit down.

Where was he? He looked for a street sign and couldn't see anything. His basic knowledge of York meant he had some idea which direction the shops were in. He turned a full circle, looking for the Minster, but couldn't see it. Where had Peter put the map they'd bought? He rooted around the various bits of the buggy where things could be stored. Not there. Must be in Peter's pocket. Of course it would be! He turned back the way he'd come. If he retraced his steps, he'd eventually see something he recognised.

Zac yelped and shuffled, and Joe's heart knocked against his ribs as he fully realised the implications of what he'd done.

After walking around for another twenty minutes, he passed a small café. He was sweating badly now. It would have to do. He needed a drink, somewhere to sit down and regroup.

He went in, getting the buggy stuck several times on the door, and sat at a table in the window. He and Zac were the only customers.

'I'll be over in a sec,' the man behind the counter called, his phone jammed against his ear.

Joe reached for the menu. As he opened it, Zac, still in the pushchair, made a grab for it.

'No!' said Joe, pulling it away.

Zac grabbed again and missed. Was he too young to drink out of a cup? Joe wondered. It struck him just how little he knew about kids, having paid scant attention to his own when they were little. Or at any time, really. He'd kind of just done his own thing, mainly tuning them out as much as he could.

He glanced towards the counter, but the man had his back turned and was still on the phone. Zac was struggling, plucking at the straps holding him, trying to get out. Joe had only seen Zac crawling. He couldn't walk yet. He couldn't put the kid down in here, surely. What did people do?

'Would you like a high chair?' the man called over, his call now finished.

Of course. High chairs.

'Yes, please,' he said, as he got Zac out, sitting him awkwardly on his lap.

The man brought a chair over, and, after several attempts to guide Zac's legs through the holes, Joe slotted him in. Zac seemed fascinated by a row of beads on the front of the chair and busied himself pushing them about.

'What can I get you?' the man asked.

'Just a coffee, please.' He looked at the counter again. 'And a Kit Kat as well.'

'Coming up. He's a bonny little feller,' the man said.

'Yes. My grandson.'

'What's his name?'

'Zac.'

'How old is he?'

Shit, thought Joe. He didn't know exactly. So many months. He had a stab at it.

'Oh, he's not one yet.' That would do.

'Ah, right. I'll just get your order.'

The man walked off. If he thought it was a strange answer, he didn't say anything. Good. The customer was always right. That's what they said, wasn't it?

The coffee and biscuit came quickly. Joe hesitated. Could Zac eat chocolate? He tried to think back to what he'd seen Zac have in the past. Peter had given him all sorts of things. Like… bread and fruit and cake. So it must be okay.

Zac squealed and reached for the Kit Kat. It was four fingers. Joe unwrapped it and gave a finger to Zac, who examined it for a second, then sucked and nibbled on the end. Satisfied he'd have a minute's peace, Joe sipped his coffee.

He took out his phone, a new pay-as-you-go Gerry had given him. A burner phone, Daz had called it. Joe had liked the sound of that. So far, he hadn't sent Colin anything from it. He snapped a picture of Zac. When to send it to Colin? When would Colin get the opportunity to see the pictures? His fingers drummed on the tabletop—it might be ages before Colin saw it.

The coffee revived him, and he sat there, thinking through his options. He couldn't walk around endlessly. He didn't have a child seat in his car, so that was a no go. He envisaged turning up at Gerry's with him. Gerry's face would be a picture.

What was Peter doing right now? He wished he could see him. All morning, he'd fed Peter lie after lie about his family and life history. Having a daughter that had gone to university? His real daughter couldn't have even spelled it. Working for Whitehall on secret defence projects? Peter had swallowed all of it. The man was a gullible idiot. He deserved to lose his grandson. All he'd done for the past few weeks was grumble and complain about his lot in life. Joe's hand curled into a fist, and he bumped it up and down loudly on the tabletop, as a tight curl of anger began to uncoil deep inside him.

'Everything alright?' the man behind the counter called across, his eyes sliding from Joe to Zac.

'Yes. Thank you.'

The man frowned. 'Are you okay? You look a bit hot.'

Did he? He did feel a bit hot, come to mention it. It must be all that rushing about.

'Would you like some water?'

'Yes. Yes, please.'

The man ran a glass under the tap and brought it over. Joe gave Zac a second finger of Kit Kat. A lot of the first had ended up down his front, as well as his face. His pale blue T-shirt was now brown.

Joe gulped at the water, aware that the man was still watching him. The door opened and a young couple came inside.

'How old did you say he was again?' the man asked, nodding at Zac. He hadn't looked at the other customers yet.

'He'll be one, soon.'

The man looked at Zac, his brow creasing. Joe was getting an uneasy feeling. The man was fast growing suspicious. Although not yet rested, Joe wanted to leave. The man went back to fiddling behind the counter. Joe couldn't see his hands. Maybe he was reaching for a phone.

He stood up, yanked Zac out of the highchair, pocketed the Kit Kat, and bunged him roughly back in the buggy, not bothering to do up the strap. He managed to get out of the café a damn sight faster than he'd got in.

Zac was still guzzling the biscuit, giving it his full attention.

He hurried away from the cafe, but he still didn't know what to do. All he really wanted to do was scare and hurt Colin, not the kid. Maybe he could do that now. He sat on a low wall in front of a small church and took the phone out again. Zac protested and started snivelling as he lifted him from the buggy, sat him on his lap, and took a selfie of them both. A picture of Zac looking upset might be just the thing. Zac crying and Granddad smiling. Nice. He had quite a collection of pictures of Zac now. Sending the pictures from this phone would surely confuse Colin further. He hadn't answered the *Who are you?* message Colin had sent to Gerry's phone. These pictures would answer it for him.

No point waiting any longer. He opened his WhatsApp screen and sent all the photos one by one. Then, for good measure, he typed '*Hello Colin. Have ya met youre son? Seems I'm a grandaddy. Did you forget to tel me. Shame.*' Smiley face icon.

He laughed harder as he pressed Send. Hopefully, this time, he'd get a response. If he didn't, he had no idea what to do. It wasn't a good thought. He pushed it away and fed Zac a third, by now melted, chocolate finger.

47

Peter

THE DOOR EXPLODED AGAINST the wall as he burst through it, startling several diners. What could he tell Sarah?

'Peter?' Claire asked from behind the counter. 'Are you okay?' Her eyes dropped to where the buggy should be and widened: Peter's hand was clutching the red rabbit. 'Where's Zac? Sarah!' she called behind her. 'Come quick.'

Peter's knees threatened to give way as his daughter came flying out of the kitchen.

'What? What's the matter?' She followed Claire's gaze and took in Peter's haggard face. He looked ill. 'Dad? Where's Zac?' Her hands flew to her face, and her mouth stretched wide.

'Come into the kitchen,' Claire said, coming out from behind the counter and ushering Peter in. Peter, having no idea what to do, and having totally lost the capacity to think and act for himself, gratefully let her.

'Dad, sit down. Where's Zac?' Sarah asked, her voice high and tight.

Peter's knees buckled, and he dropped onto a stool. 'I don't know. I went to get a steak bake and some potato wedges for Gerry, and a tuna sandwich for me, and when I came out, he'd gone. I mean, they both had.' His breath came in ragged heaves, and a mist swam in front of his eyes. He blinked to clear it. It didn't go.

'Dad, you're not making sense. Where were you? And where's Zac?'

Peter shook his head and tried again. 'I… I'd left him with Gerry outside the shop. I'd gone in. I didn't take the buggy in. It was crowded inside. Gerry said to leave it with him. He was just outside… he…'

'Oh my God, oh my God! Are you saying Gerry has him?'

'I don't know. They'd gone when I came out. I thought maybe Gerry needed the toilet and… and… I don't know. He said he had a heart problem. He might be ill…'

Ellie had come into the kitchen now, along with Olwyn.

'There's probably a reasonable explanation,' Ellie said.

'Like what?' Sarah's face was white, like porcelain. Peter shook his head again. This couldn't be happening. Stella would kill him. He'd lost his own grandson.

'Dad!' Sarah's voice was sharp. 'Which shop? Whereabouts?'

'That pie shop at the top of the Shambles.'

'When?'

'I don't know. Half an hour ago? I walked around for a bit then came back here. Maybe longer than half an hour. I just don't know.'

Sarah pulled out her phone. 'I'm calling the police.'

No one stopped her. All Peter could do was look on in terror. They had to find Zac. They had to.

48

Chris

CHRIS SAT, LOST IN his own world, on the edge of his bed. No one had been to check on him about his fictitious tummy bug. Just as well he'd made it up. Every hour, he turned the phone on to check. Nothing. Then he'd turn it straight back off. It was coming up to one o'clock. Time for another update. Two minutes wouldn't make any difference. Twelve fifty-seven. Twelve fifty-eight. He turned it on, making sure his bedcovers muted any noise it might make. When it loaded, he gaped at the screen.

Four WhatsApp messages, from a different number this time. Another new one.

His hand shaking, he opened them. Pictures. Of the kid again, this time with his dad. He read the message his dad had typed. Oh my God! It sounded like he'd snatched the child! How?

He typed one back:

Dad, what have you done? What are you saying? I don't understand. I don't have a son.

He sent it. Five minutes later, a message came back.

Sure ya do. With that pritty little piece, Sarah. Kept quiet about her, din't ya! I'm just spendin some qualitie time with my granson while his daddys indesposed.

Chris clutched his head. What could he do? He knew instantly what his dad was doing. It was all a game, to get back at him. Joe Gillespie had been the most vengeful, vindictive person Chris had ever known, and now he knew what Chris had done all those years ago, there would be no stopping him. His dad wouldn't rest until he'd got his own back and won. It was how he'd always been. He had to let Sarah know. His dad wasn't safe to be around, not for anyone. But especially not for a baby. There was no telling what he might do.

What time had his dad done this? Could have been hours ago. Could have been yesterday, and he'd only just sent the photos. Every hair on Chris's body stood up as a prickling sensation crept over him.

He opened his text message app. Typed in Sarah's number, that was imprinted on his memory. Please God, don't let her have changed it.

Sarah, it's me, Chris. Add this number to your contacts, I need to send you some pictures on WhatsApp. It's urgent. About your baby. And DO NOT ring me.

He sent it.

49

Sarah

I GRABBED DAD'S SHOULDER and shook it, wishing Mum was here. She'd know what to do. But she wasn't answering her phone. All the time I'd been speaking to the police when I'd called 999, Dad had sat there, shaking and moaning to himself. And then he'd started crying and now wouldn't stop.

'Dad!' I said again. 'I need you to talk to me.'

It was no good. He was on another planet. My phone beeped, and I slid it out of my apron pocket, my hands shaking so badly I almost dropped it. It was a text message from an unknown number.

When I opened it, I almost screamed. Then, I did what it said, and added the number to my WhatsApp, under 'Chris'. He'd better not be joking. If he was, I'd kill him. If he thought this was funny, I'd rip him limb from limb. How had he found out about Zac? None of this was making sense.

Another message came:

The man who has the baby is my dad, Joe Gillespie. He is out of prison. He is sending me pictures right now. I haven't got a clue what is going on, but he's doing it to get at me. He says the baby is mine, and he's taken him. I don't know anything else. DO NOT trust him. He is dangerous.

Pictures began to come in. Me at my mum and dad's flat, holding Zac, standing near the window. The one Gerry took.

A picture of just me, outside the shop. Looked like it had been taken from the other side of the street when I'd been working. Dad with Gerry, taken like a selfie, the two of them laughing. Then Gerry with Zac, blurred; another selfie. More with Zac. One in a cafe somewhere, with chocolate smeared all over Zac's face.

I peered harder at the picture, trying to see the view outside the cafe window but only a sliver of glass was visible, and I couldn't make out where it was. I went back to the others and scrutinised the backgrounds. Shops I thought I knew, streets that seemed familiar. But nowhere concrete. Another message:

Whatever he sends me, I'll send straight to you. I have a contraband phone. If they find it, they'll take it off me. Again DO NOT RING.

I sent back *OK* then set off down the street at full pelt, going nowhere in particular, but looking for Gerry and Zac. According to Dad, Zac had been gone almost an hour now. He could be anywhere. All I could hope for was that he'd keep sending Chris pictures, and Chris would send them to me. Best case scenario, they'd still be somewhere in York. Worse case… I couldn't think about it now. I'd run from one location to the next, if I had to.

'Sarah! Wait.'

A voice behind made me turn, but I didn't stop. Didn't even slow down. Dad was trying to catch me up, red-faced and panting.

'Where are you going?' he said. 'Stop.'

I glared at him. I felt like crying, but there was no time for that. Instead, I slowed.

'Your new best friend has taken my baby,' I yelled. 'And you let him.'

Then I set off again.

50

Joe

JOE WIPED THE BEADS of sweat from his hairline, trying not to notice how shaky his hands were. The adrenaline was rushing through him like speed. It had been almost three hours since he'd taken Zac. He'd taken refuge in the Jorvik Viking Centre, to get him off the street. The entrance fee had been exorbitant, although Zac got in for free. He'd been hoping it was dark inside, and he'd been right. A lot of it was. Most of the staff and tourists inside hadn't looked twice at the grandad pushing his grandson around. After a long period of whining, Zac had quietened down, being entertained by the new sights and sounds. Or maybe not the sounds. Joe thought back to what Peter had said about Zac being deaf. It was a shame for the kid.

He checked his watch. Four o'clock. He groaned; his back was killing him. He'd found a few places to sit in the Centre, whether or not you were supposed to. Then he realised and his heart gave a lurch—four o'clock! He should have been starting his shift! What with everything, it had gone clean out of his head. He clutched at his head, thinking. If he lost his job, then what? There was no Plan B. As it turned out, he hadn't even had a Plan A. Because he was a stupid bloody fuck-up, and there was nothing he could do about it now anyway, even if he wanted to.

Why had he grabbed the kid? He shuffled back on the straw bale he was sitting on, and an agonising pain shot up his spine. He stood up, still thinking. Zac had fallen asleep again. Joe looked down at him and wrinkled his nose at the shit smell coming off him. The kid's face was still smeared with chocolate, even though Joe had tried to clean some of it off with the bottom of Zac's T-shirt.

He wondered if he should just leave Zac here and walk away. He manoeuvred the buggy tight behind the bale to see how it looked, and snapped another photo. This time he didn't send it. He was getting tired of it all. Colin had sent some frantic messages back, but it was now wearing thin, the whole damn thing. All the hassle meant he was getting little satisfaction. Maybe it wasn't worth it after all.

'Sir, you can't go in there with the exhibits.'

He turned to see a female staff member he hadn't noticed staring straight at him.

He grabbed the buggy, left the Jorvik Centre, and emerged, blinking, into the daylight. Outside, he stopped and looked all around, the idea of leaving Zac somewhere to be found still in his mind. But what if someone saw him? There must be cameras around here. They were everywhere these days.

He looked helplessly at the roof lines of the shops around him. If there were any, he couldn't see them. Then again, they could be hidden, couldn't they? Wasn't that kind of the point?

He had no idea. The world had been a less complicated place when he'd been banged up all those years ago. People didn't walk around glued to phones all the time, for a start. He sighed, feeling suddenly old and exhausted, and like he didn't belong. He'd never looked after his body, and it wasn't thanking him for it now.

He started walking, with no idea of where to go. It was hours until nightfall. What would he do then? The best plan would be to get away from the shops and crowds of people.

Were more and more people looking strangely at him, or was it just in his head? He felt scrutinised, vulnerable, exposed.

He walked faster, ignoring the blisters on both feet that rubbed with every step. Zac was quiet, his fingers gripping the front of the buggy, pushing the coloured beads first this way then that. When he turned and saw Joe looking down at him, his bottom lip wobbled before he turned back.

'Don't start, kid, just don't fucking start,' Joe muttered, pushing the buggy into the road and causing a van driver to swerve and yell something out of his open window.

The inside of Joe's head was hurting with the tension that was building up and making the blood pound in his ears. Both the buildings and the open spaces between them taunted him, and he wished he was anywhere but here: Gerry's flat, his little car, even his prison cell; all would feel safer than this. He concentrated on putting one foot in front of the other, not caring where it would lead. *Just keep walking, keep walking.*

The shout of a child made him look up, and he was astonished to find he was down near the river, on a leafy, quiet path. A small girl was pedalling towards him furiously on a pink bike with purple streamers billowing from the handlebars.

'Mummy!' she yelled. 'Keep up!'

A woman was following, pedalling her own bike much more slowly.

'Jessie, don't go too near the water,' she called. 'Stop and wait for me.'

The woman shot Joe a quick smile as she cycled by. His mouth stretched in response, but it felt tight and humourless. His grip on the buggy tightened as his eyes slid to the water. There was no one else on the path in either direction. Zac squealed and Joe jumped. The fucking kid was a nightmare. Joe edged the buggy closer to the river until he stood right at the edge, watching the water swirl and rush by. Even on a calm day, the pace of it was fierce. One small shove and it would all be over.

He let the handle go and the wheels inched forwards, down the slight incline. He glanced both ways: still no one. Zac let out a wail then fell silent again. Joe stood, mesmerised by the water, watching as one of the pushchair's front wheels passed the kerb that edged the path, until it was suspended over the river. Zac shuffled around, causing the buggy to wobble and lurch forward, beginning to tip. Joe's hand shot out, grabbed the handle and pulled the buggy back to safety. Panic rose in him, rushing up from his feet to his head. Of all the things he was, he wasn't that: a child killer, like his son. In his mind, he saw the pushchair going over the edge and disappearing into the dark water, with Zac still strapped in. Shaking, he took several steps backwards, away from the edge. That wasn't the answer. If he killed Zac, how would that hurt Colin the most? The ones he'd hurt would be Sarah, Peter and Stella, and they'd showed him nothing but kindness. But what should he do now? He couldn't leave the buggy here.

He walked away from the river, trying desperately to think where he could go, and eventually ended up somewhere near Clifford's Tower. Zac had dropped off to sleep again. Not far from there, standing high above everything else, was some monument or other, to God knows what. He'd walked past it loads of times and never bothered reading the plaque at the bottom. He made for it and stood looking up at it. There were at least fifty or sixty steps leading up to it, maybe a hundred. He doubted he had the strength to climb them. But maybe, if he could see the view from the top, it might bring with it inspiration as to what to do next. Some answer might be revealed. He knew it was a barmy thought, but he didn't have a better one. And, if inspiration didn't strike, he could hide out there until dark, then find somewhere to dump the kid, where he'd be found, safe and well. He could tell them at work that he'd been ill, or make something else up, or whatever. It would be okay.

Having made a decision of sorts, he felt better. He took Zac out of the pushchair and slung him over his shoulder.

His stomach turned over at the smell emanating from the kid's trousers. Zac didn't wake up. Joe tried to collapse the pushchair with one hand but the damn thing wasn't having any of it. If he left it down at the bottom, it'd get stolen, for sure, then he'd have to carry the kid about. He'd just have to summon up the strength to lug them both up to the top.

The climb was steep and hard, but he kept going, even as his heart punched faster and his knees creaked. Every step was harder than the one before, but he kept climbing steadfastly up. He wasn't thinking straight. He wasn't really thinking at all. Exhaustion overcame him. He hoped there was somewhere comfortable at the top to sit and have a breather.

There wasn't. He hauled himself up the last step, gripping the handrail while his heart fought its way out of his chest. His lungs heaved as he took in what was in front of him. It didn't take long.

There was only a sculpture of something in the middle of a large paved area, maybe ten feet square, with narrow, waist-high railings that ran around the edge, breaking only for the steps. He sank down onto the top step. There wasn't a soul up there but him and the kid. As he gasped for breath, his lungs began to re-inflate and his heart rate slowed. He felt drained but slightly better, and the fog that had descended over his eyes was slowly clearing. He blinked. Might as well take another picture now he'd dragged them both up here. The view over York really was spectacular, with the Minster in the background.

He stood up again and pasted a smile on his face for another picture. He typed *Hello daddie, weer on top of the world* and sent it. Then, he hutched a still-sleeping Zac higher up, walked over to the other side, away from the steps, sat down with his back against the railings, lit a cigarette, and waited for inspiration to strike.

51

Sarah

TWO HOURS HAD PASSED without a single picture. I'd messaged Chris numerous times, but the answer was always the same: no news. I'd walked every street I knew in York but not spotted a thing. Dad had trailed after me, barely speaking and looking suicidal. Mum was now back at the cafe, talking to the police. Every so often, Dad's phone would ring and he'd relay information to me. Always questions from the police, but, so far, zero answers. They wanted me to return to the café, but I'd refused. Nor would I answer my phone to them. I had to keep it free, and the battery life up, in case Chris got in touch.

Dad's face was grey, ashen, but I wouldn't look at him. I wasn't being fair—ultimately, it was Chris again; him and his stupid, horrible family. What I couldn't understand, though, what angered me more than anything, was that Dad could leave Zac outside with a near-stranger looking after him. Because what did he know about Gerry, really? Nothing. Not even his real name. None of us did, but it was Dad who had trusted him the most.

I'd been so shocked when I'd found out who Gerry really was that I could barely speak. I'd known Chris's dad had been a bad lot, he'd told me so, but I'd never given him a moment's thought. He'd been so far off my radar, he could have been on another planet. Dad now knew as much as I did about who his friend was. When I'd told him, he'd been aghast. As had Mum.

I felt like I'd aged twenty years in the last few hours. There was so much adrenaline racing through my body, I felt dizzy and sick. The bone-deep fear that gripped me was the same as when he had meningitis. I might never see him again, due to a maniac. If the loss of the other baby had been bad, what would losing Zac be like? I wouldn't want to live. I wouldn't live, I'd make sure of that.

'Sarah,' Dad said.

'What?' I snapped.

'Do you think we should go back to the cafe?'

'Why? Is Zac there?'

Dad hung his head. 'No.'

'Well, why would I go back, then? You go back if you want. I'll keep looking.'

Just then, my phone beeped. It was already in my hand, damp with perspiration from being squeezed for so long. I whipped my hand up. WhatsApp. I stopped. Dad bumped into me, peering over my shoulder.

A picture loaded. Joe and his hateful face, Zac with his cherubic one. I looked at the picture in more detail. My head snapped up.

'I know where they are.'

'Where?' asked Dad.

'The Queen's Jubilee Monument. Near Clifford's Tower.'

I sprinted off, my steps lighter now I knew where I was going. Dad wouldn't be able to keep up. I couldn't worry about that now. Getting to Zac was all that mattered.

I knew exactly where it was. I'd been there with Leanne, and I'd hated it. It was so high up. The sculpture was clear in the background. All those steps. How the hell had Joe even got up there? I hated that old bastard more than I'd ever hated anything or anyone, and that hate fuelled my legs. I powered down the streets, my feet pounding the pavements as if Satan himself were after me. Instead, I was after him.

52

Joe

SITTING IN THE SUN with his back against the railings, Joe smoked and slowly got his breath back. Zac, somehow, was still asleep, heavy in his arms. The kid stank of piss as well now, right under his nose. He moved his head to one side, where the air was fresher. Every last bit of energy seeped out of his body as his adrenaline levels fell, and the sun's warmth relaxed him.

It was peaceful up here, the main noise just birdsong. The road noise sounded far below him. If he could just have a rest, a quick nap, maybe when he woke up, he'd know what to do.

His eyelids grew heavy, and his chin dropped onto his chest. He couldn't fight the tiredness. Didn't want to. Even though the concrete underneath him was hard, it was warm. He was comfortable enough. His breathing slowed, grew deep and even, and he closed his eyes and drifted down. His grip on Zac loosened as his muscles relaxed.

As Joe's arms went slack, Zac's eyes sprung open. His trousers were wet, as were his legs. His nappy was bulky, cold, and uncomfortable. He wriggled about and the arms enfolding him loosened further. The body against his didn't move, but emitted a loud snore.

He wriggled again, harder this time. The arms slid completely away from him. He was free.

He slid off the body and sat on the floor, blinking in the sun. His world was silent, but there was lots to see. He turned his head and looked around. Then he began crawling towards the top of the steps.

53

Sarah

I NOTICED NOTHING AND no one as I ran for the monument, dashing over roads and between cars and people without slowing. They would have to stop for me. A few cars beeped their horns at me and a bus swerved at the last minute.

I left the shops behind. I could see the monument now, towering over everything else. The sight of it spurred me on. I had to get to it before the sick bastard left and took Zac with him. What if he'd already left?

The thought made me take more notice of everyone else. He could walk right past me. The monument was growing bigger now as I ran. I shielded my eyes from the sun. At the top was what looked like a speck of red. A buggy?

And then I was there, at the foot of the steps, my lungs on fire. I took off up the steps, clearing them two at a time, my muscles burning and screaming from the effort. In no time, I was a quarter of the way up, then almost halfway.

I looked up at the top again. Joe was nowhere to be seen. My God, had he left Zac here on his own? Was he in the pushchair? Then something up there moved. I could just make out a tiny shape, getting closer and closer to the edge. Dressed in pale blue, with dark, curly hair.

Zac was so close to the edge, he was going to fall. I screamed at him to stop where he was, knowing he couldn't hear me, but doing it anyway. Even faster, I pushed on and up with almost superhuman speed and strength. I had to get there.

'Zac! No!' I screamed again. Three quarters of the way up.

Zac was leaning forward, reaching for nothing with his tiny hand. He saw me and stopped. Then he tumbled over the edge. It was horrific, and I moved into a gear I didn't know I had. My baby. He wouldn't die. He couldn't. I wouldn't let him.

But he was still falling. Five, ten steps down. Then more. Over and over. Getting closer to me, gaining speed. I reached out, blocking his way with my whole body, and he fell into my arms. My fingers gripped his clothes and I hugged him close to me, leaning against the banister railing and holding him tight. Slowly, I sank down onto the step I was standing on, my legs unable to hold me up any longer. I peeled him away from me, checking for broken bones. Miraculously, he seemed fine, but his beautiful little face was cut and bloodied. A nasty cut on his temple was bleeding quite heavily. He was looking at me in shock. My heart felt wrenched in two as I saw him fall, over and over again, in my mind. I looked up to see Joe Gillespie standing there, looking down at me. An ugly sneer twisted his face. Everything inside me clenched tight.

I heard panting behind me. Somehow, Dad hadn't been all that far behind me.

'Have you got him? Is he okay?' he said, puffing so hard he could barely speak.

'I don't know. He's moving, at least.'

Zac began to cry then and wouldn't stop. I hugged him again and buried his face in my neck, soothing and shushing him. He was here, in one piece. Anything else, we could cope with.

Dad heaved in air, then straightened up and began to climb the steps past me, a look of fierce resolve on his face. I'd never seen him look like that before. What was he doing?

'Dad?' I shouted.

I got up and managed to make it to the top by clinging on and hauling myself up the banister rail with one hand, Zac bundled in my other. Joe and Dad were standing there, facing each other at the foot of the monument. Joe was laughing. Dad was trembling all over. I stepped onto the top. If I could find the strength, I'd throw Joe Gillespie over the railing without a second thought, and feel no guilt.

He and Dad were arguing now. I couldn't make out what they were saying as they shouted over each other. I stayed out of the way, near the railing. Joe began to walk off, and Dad followed him. Then Joe turned and laughed again. Laughed at him. At us.

'You're a loser,' Joe said.

They were both standing near the top of the steps, inches from the edge.

'Dad. Come back,' I said, alarmed.

Dad's eyes swung my way, then back to Joe again. The look in them frightened me.

'I can't believe I ever trusted you,' Dad yelled. 'I know what your son is. You're worse than he is.'

Joe turned away, but his eyes were blazing. He looked nothing like Chris. I would never have known.

'Don't you walk away from me,' Dad shouted, stepping forward to grab his arm. 'I haven't finished.'

He wrenched Joe back, and Joe turned and punched Dad in the face. Dad's head flew back.

I screamed. 'Stop!'

Joe swung another, harder, punch at Dad, putting his full weight behind it. Dad stepped out of the way as Joe carried on, off-balance now, and stumbled in a full circle. His foot slipped off the top step and his arms cartwheeled. He tried to grab Dad's shirt. Dad stepped back once more as Joe's fingers grasped for the fabric then slid off.

He was falling now, toppling backwards. It was horrendous, but I couldn't tear my eyes away. Dad was watching too, his eyes wide. He took another step back, away from the edge.

I ran over to Dad, and we both watched in horror as Joe fell, gathering speed, hitting step after step on his way down. His head made a sickening crunch. He fell right from the top to the bottom, where he lay in a crumpled mess, unmoving. Bright red blood smeared the pale concrete steps. I couldn't tear my eyes away.

Dad went to go down, but I held him back. I was trembling badly, and so was he.

'Stay up here,' I said. 'Ring an ambulance.'

He nodded, and pulled out his phone.

'Did you see that?' he said, while waiting for the operator to answer. 'He could have taken me with him. He tried to. He tried to grab me.' His voice was tremulous and his face ashen.

'I saw.'

We both sank onto the floor, not wanting to look down at the figure at the bottom, and waited for the ambulance to arrive, while the sound of Zac's crying filled my head. And, by God, he stank.

54

Sarah

A WEEK AFTER 'THE kidnapping', as I called it, Zac had mostly recovered. He'd been taken to hospital straight from the monument, as they were worried about concussion. We all were. But, apart from cuts and bruising, he was fine. Dad's worst injury had been a large bruise on his cheek, the remnants of which was still there. The pair of them still had battle scars. But they were slowly fading. The horror, however, wasn't.

I sat on the sofa watching Zac crawl after Lulu on the living room carpet, babbling away to himself. I would never forget the horror of seeing him tip over the edge of those steps and plummet towards me. How he didn't suffer any broken bones, I'll never know. The doctor said it was because babies' bones are soft, so they tend to bend more than break. His, though, hadn't even done that. His little face and head had come off the worst, as they'd bashed on every step he hit.

So did Joe's, but he wasn't so lucky. He was dead long before the ambulance arrived. Maybe he was dead before he hit the bottom. Not that I went down to find out. Dad and I were huddled together at the top when the paramedics arrived with the police.

Zac pulled Lulu's tail hard, and she yipped at him before gazing dolefully at me.

'Zac, stop that. It's naughty.'

I picked Lulu up and sat her on my knee. Zac pulled himself up to his feet, using the edge of the sofa cushion, before falling back onto his bottom. I passed him a squashy fabric book, which he stuffed straight into his mouth.

I stared out of the window, unable to stop reliving the horror. We spent a long time going through everything, over and over, while the police got it all down. In the end, there were no charges to face. The guilty party was dead, and that was that. But my poor dad was a mess. He blamed himself, and me shouting at him hadn't helped. Even though I'd apologised a thousand times, he couldn't forgive himself. Nothing Mum or I said made any difference.

'There's no fool like an old fool,' he said, over and over. 'That's what I am. The biggest, oldest fool of them all.'

Mum said he'd cried all night that first night. None of us got any sleep. I don't really know what will happen from now, but life goes on, as they say. Ours will. But Dad needs more time to himself, and we'll make sure he gets it. The doctor gave him some anti-depressants. Thankfully, he's taking them.

As usual, my staff at the cafe were wonderful, and just got on with things. They only know half the story, though. To everyone else, Gerry was just a friend of Dad's who lost his marbles one day and did a terrible thing.

The door opened and Mum came in. Her eyes went straight to Zac until she was satisfied he was okay.

'How's Dad?' I asked her.

He was at home. He'd barely been to my flat since it happened. Had barely been out anywhere.

'Same,' she said.

I covered my face with my hands, and Mum pulled them away.

'He does know you didn't mean what you said. He doesn't blame you.'

'Well, he should. I can't forgive myself. It was my fault, if anybody's, not his. I was the one who brought Chris into our lives. If I hadn't done that, Joe wouldn't have come after us, would he? Everything he did was to get back at his own son. Poor Dad just got caught in the crossfire. That man manipulated him.'

I thought of how manipulative Chris could be when he wanted. Perhaps he was more like his dad than he realised.

Mum sat down next to me and Lulu, the little traitor, left my lap for hers.

'I'm going to arrange some counselling for him. I think he'd benefit from talking to someone other than us,' she said.

'Do you think he'll go, though?'

'I've already asked him, and he said he will. We need to move on. Joe is gone. Chris is in prison. It's over, Sarah. We can focus on Zac now.'

'I know. It'll just take time, that's all.'

She paused, her eyes fixed on mine. 'Have you decided then?'

'Yes. I'm not going to see him. I'm going to say everything I need to in a letter. I'm not taking Zac to that place, and he can't make me. He'll never see his son; it's that simple.'

Mum grabbed my hand and squeezed it. 'For what it's worth, I think you're doing the right thing.'

I took a deep breath in. She wasn't going to like what was coming next.

'Um, Mum… I have something else to tell you.'

Her mouth tightened. 'What? It's nothing bad, is it? I don't think I can take any more bad news.'

'No. It's not bad. But I've found a child minder. I think you and Dad need more time to do things together. Your retirement shouldn't be all about looking after Zac. It's not fair on either of you.'

To my amazement, she nodded. 'Okay. I agree, actually. Much as I love having him, I think it's what your dad needs. I've neglected him, and that's on me. He felt shoved aside, pushed out. I shouldn't have made him feel he didn't matter. Because he does. Of course he does. He's my rock.'

'He's mine, too. And I'm glad you agree. So, she's called Sharon, and she's lovely. She has six children she looks after, all pre-schoolers. One of them is around Zac's age. I think he'll benefit enormously from mixing with the other kids. I want to work out with you how many days I'll need her for.'

Mum narrowed her eyes, thinking. 'What if she had him four days, and we had him two. You have him when the cafe's closed on Mondays, of course.'

'I think that'll be brilliant. We can work out all the finer details later.'

'Great. I'll go and tell your dad. I think he'll be relieved. It's really knocked his confidence, all this. He thinks he's no good at looking after Zac anymore.' She lifted Lulu down and stood up. 'I'll be back in the morning. And stop worrying. Everything will be alright. What are you doing tonight?'

'I have a letter to write. A very long one, I think..'

'Ah. Okay. Probably better to just get it over with.'

After she'd gone, I grabbed a pen and some paper. It took me ages to work out what to say, but finally I finished. I had to write it wondering if prison staff might read it first. Then I thought *what the hell!* Better to be truthful.

When it was done, I picked up my phone. There were messages from men on some of the dating websites I'd joined. I deleted them all without reading them. Maybe one day. But not today.

55

Chris

CHRIS SAT ON HIS bed as the screw exited his cell and locked the door. He stared at the already opened envelope he'd just been handed in disbelief, gripping it with shaking fingers—his name in Sarah's neat, cursive handwriting. Even though he'd waited for a letter from her for so long, he couldn't open it. What if it was bad news?

He set it down on the bed beside him and stared at nothing out of his small window. Until he read her words, he still had hopes and dreams alive. After reading it, would they be gone?

It had been two weeks since the debacle with his dad. Miraculously, he still had the phone hidden under his mattress. They'd find it one day for sure. He hadn't turned it on since that day.

He'd felt nothing when they told him his father was dead. Phil had asked if he wanted to go to the funeral. Nope, he did not. They'd left, and he'd lay on his bed, thinking about it all.

If anything, the world was a better place now his father was dead. He'd never contributed anything to society. He was just a leech.

His fingers found their way to the envelope on their own, while his eyes were still fixed on the window. He extracted the letter. It was folded neatly in half; thick, unlined paper.

His heart dropped at the realisation there was just the one sheet. He sniffed it, hoping to catch the scent of her, but there was nothing. He unfolded it and began to read.

Dear Chris,

I don't really know where to start. We both know what happened with your dad that day, so I won't rehash all that. That said, it was quite ingenious how he wormed his way into my dad's life to get to me, ultimately to get to you. I still can't quite believe the deviousness of it. The silly thing is, until he did what he did, I'd quite liked him. He'd certainly charmed both my mum and dad. All of us, I suppose. And me, with my trust issues… he played a blinder there.

Chris paused. Trust issues? She had them because of him. She'd never had them before. His cheeks felt hot.

Anyway, I'm sorry you had to find out about your son in the way you did. I'm assuming you know that Zac is yours. I hope you understand that I can never bring him to see you. Just trust that he will want for nothing and will have the best life ever. Please don't try to have any rights over him, if you were thinking about it. I'd fight you all the way.

I want to keep this letter fairly short, so I'll try not to ramble on. The only thing that worries me is your sister, Shay. I don't know why, but your family has a history of targeting me and coming after me. I need to know she won't do that. What if she does? She scares me, and I don't know what to do about her. There again, I may be overreacting.

This letter is to say goodbye for the final time. I won't correspond with you, answer any calls or send you pictures of Zac. I think a clean break would be best. I confess I have no idea what I'll tell Zac about you. I suppose one day I'll have to tell him the truth. I'm not one for making up elaborate lies, as you know.

So this is it.

Goodbye Chris. Forever.

Sarah

When he put the letter down, his eyes were wet. As he'd thought, his hopes for the future were now completely dead. But there was one last thing he could do for her. He pulled out the phone from under his pillow and sent one last message to her.

Shay is dead. Don't worry. Goodbye.

That was it. She could change her number and he'd never know.

There was one last thing to take care of. When you'd taken away everything a man had, including hope, there was nothing left. So he had nothing to lose. He'd already lost it all.

***

The next morning, he was up and ready for kitchen duties, hoping fervently Tommy would be there. He left the phone in full view on top of his bed. He wouldn't be needing it anymore. His luck was in. When he arrived, Tommy was there at his workstation.

'Alright,' he said when he saw Chris.

'Alright,' he said, taking out his first potato.

They worked in silence for half an hour, while Chris kept his eye on where the two attendant screws were. Then he went for it.

'Erm, so what's the deal with that phone you got me? Who else knew the number?' he asked, quietly, watching the screws from under his brows.

'What do you mean?' Tommy did a really unconvincing job of looking surprised.

'No fuckin around anymore. Just tell me.'

Tommy looked Chris square in the eye. 'Why do you wanna know?'

'How did my dad get that number? How did you give it to him?'

'Why does it matter?'

'Cos it got him killed,' Chris shot back.

Did Tommy already know that? It had been two weeks. Who might he have spoken to in that time?

'Please. Just tell me. I want to know.'

Tommy grinned. 'Alright. No skin off my nose, is it?'

It might be, Chris thought. 'So? Tell me, then.'

Tommy looked to where the nearest screw was and then back at Chris, a sneer pulling at his mouth. 'Something you don't know. Your old man and my Uncle Gerry were old cell mates. Now they're both out. Family connections, mate. I told you they were everything, but you didn't value yours.'

Chris turned it over in his mind. The conniving bastards. They'd cooked all this up between them, and he'd never suspected a thing.

'So what happened?' Tommy asked. 'How did it get him killed?'

'Why don't you ask dear old Uncle Gerry, seeing as you're so close?'

Tommy bit down on his bottom lip and narrowed his eyes.

'All this time you were passing on what I told you?' Chris said, realising just how much he'd been played.

'Every last bit. But no need to get sore about it.'

No need to get…? The man was insane. He thought about everything he'd told Tommy. He'd confided the fuckin lot. Even down to supplying the overdose money for Shay. Had his dad known that, as well? He must have done.

'Why are you so pissed, anyway? You didn't give a shit about your dad. You told me that.' Tommy reached for a handful of carrots.

'True enough. I'm glad the old fucker is dead.' He thought of all that Sarah had suffered because of this prick, and felt his temper rise.

'Oh, while we're on the subject of confessing… how's the ribs? All healed up now?' Tommy gestured to Chris's torso. 'I've been forgetting to ask. Bit remiss of me.' He winked, and the realisation of what he was saying dawned on Chris. He swallowed down the bile that rose in the back of his throat.

'That was you! You arranged for me to get jumped! But why?'

Tommy shrugged. 'You needed to trust me. I rode in on my white horse and saved you. Pretty good, eh?'

Chris gripped the potato harder. His knuckles were bloodless. He watched from the corner of his eye as a carrot Tommy had plucked from the pile rolled onto the floor and landed at his feet.

'No hard feelings, eh? All just water under the bridge now.'

Tommy laughed as he bent down to pick it up. The nearest screw was right across the room, with his back turned, dealing with some altercation or other; two cons were going at it over something, arms waving and yelling. The other screw was going over to join him. While Tommy was still bent down, Chris grabbed the back of his neck with both hands and drove his face hard into the edge of the metal workstation. Showers of blood erupted from his nose. Chris did it again and again, losing count of the number of times it hit. He put every last inch of his force behind it, anger and fury fuelling every blow, and compelling him to carry on. When he let go, Tommy crumpled to the floor. Where his face had been was now a dripping mass of red meat.

'Hey!' one of the screws shouted. 'Pack that in!'

Before either of the officers could get there, Chris kicked Tommy hard several times, in the face, the head, the stomach, and the back. Any angle which presented itself, really. Chris wasn't fussy. And to say Tommy had more or less insulted his size and physique, he wasn't laughing now.

The two officers dragged him off, and more poured in. Chris still aimed kicks, blows and punches at anyone who got in his way. Those times he'd spent in the gym lately had paid off. He was in better shape now than he'd been in ages. He managed to head butt one of the officers right on the brow bone, and the man howled before letting him go. Another one took his place and hit Chris square in the kidneys with a baton. Chris welcomed the pain that bloomed in his back. He didn't care what happened to him. Tommy's cronies could finish him off. So what?

While they dragged him away, he screwed his head round and looked back. Tommy was still on the floor. But he was moving. He wasn't dead. Shame, because that had been his one and only chance. He'd known it was a long shot, though. Not enough time. Pity he didn't have a gun. That would have done it.

'You'll have a long time to sit in solitary and think about this,' one of the screws said.

'Yep,' Chris said. 'I sure will. Maybe it was worth it, though.

***

The screw wasn't lying. In the month he spent in solitary, he learned to clear his mind and go someplace else. Maybe it was what they called meditation. Or maybe it wasn't. He preferred to think of it as shutting off. Time passed with no meaning, and with the cell being underground, there was no day or night. No window. No natural daylight.

After a month, the door opened, and an officer came in. It wasn't a mealtime. Chris sat up from where he'd been lying on the hard, narrow bed.

'Just letting you know. You're not going back on the wing. You're being shipped out.'

'Where to?' He knew what this was about. They weren't putting him back on the wing, as he'd be a target. Tommy's lot would kill him for sure. Shame. He was ready for it. It would be welcome.

'Woodhill.'

'Where the hell's that?'

'Milton Keynes.'

'Right. How's Tommy?'

'Not dead yet. But it's not looking good for him.'

Oh dear, he thought. What a shame.

The door clanged shut again. Looked like that was all the information he was going to get for now. He'd probably never get out now.

He lay back down on the bed, staring at the low ceiling. He had a decision to make. Should he let Sarah know where they were moving him to? Did he have a duty, what with them having a kid and all? Probably.

But he wasn't going to.

Her letter had been final. If she ever needed or wanted to find him, she could track him down through the prison system. It couldn't be that hard.

He closed his eyes, rolled onto his side, breathed out slowly, and shut out the world.

READ ON FOR AN EXCERPT FROM THE DARK PLACE, A STANDALONE PSYCHOLOGICAL THRILLER

SHE PULLS UP IN the car, turns off the engine, and sits outside the house for a minute, her heart skittering a brief, crazy rhythm at the sight of it. The house is a neat, small semi, with a well-manicured front garden; nothing special or remarkable about it. Bright sunlight reflects off the gleaming windows, causing Issy to shade her eyes. Home. The place that's supposed to be a sanctuary. She tries to quell the tremors in her hands by jamming them under her thighs, while thoughts of what's to come crowd her mind.

When the front door opens and three-year-old Noah appears, she opens the door and gets out. He belts down the drive past her mother's car in a war charge, in T-shirt, shorts and bare feet. His over-long blonde curls flap behind him. The muscles around her heart clench tight at the sight of her son.

'Waah!' he roars, putting on a spurt and heading straight towards her.

Issy's mother chases after him as best she can, but he's too quick. He careens straight into Issy and she picks him up before he can run into the road.

'He's heavy,' she says to her mum.

Issy has no hips to speak of, certainly not child-bearing ones, and he continually slides down. His chubby little arms grasp tight around her neck and she turns away from the little boy smell that's making her stomach flip over.

'Darling, welcome home. We're going to have a great summer. Dad's been so excited.' Her mother beams at her and pulls her into a hug.

Issy puts a struggling Noah down, and he's instantly drawn to a beetle crawling along the base of the front garden wall. He pokes it with a tentative finger and squeals when it flips over onto his toe. Issy smiles brightly at her mum. Her mother won't notice she's not right. She's missed so many clues along the way. People only see what they want to see.

'Is Dad at work?'

'Yes, but he's arranged to come home early. We're all going out for tea. His treat. Aunty Pam and Uncle Justin are coming too. And Sammy and Joey. Carl's got football practice, as usual.'

Playing happy families then. Her heart thuds once, hard. She nods. 'Mmm, lovely.'

Noah tires of the beetle and scurries back inside the house, holding an imaginary sword aloft and yelling, 'Charge!'

Her mum tuts. 'He's got that from your dad. They've been playing 'battles' again. Oh, it's so great to have you home, love.' Her mother pulls her close and hugs her tight again, her hair tickling Issy's face. The smell of *Charlie* gets up her nose and Issy tries not to breathe it in. She's never liked it. For God's sake, who uses *Charlie* these days, anyway?

Together, they unload the boot, dropping a jumble of plastic bags, holdalls and suitcases onto the pavement. The accumulation of a year's worth of life.

'Crikey, Issy, I'd forgotten how much stuff you'd taken to uni,' her mother says at the sight of it all.

They gather up the luggage and struggle up the drive with it, dumping it in the hallway. Issy looks at the massive pile—why did she need all this stuff, anyway? She won't need any of it soon. She wonders if her mother can sense she's different. Doesn't seem like it. Noah runs out of the kitchen, straight past them and up the stairs, clutching a toy car in his fist. At the top he stops, turns and tosses the car down the stairs. It hits the bottom stair, bounces off and smacks Issy on the shin, then drops onto the floor where it lays upside down like an overturned insect, abandoned and forlorn, its wheels still spinning.

Issy looks up at him, ignoring the sting in her leg where it hit her. He watches, biting his lip, waiting to see what she's going to do. Issy picks it up, walks into the kitchen and throws it into the bin, right into a blob of what looks like discarded custard. Through the spindles of the staircase, Noah sees her and shrieks. *Serves him right*, she thinks, as she rejoins her mother at the bottom of the stairs.

Her mum is looking at her in dismay. 'Issy! You didn't have to throw it away. He'll carry on forever now. It's one of his favourites.'

'Well, he should have thought of that before throwing it. He's nearly four!'

'I know and I've been telling him,' her mum says. 'It's just a phase.'

Issy rubs her leg while Noah's cries continue. 'Want car! Want car!'

She blanks the noise out and goes back to the kitchen to get a drink of water. Her mum is making her way up the stairs to him. She's way too soft with him, and it's about time he learned. Issy leans against the worktop, gulping down a full glass of water. Her mum gave up her job when she had Noah, so she could carry on at school and then go to uni, and Issy still feels bad about it. Her mum loved that job. She'd thought, when she'd got pregnant, that she would be able to cope, that she would get used to Noah, but it hadn't happened. She fills the glass again, and it clinks against her teeth when her hand shakes with the thought of what she's about to do. She'd planned to do it tomorrow, but she knows without a doubt that she can't stay a night in this house, delaying things. It has to be today. Soon. Before she can change her mind. She won't change her mind.

Acknowledgments

I have a couple of people I want to thank.

Firstly, my husband Adrian., who reads all my books because I need and want his feedback. It's sometimes brutal (but I'm sure he doesn't mean it!), and usually right. Sometimes! I appreciate the time he spends reading it, as psychological thrillers aren't his bag at all. But he has oodles of common sense, and that's what I need.

Also, a huge thank you to Paul Baker, whose advice in all things prison-related was invaluable, and well worth getting up at 7AM for, for our long-distance conversations. Paul, you rock! Any mistakes in the prison bits are mine alone.

And thanks to you, my reader, for getting this far with me. Long may we journey together...

From the Author

I am a thriller writer living in Yorkshire in the UK. After years working as a dog groomer and musician (not usually at the same time), I discovered a love of writing that now won't go away. I recently decorated my office in a lovely shabby chic pink wallpaper, as I wanted to have a beautifully inspiring place in which to sit and plot how to inflict unspeakable suffering on my poor unsuspecting characters. Only they don't know that yet… I love connecting with readers. As a new writer, it's one of the best things about the job. It makes all the time spent thinking up stories to share worthwhile. I'd like to say a massive thank you for taking the time to read this lil' ol' book of mine. I hope you enjoyed reading it as much as I did writing it. If you feel moved to write a review, I would greatly appreciate. It really does make a difference to authors.

I strive for perfection. If you find a typo, I'd love you to tell me at info@stephanierogersauthor.com I hope you'll stay with me on this journey. We're gonna have a blast!

Printed in Great Britain
by Amazon

22680406R00182